MW01595313

BOUNTY HUNTERS

(Cade Korbin Chronicles, Book 5)
(1st Edition)

by Jasper T. Scott

JasperTscott.com
@JasperTscott

Copyright © 2023

Cover Art by Tom Edwards
TomEdwardsDesign.com

CONTENT RATING: R

Swearing: Some strong language
Sexual Content: Mild
Violence: Moderate

Author's Guarantee: If you find anything you consider inappropriate for this rating, please e-mail me at JasperTscott@gmail.com and I will either remove the content or change the rating accordingly.

ACKNOWLEDGMENTS

Writing this book was an encore for fans of the original series. Several years after finishing the original Cade Korbin Chronicles series, I realized that I missed writing about Cade's adventures. Thanks in part to fans like Elmi Hassan and Jay Smith, I decided to write a sequel that would be equally accessible to fans of the original series and new readers. Thus, Bounty Hunters was born. Hopefully, the coming years will give me many excuses to revisit this series with subsequent installments.

As usual, finishing this book on time was a challenge in itself. I couldn't have done it without the support of my family and the speedy work of my editor, Aaron Sikes. And a big thanks to my proofer, Dani J. Caile, who always manages to proof my work in record time.

My heartfelt gratitude also goes to my advance readers for their early feedback. And finally, many thanks to the Muse.

PROLOGUE

I check the timer on the shuttle's nav display: ten minutes and counting until our reversion from FTL. *Finally.* I look up from the ship's displays and stare off into the swirling kaleidoscope of starlight beyond the cockpit.

We've had the same dizzying view, with only brief respites, for the past three hundred and twelve days—ten months give or take. In that time we've made forty-two separate jumps and flown more than six thousand light years from the edge of Coalition Space to our destination: the Nidus System in the heart of the Hadros Sector.

We spent most of the past ten months frozen in the stasis tubes at the aft end of our long-range ERAS-3 Javelin-class shuttle, but we still had to wake up for each transition to and from FTL. Now and then the ship would also wake us to stretch our legs and to double-check that everything on board is running smoothly. If not, well, we have plenty of spare components on board, and the repair drones to swap them out.

We also have Operative Brix Rylo, a certified systems engineer, and Operative Sia Dust, a better-than-average ship's mechanic, and pilot. I would still feel a whole lot better about this mission if the Coalition had sent *two* shuttles instead of one. Maybe that's more expense than they could justify rescuing a team of eight researchers.

Or maybe it's because you have to tread lightly when you're venturing into the recently re-claimed sacred territory of a hostile alien empire.

The Cath Imperium recently laid formal claim to the entire Hadros Sector with the pretext that their ancestral home, Cythos, lies within it. The Cath are an interesting species: tall, bipedal apex predators with tails and sharp teeth. They evolved about three thousand light-years from Earth, only to mysteriously up and leave their ancestral home soon after developing the FTL tech to do it. Their entire species migrated more than six thousand light years away—nearly ten thousand light-years from Earth—and they made the exodus at a time when we were still a pre-FTL society, struggling to establish permanent colonies on the Moon and Mars.

Whatever their reasons for putting so much distance between us, I can't say I'm sad about it. The Cath are xenophobic, militaristic, and technologically advanced, which is a great combination for a war of extermination. At least now, with their Imperium so far from us, it's a logistical nightmare for either species to contemplate war. It's a two-year trip through FTL for either side to reach the other. One way. And there's no upside to it. Whatever we could hope to find over on their side of the galaxy, we can find it closer to home.

Except, apparently, for one thing: the Priors' artifacts. They were an unknown space-faring species that spanned thousands of star systems as recently as 97,000 BC, before mysteriously disappearing without a trace. They left behind hundreds of mega-structures in various states of repair: ring-shaped orbital habitats that completely encircled planets; vast-solar collecting Dyson spheres that completely enshrouded stars, and a handful of mysterious space stations that were shaped like giant donuts.

A little over two years ago, the Coalition found one of those donut-stations out here in the Nidus System of the Hadros Sector. Code-named "Terminus" Station, it was still powered up and running, and in seemingly perfect condition.

Terminus Station sits at roughly six thousand light years from both the Cath Imperium and the Coalition, so I guess it seemed innocent enough for us to occupy the station. That was until about a year ago when the Cath showed up with a long-range scout ship.

In all that time, they haven't even attempted to approach the station—at least as far as I know from our last contact with Terminus about a month ago. We suspect that they're waiting for reinforcements to arrive.

In response, the Coalition, treading lightly to avoid angering our more technologically advanced neighbors, dispatched a covert ops team of Paladins.

My team.

Our orders are to evacuate the researchers and their research and to make sure that Terminus Station doesn't fall into enemy hands.

The reasons why are above my pay grade as an E-7 Chief Operations Officer, but what little I've been told is that the researchers aboard Terminus Station are studying FTL Rifts, volatile tears in space-time that allow near-instantaneous (if unpredictable) travel between two distant points in space.

Whatever the reasons behind it, the mission is simple enough: get in, get out, and rig the place to blow.

The sound of the cockpit door sliding open precedes the booming voice of Brix Rylo. "What's our ETA to reversion, Chief?"

I turn to see the bald, dark-skinned operative stepping into the cockpit in full combat armor. He has his helmet tucked under one arm. No sense in breathing more canned air than we have to. I nod to the nav as he eases into the co-pilot's seat. "Five minutes and change."

"Guess I'm right on time," Brix says as he tugs his helmet on and twists it to engage the seals. With a rueful grimace, I reach over beside my seat where I left my helmet and slip it on too. Holographic icons and readouts flicker to life on the heads-up display, crowding the edges of my visor.

"Is the rest of the team ready to go?" I ask via external speakers.

"Locked and loaded," Brix confirms.

I nod wordlessly. My gaze is back on the jump timer.

"Moment of truth," Brix sighs. "Think the Cath beat us there?"

"I hope not," I reply. "It'd be a helluva a pain in the ass to have come all this way for nothing."

Brix grunts. "Not for nothing, boss. Our orders are the same whether the station's occupied or not."

"Maybe, but the odds of us completing the mission successfully are a damn sight lower if the place is already teeming with hostiles."

Brix frowns dubiously. "Nah. They'd never even see us coming."

I shake my head. "We don't want to be responsible for kicking off an interstellar war. If Cath are on board, the rules of engagement change, and this operation becomes a lot more delicate."

"That's why they sent us, Chief. We slip in on a cloaked shuttle, sneak aboard with cloaked exosuits, in and out and no one ever knows we were there. We'll make it look like a reactor failure took out the station. Easy as sniping rockrats off a mauler's back. *In omnia paratus!*"

I fix Brix with a skeptical look that I hope he picks up, despite my visor concealing my face. He just quoted one of the Paladins' mottos: it means *ready for anything*, but he's deliberately forgetting the other one: "*Vita brevis,*" I reply. *Life is short.*

Brix waves away my objections, and our conversation lapses into relative silence.

The jump timer hits three seconds and becomes an audible countdown over the cockpit speakers.

"Three, two, one…"

A jolt kicks through the deck, and the swirling tunnel of light becomes a fixed, glittering field of stars with a blank black circle in the middle. That hole is the dark side of the Nidus System's gas giant: Icarus. At point three astronomical units from the system's sun, it's a super-heated ball of fiery reds and yellows, but the dark side is all we can see right now.

Seizing the flight controls in both hands, I hurriedly set the shuttle to scan the area, checking to make sure the Cath didn't have any ships around to see us emerge from FTL.

With another hand, I engage our ship's cloaking shield and plot a low-powered trajectory that will bring us into line with Terminus Station.

"All clear," Brix announces, reading the results of the scan.

I nod absently with his analysis, watching as our orbit brings us around to the day side of Icarus. A shining red crescent of Icarus's mottled surface appears along the far right edge of the planet, then the sun crests over that: a blazing orange orb. It casts progressively broader swaths of light across the fiery surface of Icarus. Soon after that, Terminus Station appears, a darkly-gleaming ring locked in a high geo-synchronous orbit above the gas giant.

Moments later, we detect the Cath's scout ship: a dark red rock, oblong and misshapen, at about two hundred meters long. It's a hollowed-out asteroid, which is not a bad disguise for a scout ship when you think about it. But by now we're wise to the Cath's tricks. This particular ship is locked in a distant orbit around the Nidus System's sun, and we calculated the timing of our exit from this jump to coincide with when Icarus would be between us and them, so they wouldn't detect our exit from FTL. Now we have our EM cloak engaged and we're running on low power, using the gas giant's gravity to guide us to Terminus Station. It would take a small miracle for the Cath to spot us on their sensors.

Brix lets out a heavy breath. "So far, so good. Just the one ship. Although... you ever think that maybe it really is just a rock?"

I arch an eyebrow at him.

"Hey, I can dream, can't I?"

"Sure you can," I agree. "Just so long as you remember to wake up."

Brix snorts at that.

My hands are busy sweating inside my gloves despite the adaptive lining in my exosuit. I'm anxious to board the station and get this mission underway. But the closer we get to Terminus, the more apprehensive I begin to feel.

"I'm going to check in with Pixie and Gunner," Brix says after a while.

"Keep me posted," I reply. Pixie is what we call Operative Second Class Sia Dust, and "Gunner" is Kraug Hammer, a giant of a man at about seven feet tall, with arms as thick around as my legs. He's a genetically enhanced super soldier who does his level best to make the rest of us look bad. He's also our demolition expert.

About thirty minutes later, the shuttle glides into line with a yawning hangar bay along the outer circumference of Terminus Station. Ancient blast doors have been forced open, leaving a hazy blue gap that the researchers sealed off with a buzz shield to keep the hangar pressurized.

My heart races as we slip through the massive doors—at least fifty meters high and maybe a hundred across. You could fit a fifteen-story building in here. Or a Coalition frigate. Buzz shields sizzle softly against our hull. The inside of the station is dark. Everywhere I look, the walls and floor are made from the same nearly-uniform glossy black alloy. Illumination is dim and mostly provided by portable spotlights that the researchers set up after they arrived. The hangar is massive, and at the moment it's empty, although I can see spare fuel containment tanks, stacks of hover crates, and other gear that implies several other ships were landed here recently.

That puts a tight knot between my eyes. The researchers brought two shuttles of their own, also long-range Javelins like the one I'm flying, but they've long-since depleted their fuel to the point that those ships can no longer return to the Coalition. And for some reason, neither shuttle is currently landed in this hangar. Maybe they're using another hangar? I didn't see any on the way in, but maybe it's hiding on the far side of the station. Either that or the researchers left in a hurry. My credits are on option two, and that's bad news for the mission.

I land the shuttle on one side of the yawning hangar. The landing struts touch down with a muted *thump*, and I quickly power down the thrusters but leave the cloaking shield engaged and the reactor running on standby for a speedy exit.

I hesitate before unbuckling and rising from my seat. I can't shake the feeling that something is very wrong here. Maybe we're too late, and the Cath have already boarded Terminus. The researchers might have fled and been shot down by the Cath on their way out.

Whatever the case, I can't risk getting on the comms to see if anyone's home—or nearby—so there's only one way to find out what happened: we have to explore the station on foot.

* * *

Three shaded translucent green shadows are moving swiftly down the corridor ahead of me, cloaked, and planting charges as we go. Our orders are to blow the station just as soon as we've evacuated the researchers. If it's already empty, then there's no reason we can't skip to the punch line. But I'm still verifying the situation. No way to be sure until we've done our rounds. First up: the station's control center. The green diamond of the waypoint that I placed there is floating on my HUD, up ahead and to my right, 562 meters away. A green arrow at the bottom of my HUD points the way whenever that diamond dips out of my field of view.

The ceiling glows with a faint illumination that flows ahead of us, lighting the way like a living entity. The light reflects dimly off the glossy black walls and floor. Our exosuits are holo-plated to seamlessly transmit that light from one side of our armor to the other, making us perfectly invisible to hostile sensors and the naked eye, but special line-of-sight transmitters enable us to keep track of each other with the shaded green overlays. Aiding our covert insertion, are the acoustic dampeners that make our footsteps utterly silent. Our laser rifles are also holo-plated as well as mag-silenced and spectrum-shifted to make our shots both silent and invisible. If we run into anything down here, we could kill it in a whisper. Not that we're authorized to use lethal force against the Cath, but if we can get away with it... maybe.

Artificial gravity on board is light, maybe just a quarter of standard. I guess the researchers didn't figure out how to adjust the grav generators. Fortunately, the emitters in our boots are making it easy enough to keep our feet on the ground.

Our rifles are up and tracking, checking corners, doors, and intersecting corridors as we go. Gunner is bringing up the rear, planting compact antimatter bombs the size of my thumbnail every one hundred meters.

No sign of anyone on board yet, Cath or otherwise. I give the occasional hand signal, directing my team, but everyone already knows what to do without being told. We've practiced this op a hundred times in the Javelin's VR pods. And we were also thoroughly briefed in advance and given access to full station schematics.

Those schematics are projected on the small

flat circle of a map in the top left corner of my HUD. The four green dots that represent my team are busy racing down a gently arcing corridor to the station's control center. The arrow at the bottom of my HUD tells me we're almost there. A hundred and sixteen meters away.

Thirty seconds later, we reach a set of deep obsidian blast doors illuminated by a pale white square of glow panels. A quick look at my map confirms the control center is behind these doors. A jury-rigged touchscreen control panel is a testament to the fact that the researchers have already adapted the alien controls to a more familiar interface. I gesture to Brix and he moves toward the panel.

Signaling to Pixie and Gunner, I take up positions with them on either side of the doors. With no actual cover besides the narrow frame around the entryway, we paste ourselves to the walls, and I drop to one knee to make myself an even smaller target. Just in case.

Brix is standing by. I nod to him, and he triggers the doors. They rumble open, revealing a massive chamber with broad, curving walls of viewports on either side. One side, to our left, looks down on the angry red swirls of Icarus below. The other has a clear view across the empty center of the ring-shaped station, but in the middle of it, I can see a glossy sphere of distorted space-time that looks almost exactly like a giant glass marble. *What the hell?* I wonder idly at the sight of the anomaly.

No sign of any hostiles inside the control room, but I am picking up two *human* signatures.

Thank Deus. Someone is still here. My sensors shade them yellow through the walls of the station. Signaling to the rest of my team, we push up into the control room. As soon as we're in, I order Pixie and Gunner to hang back and cover the entrance while Brix and I continue.

Circular cubicles with glowing screens and oddly-shaped chairs are spaced almost evenly across the giant deck. One of those cubicles is occupied by the two humans I detected. Hurrying to reach them, I manage to make a positive ID from their faces: it's Christophe Zabelle and Ivy Rox, two of the eight researchers we came here to evacuate.

Christophe is about average height with skin the color of burnt caramel, blue eyes, and thick, wavy dark hair, while Ivy is tall and slender with straight dark hair cut short and a wall of bangs across her forehead. She also has blue eyes, but they're a much lighter shade than Christophe's.

If these two are still here, then maybe we're not too late, but where the hell are the other six?

I glance about quickly to make sure that we're clear before disengaging my cloaking shield. "Mr. Zabelle," I say, my suit shimmering as the holo-plating turns from invisible to opaque.

Christophe Zabelle flinches at the sight of me,

and his hand flashes down to a laser pistol on his hip.

I subtly turn and point to the Coalition flag projected over my left shoulder—a rising phoenix, surrounded by a circle of forty-seven stars, one for each of the colonized worlds that make up the Coalition.

"Oh, thank Deus," Christophe breathes shakily. "I thought you'd never get here!"

"It's a long trip," I reply, setting the polarization on my visor to clear so that these two can see my face. "We need to evac immediately. Are you ready to go?"

"Why? Did the Cath spot you on your approach?" Christophe asks quickly.

I slowly shake my head, and Christophe's whole body slumps in relief as if I just gave him the best news he's heard all week.

Brix materializes beside me, and Ivy's eyes snap to him.

"Where are the others?" I ask, still speaking to Zabelle.

He winces. "Not here."

"They left on the shuttles?" I suggest.

He nods.

"Are they close by? We're on a tight schedule."

"Yes and no..." Zabelle replies, glancing pointedly at the giant glassy sphere suspended invisibly in the empty void at the center of Terminus Station.

"What the hell is that supposed to mean?"

Brix asks. "Are they close or not?"

"Not," Ivy answers without skipping a beat. "They're in the Small Magellanic Cloud."

My jaw drops.

"What is that? Some kind of local nebula?" Brix asks.

Christophe pushes the silver circlet of a holo band higher up on his forehead, his expression looks like it could have been carved from stone. "It's a satellite galaxy, about a hundred and ninety thousand light-years from the edge of the Milky Way."

That makes my 10-month-long journey to get here look like a stroll around the block. Crunching the numbers with my Neuralink, I discover that it would take us twenty-seven years to reach that galaxy—assuming we didn't run out of fuel long before that, which we would.

"How the hell is that possible?" Brix asks.

Christophe points to the glassy sphere that he's been stealing glances at. "They didn't tell you what this station can do, did they?"

"No," I reply shortly.

"It's a jump gate. The Priors' version. It can make a stable connection to any other rift in the galaxy. You can travel almost anywhere—" Christophe snaps his fingers. "—in the blink of an eye."

"That's impossible," Brix mutters.

"Not for the Priors," Christophe replies. His eyes are glittering brightly. "Now you know why the Coalition sent us out here."

Ivy frowns. "What my colleague is neglecting to mention is that we still haven't figured out how to operate the gate. The only rift we can connect to is in the Small Magellanic Cloud."

"And you decided to send your people through it?" I growl at her. "Right around the time we were due to arrive for your extraction."

"Well, slag me..." Brix mutters.

"We had a good reason," Ivy objects. She points to the shining sphere. "Something came through the gate right after we figured out how to activate it. We think it could be one of the Priors—a real, living Prior! Can you imagine the things that they could teach us?!"

I can feel the beginnings of a headache pulsing in my temples. "Let me get this straight, you went chasing after some ship full of long-extinct aliens, thinking, oh I bet they'll want to be our friends! Because that worked out so scragging well with the Cath, right?"

Ivy scowls at me.

Christophe puts in, "They were supposed to be back by now."

"Even better," I mutter. "How long ago did they leave?"

"About twelve hours?" Christophe asks, looking to Ivy for confirmation. She nods.

"All right," I sigh. Spinning away from them, I gesture to the pair of translucent green silhouettes by the doors and raise my voice, "Pixie, Gunner, stay here and guard the station. Brix and I are going after the missing researchers. If we're not back within 24 hours, or if the Cath try to board the station before then, you know what to do. We can't allow this facility to fall into the Cath's hands. Especially not now that we know what it's capable of."

"Copy that, Chief," Pixie says. Both she and Gunner de-cloak, shimmering into view beside the doors. I know I can count on them to do what needs to be done. The Coalition vetted my team carefully before selecting us for this mission; they knew, just as I do now, that each of us is willing to die for the cause. Going down in a blaze of glory to prevent a bloody interstellar war is exactly the kind of thing that we signed on for when we joined the Paladins.

Looking back to Christophe and Ivy, I say, "You're coming with us."

"We can't *both* go," Ivy objects. "Someone needs to stay here and make sure that the rift stays open. Just because it's stable right now doesn't mean it'll stay that way."

Christophe nods. "I'll stay. You go."

Ivy appears to hesitate. "Are you sure? If they blow the place while we're gone..." She trails off, shaking her head.

I know what she's getting at. The people on our shuttle will survive—even if we wind up stranded in a neighboring galaxy. Not a much kinder fate, if you ask me, but at least we'll be alive.

"Aster is still out there," Christophe adds. "You'd do the same for me if it was Nadine."

Ivy's gaze softens with gratitude. "Thank you," she breathes.

"All right then. Let's move out," I snap at her.

"Do I have time to grab something from my quarters?" she asks.

"No," Brix answers for me.

She scowls at him, but there's no time to argue. I lead the way, sprinting from the control room and back down the corridors to our ship. We're no longer cloaked or making any kind of effort to quieten our steps. Makes no sense to stay hidden when Ivy is perfectly visible running beside us.

I can't help thinking as we go, why did they send *both* of their shuttles through that rift? It seems far too careless, even for civilians.

But gradually, it dawns on me that there's something these researchers haven't said.

"Why did you send two shuttles?" I ask, looking to Ivy.

A sheepish look crosses her pale face, which is now blotchy and flushed from all the running. "Because…" she takes a moment to catch her breath. "We were trying to rescue the first expedition."

Oh hell no, I think to myself. Shuttle one ran into trouble. Then shuttle two was sent to look for them, and now they're also overdue to return.

"How long has it been since the first shuttle left?" I demand.

"A little over a week," Ivy admits.

Brix looks at me and gives his head a slight shake.

I know what he's thinking. This is a scrigg's errand. But our orders were to extract the researchers and *then* blow the station. We can't accomplish A if we skip straight to B. And besides, shuttle two only left twelve hours ago, so there's still a good chance we can find them and bring them back before the 24-hour deadline I gave Pixie.

But if Pixie or Gunner decides to wait longer than that, or if the Cath surprise them here, we could wind up failing our mission entirely, and then Terminus will fall into our alien neighbors' hands—or paws, I suppose.

If they figure out how to use Terminus, their fleets will gain a deadly first-strike advantage, and I have a bad feeling they'll use it. Visions of war dance through my mind's eye—of Cath war fleets jumping to Earth and bombarding us from orbit until nothing but smoking craters remain.

"Please," Ivy pleads, as if she can sense my weakening resolve to rescue her colleagues. "You have to try. My husband, Aster, is on the second shuttle. We can still find him and bring him back."

"It's your call, Chief," Brix whispers to me over a private channel. "What do you want to do?"

PART ONE: THE BUBBLE BURSTS

CHAPTER 1

Forty-five Years Later...

The Year 577 UGC
Pyria, Alliance Space

"**L**ean into it, Dad!" Callista shouts at me from a few yards away, where she glides over the water on her grav board.

Wobbling a bit, but staying upright, I yell back, "I'm leaning, damn it!" My voice still sounds wrong, even after all these years. But you can't change your name without changing the rest. At least I already had the vocal implant. Sculpting my face was the worst part. People talk about phantom pains from a missing limb. As far as I know, no one's ever mentioned phantom reflections from a missing face.

The blinding crimson sun catches my eye, forcing me to squint. I'm racing over the water, pushed by the wave surging under me. The grav board tilts fractionally beneath my bare feet as

I take my daughter's advice, *leaning into it,* as I follow the racing roar of the water that's cresting over me.

I can hear my daughter's friends laughing and jeering in the background, probably thinking I'm too old for this. Youth and ignorance go together like stink on a tobra; you can't get rid of one until you get rid of the other.

If they only knew the things I was doing at their ages: orbital insertions in an exosuit, skulking in alien jungles for weeks on end with nothing but a pack of emergency rations and a mag-silenced bolter rifle to keep me alive; sleeping in the trees to avoid the monsters that come out at night. Neutralizing, by which I mean *killing*, countless targets, all in the name of peace and freedom.

The wave forms a shimmering tunnel around me, and there's a moment of plunging silence as cool water surrounds me, turning the world into blurry smears of color. A bright circle of sand and water is the light at the end of the tunnel. I can hear the rush of the water chasing me toward it. I crouch and lean forward just a little—

Causing the board to dip and dig in. Before I can blink, I'm tumbling. The water swallows me with a roar, and the wave rolls me, showing me the soles of my feet a few times before leaving me to drift along the sandy bottom. I linger there, staring at the wavy patterns imprinted on the ocean floor. A colorful reef of alien coral drifts into my peripheral view. It crackles like popcorn.

Dark red swirls appear below me, blooming like crimson flowers before my eyes and quickly spreading in greasy swirls. But only a dim echo of pain accompanies those spurts of blood. I blink a few times rapidly, and the apparition is gone. Just a memory.

My body drifts back to the surface, and I pop my head up for a gulp of air.

The sun and reflections off the water blind me. "How was that?" I ask, smiling tightly as I flick the water from my eyes. I glance about wincingly, treading water while I look for my grav board and my daughter.

"It was *flashin'*, Mr. Hale!" our next-door neighbors' son, Terrin Cushing, says as he drifts alongside me. Terrin smooths his hands through a mop of thick, wavy blond hair, accidentally-on-purpose flexing meaty biceps around his ears for Callista's benefit as she comes cruising toward us on her grav board.

One side of my face falls into a scowl. There's just something about Terrin's perfect tan and impossibly symmetrical features that rubs me the wrong way. His parents invested a little too heavily in engineering him to perfection before he was born, and somehow, they managed to achieve the opposite of what they were probably going for, making him annoying to look at.

Callista drifts alongside Terrin, wearing a green bikini that's much more revealing than I would like. At seventeen, she's all grown up: a knockout beauty with blonde hair, green eyes, and elfin features that closely resemble her mother's.

"Hey, Sparkles," Terrin says, calling her by a pet name I don't care for, and giving her a look that makes me want to gouge out his eyes with my thumbs. I let out a stale breath as he leans over for a kiss.

Callista pushes him away playfully, but Terrin won't take no for an answer, with his arm locked around her waist. She giggles, whispering, "Terrin! Stop. My dad is watching…"

I can tell by the way Callista smiles as he pulls away that she likes him. A lot.

My scowl is twitching now. Is it the fate of all fathers to loathe their daughter's boyfriends?

I clear my throat, drawing their attention away from each other. "I'd probably better head back to the beach and keep your mother company."

"Oh, sure. That's a good idea, Dad!" Callista says brightly. Her smile lingers on me. "Thanks for joining us. You're pretty *stag* on that board!"

"Oh, yeah, Mr. Hale, coming out here was really *creed* of you!" Terrin adds.

Creed. Kids. They probably don't even know what a creed is, but I guess they'll never have to live by one, so what does it matter?

I nod and force a strained smile for Callista's benefit. "It was fun. We'll do it again sometime."

With that, I turn around, tuck my head, and swim for the shore. Finding my grav board drifting near the beach, I use my neuralink to toggle it to follow me.

Two minutes later, I'm running up the beach, spraying hot sand from my heels. Aurora looks up at my approach, blazing copper eyes and fiery red hair catch my eye. She smiles a perfect grin that Terrin Cushing could learn from.

"It was nice of you to join them," she says. "Thank you."

"Yeah. Good times." I drop down on the empty towel beside her and lay back, shutting my eyes against the sun and waiting for it to sizzle me dry.

"Callista *really* wants you to like him," Aurora adds. I can feel her eyes boring into me.

"Mmmhmm." I hope Aurora takes the hint and drops it there.

And of course, she does. Reading body language from meatbags like me is one of my wife's hidden superpowers. A warm hand touches mine, and I realize that I've clenched my fists full of sand.

I force myself to relax, letting sand trickle from my hands as I drag a deep sigh from my chest. The Pyros System's sun is warming me steadily. Waves boom and swish rhythmically in the background. Sea shrikes are hooting. The water from the ocean is fast evaporating on my skin. It feels like a vacation. The problem is, I've been on this beach for so long that I've forgotten how to be on anything else. It's true what they say: you really can have too much of a good thing. And somehow, after fifteen years of lounging in a deep puddle of leisure, it just feels like a slow, creeping death to me.

How did I get so old, anyway? At sixty-seven, I'm approaching middle age, even if the gene-therapies have managed to keep my face looking thirty-five years young for the past three decades. But now I have a seventeen-year-old daughter and a wife of twenty years, so I can't pretend anymore. And I'm also *retired*. Another sigh builds up inside my chest like a ticking time bomb.

I crack my eyes open, then wince and lift a hand to shield my face as the sun blinds me. The afternoon sky has deepened to a magnificent shade of indigo between scudding white mountains of cloud.

A trio of IF-21 interceptors streak across the blue, their dual thrusters winking red as they bank through a lazy turn toward Coral City. Rumbling along behind them is a blocky hammerhead gunship. Pyrian System Patrol. Judging by the plodding pace they've set, they're not after anyone, just doing their rounds.

My mind wanders, and I imagine slicing through the clouds in the *Cloven Hammer*, my modified Type-9 Corvette, with that patrol chasing me as I blast out of Pyros with a wanted criminal in my hold...

Maybe they'd shoot me down, and I'd be forced to bail out with nothing but my exosuit and a survival kit. A smile twitches to my lips as the memories come parading through my mind's eye.

Back then, I thought I was doing the galaxy a favor. I bought right into the Coalition's recruitment propaganda: fight for peace and justice across the galaxy, defend the innocent, strike down the oppressors, and defend our utopian way of life. I was like a naive child trying to help a baby bird back into its nest, only to find that I'd sealed its fate by smearing my human stench all over it.

Some things you only make worse by touching them, no matter how good your intentions might be. And the Coalition's intentions were rarely ever as good as they seemed. I'm living proof of that. Dishonorably discharged for a shitstorm that they started and then sent to ARCmax on Mars because the only jobs I could find after the Paladins were the illegal kind.

To be fair, I probably could have left the Coalition a lot sooner than I did and avoided that whole ugly mess. Laws out here in the Free Systems Alliance are more like suggestions.

The sigh that's been building in my chest rattles out, but somehow I still feel like I'm holding some of it in. I can't ever seem to catch my breath these days.

Pushing those thoughts from my head, I turn to admire the gorgeous redhead lying beside me. My wife, Aurora. Her face is different than it was when we first met, but she kept her hair and her eyes the same.

With over twenty-seven trillion people in the galaxy, maybe we needn't have bothered changing our faces. For every bio, bot, and cyborg, there must be at least a dozen faces that look the same. Digital IDs are much more reliable, but even those can't be trusted. You can buy a new name for the price of a blaster on some planets, although we paid a lot more than that for ours.

Before we retired, I went by Cade Korbin—and a dozen other aliases—but now I go by just one: Corvus Hale. And Aurora is Aura Hale. That one is a bit too close for comfort, but Pyria feels so far removed from the life we left behind that we've never worried about anyone following us here.

Seeming to notice my scrutiny, Aurora rolls toward me. Her glowing orange eyes flick open like two drops of molten copper. Her lips curve into a smile, revealing perfect white teeth. Her hand slides into mine, caressing and then squeezing gently.

"Getting nostalgic, are we?" Aurora asks. "You miss it, don't you?" She nods to the sky. "Nothing but you and your ship against the galaxy."

I cock an eyebrow at that. I'm always

surprised by how easily she can read me, but maybe I shouldn't be after all these years. And Aurora is a resurrected *bot*, equipped with more hidden abilities than I can name.

"Miss it?" I ask. "What's to miss? Getting shot at, always watching my back, nearly dying a dozen times before lunch..." I slowly shake my head, rocking it from side to side on my beach towel. "You and Callista are enough for me."

I hope she bought it. We've argued about this before, with Aurora accusing me of secretly wanting to go back to bounty hunting, and with me stubbornly insisting that nothing could be further from my mind.

Aurora turns away, looking straight up at the sun and making no attempt to shield her eyes from the glare. Bots are lucky: they don't need sunglasses or UV shields, and they don't sweat or get dehydrated. Going to the beach must be like heaven for Aurora. But sometimes I have to wonder: does the sun on her skin and the sand between her toes still feel the same as it does to me?

All the big resurrection companies swear high and low that life as a bot is ten times better than it is as a bio, and resurrected people typically agree, but I still can't wrap my head around it. Transcending just seems too much like dying.

But does that mean my wife is dead? I study her surreptitiously out of the corner of my eye. We met when Aurora was already a bot, and except for those glowing eyes, her appearance is perfectly human. Elaborate window dressing for a resurrected human mind that was long ago digitized and encased in metal. A mind that I subsequently fell in love with. Somehow, despite all the odds, she fell for me, too.

Bio-bot couplings aren't exactly rare, but most of them were couples *before* one of them died and came back in a synthetic body. That makes perfect sense, but a romance developing out of a vacuum between a bot and a bio? Now *that* is unusual. There are so many little nuances that you wouldn't even think about. It's like we're from two completely different species.

How do you relate to someone who looks human, but who effectively shares none of your biological urges and needs? Bots can simulate almost anything they want to from their old meatbag bodies. Aurora can eat and drink when she wants to, and supposedly she gets to savor all of the same flavors and even the digital equivalent of the same dopamine rush, but unlike me, she doesn't *need* to eat, and she can get that same rush whenever she wants to, with or without chewing up a tasty meal first.

So why waste credits on food?

The answer is that she doesn't unless we're out on a date, or it's a special occasion. And what about sleep? Sure, she can lie next to me and charge for eight hours if she wants to, but why bother when her power cells go from zero to a hundred in just thirty minutes?

On that score, we've come to an arrangement. She goes to bed with me and charges while I fall asleep. Then she rolls out of bed to indulge in a very active night life without me. She has other bot friends. And hobbies, like running along the promenade in Coral City.

I have to admit, that particular ability—being able to get by with little to no down time, makes me pretty jealous sometimes.

But there are other more insidious issues that we've had to deal with over the years. For example, when Aurora kisses me, does she do it because she loves me and craves physical intimacy, or because that's what a meatbag wife would do, and she's adapted for my sake?

It took me a while to adjust my thinking on that score, and I guess in some twisted kind of way, *choosing* to desire your spouse is more romantic than having it come naturally. Meatbags are slaves to our natures, but bots aren't, so everything they do is much more deliberate. The nearest equivalent for bios is behavioral clinics. A *minder* can get in and tweak my natural impulses almost as readily as Aurora can adjust hers by herself.

By this point, we've overcome most of our fundamental issues. Aurora keeps up some of the pretenses of humanity for my sake, and I do my level best to understand the idiosyncrasies of her synthetic life.

Meatbags like me would say that we must be soul mates to go through all of that for each other, but that can't be true, because supposedly, bots don't have souls.

And it's even worse than that. Aurora is an illegal copy of a bio who is still very much among the living: Bella Zabelle of Zabelle Enterprises, the daughter of one of the wealthiest families in the galaxy. We can't even pretend that Aurora's immortal soul was somehow inexplicably transferred to her new, synthetic body.

"You're doing it again," Aurora chides.

"Doing what?" I ask.

"Dwelling on the past."

"Not exclusively," I reply.

"Your past is full of skeletons. Are they better company than me?" Aurora turns to look at me once more.

"No one's better company than you, Aura," I say.

Her eyes narrow at me. "Live life forwards, not in reverse. It's a beautiful day," she adds, nodding to the sunny sky. "This is why we came to Pyria: to put the past behind us, remember?"

I smile tightly and nod. "How can I forget?" It's been fifteen years since my last bounty-hunting gig, and twelve since I took an independent contract of any kind. It's been about the same for Aurora. After we decided to have Callista, it wasn't long before we realized that we couldn't keep doing what we'd been doing for a living. Bounty hunting tends to make you a lot of enemies—especially *our* brand of bounty hunting.

Rather than taking contracts from the galaxy's lowlifes, we *targeted* them, making it our job to clean up the proverbial streets, a job that Alliance patrollers are loathe to do because they're getting big kickbacks from the stim cartels.

Eventually, we built ourselves quite the reputation, and we founded the Templars, a bounty hunters' guild that put justice before credits. But taking active contracts personally, and running a guild that does so en masse wasn't any less dangerous, so Aurora and I set up the Orion Shipping Co. as a front for the guild, and then we left the Templars in the capable hands of Brix Rylo, an old buddy of mine from the Paladins.

Then we changed our names and faces and picked a tropical Gaia world to retire on, somewhere far from the major trade lanes and the galaxy's most populous worlds.

Pyria fit the bill perfectly. Right on the edge of charted Alliance Space, all of the Alliance's wealthiest families have homes here. Some of them live here full-time, like us, while others leave their massive beach front mansions in the care of their staff. Adding to the appeal for Aurora and me, Pyria is a restricted-access world. You have to own property to get past the orbital checkpoints. But to buy that property, you need an invitation from an existing owner and be vetted by the planet's governing council. One of the more regrettable requirements is that you need a net worth of over ten million credits just to be considered for residence, which means my neighbors are all entitled assholes.

Ordinarily, I wouldn't be caught dead on a planet like this, but as it happens, few people do security like the galaxy's rich, and we came here to keep Callista safe, after all.

Propping myself up on my elbows, I place a level hand against my brow to shield my eyes from the slanting rays of the sinking sun. I scan the shining lavender-white sand and the sparkling, frothing sea for signs of a bright green bikini or a slick mane of wet blond hair.

But there's no sign of her.

I frown at that. My daughter was bobbing on the waves with the other grav surfers just a few minutes ago.

Aurora seems to notice my concern. "She went out with Terrin and his family on their hoveryacht."

"What?" I send her a sharp look. "She left without telling us?"

"She told *me*," Aurora replies, and taps the side of her head as if to remind me that she can take comms calls silently inside her head. I can, too, but I need my holoband for that, and I left it at home.

"Why am I only finding out about this now?"

"Because we know how you feel about Terrin, and you came out here to relax. I didn't want to upset you on your day off."

My day off. Every day is a day off. Taking a few calls and watching routine operations for the Orion Shipping Co. from my office doesn't count as work.

"Terrin's a scrigg," I say.

"See?" Aurora says.

"I can count his brain cells on one hand," I add.

"He's a nice boy and you know it."

"I never said he wasn't nice, but I swear I'll never understand what Callista sees in him."

Aurora thinks Callista fell in love with Terrin Cushing because he has some secret hidden qualities that make him lovable to *her*, but I know the truth: he's a regrettable side effect of the bubble that we raised Callista in. We've kept her so close and sheltered that she fell in love with the boy next door, not because he's such a great catch, but because we never let her wander any farther afield than that. I just hope it's not too late for her to realize it's a big galaxy and she has other options.

Aurora sighs. "Well, they say love is blind, don't they?"

"And stupid," I add. "Don't forget stupid."

Aurora narrows her eyes at me. "We don't get to choose who we love, Cade," she whispers.

Adrenaline sparks dimly through my veins at the sound of my real name. But we're alone on the beach, and Aurora would have detected it if there were any drones nearby watching us.

"Do I have to remind you how *we* met?" she asks.

"As I recall, you were the bait in a plot to kill me."

"And you fell in love with me anyway, but somehow Terrin is the scrigg?"

It's my turn to glare. "Are you saying I was a fool to fall for you?"

"No, I'm saying that from the outside, love makes no sense to anyone. You have to experience it for yourself."

I let out another sigh, and Aurora rolls over onto her stomach. I can't help but notice the burgundy-colored thong that she's wearing. She crosses her arms for a pillow and turns her head to watch me surreptitiously with one glittering orange eye. A sultry smile curves her lips.

"What is it?" Aurora asks innocently.

"You're doing it on purpose."

"Doing what?" she asks again, smiling smugly and shrugging as she props herself up on her elbows, leaving her cleavage to droop.

I tear my eyes away from her curving figure, up past the sparkling sand to the hanging red blossoms of the lorus trees at the ocean-facing end of our property.

"Let's go. It's getting late, and I need to make

dinner."

"Let's start with dessert," Aurora says with a wink.

"Perfect."

We stand up together, brushing off the sand and picking up our towels, and shaking them out. We put on our sandals, and I gesture absently to the cooler cube and my grav board, both of which follow us up the beach. We cross beneath the hanging fronds of the lorus trees, leaving the sparkling lavender-white sand behind.

A bright green lawn of chroma grass envelops us up to our ankles, and long, motile blades flow toward our feet, tickling the sand from between our toes, and in my case, nibbling away at layers of dead skin. As dusk falls, the grass will gradually turn blue with the setting of the sun, and then to silver, as it begins to luminesce with ethereal light. Chroma grass is native to Pyria, but somehow it still cost me a small fortune to pave my lawn with it. Chalk it up to an economy flooded with more money than sense.

We cross from the lawn to a lighted cobblestone path that winds down from our home to the beach. Lex, our gardener, is busy trimming hedges and fertilizing flowers around decorative lily ponds. The name stands for LX-9 —the landscaper version of the X-9 bot chassis. I wave to him. He smiles and waves back mechanically. "Hello, Mr. Hale!" His smile lingers, looking forced. Those flaws are worked in deliberately to differentiate AI-powered *drudges* from resurrected bots like Aurora.

Since only the ultra-rich are allowed on Pyria, we need drudges to do all of the actual work, just like they do in the Coalition. Drudges like Lex are foundational to the utopian lifestyle, but I can tell you first-hand that sitting around all day with nothing to do isn't all it's jacked up to be.

As we walk past Lex, Aurora doesn't even acknowledge his presence. Being a bot herself, with a fine line artificially drawn between her and *it*, I've often wondered how she sees the prevalence of robot slaves in our society. We've talked about it, of course, and she pretends not to care, but deep down I suspect it makes her uncomfortable.

I let my gaze rise from the garden to take in our relatively modest one-floor home perched on a rocky ridge. Our infinity pool cascades from those obsidian cliffs into a deep, secondary pool surrounded by lush greenery in a fern-lined grotto at the base of the cliffs.

Reaching the top of the stairs, our home sweeps into view: a wall of highly reflective palladium glass set in a terantium alloy frame that reflects its surroundings like a mirror. Right now it's a jagged slice of the indigo sky, freckled with clouds. We built up on this cliff, despite the relatively small footprint that it allowed, to maximize the view and our privacy. Sitting almost a hundred feet above our neighbors, we have the illusion of solitude and a three-hundred-and-sixty-degree view of the ocean on both sides of the peninsula.

Everyone around us built sprawling mansions on the flatlands around the ridge. I could have done the same, but what the hell does a family of three do with ten bathrooms, anyway?

I guess our neighbors must be full of shit.

Aurora grabs my hand and leads me through our bright, sleekly-furnished living room to the bedroom, where she promptly gives me better things to think about.

A few hours later, we're lying naked in each other's arms, watching the sun slip below the horizon. An empty pizza box and two beers lie on the floor beside me. Aurora had that questionable dinner delivered from one of my favorite joints in Coral City, so I wouldn't have to get out of bed and cook.

Aurora whispers something from where she lies with her head on my chest. My mind is hazy and numb from a lazy day, and at first, I don't catch what she said.

"Hmmm? What was that?" I mumble.

"I said, I have something that I need to tell you."

"Go for it."

She sits up, distracting me with her nakedness. Then she frowns and pulls the blankets up. "It's important. Focus."

"Hey, I'm trying, but you don't make it easy."

She bites her bottom lip and looks out at the view, stalling for time. Maybe steeling herself for my reaction. That puts me on edge and I sit up now, too, feeling suddenly wide awake.

"Aurora? What's going on?"

"Something happened last night while you were asleep."

"Okay…"

"Before I tell you about it, you have to promise me that you won't get mad."

Aurora's gaze tracks back to mine. Her eyes are big and round, and I can tell that she's scared—*of me?* I wonder. My heart is pounding. Was this afternoon her way of making up for something that she did?

"I can't promise I won't get mad," I say. "But I'll try to dial it back if I do."

Aurora sucks in a deep breath, and suddenly I'm aware of just how strange that is; she doesn't need to breathe. Just like she doesn't need a heartbeat, or skin that's warm to the touch.

That leaves me wondering how much of Aurora is real, and how much of her is fake.

What has she been hiding from me?

CHAPTER 2

"Just spit it out, Aura," I growl, bracing myself for whatever she's about to reveal.

Is she having an affair? It's not unheard of, but we *agreed* to be monogamous. Faithfulness is supposed to be hard-wired into her.

"Maybe it would be best if I just showed you," Aurora says.

Show me? I wonder. "Fine," I grunt.

Aurora eases out of bed and I follow her to the walk-in closet. We both slip into comfortable pants and t-shirts. She puts on slippers. I leave my feet bare but slip on a thin silver circlet. My holoband chimes silently through bone-conduction speakers as it wakes up. Glowing icons and displays swirl to life at the edges of my vision: my vitals. Workout logs. Sensors. Wireless connections to the Galnet and Hypercomms.

Aurora leads me out and down the bedroom hall, through an open living area and kitchen, and down the opposing hallway where our offices lie. Mine is on the left, facing the pool and the view, while hers is to the right, up a short flight of stairs. Aurora leads the way up. My feet feel like they're stuck in castcrete, each step heavier than the last. My gut is churning with apprehension at whatever Aurora is about to reveal.

She pauses at the top of the stairs, hesitating before she opens her office. I turn to look through the glass door across from it, to the rooftop deck. A retractable flexiplast roof stretches above three hammocks and some cozy lounge furniture, as well as an outdoor kitchen and a clay brick pizza oven.

I remember countless evenings spent out there, cooking dinner for Callista and myself while she and Aurora played holo games at the table. Or sipping a glass of wine with Aurora after putting Callista to bed, watching the stars come out, and listening to the waves crash and the sea shrikes hooting in the background...

Suddenly I'm no longer bored by our life but terrified that I'll lose it.

"Cade?"

Aurora's voice startles me from my reminiscing, and I turn from the deck to see her standing by her desk. She beckons to me, and I put one leaden foot in front of the other, breezing through the open doorway. Her desk is facing the pool and our slice of the private beach that we came from just a few hours ago. Her office is built on top of mine, with slightly more square footage to accommodate a charging pad and a maintenance pod which she uses to make any minor modifications and routine repairs to her body.

As soon as I reach Aurora's side, she peels away from the desk, heading for the wall behind it. That wall faces the landing pads behind our home and the indoor garage beneath them, but there are no windows directly behind the desk, just the two wall sconces and a holoframe hanging between them that cycles endlessly different holograms of us and Callista.

Aurora stops to admire a particular memory, and the image comes to life as a video, replaying a recording of us at the zoo on Ataris IV.

"It's freezing!" Callista cries with delight as fat snowflakes begin spiraling down from the sky. "Daddy, pick me up!"

I scoop her up into my arms, hugging her close to keep her warm. "Turn on your thermal shield, honey," Aurora suggests.

"No, I want to feel the cold. It's *never* cold on Pyria!" Callista looks up wonderingly, craning her neck to watch the snow fall. "It's so pretty..."

The recording of me smiles, and I swing Callista up over my shoulders for a better view.

She leans forward and opens her mouth to catch a snowflake. "Delicious!" she announces.

Aurora loops an arm through one of mine,

watching Callista with a grin. The image freezes there, with all of us smiling.

"Do you remember that trip?" Aurora asks, her tone wistful.

"Yes," I say simply.

"It was so long ago, and yet somehow it still feels like it was yesterday. How did Callista grow up so fast?"

"Aurora," I intone darkly, growing impatient with her. "What the hell is this about? What's the secret?"

Aurora flinches and a guilty look flits across her face. She steps sideways and grabs the wall sconce to her right, pulling it toward her.

I blink in shock as a soft *thunk* sounds beneath my feet. The floor tile I'm standing on sinks down a few inches, and I leap back just as it slides away to reveal a dark, circular shaft with a one-meter circumference, the same as the width of one of our tiles. It plunges straight down into unfathomable depths.

But that's impossible. I was on-site with Aurora when our house was being built. We took turns supervising, and I saw the plans. No tunnels were going down into the ridge. A few crevasses, mind you. Is that what this is?

Dim blue rings of light flick on in a cascading sequence, illuminating the length of the tunnel below. Even without my holoband to measure the distance, I can tell it goes down a *long* way. About fifty meters. Well below sea level. No, this had to be *built,* whether it was cored out of solid rock or not.

Rather than ask how in the galaxy Aurora built this without me finding out, I nod to the tunnel and ask the more relevant question. "Where does it go?"

"Come on down, and I'll show you."

With that, Aurora crosses her arms over her chest and hops into the shaft. Those blue rings of light flash brightly around her as she falls. They're grav generators. The sequence slows along with Aurora as she nears the bottom.

It's a drop tube. Much more compact than an elevator, but unnerving to some. And these require more energy to run. Not to mention a backup power bank, in case the grid fails and the grav fields fail while they're in use. *Splat—* though I suppose in Aurora's case it would be more of a *crunch.*

Taking a deep breath to steel myself for whatever I'm about to learn, I cross my arms and hop into the drop tube.

CHAPTER 3

Rings of light flash brightly around me as I fall, then quickly arrest my momentum, as I near the bottom of the shaft. The sleek walls of the tube vanish, leaving nothing but four skinny columns tracking me down the last ten or twelve meters to the ground.

My feet touch the bottom of the drop tube, and I turn to see Aurora standing sheepishly to one side of the open platform, just outside the glowing ring in the floor that defines the edges of the grav field generator.

My gaze only lingers on Aurora's face for a second before I notice the familiar sight of a modified Type-9 Corvette, the *Black Augur*, sitting on a landing pad in a vast, rocky cavern behind her.

As far as I can tell, that's pretty much all that's down here. I step woodenly off the platform, walking by Aurora, my jaw agape and eyes darting to take in the underground hangar that's secretly been lurking beneath our house for who knows how many years. The cavern appears to be naturally-formed, complete with stalagmites in the floor around the landing pad, and stalactites in the ceiling. Dripping water echoes through the silence, punctuating my thoughts.

"You've been working again."

Aurora nods, chewing her bottom lip.

"And you accuse *me* of reminiscing about the good old days?!"

"Accuse you?" Aurora echoes incredulously.

I stop at the edge of the landing platform, looking up at her ship. Matte black, twenty-five feet high, with a classic Y-shaped fuselage leading to two main thrusters at the back, and a small docking bay for an interceptor-class getaway vehicle stowed beneath the cockpit.

"I never *accused* you," Aurora whispers. "I've been looking for a way to tell you about this. I thought that maybe if you admitted to missing our old life, then I'd finally be able to tell you about all of this, but you always swore you were happy, that retirement was the best thing that ever happened to you. And I could never really tell how much of that was true. Besides, even if you *did* miss our old life, I wasn't sure you would understand. We came here to protect Callista. And this..." Aurora gestures to her ship with one hand, and shakes her head, looking miserable. "I thought you'd accuse me of being selfish and putting our life here in jeopardy. So that's why I never told you about it."

"How long have you kept this a secret?" I demand, rounding on her.

Aurora winces. "Four years."

"Four years!" I thunder. "How… when did you…" I gesture helplessly to her ship.

"You remember that business trip you took to the Virgil System to resolve the trade dispute between Orion and Luxor?"

That was six years ago. Holy shit. This has been going on right beneath my nose for a *long* time. "I was only gone for two weeks!" I thunder at her.

"The cave was always here," Aurora explains. "I found it one night while I was out diving with Jana. And the crevasse that I used for the drop tube was also there, I just had to widen it at the bottom, then seal the entrance of the cave, and pump out the water." She gestures to a pair of heavy metal doors facing the nose of her ship.

I can only assume that there's another set behind those, allowing it to function like an airlock so she can keep the cave dry.

As mad as I am, I have to admit, this is impressive. I almost wish I'd thought of it instead of her. But then, I'm the meatbag who needs to sleep for eight hours while she's slinking down here to live a double life.

Except that isn't enough time. Seven hours would barely get Aurora to the neighboring system, let alone give her enough time to work a contract and still somehow make it home before I go stumbling into the kitchen looking for coffee. And she's usually the one to wake me up and put that first cup in my hands.

So what the hell is going on here?

My mind is spinning through the possibilities again, and suddenly an affair jumps back to the top of the list. Maybe she can't make an interstellar trip while I'm asleep, but she could go somewhere more local. Maybe to one of the Pyros systems' other planets—like Ataris IV. Is *that* why that particular memory from the holoframe caught her attention?

I struggle to put the clues together in my mind. How many times have I woken up in the middle of the night and found Aurora missing, only to give her a call and find that she's out with one of her bot friends, or out in Coral City, buying groceries for me and Callista? How much of that has been a lie?

Anger and outrage come simmering back to the surface. I cross my arms over my chest and jerk my chin to her ship.

"What's his name?" I ask.

Aurora blinks and shakes her head, looking suddenly confused. "My ship? The *Black Augur.*"

"Don't take me for a scrigg. The guy you're cheating with."

Laughter bursts from Aurora's lips. Confusion gives way to a smile and rueful amusement. "Oh, Cade, I'm not cheating on you. I would never do that."

Relief flutters through me, but now it's my turn to be confused. I'm back to my original assumption. "You've been taking contracts and working them while I sleep?"

Aurora nods.

"How? I mean… the average job takes what, a few weeks to complete between prep and travel time?"

"About that."

"And we used to track our targets across several systems, so unless these are local contracts…"

She shakes her head.

"Then it's impossible," I say. "You can't sneak out and do all of that while I'm asleep."

Aurora cocks an eyebrow at me, waiting for me to figure it out for myself.

"Unless…" My gaze sharpens accusingly on her. "You're in two places at once."

"Bingo."

"You copied yourself?"

She nods.

"And left *me* with one of them. Are you fucking kidding me right now? Which one are you?"

Aurora winces. "I'm the one you've been living with. But we're the same person. I mean, we'd reconcile our neuro data between jobs, so I know everything that she does and vice versa. It's not like you don't know who you've been married to." She reaches for one of my hands, but I recoil from her.

"Are you sure about that?" I look around suddenly. "So where's the copy? Or the original?"

"Copy," she confirms. "And that's what I needed to tell you. I said something happened last night, remember?"

"Uh-huh." I think I know where this is going.

"My copy got killed."

"On a job."

"Not exactly. The job was over. She—I mean *I*—" Aurora corrects herself hastily. "—returned safely to the Shroud. She was busy syncing her neuro data over the Galnet when someone broke in and shot her with a plasma blaster."

My anger fades as confusion surges once more. "This happened *in* the Shroud? Are you sure?"

"I'm positive."

Guild members are off-limits to each other. That's one of the more fundamental rules of our trade. Our headquarters are sacred. They're supposed to be safe places where we can regroup. We're not even allowed to take weapons into them.

"One of our hunters?" I ask.

"I don't know. His face was covered."

"With a biomask?"

"More like a helmet."

"No ID?"

Aurora shakes her head.

"What did Brix have to say about it?"

"He's on his way here right now. I made him promise to let me be the one to tell you."

I blow out an angry breath. "What was your last contract?"

"I don't know. I only got a partial download from my neural net. The data was corrupted."

"But the Templars must have a record of the job."

"Brix said there was nothing on the board. I was supposed to be between jobs."

"You took a job off the books? Do you have any idea how dangerous that is?"

Aurora scowls. "Don't patronize me. I don't know, okay? My copy got disintegrated before I could get all the details. Brix says there's evidence the Templars' logs might have been tampered with."

"So your double only syncs up with you after she completes a job. Kind of a scrigg move for an old pro like you, isn't it? If you die, you'll never know who might still be out there looking to make it a permakill."

"That's what guild records are for," Aurora insists. "I should have something to go on."

"Except that you don't."

"How is that my fault?" Aurora demands. "The guild has obviously been infiltrated."

"Yeah... okay..." I absently stroke my jaw, thinking it over. "Wait a minute." My gaze snaps to Aurora's ship. "What is the *Black Augur* doing here if your copy never made it back?"

"She took my heavy fighter this time." Aurora points to a smaller landing pad that I can now see peeking out behind the corvette. "And we only meet up here in person very occasionally," Aurora adds. "It's too risky, otherwise."

"No shit. Have you ever thought that you could be putting Callista in danger?"

Aurora frowns. "Pyria is the safest planet in the Alliance. It's not like just anyone can visit."

"The Shroud was supposed to be safe, too, and look how that worked out for you. If the Templars have been compromised, then whoever killed you could know about our life here."

Aurora's expression flickers uncertainly. "Only Brix knows where we live…"

"You mean other than you and your clone? Who's to say that whoever killed you didn't figure out where we live *before* they disintegrated you? For all we know, they're on their way here now to finish the job."

"Cade, I…" Aurora falters, looking scared.

"How do we know that Callista is really on the Cushings' hoveryacht right now?"

Whirling away from my wife, I dash back into the drop tube and touch the side of my holoband, saying, "Call Callista Hale!"

"Calling Callista Hale," the device replies through its bone-conduction speakers. I activate the drop tube and go whirring back up to Aurora's office with the call ringing over and over in my ears.

Callista isn't answering her comms.

CHAPTER 4

I reach the top of the drop tube and step quickly out of the grav field.

Aurora is right behind me. "Is she okay?"

Before I can reply Callista's face appears in the top right corner of my holo display.

"Hey, Dad!" she says, smilingly.

Relief billows out of me at the sight of her. "Callista, where are you right now?"

Her eyebrows drift up, and she slowly shakes her head, looking confused. Her green eyes are bright, and she's sipping a fruity-looking drink with an umbrella in it. She has her mother's dimples and cute, elfin features. Like most bots or bio-bot couples who want to have children, we had to use digital records of Aurora's DNA to synthesize the embryo, and then rent a synthetic womb.

"Ummm..." Callista trails off. "I don't know. Somewhere between Dash Point and Coral City, I think."

I can hear people chatting in the background. Smooth jazz music is playing. There comes a squeal of laughter and then a splash, followed by another one as someone is either pushed or jumps overboard. Terrin waltzes through the background, dancing to the music with an imaginary partner. He has a beer in one hand and a towel draped over his shoulder. As I'm watching, he swoops in, trading his imaginary partner for Callista, and spinning her around. She giggles and some of her drink sloshes over the sides of the glass. The background blurs behind her as the holoband and its cameras follow her head.

Callista deploys her holoband's camera drone and puts it on speaker-mode. My viewpoint detaches from Callista's head just in time for me to get a good look as Terrin pulls her in for a sloppy, lingering kiss.

I clear my throat. "Callista?"

She pushes her boyfriend away with mock annoyance and a fading grin. "Sorry, Dad."

"Oh, heya, Mr. Hale!" Terrin smiles sheepishly and waves to the drone. He's about my height at six-foot-two, with a classically handsome face, genetically-engineered to perfection, and still annoying to look at. Right now he's shirtless and sporting a flawless tan that he actually earned the hard way by lounging around the pool and on a grav board. Which is more than I can say for his six-pack abs and bulging biceps. Dimples in his chin and cheeks, bright blue eyes, and thick wavy blond hair complete the picture of a holo star that his parents paid handsomely for him to cultivate.

Speaking of, I can see Destine and Prentice in the background behind him, chatting with another couple that I vaguely recognize. I think it's the Ferrols, who live four houses down from us. Just then, his father leans in to kiss Mrs. Ferrol on the lips, while Mr. Ferrol and Mrs. Cushing look on with inane smiles.

They're swingers. Aurora and I got the memo soon after we first met, and we've promptly avoided them ever since. Callista has assured me that Terrin doesn't share his parents' liberal views, but I'm not convinced. It's so much easier to prove what you are than what you aren't.

"Send me your location," I say to Callista. "I'm coming to get you."

"What?" Callista looks annoyed now. "What for?"

"It's late, and you should be home already."

"I'm almost *eighteen*, Dad. And anyways, Mom's here. What do you think is going to happen?"

Suddenly, my blood turns to ice and my skin prickles all over. Time seems to slow to a crawl, and my heart begins hammering loudly in my ears.

"What did you say?" I ask quietly.

"I *said*, I'm almost eighteen. Or did you forget

that my birthday is next week?" Callista lets out an irritated sigh. "Look, why don't you just talk to Mom about it? I'll come back with her later. Mom!" Callista calls out.

"Cally, stop!"

I see her spin away from the camera drone, searching the deck of the yacht for her mother, but there's no sign of her.

"What's going on?" Aurora asks from my end, crowding in to get a glimpse of the visuals being transmitted to the holoscreen that's being projected a few inches in front of my face.

Callista suddenly freezes, having noticed her mother standing in the background beside me. "Mom? When did you go home? I thought you were in the kitchen with Jana?"

Terrin sips his beer and glances about idly, looking bored by the conversation.

Aurora whispers beside me, "Callista, I've been with your father ever since you left the beach."

"What? That's impossible. I just saw you here a few minutes ago…"

I shake my head quickly. "Cally, the woman on the yacht is not your mother."

CHAPTER 5

Callista's eyes fly wide, and she glances about furtively. Terrin, like the scrigg he is, still hasn't realized what's going on.

"Hey, doll, I'm gonna go grab a snack. Be right back." He drops a kiss on Cally's cheek and then drifts out of view.

Aurora asks me over a text to invite her to the call, but I do one better than that and deploy my own camera drone.

Callista looks even more shocked now that she can see her mother standing beside me in her office.

"Take us off speaker," I say. "And find somewhere more private where we can talk."

Callista nods and slips away from the sights and sounds of the party, walking to the edge of the deck and down a stairwell to a private alcove that's tucked away along the starboard side of the ship. "Someone is impersonating you?" Callista whispers to us once she's sure that no one else is around.

"Yes," Aurora answers.

"Why?"

"We think they might be there for you," I explain. Scanning her surroundings, I notice a door behind Cally and banks of three windows to either side of it. The lights are on in two of the ones to the right, but they're curtained for privacy, which makes me think that they belong to a guest room. Probably safe. What would the impostor be doing in there?

"You need to get out of there," Aurora says.

"Is there an air car you can take to get home?" I ask.

"Or a waveskimmer?" Aurora suggests.

"Uhh, well, Mom—I mean, the woman who looks like her—brought her car."

"You recognized it?" I ask.

Callista nods.

Whoever is behind this has gone to a lot of trouble to get to us. Or more specifically, to our daughter.

"Does anyone else have a vehicle?" Aurora asks quickly.

"Terrin's dad has one."

"Ask Terrin to borrow it and bring you back here. Quietly."

Callista nods and begins drifting back toward the party. "Where is the woman who looks like your mother?" I think to ask.

"She was in the kitchen on the deck above this

one."

"Good. If you run into her, act normal."

Callista nods again. The camera turns with her as she leaves the railing and heads for the stairs to the upper deck where the party is. Just as she's leaving, the door slides open behind her, and an intimately-familiar woman comes striding out in a loose white cotton wrap and a fire-red bikini that matches her hair.

"Hello, Cally!" Aurora's copy calls to her. She's holding an ice-blue margarita that's steaming with dry ice. She's smiling lazily, and her glowing copper eyes look dimmer than usual. Her gait is slightly unsteady, too. It looks like she's simulating a nice buzz.

Aurora's and my faces wink off the call as my wife wisely decides to kill the visual from our end.

Callista flicks a nervous smile over her shoulder and slows her pace. "Oh, hi, Mom." There's a detectable quaver in her voice. "I've got to go... Terrin is probably wondering where I went."

Aurora's copy hurries after her. "Hey, slow down! Who are you talking to?" the copy asks, pointing to the camera drone hovering ahead of her—it's a tiny silver ball no bigger than the tip of my thumb, but trust a bot to spot even the smallest detail.

Shit, I think, my mind racing. "Tell her it's just a friend."

"It's just a friend," Callista says.

"Oh? I thought I saw your dad on your holoscreen..." Aurora sounds perfectly sober now.

Callista drops the charade and breaks into a sprint, but Aurora's copy is much faster than her. She catches up and yanks Callista back by her arm before she can reach the stairs.

"Let me go!" she cries.

"Quiet," the impostor hisses as she drags Callista back to the railing. "If you call for help, your boyfriend and his family die. Got it?"

Callista nods woodenly. I catch a glimpse of the bot reaching into a hidden compartment that Aurora has in her abdomen. She pulls out a matte black laser pistol with a spectrum shifter affixed to the barrel so that it can fire both silently and invisibly.

"What do you want from me?" Callista whimpers as the impostor jams the barrel of the weapon into the small of her back.

My heart turns to stone. "Put us back on speaker," I say, and Callista promptly does so.

"Let her go," I say.

"Ah, so it is your father! Corvus Hale." The impostor smiles prettily at the camera drone. "Or should I say... Cade Korbin?"

She knows my name.

"Who?" Callista asks.

"What do you want?" Aurora cuts in.

Before the copy can answer, I notice the lights

flick off in the windows in the background, and Aurora's meatbag friend, Jana, comes stumbling out, laughing and hiccuping as she almost trips over the raised threshold.

"Oh, I think I'm going to be sick..." Jana mutters loudly as she crashes into the railing beside Callista and Aurora. Her cheeks bulge, but she swallows thickly and manages to resist by putting a hand to her lips. "Be thankful that you're a bot, Rory," Jana says. "You can drink all the colors of the rainbow without ever seeing them in reverse."

The impostor smiles thinly at her and deftly tucks the gun out of sight.

"I'm sorry, Jana, but Cally and I are having a private moment right now. Would you mind leaving us alone for a little while?"

"Oh, sorry! No problem. I should go find a bathroom, anyway."

"That's a good idea," the impostor says as Jana is leaving. "End the call, Callista," she growls next to my daughter's ear.

"Wait!" Aurora cries.

Jana spins around. "Yes, hon?"

My wife grows still beside me, having realized her mistake.

"Oh, nothing, Jana," the impostor assures her. "Sorry, I was talking to Cally. You can go."

"All right, all right, I can take a hint!" she says.

I can see where this is going, and I'm on the move. Crossing my arms over my chest, I jump back into the drop tube, racing down to Aurora's underground hangar. I look up to see that she's right behind me. We need to get to that hoveryacht.

Just before we reach the bottom, Jana comes lurching back over to Cally and the impostor bot. She bumps into them, slapping her friend on the back. "Oh, before I go, I almost forgot, Rory! I met this *amazing* bot tonight. You'd love her. She's just like you. Married to a bio, so she has lots of free time to kill at night, and she can't wait to meet you! I bet she's still here if you're..." Jana trails off, noticing the gun that the impostor is holding, now pointed at her.

"What? Where did you get that?"

Suddenly Jana is clutching a smoking, char-blackened hole in her bare stomach and looking confused. "Rory?" Jana's breath seems to catch in her throat.

Aurora curses viciously as she and I sprint through the cave to her ship.

Another smoking hole appears invisibly over Jana's left breast. Cally screams as her mother's friend crashes into the railing beside her. The impostor yanks her overboard.

And then the feed cuts out.

Aurora and I pound up the ramp to her ship. She triggers the airlock open, and we fly through both sets of doors and into the main cabin.

"This is all my fault," Aurora mutters miserably as we race to the cockpit.

I'd like to argue the point and tell her we're both the victims here, but that would be a lie.

CHAPTER 6

"**C**all the police," Aurora instructs as we crash into the cockpit. She takes the pilot's seat, mostly because it's her ship. Holding in every curse and accusation I can come up with, I drop into the co-pilot's station beside her. If she'd been honest with me from the start, this would never have happened.

But even as I think that I know it's not true. When people want to find you badly enough, they'll do it. I should know.

That gives me something else to think about.

"If I call the authorities, you'll be charged with doubling." I don't need to tell her that it's a crime to make simultaneous copies of yourself.

"We can deal with that later," Aurora says. "Call the police, Cade."

"On it."

She cold-starts the reactor while I run my comm logs through a signal tracker to get Callista's coordinates. It's just like she told me.

The Cushings' yacht is right between Dash Point and Coral City, about a kilometer off the coast of a popular beach, and thirty-two klicks from our present location.

Armed with that information, I place a call directly to the authorities.

Aurora raises the landing ramp and hovers a few inches off the landing pad.

The giant pressure doors ahead of us begin sliding open. Aurora waits, flexing her hands impatiently on the flight stick and throttle, while I grind my teeth listening to the comms ringing one too many times at the Coral City police department.

I'm pissed as hell at the whole damn situation. We may as well have both kept working with the Templars and trained Callista up to join the family business, instead of spending the last fifteen years lying on a Deus-forsaken beach, growing soft and old.

"If something happens to her…" I trail off angrily with a sideways look at my wife.

Aurora shakes her head, and a synthetic muscle twitches convincingly in her cheek. "The guilt and blame can wait until after we get her back."

She's right. Whoever is gunning for us hasn't made any demands—at least not yet. Those might still be coming, but I have a bad feeling that this is about more than just credits. Whoever is behind this, it's good that they didn't simply kill Callista, which means it isn't a hit. But that's also bad because in this galaxy there are a hundred fates worse than death.

Pushing those thoughts from my mind, I let out a ragged sigh and focus on what's ahead. We need to catch up with Callista before her abductor can escape.

"Coral City Emergency Services, my name is Ella, how may I help you, Mr. Hale?"

A visual appears in the top right of my holo display of a pretty humanoid bot with brown hair and glowing blue eyes. From her blank expression and lifeless gaze, I can tell that she's a drudge, but what else would she be on a planet that's only populated by excessively wealthy people? It almost makes me sick that I'm one of them.

"My daughter is being abducted. She was last seen at these coordinates, about five minutes ago." I send the location data.

"I see. Bringing up security footage now…" Imagery flickers brightly across the drudge's eyes.

The pressure doors are finally open wide enough for the *Black Augur* to cruise into the airlock. Aurora jack-rabbits through the gap, scraping paint off the engine nacelles.

I lean forward to flick a switch, powering up the shields. The doors begin rumbling shut behind us.

"I have multiple holo recordings from

workers on site that show Callista Hale and her mother, Aura Hale, leaving the yacht together and entering an air car registered to Mrs. Hale. No one else accompanied them. They took off three minutes and six seconds ago. There were no signs of a struggle, and I have no record of either a restraining order or a custody agreement which might limit Mrs. Hale's rights with regards to her daughter."

"That was not her mother!" I snap at the drudge.

"All of the workers who saw her made a positive ID, Mr. Hale."

"That's because she's a duplicate. Someone jacked the copy, and now they're using it to abduct our daughter."

"Doubling is a serious crime, Mr. Hale. Are you reporting your wife? Please note, this call is being recorded and can be used as evidence in a court of law."

"Fuck this," I mutter to myself and promptly end the connection.

"Cade, get them back on the line!" Aurora demands.

"Forget it. By the time that scrigging drudge sends cops to the scene, the trail will be cold and Callista will be long gone. And even if I'm wrong, what do you think happens to Callista if authorities corner her abductor?"

The airlock seals behind us with a muffled *boom,* punctuating that thought.

Water comes frothing in and swirling through vents in the floor and ceiling. I can tell by how slowly the massive airlock is filling up with water that this is going to take a few minutes. Ten or fifteen, at least.

"Aura, we don't have time for this!"

She sets her jaw and stabs a button. The outer doors *thunk* as the locking mechanisms release, and they begin parting with a groan. A column of pressurized water comes roaring through the widening gap and explodes against the cockpit. That blinding torrent draws shimmering light from the shields. Hovering on grav lifts, there's not enough friction to hold us in place, and the corvette is slammed into the rear set of doors with enough force to clack my teeth together.

"Sorry," Aurora mutters, and pushes up the slider for the inertial dampeners, setting them to seventy-five percent. "How are we supposed to find her without the police? The police can track my car and even force it to land."

"If they found a way to jack into your copy, you can bet they did the same with your car."

I pull up a map on my holoband, checking for locator pings from Callista's peripheral devices or her mother's car. Her holoband is busy broadcasting from the bottom of the ocean. No surprise there, but her neuralink has a beacon, too. It's a lot shorter-ranged, though, so I'm not getting anything from it yet.

As predicted, Aurora's car is reporting that it's

still parked in the garage below our driveway. A quick look at the holo feed from the camera in there confirms it, which means that the vehicle the abductor is using was purchased recently, likely the same make and model. That might give me a trail to follow later, but I'm hoping it doesn't come to that.

"Fly to the yacht. I've marked the location on the map. I'm going to call Terrin and see if he can tell me which way they were flying when they left. If we can get close enough, we can pinpoint Callista's location from her neuro beacon."

Aurora nods mutely, while I place the call to Terrin. Water is still swirling around us as Aurora sends her ship jetting out into hazy black depths. Tracking lights snap on, and colorful schools of fish dart away from us.

"Anything yet?" Aurora asks.

I slowly shake my head. Terrin isn't answering his comms. A moment later, the call ends, having timed out. An annoyingly cheerful answering service with a pretty drudge for a face asks me if I would like to leave a message, but I end the call and place one to his father instead. At worst, Terrin is dead like Jana. At best, he took off his holoband and went for a swim with his friends. Either way, I don't have any time to waste.

After just a few seconds, Aurora pulls up and the *Black Augur* explodes from the surface of the ocean. She ignites the main thrusters with a meaty roar, and a sharp jolt of acceleration pins me to the back of my seat.

We are immediately hailed on an emergency channel. The message crackles obtrusively over our comms without us even needing to accept the transmission.

"*Black Augur,* this is Pyria Traffic Control. You are not authorized for launch and be advised that firing primary thrusters below ten thousand feet is in direct violation of sub-orbital traffic law 1056, Article C. Please shut down your drive system immediately and cede control of your vessel to us."

A blinking request appears at the bottom of the cockpit canopy, as well as on the autopilot.

Aurora responds notching the throttle higher. She levels out at just over five hundred feet, and we break the sound barrier a few seconds later with an insubordinate *boom* that ought to scare the piss out of our neighbors.

A cottony silence envelops us as we leave the noise of our thrusters behind, but the insistent squawking of the comms makes up for it. I stab the mute key.

"Looks like we won't have to call the authorities, after all," I say, nodding to the sensors, which show three IF-21 interceptors and a hammerhead gunship rocketing down from orbit on an intercept course. It's the same patrol I saw earlier.

"Nothing from Prentice?" Aurora asks.

My call to Terrin's father times out, too, and I'm left listening to the same annoying answering service that his son uses.

I scowl and shake my head. "Like son like father," I mutter. I'm fairly certain that Prentice is wearing his holoband. He doesn't even unplug to go to the bathroom, but he saw that it was me calling and decided to ignore it. I send him a text, indicating that it's urgent, and then I try calling him again.

This time he answers, and his head and shoulders appear, looking insouciantly drunk as he sips a frosty glass of white cordite wine. His glowing blue eyes narrow slightly at me, and he purses his lips. He has a broad jaw with dimples in his chin and cheeks. Shoulder-length blond hair completes the picture. He could be his son's older brother, but unlike Terrin, he's a cyborg and a very old one at one hundred and six chronological years of age. His thickly-muscled arms are draped over the back of a plush white couch—one behind his wife, Destine, and another behind his neighbor, Mrs. Ferrol.

"Corvus!" he thunders as if he's happy to see me. "Your ravishing wife just left, if you're looking for her."

"I am, but that wasn't my wife."

"I beg your pardon?" Prentice asks, his eyebrows lifting mildly as he takes a slow sip of his wine.

CHAPTER 7

"What do you mean that wasn't your wife?" Prentice insists. "I saw her leave. I waved, and she waved back. Terrin went to say goodbye to her and Callista both. If that wasn't your wife, then…" He trails off uncertainly as if he's just realized that something illegal could be happening in front of his nose. But then a giant grin springs to his lips. "You're spoofing me, aren't you, Corvus? You old slagger!"

Prentice is just as dumb as his son is. "Listen, I don't have time to explain. I need to know what direction her air car was flying when it left."

"Have you tried checking the vehicle's locator beacon?"

"The tracking system is disabled," I lie.

"Then why don't you just call your daughter and ask her to send you her coordinates?"

I grit my teeth and smile thinly. "Prentice, I wouldn't be calling if I hadn't already tried the obvious methods. Callista is being abducted, and I need to see all of the sensor data from your yacht since the party began, up until my daughter left."

Prentice appears to sober slightly with the unusual request. "Abducted? By her mother?"

"It wasn't her, Prentice!"

"But I made a positive ID. Are you saying that your wife copied herself to a second body? Corvus, you sly *crobbin*, and here I thought you were too staid for that kind of *slaggery*. Meanwhile, you've got us all beat! This is why doubling is a crime, Corvus... because your copy thinks it has all the same rights to your life as you do! And technically, it does."

I'm choking on bile as Terrin's father prattles on.

"Now your wife's double is stealing your daughter away, and she has every right to do so, doesn't she? You're going to have to work it out behind closed doors, I'm afraid. It's that, or confess to the authorities, pay the fine, and serve the time."

Suddenly Prentice's hair whips back from his head and his drink splashes all over him. I hear glass shattering as people jump up screaming all around him. Even he looks terrified.

A sonic boom thunders over the comm speakers a few seconds later. Aurora slows right down and banks back around for a second pass, then stops to hover low overhead.

Our running lights bathe Prentice's face in

a blinding azure glow as he looks up in awe and horror at our ship. It's a damn sight more impressive and expensive than his hoveryacht— by a factor of about ten. While the Cushings live off their investments and have a giant mansion that they built by selling their family business, we have a significant active income from both the Orion Shipping Co. and the Templars.

"Is that you up there?" Prentice asks wonderingly as our idling grav lifts buffet him and his guests with violent gusts of wind.

"Send me the data, Prentice," I intone darkly. "Before I poke your little boat full of holes."

"There's no need to be rude about it..." A data transfer request pops up on my screen, and I accept.

"Thanks," I say and promptly end the call.

"We've got incoming!" Aurora warns as she pushes the throttle up and rockets away from the yacht with another burst of drink-spilling wind.

My gaze dips to the sensor grid. Those system patrollers are right above and behind us, and coming in hot at 6.2 km away, which is well within atmospheric effective laser range.

"Hold them off! I need a minute," I say as I use a secondary holo display to skim through the sensor data that Prentice sent.

"I don't think we have a minute!" Aurora warns as she commences an evasive flight pattern. Our comms are flashing insistently once more. A split second later, crimson lasers flicker by on all sides of us, soaking the cockpit in a ruddy light, and hissing violently against our shields.

I ignore those signs of imminent danger as I check the holo feeds from the Cushings' yacht. I watch the car that left with Callista rise swiftly from one of the landing pads on the upper deck. It made a beeline for the shore and landed on the secluded beach where the yacht dropped its grav anchors.

Zooming in on the beach, I watch the car land and see two people emerge from the vehicle. It's Callista and the copy of Aurora, who has a blaster aimed directly at her back. They're met at the tree line by two bots with glowing eyes. I zoom in still further to see that they're both heavily armed with plasma rifles which they're aiming directly at Callista.

The four of them promptly vanish into the jungle. About a minute later, a heavy fighter jumps above the shadowy jungle canopy.

"That's my ship!" Aurora objects, her eyes narrowing on the feed.

I glance at her. "Your other ship, you mean." I recall Aurora telling me that her double took a heavy fighter instead of the *Augur* the last time the two of them met up here on Pyria.

The fighter pulls up sharply, aiming for orbit, and then vanishes behind the clouds. Its main thrusters stay dark and dormant the whole time, playing by traffic control's rules. That's good. It means we might be able to catch up before they make it past the orbital checkpoints and Pyria's FTL inhibition field.

I notice the fighter's SID codes and blink in shock at the name. "The *Korbin's Folley?*" I ask aloud, even as I set our sensors to scan for it.

"The what?" Aurora asks. "They scrubbed the SID codes?"

Of course, they did. Why keep the old ship ID codes and make it easy for us to track them? "It's already in orbit!" I shout, just as our sensors get a ping.

"I see it." Aurora yanks the stick back and pushes the throttle past the stops into overdrive. The engines roar and the reactor whines sharply in protest. The sudden boost of acceleration has me seeing stars.

Dead ahead, beyond the gauzy black curtain of clouds that are now billowing around us, is the neutral yellow target box of our daughter's kidnappers. I mentally re-designate the target as *enemy,* and the box around *Korbin's Folley* turns red.

Whatever this is, I was right: it's not about credits, but I'm no longer convinced that it's Aurora's fault.

It's mine. This is about revenge. Someone is gunning for me, and they're using my daughter as the bait.

Again.

CHAPTER 8

A bright dome of stars sparkles ahead of us, darkening steadily as the atmosphere grows progressively thinner.

"What are you doing?" Aurora asks, eyeing me as I deploy the controls for the *Augur's* weapon systems. She's busy weaving desperately from side to side to evade laser fire from the patrollers. She's also deploying a refractive mist to buffer the inevitable impacts of high-powered laser beams. Like that, our shields are holding, but only just.

"I'm going to shoot out their thrusters," I reply.

"Don't be a scrigg, Cade. Pyria's orbital defenses will vaporize us if you fire weapons within the planet's security cordon. We have to play by the rules, and so do they."

I blow out a frustrated breath. "We're already breaking the rules by firing our thrusters below 10,000 feet!"

"It's a traffic violation. They're not giving us everything they've got because we haven't broken any other laws, but you fire our guns, and all of that is going to change."

Shit. She's right. "Then what are you planning to do?" I demand of her.

"We follow them up to the orbital transfer checkpoint. If they make it past that, *then* we open fire."

"ETA two minutes, twelve seconds before they reach it," I say, reading off the sensor display on my side of the cockpit.

Aurora gives a shallow nod.

Either way, it's not much of a plan. Pyria's security cordon and its FTL inhibition field both have a radius of 100,000 klicks. And the orbital transfer checkpoint is smack in the middle of it. Effective laser range in vacuum is also about 50,000 kilometers, so that means that any patrollers and orbital defenses near the checkpoint will be able to vaporize us just as easily up there as down here. It doesn't matter when we choose to take offensive action against *Korbin's Folley,* the outcome will be the same. And if we wait for them to leave the security cordon entirely, then we won't have more than a couple of minutes before they go to FTL. All of which adds up to the same conclusion.

"We need to bring the authorities in on this," I say.

"Do it," Aurora says.

I activate the comms, and an angry-looking man with ice-blue eyes, short silver hair, and a matching goatee appears sitting in the command chair of a hammerhead gunship. The bridge is dimly lit around him, and a few of the other control stations are visible in the background. In contrast to his hair, the man has a smooth, young-looking face.

"*Black Augur*, this is Captain Nevos of the *Iron Helix*, flying for Pyrian System Patrol. *Black Augur*, you are charged with multiple violations of sub-orbital traffic law and are ordered to cede control of your vessel to us immediately."

"No can do, Nevos. My daughter has been abducted. Her captors are on an escape vector aboard a HAF-30 designated *Korbin's Folley.*"

Nevos appears to hesitate, and his eyes narrow fractionally.

"Do you have any evidence of these accusations, Mr. Hale?"

"Sensor logs and holo feeds from the hoveryacht she was taken from."

"Send it to me. I'll have the vessel intercepted and searched before it even reaches the checkpoint."

"Thank you, sir." I send the log data and mentally prepare for the interrogation that will follow when they realize that Callista was taken by her own mother.

Holo imagery appears on the captain's holoband, blurring his features.

"There is one other thing, Captain... With your permission, we'd still like to fly up to orbit to meet our daughter when she is rescued. After that, we'll happily submit control of our vessel to you."

Nevos's features darken. "Negative, Mr. Hale, You are to send us your remote access codes immediately. If you do not comply, we will be forced to disable your vessel. You have five seconds."

I spend a moment grinding my teeth, still watching the holo imagery flash across the captain's face.

"I'm getting a positive ID on the girl's mother."

Aurora extends our comms' visual recording radius to include herself. "Her mother is right here. The one in the holo feed is an impostor."

Nevos scowls. He wipes the holo recording from his display, giving us a clear view of his features. "Doubling is a serious crime, Mrs. Hale."

"You can convict me later. Are you going to stop them, or not?"

"I said that I would," Captain Nevos replies. "Now, please power down your drive system and surrender your vessel. I will not ask again."

"Fine." Aurora blows out a shaky breath and hauls back on the throttle. A heavy weight leaves my chest, and I suck in an aching breath. Aurora activates the autopilot and sends the access codes. The *Augur's* nose immediately drops back to level with the horizon.

"Thank you," Captain Nevos says, smiling tightly at us. "Stand by for boarding."

The visual disappears as he kills the communication from his end.

Aurora gives me a shaky smile. "At least we're going to get Cally back."

I can't bring myself to smile back. This isn't over yet.

"Is the *Korbin's Folley* being intercepted?" I ask.

"Let me check."

Aurora pulls up an enlarged sensor grid on the secondary holo display between us. It shows a gridded map of this side of Pyria and the space around it. The grid is a flat plane that bisects the planet, with hundreds of icons representing ships appearing both above and below that grid. System Patrollers are shaded blue, while everything else is yellow. The *Korbin's Folley* is the only red icon on the map. It's rocketing steadily along the priority clearance corridor with a handful of other ships. For them to have entered that exit corridor means that they've been pre-cleared, so they won't have to stop for scanning in orbit.

My gut churns uneasily with that realization.

"Who the hell cleared them?" Aurora asks.

Having priority clearance usually means that a ship and its passengers were scanned by customs officers at a spaceport before take-off, but since I know for a fact that the *Korbin's Folley* didn't leave from a spaceport, there's no way that they've been pre-cleared.

"They must have bribed a high-ranking patroller to get clearance."

"You mean like a *captain?*" Aurora intones darkly.

"Look," I add, pointing to the *Folley* on the grid and drawing a sloppy circle around it with my index finger to indicate all the nearest patrollers. "There's no sign of any of them moving to intercept."

"Then Nevos lied," Aurora growls.

"I guess we know who granted their clearance," I add.

"The hell with this." Aurora cancels the remote access codes she sent and then slams the throttle back up to the max. I'm plastered to the back of my seat once more, and the stars pinwheel around me in blurry streaks.

The comms immediately squawks with an incoming message from the *Iron Helix,* but this time neither of us is answering. Whoever took Cally also went to the trouble of bribing the authorities to look the other way. I think back to when I saw this exact patrol squadron flying overhead when I was lying on the beach with Aurora. The fact that they're on our tail now is no coincidence. They weren't just paid to look the other way. They were paid to make sure that the *Folley* escapes.

I seize the weapons control yoke just as the

atmosphere falls away. This time Aurora doesn't try to stop me from bringing our weapons online. Instead, I can see her maneuvering away from the nearest orbital weapons platform, and a pair of patroller frigates in orbit—any one of which could take us out in a matter of seconds. Besides the patrollers on our six, who are now tearing into us once more with their lasers, the closest threat is the defense platform at 25,622 kilometers away. Standard effective laser range is about 50,000 klicks, but up against the *Augur* with its heavily modified drive system and a max acceleration in vacuum of 180mpss, it's pretty hard to get a lock on us at this range.

We're safe for now.

Our range to the heavy fighter that has Callista is just 2,250 klicks—well within ELR. The range is increasing slowly, which means that despite the vessel's smaller size, it's only slightly faster than ours.

I target the *Folley's* thrusters and power up the corvette's port and starboard laser turrets. Each of them is mounted with dual RS-12 "Shredder" lasers packing a megawatt each. Compared to our rail guns and missiles, that's nothing, but it's more than made up for by the fact that we're guaranteed to hit the target with lasers, as opposed to missiles and rail guns which would either be intercepted or simply miss the target by hundreds of kilometers.

But that's also true for the patrollers firing up

at us. Despite Aurora's best efforts and deploying state-of-the-art refractive mist, we're getting hit almost constantly, and our shields are dropping steadily.

Given how close they are, I'm surprised they haven't fired on us with rail guns or missiles. But I suppose we're still a long way from reaching the edge of Pyria's FTL inhibition field, so there's no point wasting expensive munitions.

Lining up the *Folley* in my sights, I pull the trigger and hold it down. Alternating bursts from the laser cannons flash by on either side of the cockpit with sharp, cracking reports and dazzling red beams of light. The sounds and visuals are simulated by the combat computer.

"Target's shields are dropping steadily," I announce, watching as the *Folley* initiates an evasive flight pattern that is almost entirely useless at this range. My lasers are locked on and tracking, scarcely ever leaving the thrusters.

In retaliation, the *Folley* deploys a sparkling cloud of refractive mist and returns fire with its laser cannons—not an illegal act now that it can be considered self-defense.

"Taking fire," Aurora announces.

Now we're caught in a pincer between the targets on our six and the ones in front.

"Shields at 75%," the *Augur* announces helpfully.

The *Folley's* shields are at 92%. I run a quick calculation through the ship's computer based on the rate of drain to both sets of deflectors to see whose shields will fail first. The *Folley's* will, but ours will fail about five seconds later, which means the patrollers behind us are going to poke us full of holes long before we can board our target and save Cally.

"This isn't going to work," I say tiredly. "We're out-gunned. Even if we could disable and board the *Folley* here, those patrollers would board us next. If that happens, we'll go straight to jail, and Cally, being a minor, will go to a foster home. It will be easy for whoever is after her to abduct her again after that. They'll probably just pay her foster parents a tidy sum to pretend she ran away."

"Get to the point, Cade!" Aurora snaps at me.

"The point is, we need to dump all the power we can spare into engines and shields, and follow them to their destination."

"And what if we lose the trail?" Aurora demands of me.

"Get up as close as you can and plant a tracker. Make it look like we're trying to hit them with our rail guns."

"They'll detect the tracking signal and remove it."

I smile darkly at that. "Exactly. But they'll have to drop out of FTL and go EVA to do that. And that's where we catch them."

Aurora glares steadily at me, then gives in with a stiff nod. "You still have to drop their shields to attach a tracker."

"I'll get them down," I say.

Our ETA to the edge of Pyria's FTL inhibition field is 16 minutes and change. At the current rate, our shields will fail in just over 15 minutes, while the *Folley's* will fail in 14 minutes and 31 seconds. They'll reach the edge of the inhibition field just ten seconds later. Assuming they pre-calculate their jump and spin up their FTL drive in advance, I won't have enough time between their shields failing and them jumping out to pin a tracker on them. Furthermore, the tracker needs to be already fired and tailing them before their shields fail because we'll still be separated by thousands of klicks by the time they're ready to jump out.

The timing needs to be perfect.

I leave the targeting computer to auto-track and fire our lasers at the *Folley* while I prep the tracker. It's a guided projectile fired from a rail gun, but it needs to be fired as accurately as possible, with me effectively guessing from the target's trajectory where they'll be by the time it reaches them. At the last possible second, the tracking dart will fire thrusters to guide it to the target, but at that point, the *Folley's* sensors will see it coming, and point defenses will shoot it down. I need to fire as many as possible to be sure at least one of them will latch onto the target.

Odds are we won't get another shot at this, so I'm going to fire all but one of the 24 trackers we have on board.

I get firing solutions from the targeting computer, calculated probabilistically from their trajectory. They're not maneuvering much, so guessing where they'll be is easy enough.

And then I launch the trackers one after another, as quickly as possible. The projectiles are too small for the *Folley* to detect and intercept until they engage their thrusters to guide them to the target.

Having launched them all, I sit back watching the laser turrets slowly drain the target's shields. Peripherally, I notice we have more patrollers incoming off our port side—high-speed interceptors like the ones behind us, which are busy firing their lasers at point-blank range. At twenty-five thousand klicks out, the newcomers add their fire as well. Aurora is maneuvering expertly, but even so, some of those lasers make glancing hits, adding to the rate of drain on our shields, and making it even less likely that we'll escape to chase the *Folley* through its jump.

"Shields at 50%," the *Augur* announces helpfully.

I pull up the ship's engineering panel and shunt emergency power from the reactor into the shields to even the odds again.

"This is going to be close," Aurora says.

I nod grimly, not risking a moment of inattention for a reply. At the current rate of drain, our shields will fail just a few seconds after we cross the jump line, which puts us at risk of being disabled before we can get away.

I could bolster the deflectors further by redirecting power from the lasers, but then we won't be able to take down the *Folley's* shields in time for one of the trackers to latch on.

We're going to have to risk it. The *Augur* can take a few lasers breaking through our shields at the end. Just so long as they don't hit our FTL drive or our reactor, we'll be fine.

But there are other possibilities. I'm not wearing a vac suit. If they poke a hole in the cockpit, I'll be huffing vacuum.

Setting the inertial dampeners to 100%, I unbuckle my restraints and jump up from my seat, heading for the emergency lockers at the back of the cockpit. Aurora glances over her shoulder to see me hurriedly yanking on a sleek white jumpsuit.

"Good idea," she says.

I trade my shoes for grav boots, then complete the ensemble with a helmet. I return to the co-pilot's seat and air tubes in the headrest automatically snake out to the back of my helmet. Now I'm ready for anything.

A quick look at the sensor grid gets me back up to speed. We're just five minutes from the jump line. Our target will beat us there by a couple of minutes, but all twenty-three of the trackers are inbound and set to reach the *Folley* just after its shields fail, at the edge of the jump line.

It's all carefully coordinated and calculated by our combat computer, with an intricate balance of velocities, accelerations, shield strengths, and laser wattages.

But then it all goes to hell as one of those variables exceeds the previously measured parameters, and the *Folley* pours on a burst of speed by deploying an emergency thruster. It blazes to life between the fighter's two primary thrusters, a bright crimson eye glaring at me between the two glowing blue jets on either side.

"Shit!" Aurora cries. "We're going to lose them!"

Their acceleration was 202 mpss, which is just slightly better than ours at 180, but now they're roaring away at 236 mpss, and that extra impulse is throwing everything off. Now their shields won't fail before they jump out, and the trackers won't intercept them unless they ignite their thrusters early, which puts them at imminent risk of interception by the fighter's point defenses. But it won't matter anyway, because they can't latch onto the *Folley's* hull while its shields are still active.

"Cade, what are we going to do?"

"I don't know!" My mind is racing to come up with a solution. The *Folley* played us, waiting until the last possible moment to fire that concealed emergency thruster.

CHAPTER 9

I need more firepower to counter that. I could drain power from engines to add to the lasers, overcharging them so that they'll still take down the target's shields before they escape, but that means we'll take heavy damage before we reach the jump line. We might even take enough damage that we won't be able to jump out, which means we'll get arrested and we won't be able to follow the target whether we have a tracker on it or not.

We can still follow them without a tracker by calculating their jump vector and following the tachyons in their jump stream, but it'll be a lot easier for them to shake us off their tail.

No matter what we do at this point, it's a gamble, but the safest bet is on our shields and engines, and following them through their first jump.

"Forget the trackers," I say as I shut down the weapons and shunt the power to our engines and shields. "We'll have to hunt them the old-fashioned way."

"Cade, a heavy fighter is faster in FTL than a corvette. They'll just drop out of FTL and change course. By the time we get there, the jump stream will have dissipated."

"We don't have a choice, Aura. If we don't let them go, we're going to get boarded and arrested. At least this way we'll be free to catch up with Cally later."

Aurora licks her lips, holding my gaze while her hands move automatically across the controls. I know what she's thinking. It's a big galaxy, and we've both tracked enough targets to know sometimes later is too late.

Aurora looks away, her eyes unblinking, and her jaw set. I focus on managing power to our shields, shunting power from the starboard array to the port and from the ventral to the aft and dorsal arrays.

We're still getting hammered by patrollers, but it's easy to see that with the added power from weapons, they're not going to be able to drain our shields before we reach the jump line. I'm still surprised that the gunship on our tail isn't trying its luck with rail guns or missiles. Obviously, at this range, our sensors and point defenses would see them fire and we'd intercept the projectiles, but it would just take a couple of rail gun rounds reaching us to knock out our shields. It's almost like they want us to escape.

"Here comes the moment of truth," Aurora whispers.

I see what she's talking about. The *Folley* is just about to reach the jump line.

The comms chirps with a message from them, and I immediately put it on-screen.

The face of Aurora's double appears, smiling smugly at us. "Hello Korbin," she says.

"Who are you?" I ask.

"Don't you recognize me, baby? I'm your wife, Aurora." With that, the impostor winks one glowing copper eye at me.

"What do you want?" Aurora asks.

"What do *I* want? Oh, this isn't about me, darling. It's about your husband." Her gaze flicks back to mine as she says that. "Cade Korbin, the legendary founder of the Templars: a guild that fights for justice rather than credits…" The impostor laughs gratingly. "But you get what you pay for, don't you Korbin? And you've cheapened justice, auctioning it off to the lowest bidder. Well, it's time to pay up, Korbin! You took something of mine, and now I'm taking something of yours."

With that, the camera swivels away from the impostor's face to show Cally sitting in a jumpseat at the back of the cockpit. Aurora sucks in a sharp breath, and suddenly I'm seeing red. Cally is bound and gagged, her face streaked with tears. One eye is swollen shut, and a bloody gash is running through her eyebrow. The impostor swivels the camera back and smiles once more. "I wonder what she's worth on the open market? A beauty like her. I bet she'd fetch a small fortune."

"Whatever you think you can get, we'll double it," Aurora puts in quickly.

"Isn't that sweet? A mother trying to buy her daughter like a commodity. But that's what you did, isn't it? A sterile, soulless machine like you can't have children without paying a small fortune to have them cooked up in a petri dish and then implanted in a synthetic womb."

My eyes narrow sharply at that, filing away bits and pieces of what Cally's abductor just said. Whoever it is, they hate bots, even though they clearly are one. And they know how we conceived Cally. How do they know we didn't use a living surrogate?

"No, I'm afraid it won't be that easy. As they say, the most valuable things in life are priceless. But don't worry. You're both famous bounty hunters. It should be easy for you to find your own daughter. Unless... well... unless you've finally met your match." Another smile. "Callista, is there something you'd like to say to your parents before we go?"

The camera pans back once more, and one of the two bots who met her on the beach steps into the cockpit. He yanks Cally's gag down. She coughs and grimaces. "Mom, Dad, they're going to sell me! They're headed for—"

Smack. The bot's fist is almost faster than my

eyes can track and it sends Cally's head thumping into the padded headrest on the bulkhead behind her. I wince as if I'd taken that blow myself. The bot yanks her gag back up, and the camera swivels away, bringing Aurora's impostor back front and center on the screen.

"Oops. We almost gave the game away. That wouldn't be any fun, would it?"

"I'm the one you want," I say. "Let's trade. Callista for me."

"Again, that's too easy, Korbin! Any decent parent would sacrifice themselves for their children, but it's much harder to take when it's the other way around, isn't it? One day, when you're old and tired from searching, I want you to ask yourself: was it worth it?"

"I'm going to catch up with you," I grit out darkly. "And when I do, you'll beg me to kill you."

"Maybe you will, maybe you won't… but it's time to find out, isn't it? Tag. You're it."

The comms end abruptly, and my gaze snaps to the sensor grid. The *Folley* has just crossed the jump line. I'm counting down in my head, figuring that they've already spun up their FTL drive. I reach five, and then the *Folley* winks off the grid.

"Scan their jump stream while I spin up the FTL," Aurora says.

I nod and pull up the jump scanner from my control station. I target it on the spot where the *Folley* was.

But there's nothing. No jump stream, no decaying tachyons. I frown at that and widen the radius…

The scanner beeps sullenly at me. No results.

This time Aurora glances over at the results. "That's impossible," she says. "Try again."

"I just did!" I snap. But she's right. It shouldn't be possible. Our sensors are state-of-the-art. We should be able to track a jump for a ship the size of the *Folley* up to at least half an hour after they've left.

"Get me something, Cade! We can't stick around here forever."

We're coming up on the jump line ourselves, and we need coordinates to feed into our FTL drive before our shields fail and those patrollers disable us.

"Shields at 25%," the ship adds as if to emphasize my concerns.

CHAPTER 10

"I'll have to track their jump trajectory," I decide. Pulling up the sensor logs, I get the ship's computer to analyze the *Folley's* heading and give me a list of possible destinations. FTL drives are a linear propulsion system, so a simple way to figure out where a ship went is to see where its nose was pointing before it jumped.

I get a list of possible destinations, all of them too far away for a heavy fighter to reach. Ships like the *Folley* get about three-quarters of a light year per hour, and the habited systems in front of them when they jumped are all over a hundred light years away. It would take more than ten days to reach even the nearest one, and they'll run out of fuel by about day six. That means their first jump was a decoy or to a rendezvous with a larger vessel. They'll probably drop out of FTL, after a fraction of a light-year and then re-route somewhere else so that we can't follow them. This wouldn't have been an issue if we'd been able to analyze their jump stream, lock onto the signature, and follow it to its end point.

The fact that we can't is still bothering me.

"Cade?" Aurora prompts me. "Where are we going?"

"They jumped through a rift..." I realize.

"What?" Aurora looks sharply at me.

I can imagine what she's thinking: that Cally could be dead, or stranded so far from civilized space that she may as well be. FTL rifts are space-time anomalies left over from the Priors, a long-extinct alien civilization that preceded ours.

Rifts are a bit like traversable wormholes, but with spatial and temporal connections that are constantly shifting. Some of them are big enough for ships to jump through, only to find that they've traveled hundreds or even thousands of light years in the blink of an eye. Rifts can slow down time for the traveler, and sometimes speed it up. The real problem is that rifts can't be reliably mapped. They're unpredictable, and constantly shifting, so you never know where you're going to end up. But one thing they're excellent for is losing a tail. Jumping through a rift doesn't leave a jump stream to analyze. Which is exactly what we saw happen when the *Folley* jumped out.

"She could be anywhere!" Aurora rages.

"No," I say, shaking my head. "They knew where they were going." Even though the rifts are constantly shifting, if you traveled through one recently, you can be reasonably certain that it still goes to the same place.

I pull up the jump scanner again, this time to check how many rifts are around the spot where the *Folley* jumped out.

Four, and only two of them are big enough for a ship to enter.

It's impossible to know which one they took, so the odds of us picking the right one are fifty-fifty. We could end up a million miles from where Cally was taken. But if we get lucky, we'll be right on their tail again, and this time we'll have a much better chance of disabling them or tracking them through their next jump. Picking one of the two rifts at random, I target it and feed the coordinates into the nav computer.

As I do that, the ship reminds me we're not just flying free and easy.

"Shields at 10%."

We're two minutes from the jump line, and Aurora is staring at me. "Cade, if you picked the wrong rift…"

"This is our best shot," I insist.

And it is. We both know that.

"I hope you're right…" Aurora says.

I sit watching the stars as I manage what's left of the shields. Crimson lasers flicker around us, lancing off into the void. At this point, only a handful of those shots are missing, but it doesn't matter. We made it.

The *Augur* crosses the jump line.

"Jumping in five," Aurora announces. "Three, two, one..." She pushes the jump lever forward and the stars vanish with a bright flash before returning as a swirling vortex of multicolored light. There's no telling how long this jump will last.

Aurora looks at me. I reach over and grab her hand, squeezing it gently. "It's going to be okay."

She nods uncertainly back.

We sit in silence for several tense minutes, holding hands, and trying not to think about what will happen to Cally if I picked the wrong rift.

At five minutes and forty-two seconds, the tunnel of light vanishes abruptly, and we're hurtling toward a bright blue world that is far too close for comfort.

"Warning, impact imminent! Reduce speed. Warning, impact imminent! Reduce speed."

"Shut that thing up!" Aurora snaps at me, even as I mute the alert.

She's pulling up hard, drawing a fiery cone of friction around our cockpit from the planet's atmosphere. She's firing the thrusters at 90 degrees, supplying vertical thrust to push us away from the planet that's now below us. An arcing red line appears across our field of view, helpfully supplied by the nav computer to indicate when and where we're going to crash. I hurriedly dump as much power into the engines as I can, and the line flattens out just enough that we'll go skipping off the upper atmosphere.

"Run a full sensor sweep," Aurora says.

"Already on it."

So far, our sensors are blank. There's no sign of the *Folley,* or anything else. A minute later, the sweep confirms it.

"Merde!" Aurora shouts angrily, slamming the armrest of her chair.

I feel hollowed out and empty. This is bad. I picked the wrong rift, and we've jumped to an uninhabited system. We could be anywhere.

I pull up a star map with a heavy sinking feeling in my gut, only for my worst fears to be confirmed. We're in uncharted space—nine hundred and sixty-two light years from the nearest settled star system, and while I can see from the *Augur's* clock that time was passing normally for us on board, there's no telling how much time has passed in the rest of the galaxy.

I'm reminded painfully of the last time I jumped through a rift, only to wind up stranded on an uncharted world. I met Brighten on the surface, a small food-obsessed white furball who lived with us through most of Cally's childhood. She's been dead for five years now, but thinking of her still puts a painful knot in my throat.

Is that how it's going to be with Cally if we don't find her?

I'm getting ahead of myself, and I know it. But that doesn't make it any easier to ignore the anguish churning in my gut.

"We can't jump that far," Aurora says, putting her finger squarely on the problem as she studies the map with me. "The *Augur's* max jump range is five hundred and seventy light years, and that's *if* she's fully fueled. Our antimatter reserves are down to 67%, so we can only cover about three hundred and eighty before the tank is dry." Aurora looks up from the map, her radiant copper eyes wide and full of fear. "Cade, what are we going to do?"

Somehow, Aurora isn't blaming me for this. She's just focusing on the problem and hoping that I have a solution.

Except that I don't.

We can't jump back through the rift that we came from, because there's no way to tell which one it was. We'd be guessing again, and given how well that worked out the first time, we could just as easily end up even further from civilized space than we are now.

But what other choice do we have? Either we try our luck with another rift jump, or we find the nearest habitable rock, pitch a tent, power up the *Augur's* distress beacon, and hope for the best.

Meanwhile, Cally could be anywhere in the galaxy, and neither Aurora nor I have any hope of helping her.

CHAPTER 11

"**W**e've got six rifts to choose from," I say.

"So we have about a seventeen percent chance of picking the one that leads back to Pyria," Aurora concludes. "Last time it was fifty-fifty and we picked the wrong one."

"You mean *I* picked the wrong one," I correct her.

"That wasn't your fault."

A frown creases my lips. When I thought that this was Aurora's fault, I blamed her for Cally's abduction, but now that it's clear that her abductors are trying to even a score with *me*, Aurora is going out of her way not to blame me. It's one of the reasons I love her. Aurora is always on my side—even when she shouldn't be.

"Okay. You pick."

Aurora sighs. "It doesn't matter who picks, the odds are the same."

Bot logic. "Humor me," I insist.

"Fine." Aurora studies the locations of the

rifts, then points to one of the six, targeting it. "That one," she says and engages the autopilot. The ship pulls up and away from the planet, aiming for deep space. I see the system's sun, a distant blue orb blazing off to starboard.

The FTL drive is busy cooling down. It'll be fifteen minutes before we can jump again, and that might easily be too late. Rifts fluctuate unpredictably, and the one that leads back to Pyria could end up taking us somewhere else instead.

Assuming we even pick the right one.

We watch the jump timer tick down as the autopilot brings us about on a lazy trajectory to reach the rift we targeted. It's winking on and off the grid, teleporting around as it swaps places with the other five rifts. The only way we can tell which one is which is by its unique quantum signature, and even that's fluctuating wildly. It's a miracle the targeting system can keep track of the one we chose at all. Not that it matters. It was an arbitrary choice, and we have no idea where any of them lead.

"Cade."

I look over at Aurora. Her eyes are blazing into me like two burning embers. "Promise me we're going to find her."

"I promise."

Aurora nods and looks away.

It sounds like a lie, but I refuse to believe anything else. We will find her. Somehow.

But will we get Cally back before she gets sold into slavery and scarred irreparably by the depraved dregs of the galaxy? Whoever buys her will get her hooked on stims. Probably glimmer and glo, and then they'll probably send her to work in the nearest brothel. With the advent of AI-driven drudges and realistic synthetic bodies, the slave trade should have died an ignominious death, but somehow that just added to the forbidden, exotic allure of the real thing.

The Templars have worked hard to end the slave trade, but somehow for every ring we busted up, five more would appear in its wake. It was the same thing with the stim cartels. Some vices can't be stamped out. All you do is force the roots down deeper.

Pushing those dark thoughts from my mind, I force myself to focus on the task at hand. First, we find a way back to charted space.

Then we contact our guildmaster, Brix Rylo, and figure out what the hell all of this has to do with the Templars.

In that comms call before the *Folley* jumped out, Aurora's impostor was blaming me for founding the guild, for cheapening justice by auctioning it to the lowest bidder. I must have really slagged someone's jets along the way.

In the lull we've been granted waiting for the FTL to spin up again, I think back over the brief conversation I had with Cally's abductor. What else did they say? That I *took* something from them, and now they're taking something from me...

It all sounds so damn familiar. This isn't the first time that someone has come after my daughter out of revenge. The last time it happened, it was my other daughter, Rama Drakos, who was used as a pawn in a plot to get revenge on me. The mastermind behind it was Nadine Zabelle, who was going after me because I killed her daughter, Bella Zabelle, on a mission to assassinate her husband, Christophe.

Bella was resurrected as Aurora, who, of course, is now my wife. But only Aurora and I remember this version of events because, in the process of defeating Nadine and saving Rama, I met an ancient alien entity embedded in a swarm of self-replicating nanites that called itself *Alpha.* He's the last living Prior, having long ago digitized his consciousness and embedded it in the swarm. With his help, I destroyed a time machine that the Priors had built, and in the process, I completely changed the timeline of the galaxy. Now, in *this* timeline, I never did anything to piss off Nadine. Christophe and Bella are both alive and well, and my daughter, Rama, never even got to meet me.

Furthermore, the mysterious alien empire that we call the *Cath Imperium* never wiped itself out by weaponizing the swarm in a bloody civil war, and now Alpha governs the Cath with a benevolent nanite fist, keeping the human and alien empires safely isolated from each other.

The rest of the Priors, who preceded the Cath and supposedly left behind a collection of the FTL rifts, are still long-gone. But that's probably just as well. If the Priors had survived, I doubt our human empires would have had a chance to flourish. And maybe their time machine would still be wreaking havoc in our galaxy.

An alert chirps through the ship's threat detection system, interrupting my trip down memory lane.

"Cade!" Aurora cries, jabbing a finger at the sensor grid.

"I see it." Hope stirs dimly inside of me as I recognize the ship that just appeared in orbit ahead of us.

It's the *Iron Helix.* The same system patrol gunship, with the same corrupt crew, that chased us out of the Pyros system.

CHAPTER 12

Captain Nevos's ship is 4267 kilometers away, but that's well within laser range, and they start lighting us up almost the instant they arrive. We're still burning hard to reverse our considerable momentum from Pyria and get back to that rift. At least now we know which one it is, but the added complication of that gunship makes our success even less likely.

The comms chirp as Nevos hails us, but I ignore it and hit the mute button. I can just imagine what he's going to say—power down our engines and shields and submit for boarding.

And right about now, that's looking almost inevitable. They're sitting between us and the rift that will get us out of here. We'll have to get dangerously close to them to jump back to Pyria.

"We have a serious problem, Cade," Aurora says.

"You think?" I quip sarcastically, drawing a glare from her. "Sorry," I add. Somehow I'm always the one screwing up and apologizing in our relationship. In some way that makes sense. Bots can adjust their behavior to avoid making the same mistakes. It's not so easy for us meatbags.

Lasers are flashing across our cockpit, drawing a hissing roar and shimmering pools of light from our shields, making it hard to see or even think straight. I tone down the simulated effects from the combat computer, and those distractions immediately diminish.

Glancing at the ship's engineering panel, I see that our shields had almost fully recovered, but they're getting hammered back down, and fast. Aurora is dodging and weaving expertly, but at best she's avoiding one in ten lasers. We're too close to evade anything, and that gunship has twice as many cannons as we do. Not to mention rail guns and missiles. If we get to within five or ten klicks of them, this engagement could be over real fast.

"Are we going to run the gauntlet or turn tail and make them chase us?"

My eyes dip to the rear-view display, studying the mottled blue orb behind us. Looks like a gas giant, but maybe that's just dense cloud cover. I wonder absently if those clouds have any sensor-blocking characteristics. Either way, we could use the planet's gravity to slingshot around and come back to the rift. We're faster than the gunship, so we'll be able to put the planet between them and us and use it as a shield.

But Captian Nevos is bound to realize, if he hasn't already, that we need to get back to that rift. So either he'll stay right where he is, guarding it, or he'll turn around and fly through ahead of us.

And that's even worse because then he'll have an entire fleet of patrollers waiting for us on the other side. We'll get disabled and boarded in a matter of seconds.

But... compared with all our other options, getting boarded might not be so bad.

"Cade?" Aurora prompts me.

"Okay. Here's what we're going to do. Answer the comms. Tell them we're going to power down engines and shields and wait for them to board us."

Aurora looks at me like I've just grown a second head. "Have you lost your mind? If we surrender, that's it for Cally. We'll rot in a jail cell until we're tried for breaking a hundred different laws."

I smile slyly at her. "Who said anything about surrendering?"

Aurora smirks, suddenly getting it. Captain Nevos made a big mistake by coming here. He came here by himself, without any backup, and that's because he's way out of his jurisdiction. No Alliance patroller would ever be authorized to fly through a rift to go after a criminal. It's too dangerous, and he'd lose his job. The only reason

I can think for Nevos to have followed us is that Cally's abductors promised him a handsome sum to bring us in. He's probably imagining a nice retirement for himself after this.

Well, I have something else in mind. It'll be a lot like retiring, but I'd bet he's not going to like it.

* * *

I'm crouching in the open doorway of the *Augur's* Virtual Reality and Remote Operations Center (VRROC)—or V-ROC. It's right below and across from the lift to the upper airlock where the *Iron Helix* has docked with us. Dim pulsing crimson lights are an uneasy reminder that we were forced to jettison our antimatter containment tanks before the *Helix* would risk getting close enough to board us.

I flex my hands restlessly on the repeating EMP blaster I chose from the armory. Aurora stands opposite me on the other side of the doors, armed with the same and wearing an armored vac suit like mine. She doesn't need it to guard against depressurization, but a few extra layers of armor are just as beneficial for her as they are for me.

Right above us, plasma torches crackle as they cut a hole in our airlock. That scrigg, Nevos, realized too late that getting us to jettison our fuel and shut down the reactor meant we wouldn't be able to open the door for him like civilized people.

A ringing *thunk* sounds and the plasma torches abruptly stop hissing. That's them, breaking through the first set of doors. The metallic thunder of remote patrol units' (RPUs) footsteps echoes above us as they come clattering down the ladder from the upper hatch to the cargo elevator in the ceiling ahead of us. It should still be operational, even on emergency power.

I point to my eyes, then to the bottom of the platform.

Aurora nods.

The platform *thunks* and groans to life, ratcheting down along the tracks in the walls at half its usual speed.

The feet of four RPUs come into view. My breathing and heart rate slow as I aim down the virtual sights projected on my holoband. I'm holding the stock of the rifle from around the corner. It's mag-locked to the door frame for stability, while I keep my body safely out of the line of fire.

Aurora is doing the same.

As soon as the torsos of those bots drift down into our sights, we both open fire with crackling EMP bursts that splash harmlessly across the bots' shields.

We don't have to take them out, but we need this to look good if the other part of our plan is going to work.

The RPUs duck and roll off the elevator

platform before it even reaches the deck. They come up firing. Deadly crimson laser beams vector in on our rifles, melting them to slag and silencing our ineffectual efforts.

Nevos's voice booms to my ears: "Lay down your weapons and surrender immediately!"

Instead, I trigger the doors to shut. But they groan and shudder, catching on the molten remains of our EMP rifles.

Aurora tosses a shield-disabling ion grenade into the midst of the RPUs as they begin stalking toward us.

It goes off with a hissing burst of light, followed by multiple *pops* as the bots' shields go down.

The nearest one crosses the threshold, sweeping its laser rifle into line with me. I've already drawn my sidearms, also an EMP weapon, and I pump two sparking blue bolts of fire into its chest, sending it jerking to its knees and stuttering angrily. Aurora fires another one from behind, and the bot falls on its face.

The doors finally spring free and slam behind the lead RPU which is twitching on the floor as it struggles to rise.

Aurora jumps on its back, deploys a sleek black nanoblade from one of her knuckles, and deftly slices open the access panel on the back of its neck. She flicks the manual activation switch and the bot's struggles end with a ringing thud.

One down, three to go.

Plasma torches sputter to life on the other side of the doors. Three glowing orange patches appear and begin slowly tracing out molten lines to meet each other in the middle.

An amplified voice thunders to my ears from the other side. "You are only making this worse for yourself, Mr. Hale."

Aurora looks up at me, her eyebrows raised in question. I nod once, quickly. She retreats to the shadows, behind one of the VR pods. The light in her eyes dims, and she appears to freeze on the spot.

A slow smile spreads across my face.

Several minutes pass while the remote patrol units cut open the doors. We're cornered in here and those patrollers know it, so they can afford to take their time.

Or at least they think they can.

This part is a bit of a gamble: we're betting that Nevos was paid to bring us in alive, not dead. But that's a fair bet, since whoever took Cally wants us to suffer, and we've got to be alive to do that.

As soon as a perfect molten circle has been etched into the doors, one of the RPUs kicks the severed section in, and two heavy slabs of terantium alloy fall with a boom to the deck.

"We give up!" I announce, dropping my EMP blaster and raising my hands high above my head.

Three gleaming black RPUs come stomping

in, their rifles sweeping and heads on a swivel to look for Aurora.

Glowing crimson eyes fix on me, and Nevos says, "What's wrong with her?"

"Her systems got scrambled by the EMP grenade," I say. "She has to do a hard reset and a complete file check. Could be a while."

Nevos snorts and his bot gives a hand signal to one of the others, sending them over to Aurora. Another one stalks over to me. Just as it removes my gun belt, Nevos's RPU flinches as if someone just slapped his human body inside the VR pod back on his ship.

"What the... hey! Where did she come —" Nevos's objections die suddenly with the cracking reports of blaster fire echoing over his comms. The sound isn't coming from this end.

One after another, all three remote patrol units freeze up and power down with whirring sighs, the light quickly fading from their eyes.

A slow smile creases my lips as Aurora comes back to life. She yanks her arms out of the metal grip of the bot standing behind her.

"What took you so long?" I ask.

"Three minutes and twelve seconds isn't long."

"Are they properly restrained?"

"Trapped in their pods," Aurora says. "I cut the power."

"Good job. All of them were in the VR center?"

"Apparently."

"Amateurs." I snort and shake my head at that as I recover my gun belt and EMP pistol from the bot in front of me. Nevos, being the overconfident scrigg that he is, never considered the possibility that while he was busy using RPUs to cut a hole into our ship, we might be doing the same thing with a remote unit of our own. Long before the *Helix* even docked with us, Aurora linked up with a generic RO bot and sent it out the airlock to lie in wait, armed with a breach kit, and a small arsenal of weapons. We planned it so that Aurora would cut a hole straight into their VR center and take out the pods that the crew would be using to operate the RPUs. We expected Nevos to stay on the bridge where he could oversee the operation and watch for tricks like the one we were planning, but he made things even easier by deciding to join the boarding team instead.

Holstering my EMP pistol, I hurry over to an open VR pod where we left a pair of laser rifles and plasma torches. Aurora crowds in beside me to retrieve hers.

"Let's go find out what Nevos knows," she says, clipping the torch to her belt and hefting her rifle in the direction of the open doors.

"It'll have to wait," I say. "The rift back to Pyria could shift at any minute, and then all of this will have been for nothing."

"I can deal with Nevos while you fly us out," Aurora argues.

"No, I need you on the bridge with me to keep up appearances. When we answer the comms, it's going to raise some eyebrows if I'm the only one at the controls."

"Fine, but I get the first crack at Nevos when we bust open his pod."

"Easy, Aura. He's our only lead."

"I know that!" she snaps.

I'm frowning deeply as we race out of the remote ops center together and crowd onto the cargo lift. Aurora is starting to lose her patience with the situation, and I don't blame her. The longer we take to find Cally, the worse the outcome will be.

The difference between finding her and *saving* her could be a matter of hours or even minutes, and the clock has been ticking ever since the *Folley* jumped out.

My gaze locks on the jagged hole in the top hatch above us—it's covered by the *Helix's* airlock, which I can see is gaping open into their ship. At least we won't need the plasma torches to cut our way in. That'll save us a few minutes.

I just hope it's enough.

CHAPTER 13

The rift swallows the *Iron Helix* with a bright flash, and a swirling tunnel of light appears. Again, it takes just five minutes and forty-two seconds before we emerge with another flash. A familiar gleaming, cerulean-blue world with bright green freckles of islands lies dead ahead, almost exactly one hundred thousand klicks out. Pyria.

Our comms light up with hails from nearby patrollers. They can see that we've got the *Black Augur* secured beneath the gunship, so they've likely assumed Captain Nevos has returned victorious. I take a breath and look over at Aurora before activating the comms. She's wearing a synthetic holo mask that's projecting one of the patrollers' faces—that of a pretty dark-skinned woman, reconstructed from holo logs stored in the *Helix's* surveillance system. I'm sitting beside her, wearing the meatbag equivalent—a bio mask, mimicking Nevos's features.

Additionally, we conducted a vocal pattern analysis of the people we're imitating via recordings stored in the *Helix's* internal surveillance system, and to cap it off we used one of Aurora's black-market apps to forge dossiers of their digital IDs.

It won't be enough to get us past rigorous security checks, but hopefully, the patrollers contacting us are willing to take things at face value long enough. We need to wait until the gunship's jump drive finishes cycling before we can punch out of here.

I hit the transmit button on the comms panel. An angry-looking man with pinching brown eyes and short black hair appears on the screen. He's wearing the maroon uniform of a Pyrian Patroller and the silver star of a commander.

"Nevos! You should have stayed the hell away. Now you're in some deep shit. Return to the transfer station for debriefing immediately."

The comms panel identifies the speaker as Commander Wallace, but I figure the less I say the better.

"Yes, sir."

"I assume the lawbreakers are securely detained?"

"Copy that," I add.

"Good." The commander's eyes flick to Aurora. "Lieutenant Karis, you are now the acting captain of the Helix."

"Me, sir?" Aurora looks at me uncertainly.

"You heard me, Lieutenant! Park in bay 1-D. Nevos is officially relieved of duty until further notice. I've sent an escort to bring you in. I'll be waiting for you in the hangar."

"Yes, sir," Aurora says.

Wallace ends the comms, and Aurora nods to the sensor grid. "Here comes our escort."

"I see them," I reply.

Two IF-21 interceptors. Probably the same two who were escorting the gunship before it went rogue to follow us. They won't be enough to stop us if it comes to a slug fight, which it will, but I've plotted a course along the edge of the jump line, so it should be easy to dart out of the inhibition field and jump away once our FTL drive has finished cycling.

The question is, where are we jumping to?

I've already plotted a preliminary jump into deep space to throw off any possible pursuit. These patrollers won't follow us like Nevos did, but I'm not going to risk having some local bounty hunter tag along for a quick payday. Alliance system patrol can't have one of their crews making off with a gunship without consequences, so they'll put up a sizable purse for any hunter who brings us in or provides information leading to our capture. Hell, one of the Templars might even wind up taking that contract, thinking we're a couple of corrupt officials going rogue.

"Cade, they're hailing us again," Aurora says.

"They want us to adjust course and fly deeper into the inhibition field."

"Almost like they know what we're up to…" I mutter. My eyes land on the countdown beneath the FTL control panel. It's still seven minutes and twelve seconds before we can jump. "Stall them," I say.

"How?" Aurora asks.

"Keep them talking. Fake a drive malfunction. Think of something."

"I'll do my best, but be ready for a fight if this doesn't work."

I nod silently, still thinking about our next steps. We can't directly follow the ship that took Cally, which means we're down to following leads. Nevos is one, still locked in a VR pod below decks. But the other lead is sitting right beside me. Whoever did this, jacked Aurora's double, and they did it from inside the Templars' base. The Shroud would be almost impossible for outsiders to infiltrate, so this must have been an inside job. One of our bounty hunters was responsible for jacking Aurora's double and abducting Callista. The motive is revenge, but for what?

One thing is for sure. We need to get to the Shroud and talk to our guildmaster, Brix Rylo.

"They're not buying it…" Aurora says. "I'm adjusting course. Better than having those interceptors get suspicious and disable us."

"No, this ruse has gone on long enough," I say.

Bringing up the weapons' control panel, I target our rail guns on the escorting fighters, targeting their thrusters to disable, not destroy them. Then I activate the turrets and bring our shields up to full power. Both interceptors go evasive, having detected the threat half a second before their drive systems explode in a fiery rain of shrapnel that hisses off our shields. One of them spins around with maneuvering jets and peppers us with lasers. The other one goes straight to missiles. Two splitter missiles rocket out.

The gunship's threat detection system squawks an alert. I twist the flight stick and pull up hard, firing vertical thrusters and rolling at the same time as I stomp on the right rudder pedal to fire the lateral jets.

The *Helix's* point defenses activate automatically, shooting one of the missiles down. The other one gets within fifty meters of us and splits into a dozen smaller warheads.

I slam the throttle into overdrive and barrel roll to evade.

Three of the missiles impact our shields with deafening booms and ominous shrieks from the hull.

An audible alert rattles out of the ship's computer: "Shields at 25%."

A glance at our rearview screen shows lasers are lashing us repeatedly with crimson fire. They can't miss at this range. Thank Deus those ships are two small to mount rail guns.

Another splitter missile rockets out and promptly bursts in a dozen directions. This time I deploy EM flares, catching most of them. Needle-thin lasers from our point defenses intercept the rest.

"Take them out!" I bark at Aurora, not having enough attention to spare from our evasive maneuvers to re-target the guns.

"On it!" Aurora says.

The rail guns *whirr* and then thump in tandem, one shot for each interceptor. Both of the arrowhead-shaped interceptors crack apart in glittering clouds of debris. Moments later, their pilots eject with sputtering blue thrusters beneath their flight chairs.

Rather than hitting them square in the cockpit, which would have taken those ships out pilots and all, Aurora deliberately aimed the guns to spare those pilots' lives.

"Nice work," I say.

Lasers are flashing by us from more distant ships. I manage to dodge half of them, taking the other half on our shields. The comms are going berserk with hails from system patrol. My hand flashes out to silence the alerts.

And then we're cruising over the jump line. The FTL is already spinning up, a rising whine humming along in the background as the coils charge.

Seconds later, we're vanishing once more into a swirling tunnel of light.

As soon as we're in FTL, I shoot up from the captain's chair, saying, "Reversion in thirty minutes. You think that's enough to find out who hired Nevos?"

"I'll get it out of him in five," Aurora growls as she follows me off the bridge.

CHAPTER 14

I'm leaning against the bulkhead in the V-ROC, my arms crossed over my chest, a dark scowl on my face as I watch Aurora dig around inside Nevos's head with an NSP-22—a neural probe, colloquially known as a brain spider. We're back to wearing our faces again. No need to confuse Nevos by interrogating him with a facsimile of himself.

He's awake for this, seated on a jumpseat that we folded out from the aft bulkhead of the remote ops center. Nevos is tied to the chair with a crash harness and his hands are secured behind his back with stun cords. His blue eyes are wide and bloodshot, his cheeks pale and waxy, sweat dribbling down from razor-short silver hair, his lips parted in an anticipatory scream.

The spider is a small black device the size of my thumb, clutching the back of Nevos's skull with six jointed metal legs. It drills tiny holes in his skull with a sound like a dental drone drilling cavities. It sets my teeth on edge and makes Nevos squirm like a rockrat in a mauler's den. Hair-thin translucent wires snake out of the spider, funneling through the holes in his skull and into various regions of his brain. One of those wires will jack directly into his neuralink, while several others burrow into his dorsal posterior insula, otherwise known as the brain's pain center.

"Look..." Nevos says, panting and wincing as the spider finishes digging into his gray matter. "I swear on my mother's life, I don't know who hired me."

"Are you sure that's the story you're sticking with?" Aurora asks mildly.

Nevos licks his lips, his eyes darting. "It's not a story, it's the truth! You think someone who's bribing Alliance Patrollers with two million credits would make it that easy to trace the money back to them?"

"I don't know, you tell me, Nevos..." Aurora says leadingly.

"I just did!"

Two million? That figure echoes dimly through my mind. Hell of a payday. No wonder these patrollers jumped through a rift to get to us.

Glowing displays flicker briefly across Aurora's eyes as she plays with the probe's controls. The spider twitches, and suddenly Nevos starts screaming at the top of his lungs.

Spittle flies and his eyes bulge from their sockets. Blood trickles from his right nostril.

A member of Nevos's crew, still locked inside one of the other VR pods, starts shouting and hammering on the cover, trying to bust out with blunt force. It sounds like a woman, maybe the same one that Aurora was impersonating —Lieutenant Karis. Maybe she has a romantic entanglement with the captain? That might be another angle for us to try.

A shadow appears on Nevos's trousers, quickly spreading from his crotch and streaking down his right leg, before dribbling out on the deck.

The spider beeps, and Nevos slumps against the chair's crash harness.

"That was just a small taste of what's to come, Nevos darling," Aurora purrs. "A simulation of the pain you'd feel if someone ripped out all of your teeth with pliers."

Nevos gasps raggedly and spits a clot of blood on the deck. "Listen," he whispers. "Just take the money. I'll transfer it to you, wherever you want. Use it to find your daughter."

Aurora grits her teeth and grabs Nevos by his collar, yanking him up straight to look her in the eye. "I don't need your credits! I need a fucking lead."

"I already told you everything," Nevos sobs. "I swear!"

Aurora lets him go with an angry shove, turns

on her heel, and stalks away, pacing the deck like a caged mauler.

I push off from the bulkhead and uncross my arms, moving to stand in front of Nevos.

We didn't have to do it this way. We could have just waited for the spider to finish jacking into Nevos's neuralink and then find out what he knows directly, without any of this unpleasant mess, but jacking a neuralink takes time, and right now every minute counts. So we're working both angles simultaneously.

"You have to know something. You said they set up an account for you in the neutral zone and contacted you with the access codes four nights ago."

Nevos regards me warily. "That won't get you anywhere. The neutral zone prides itself on anonymity. Everyone knows that."

"Fine, but the transfer had to come from somewhere, or are you telling me that it was deposited in person with credit tokens?"

Nevos hesitates, then begins shaking his head. "No. It was..." His brow furrows deeply as if trying to remember what he ate for breakfast last week. "The Hadros Group, yeah that was it."

Hadros. The name tickles through my brain like an itch that I can't scratch. A quick mental query to my Neuralink, which holds a digital repository of all of my memories, comes up blank. I have a bad feeling about this. Back in my days with the Paladins, I remember they had a bad habit of scrubbing operatives after missions that were so deeply classified not even the operators were allowed to remember all of the shit that went down. But if I *do* have some long-forgotten connection to the Hadros Group, I have no clue what it might be, and finding out would be next to impossible. If the Coalition kept copies of the memories that they scrubbed, they'll be buried deep in the Paladins' archive room.

I smile thinly at our subject, doing my best to hide my reaction to the name of the corporation that bribed these patrollers. "That's a lead, Nevos. See what you can do when you put your mind to it?"

"But it's not a lead," he insists. "I already checked them out. Hadros is a dead end."

"Why would you do that?" Aurora demands, suddenly standing beside me with her hand twitching restlessly beside her sidearm. We traded our EMP pistols for illegal plasma blasters from the *Augur's* armory just before we came down here. Nevos's eyes widen as he notices the weapon. Plasma blasters cause complete disintegrations, leaving no forensic evidence, which is what makes them illegal to own. It's also what makes them a weapon of choice for professional assassins like us.

In Nevos's experience, patrolling a backwater high-security world like Pyria, I doubt if he's seen more than a handful of these weapons in his life, but he knows what they are. It's hard to mistake the over-sized power packs or the bulky heatsinks and snaking coolant pipes around the barrel.

"I wasn't going to accept two million credits with no questions asked," Nevos explains. "I had to make sure it couldn't be traced back to something that would implicate me in a crime!"

"You mean other than bribery or accessory to abduction and human trafficking?" I ask.

Nevos winces at the mention of the crimes he has already committed on behalf of whoever hired him.

"What did you find?" Aurora asks.

"Hadros is an anonymous corporation. I couldn't even figure out where it was registered, much less to who."

"So that was it?" Aurora demands. "You hit a wall so you decided to stop digging and just take the payday, no questions asked?"

"What else could I do?" Nevos asks.

It takes a physical effort for me to resist the urge to break Nevos's jaw. "Let's see, you could have reported the crime to your commander and then warned us through official channels. Or you could have stopped the abductors yourself, catching them in the act... or even just got the hell out of the way while we went after them ourselves. Any of those options would have been better than what you did."

"You don't get it. Those two million credits came with strings attached. We were supposed to arrest you and bring you in. If we failed or tried to stop them, he threatened to do the same to our families as he was planning to do to yours."

"And what exactly is that?" Aurora thunders. "What did *he* say he was going to do? Who did you speak with?"

"I don't know! We only spoke once, over the comms. Whoever it was, he was using an ID scrambler, a trace blocker, a holo mask, and a vocal modulator. As for what he's planning, he said by the time he was done, you were going to wish you'd never had a daughter."

That threat makes my blood run cold, but it's just more of the same threats we already heard from Aurora's double.

Pushing my fears down deep, I do my best to emotionally detach from the situation. To stay calm and focused and keep a clear head. "How can you be sure it was a *he* if they were using a holo mask and vocal modulator?" I ask.

Nevos blinks at me and then slowly shakes his head. "I guess I can't."

Aurora lets out a frustrated breath. "He's got nothing! We're wasting our time. We should just dump him out the airlock and follow our next lead."

Nevos's eyes flare with panic. "Wait!" He licks his lips. "Give me a chance. I can use my contacts, and maybe get a warrant to look into the Hadros Group's accounts. Or at least figure out where the corporation was registered."

"Forget it. We have our own contacts," Aurora mutters. "You're useless to us. Unless... you're holding something back?"

"Hang on, uhh... I might have something else..." Nevos scrunches his eyes up tight, frantically searching his brain for something that might be of use to us.

I can tell that whatever he's about to say will be a fabrication. We've gone as far as we can with this.

"You know what, I think he said something about the Denari Clan. Yeah, that's it! Denari." Nevos nods gravely. "They're the ones who took your daughter. Must be revenge for something you did to them."

The Denari Clan is the second biggest stim cartel of the big five in the Alliance, with the Solaris Cartel being number one. Nevos probably thought name-dropping them would be too obvious, so he went with Denari instead.

"We're in," Aurora whispers to me just as a data-sharing prompt appears on my holoband. I accept it, and my holoband projects a control panel for Nevos's neuralink in front of my eyes.

Ignoring the maze of nested and cross-linked memories and holo records in the quantum storage system, I pull up a simple search prompt and query it for the Denari Clan and the Hadros Group. A bunch of recent records pop up, all timestamped within the last fifteen minutes that we've spent interrogating Nevos. Scrolling further back, to when Nevos said he was contacted by Cally's abductors and received the access codes for the bank account with his bribe money, I can see dozens of records relating to the Hadros Group, but as I suspected, there's nothing that references the Denari Clan.

Rather than confront Nevos with the lie, I pull up one of the other memories at random. I spend a few minutes watching through Nevos's own eyes as he does his digging, looking into the transfer to his account in the neutral zone. As he said, it came from the Hadros Group, an anonymous corporation. But he neglected to mention which bank they sent the funds from.

"The Bank of Kazir," I read off the transfer records.

"Oh, yes! That's right!" Nevos says. "That's where they sent the money fr—"

"Shut up," Aurora snaps at him. "Is there an account number?"

I nod. "Yeah. We've got what we need."

"See! You found it! Good. Good for you." Nevos pastes a trembling smile on his baby-smooth face. "I hope you can find her soon. If there's anything I can do to help..."

Aurora flicks a scowl at him. "You've done enough." Looking at me, she cocks an eyebrow. "So? Airlock?"

"No. Stasis," I reply. "We might need them later."

"We already have his neuro data," Aurora argues. "We don't need to be dragging around dead weight."

"All the same."

Killing human scum like Nevos and his crew shouldn't put more than a wrinkle in my conscience, but somehow I can't stomach the thought of icing them in cold blood. I'd much rather expose what they did to the authorities on Pyria and get them locked away in an Assisted Recovery Center (ARC) like the one I was sent to on Mars.

But that will have to wait.

"Stasis," I insist. "We'll deal with them later. I'll see you up on the bridge."

Aurora's eyes flash darkly at me. "Fine."

I know just how she feels. This is Cally, after all, but taking it out on four greedy yet ignorant scriggs is a poor excuse for revenge.

On my way out of the remote ops center, I hear frozen mechanisms groaning in protest as one of the other VR pods is forced open. Someone cries out in alarm, only to be silenced by the crackling report of a stun bolt. That sound is followed by a meaty thud. I'm barely halfway up the ramp to the bridge when that sequence of events concludes for the third time.

Nevos shouts something at Aurora. Maybe trying to bargain with her again. Dumb scrigg. He's just going to piss her off.

An agonized scream confirms my prediction.

Aurora must have put the spider to work again. Moments later, Nevos is silenced by a fourth and final stun bolt.

She'll put them in stasis now, just like I asked. Even if she would rather toss them out the airlock, she respects me too much to unilaterally decide their fate.

Ten minutes later, I'm sitting in the captain's chair, watching the swirling vortex of light vanish with a flash. Stars stop spinning, becoming static points of light once more. Aurora steps into view beside me, hands clasped behind her back, not bothering to take her seat.

"What's our next move?" she whispers.

"We follow the money," I say as I pull up the comms controls.

"Who are you calling?" Aurora asks.

"Brix. We need to find out more about whoever jacked your double."

Aurora nods and takes her seat beside me. "He might be in FTL. He was on his way to Pyria, remember?"

I nod quietly, not wanting to give the negativity a voice.

To my relief, Brix answers the comms just a few seconds later. He's wearing his face today, not that of one of his aliases: a broad, square jaw, dark skin, a shaved head, and violet eyes—not the glowing irises of a bot, but the wrong color to be natural.

"Hello?" he growls in a deep baritone. For

a moment Brix looks confused. He probably noticed the SID code of the ship that was calling him and wondered why a system patrol gunship is contacting him. But then he sees my face, and a familiar grin lights his face.

"Cade Korbin. Got yourself a new ride, I see. I was just on my way to Pyria, but... maybe under the circumstances we'd better meet someplace else?" He looks to Aurora, probably wondering how much she's told me.

"He knows about the double," Aurora says.

"Aha. Okay..." Brix nods slowly, his smile fading by a few degrees.

"Whoever jacked her, they came to Pyria and used the double to abduct Cally."

Brix's eyes widen and his smile vanishes. "No."

"We have a lead. A patroller who was bribed to help them escape. We need to get a look at the account that sent the credits."

Brix nods quickly. "Send me the details and I'll get one of our forensic accountants on it right away."

Imagery flickers rapidly across Aurora's eyes. "Done," she says.

"Got it. Bank of Kazir... Hadros Group. Should be easy enough. What else can I do?" Brix asks.

"We need to meet up at the Shroud," I say.

"No problem. They should still be at the same coordinates. We can rendezvous and then you can slave your nav to mine and I'll lead you straight there."

"Appreciate it, Brix."

"Anything for Cally. Shit… No luck tracking the ship that took her?"

"They jumped through a rift," I explain.

Brix lets out a shaky sigh. "That's one hell of a risk to take. She could be anywhere!"

"Not if they mapped it recently."

"Or had a rift scanner," Brix suggests.

That puts a wrinkle in my brow. Rift scanners are experimental tech, exclusively licensed to the Coalition navy. If the *Korbin's Folley* had one, that would imply that there's a much deeper motive behind this than just revenge. Something political, maybe.

Despite how ludicrous that sounds, I find myself considering the possibility.

"No." I shake my head suddenly. "That doesn't make any sense. We haven't had any dealing with the Coalition. And I cut ties with them decades ago."

Brix shrugs. "Fair enough. Just figured we gotta consider all the angles."

"Where are you?" Aurora asks.

"Routing through traffic above Pyria. About to cross the jump line. How about you?"

"We're not too far out," Aurora says, avoiding specifics in case someone is listening in on our comms.

I pull up a star map and set a spot in deep space that's equidistant from us and Brix, a quarter of a light-year away. ETA 27 minutes for us with the gunship's middling FTL speed of 0.55 light years per hour.

"I'm sending you coordinates for a rendezvous now," I say.

"Alright... got it," Brix says. "See you there."

"Make sure no one follows you," Aurora adds. "Whoever is behind this might have anticipated we'd meet with you after they infiltrated the Shroud."

Brix's hands are moving rapidly across the controls in the foreground of the holo feed. "I'll plot an extra jump just in case."

I grimace at that but nod my agreement. Having Brix revert to real space and wait for his FTL drive to cycle will delay our meeting by an extra ten or fifteen minutes, but at least we'll be able to jump straight from there to the Templars' base without worrying about anyone following us.

"We'll be waiting when you get there," Aurora says.

"Copy that."

The comms ends, and I feed the coordinates of the rendezvous into our jump drive. There are still seven minutes and change before the gunship's FTL finishes cycling from our last jump. Between that and our likely much slower FTL drive, Brix might be the one waiting for us at the rendezvous.

I look over at Aurora and find her staring

sightlessly off into the void, I reach across for her hand in an attempt to comfort her.

She looks at me with imagery flickering rapidly across her eyes, faster than any biological brain can track. I realize she's probably on the galnet, doing a deep dive into Hadros to find any peripheral mention of them. I mistook her stiff, frozen posture for idle worry, when in fact it was a sign of intense mental activity.

I risk interrupting her to ask, "Find anything?"

For a moment, Aurora doesn't say anything. Results continue flashing before her eyes, and the jump timer ticks inexorably down.

At last, she comes to life, cursing viciously. "Nothing! Hadros, the sector; Hadros Seven, the clothing line, Hadros Catering, Hadros the cosmetics brand, the Hadros Incident, but nothing that connects to an anonymous corporation with ties to The Bank of Kazir. The corps I found are all public and duly registered to their owners."

"We'll find them," I insist.

"Hadros is probably just another link in the chain," Aurora says disgustedly.

I absently nod my agreement while my gaze gets lost in the endless darkness beyond the bridge. The thing about a chain is that the links are all connected. Even a blind man can feel his way to the end of it eventually.

And we're blind to whatever's going on here.

With a sickening lurch and a bright flash, the ship jumps into FTL. *Hang in there, Cally,* I think as my eyes wince shut.

I'm going on a deep dive of my own: searching my memories to come up with a list of suspects —anyone that I might have hurt or hindered in my sixty-seven years in this Deus-forsaken galaxy.

Before I even get very far I have to start recording the names in my neuralink just to keep track. Having a digital copy of my memories to search through makes the task slightly easier, but by the time I reach a hundred suspects, I give up, realizing that the list is just too long. It could literally be anyone.

Before I retired, I executed five hundred and ninety-seven bounty-hunting contracts over thirteen years, and most of those would have pissed someone off. Before that, I was in ARCmax on Mars for a decade—probably safe to exclude that, since I kept my nose relatively clean there. But before my incarceration, I spent seven years with the Coalition Paladins where I must have run hundreds of ops, some of which I can't even properly remember since they were scrubbed from my mind to protect the classified nature of those missions.

If I have to dig through all of that history to figure out who's behind this, I'll be following leads for years. And Cally's abductor made it painfully clear that they don't want me to find out who took her. They want to have me twisting in the wind... for the rest of my life if possible. But whoever took her is in for a surprise when they realize that I don't give up so easily. We're going to get her back, no matter how long it takes.

I grit my teeth and set my jaw, steeling myself for the battles to come. I take one last glance at Aurora as she stares into the madness of FTL, her eyes imagining a future where our daughter is safe again.

We're in this together—for better or worse, until death do us part. Our search for Cally is only just beginning.

Whatever it takes—I'll find her. I swear it. Even if it means the end of me.

PART TWO: THE SHROUD

CHAPTER 15

The *Iron Helix* drops out of FTL with a flash, and I'm running a sensor sweep, checking the grid for signs of Brix's ship. Our sensors take a few seconds longer than they should to find it. A chime sounds from bridge speakers and the vessel is highlighted on our screens, but it's not broadcasting his SID code—the *Broken Halo*—maybe because energy readings indicate that it's completely powered down.

"Unidentified contact, twelve o'clock," I announce, nodding to the gray target box that appeared in front of us.

"Why did he power down?" Aurora asks.

"Maybe trying to avoid detection from pursuing ships?"

I can just make out the y-shaped silhouette of Brix's old, battered Type-7 Corvette in the middle of the target box.

"Something's off," Aurora says. "He should be hailing us by now."

"Yeah." Our shields are up, weapons primed, but space is wide open around us. Other than the derelict corvette in front of us, we're looking at nothing but vacuum.

I magnify a visual of the ship on the main viewscreen. It's drifting, dark, and silent. Definitely Brix's ship. I can see by the paint job. Or what's left of it.

Some of the hull plating has been ripped open, and the thrusters are dead. Whatever happened here was violent and sudden.

"This doesn't look good," Aurora whispers.

"No, it doesn't," I agree. "Let's go in for a closer look."

"Careful," Aurora warns. "Could be a trap."

As we draw closer, I have a sinking feeling that this is not going to go as planned. I match our speed with Brix's ship, then send out a few probes to investigate further from a safe distance.

"No life signs detected," Aurora reports.

I nod mutely, watching a live feed from the nearest probe. The cockpit canopy is shattered, but as the probe magnifies the vault of shadows within, I catch a glimpse of a crimson message smeared across the glass from the inside: *efas ton duorhS*. It's backward, but a quick mental command to my holoband flips it around.

"Shroud not safe," Aurora says a split second before the words appear before my eyes. "We need to get out of here," Aurora says. "Whoever iced Brix could still be here."

She's right. There are ways to hide a ship in plain sight if its thrusters are powered down. EM cloaks. Holographic plating. They could have their rail guns trained on us right now and we'd never know it.

But leaving Brix's ship and his remains out here doesn't sit well with me for more reasons than one.

"We're taking the *Halo* with us," I decide.

"Cade…"

"Whoever took out Brix is connected to this. There'll be evidence in the ship's logs. And besides, we don't know who wrote the message in the cockpit. It might not have been Brix."

"Why would Cally's abductors want to warn us that the Shroud has been compromised?"

"Maybe to isolate us from our resources and slow us down. Fire up the docking computer. While you're at it, spin up the FTL. We'll head to Orion Shipping first, and from there to the Shroud."

Aurora doesn't argue, her hands ablur as she follows my instructions.

Despite what I said to Aurora, I'm not convinced that Brix's attackers wrote that message in the cockpit. For one thing, it's not easy to get to the Shroud. Not even I know where it is, which is the main reason we were meeting up with Brix before going there.

The Templars' base of operations is

constantly moving around to avoid exactly what that bloody message is warning us about, but if someone boarded Brix's ship, then they might have pulled its current location from his logs, and that would also explain the message. Brix might have lived long enough to see the intruders board his ship and steal the log data. After they left, he wrote that warning for us in his own blood.

I unbuckle my harness and rise from the captain's chair, heading for the doors at the back of the bridge.

"Where are you going?" Aurora calls after me.

"To the airlock. I'm going to board the *Halo* and see what I can learn."

* * *

I'm standing in the shattered cockpit of the *Broken Halo,* listening to the sound of my breathing reverberate. My vac suit's grav boots pin me to the deck in the absence of the ship's gravity field. Flash-frozen globules of blood glitter like shattered rubies in the light of my headlamps, they're in constant motion, drifting and spinning, bouncing off each other like tiny asteroids.

"Where's Brix?" Aurora asks over the comms. She's watching through my eyes via my helmet's holo cam.

"Not in here," I reply, sweeping my head around to give her a good view. "Either they took him, or he got sucked out."

"How did he write that message for us with frozen blood?" Aurora asks.

My gaze tracks back to the warning on the jagged remains of the palladium glass canopy. *Shroud not safe.*

"He must have written it before the cockpit fully de-pressurized," I say. "Probably after the boarders left. Run a deep scan of the area. Let's see if we can find him out there."

"On it," Aurora says.

I step over to the pilot's station and try powering on the *Halo's* computer.

Status lights and holo displays flicker to life all around me. Flashing red lights pulse angrily through the cockpit. Damage reports scroll endlessly across the engineering panel. I try checking the logs from sensors and internal surveillance—but the computer spits out an error. The data's corrupted.

"Any sign of Brix?" I ask, hoping that Aurora's scan turned up something.

"I'm reading a debris cloud at just over fifty klicks and... one larger signature trailing behind it. Approximately one hundred kilos in mass with a cross-section of one point two meters. Pulling up a visual now..."

My guts clench up in anticipation.

"It's Brix," Aurora confirms. She sends the visual to my display, and I find myself staring at a shredded, blood-stained white vac suit with a glossy golden visor.

"Cade!" Aurora hisses suddenly in my ear. "I'm getting something else. A life sign on board."

"What?" Adrenaline sparks through my veins. "I thought we scanned the ship?"

"They must have been cloaked. Cade, look out! They're right on top of you!"

I yank my plasma blaster from its holster as I spin around to face the open door of the cockpit. My headlamps illuminate a dark, empty corridor. Nothing but specks of dust and debris dancing through the vacuum, but I know better than to trust my eyes. If someone is using a cloaking shield, I wouldn't see them with my eyes. Rather than wait for them to reveal themselves by shooting me, I activate my suit's occlusion-scanner. A compartment in my right gauntlet opens, and a burst of glittering silver particles erupts ahead of me like buckshot from an antique slug-shooter.

The particles quickly spread out to fill the entire cockpit and then boil away down the corridor. They're tiny self-propelled drones, physically probing the corridor for any invisible obstructions. Light can be transmitted easily enough from one side of a cloaking shield to the other, but particles with mass are not so easily manipulated. I watch as the cloud of drones vanishes into the darkness, racing down the ramp to the ship's lower deck. A moment later, the results of the occlusion scan come back clean, and I see the sparkling cloud of drones boiling back up the ramp, their tiny power cells already spent.

I relax my arm, the plasma blaster returning to my side as the drones rush back into my suit.

"Aurora, what the hell are you talking about? There's no one here." She's watching the telemetry and holo feeds from my suit, so she must have already seen everything that I have.

"According to the scanners, they're right next to you," Aurora insists.

My head is on a swivel, checking every crook and cranny of the cockpit.

"They could be outside, clinging to the hull," Aurora says.

"Check it," I say, already backing away from the jagged, gaping hole in the canopy.

Just then, the deck butterflies open in front of me and a thick mist of flash-freezing steam boils out. My plasma blaster snaps back up, aiming for the center of the cloud.

"You found me," a familiar voice rasps as someone in a white vac suit sits up. The cloud clears, revealing a concealed stasis tube. The helmet turns, and the golden visor clears, revealing Brix's dark skin, broad jaw, and violet eyes.

"Shit," I breathe, relaxing my aim once more.

"I was hoping you'd stick around long enough to find out what happened," Brix says as he pushes out of the stasis tube, drifting clear. He straightens his legs under him and drifts back down until the soles of his grav boots make solid contact with the deck.

"No sign of the bastards that jumped me?" Brix asks.

I shake my head and holster my gun. "None. They scrubbed your ship's logs, too."

Brix grunts at that. "Nah. That was me," he says, patting a sealed compartment in his suit. "All the same, I think maybe we should bug out before they get to thinking too hard about the decoy I blasted into space."

My mind flashes back to the blood-stained vac suit Aurora found, and suddenly it all makes sense.

Brix put himself in a concealed stasis tube, programmed his decoy to write that message for us, and then made it look like the cockpit abruptly lost pressure and sucked him out. His attackers probably didn't bother to check the decoy, or even board his ship. If they had, why would they leave that warning there for us to read?

I nod to the shattered canopy and the crimson warning. "You want to explain that?"

"Soon as we're aboard your ship," Brix breathes raggedly.

"You hurt?" I ask.

"How do you think I wrote the message?" Brix asks.

"Fair enough." I nod and hurry past him, leading the way to the ventral airlock.

CHAPTER 16

I'm sitting on a stool in the gunship's med bay, watching a replay of the battle from the *Halo's* logs while Brix sits on the edge of a treatment bed beside me with an FSAP medibot tending to his shredded left arm.

Four Shrike Heavy Fighters drop out of FTL, with bright flashes of light rippling across the void in quick succession. The flat-bodied, wing-shaped ships are glinting darkly in the distant light of Pyria's sun.

They're right on top of Brix at point-blank range. The *Halo's* thrusters flare with bright crimson tongues of fire in a bid to get away, but it's too little, too late. Four rail guns fire in tandem, one from each Shrike, straight into his thrusters. The *Halo's* shields fail with a bright flash, and hull plates are shredded. Then the light from the *Halo's* thrusters winks out.

This explains the damage to Brix's ship—and the fact that he didn't have a chance to fight back.

But how did mercs follow him to this rendezvous? If they had a tracker planted on his hull, it would have to have a delay built in so he wouldn't notice the transmissions until it was too late. Or they followed his jump wake from Pyria, through his decoy jump, and again, to the actual rendezvous... all somehow without Brix noticing he had a tail. It would take some serious skill and hardware to pull that off. Doubtful.

Another possibility occurs to me. A much more likely one. Someone could have intercepted his comms with us. And they got the exact coordinates of the rendezvous from that. They'd have to decrypt the message in a hurry, though—or else they tapped the *Halo's* comms.

Brix curses viciously. I pause the holo footage on my holoband just as Brix blows his decoy out into space. I minimize the feed to look at Brix. The medibot is really going at his left biceps, using pincers to remove bits of shrapnel, and a laser scalpel to cut a path for the pincers.

Brix's vac suit is lying bunched up at the foot of the treatment bed, and his jumpsuit is pooled around his waist, leaving his torso bare and glistening with sweat and blood. His right arm is gleaming silver up to the shoulder joint, a cybernetic replacement that he's had since our days in the Paladins. Just bad luck that he got hit in the left arm. The cybernetic one would have turned that shrapnel into... smaller bits of shrapnel.

"Damn you motherslagger!" Brix flinches and jerks his arm away as the bot touches some bit of flesh that it didn't properly numb before going to work.

"Please hold still," the medibot drones in a flat monotone. "I am not finished with your treatment yet."

"That's a reflex you scriggin' bucket of bolts. You want me to hold still, don't be strummin' my nerves like a guitar!"

"I am sorry. Your pain receptors must still be functioning." The bot produces a hypodermic needle with its other arm and promptly jabs it into ragged flesh.

Brix's upper lip twitches into half of a sneer, but this time he doesn't flinch.

The bot's pincer arm dips in to remove a tiny glinting shard of glass, then sets it aside on a silver platter with a ringing *plink*. The pincer retracts, and grasping digits appear in its place. The bot begins taping Brix's biceps back together with a fine synthskin mesh.

"Oh, so *now* you're done?" Brix demands. "Then what the fuck did you jab me for?"

"You were in distress. I numbed your pain." The bot says cheerfully as it sprays the mesh with a clear nanite gel that quickly fills in all the gaps.

The exchange puts a grim smile on my face.

"Slaggin' bots," Brix mutters, causing me to raise an eyebrow at him.

"I meant drudges," he quickly adds, looking at me. "You know Aurora's like the daughter I never had."

A jolt kicks through the deck, drawing my eyes to the viewport in the far wall to see that we've just transitioned back to FTL.

A split second later, the door to the med bay swishes open, and Aurora comes in.

"Speak of the she-devil!" Brix says, smiling broadly at her as he zips up his undersuit.

She nods stiffly as she stops between him and me. "Who attacked your ship?"

"Korbin's been looking through the logs." Brix jerks his chin to me. "What do you make of it?"

I shrug. "Mercenaries as far as I can tell. SID codes are scrambled, but Shrike Fighters are a favorite among mercs. They didn't make any demands?" I ask.

Brix shakes his head.

"And they didn't take your ship or anything on it," I muse while stroking my jaw.

"They were hired to take you out before you could meet with us," Aurora concludes. "But why?"

"Maybe to stop me from sharing something that could lead you to Cally?" Brix suggests.

"Doubtful," I say. "You have all your neurodata backed up on the Shroud. Kill you here, and you'll just pop back up there."

"Maybe," Brix says, "but it would still delay us."

Aurora angrily sweeps stray locks of red hair out of her face and expertly tucks them into a fresh ponytail. "Why did you write that message for us? Why isn't the Shroud safe?"

"Because the mercs' exit vector indicated that they followed me from there, not from Pyria."

That catches my attention. "Are you sure?"

"Pretty damn sure," Brix replies. "Nothing out that way besides us and reams of uninhabited space."

"Then we're more deeply compromised than we thought," Aurora says.

Brix nods gravely while rolling his shoulder and experimentally flexing his wounded arm a few times.

That has my brain churning. "I assume you re-located the base after Aurora's double was jacked."

"Of course," Brix says.

"And you left for Pyria from the new location?" I add.

Brix nods. "Don't worry. I sent an emergency alert telling them to relocate and lock the place down until we get there."

"Then they succeeded in delaying us," I growl. "Now we'll have to divert to Orion Shipping on Terra Novus and then go through the proper channels there and wait for someone to come and bring us in."

Aurora and Brix share a look.

"What was that?" I ask.

"Well, we kinda do things differently these days," Brix explains. "We leave comm buoys behind whenever we have to re-locate. The buoy will put us through a few routine security checks and then beam a message to the Shroud, telling them to send someone to pick us up. If we fail the security checks, they'll send a strike team instead. It's pretty efficient, and keeps Orion out of it, which is good because we had a few incidents as a result of using them as our point of contact."

I'm frowning at that. "And no one thought to keep me in the loop?"

A sheepish look crawls onto Brix's face. "Well, we just assumed that Aurora... I mean, that she'd fill you in eventually."

"Yeah. Eventually," I agree with a dark look in her direction.

Aurora pretends not to notice.

I guess I can't complain if the Templars have found more efficient ways to operate since I retired, but it's a painful reminder of just how long I've been out of the loop. And the fact that my wife has been living a double life behind my back.

"All right, so we head to the old location and wait," I say. "Are we close?"

Brix nods. "The new location won't be far, either. I told them to keep it tight so we wouldn't be delayed too much."

"Good," I reply. "One other thing. I was

thinking about how those mercs could have followed you to our rendezvous. They could have followed you from the Shroud, maybe been tipped off by a mole, but that's a lot of jumps to track you through. Did you check your hull for a tracker?"

Brix nods. "I did a full sweep right before I left the Shroud. I figured if Aurora could get jacked in our inner sanctum, then no one was safe. But the *Halo* was clean, I swear."

I'm shaking my head. "The fact that they dropped out of FTL right on top of you says otherwise. Those mercs were working with more precise data than a jump scanner would provide. The only other thing I can think of is that maybe your comms were tapped."

Brix's mouth opens, then shuts. "I mean… shit. I guess it's possible, but to think someone broke into my ship without me or anyone else noticing, and then still found a way to hack into her systems… that's no small feat. Especially considering all the security I have on board and what we have back at the Shroud."

"They could have tapped your comms somewhere else," Aurora says. "Some two-bit spaceport on a backwater where no one would blink twice to see a thief breaking into someone's ship."

"That would be easier, for sure," Brix agrees.

I snort derisively at that. "I wouldn't put too much faith in our security after Aurora's double got jacked right under your noses."

Brix sighs raggedly. "Either way, our base is compromised."

"We still have to go there," I say.

"Could be walking into a trap," Brix warns.

"We don't have a choice. We need to look for clues that might identify whoever jacked Aurora's double. That's our best lead right now. And whoever it is, they have Cally."

Brix winces at the reminder that she's missing. She's like family to him. Not that I ever brought Cally with me to the Shroud, but she got to meet Brix plenty over the years, back at Orion Shipping's headquarters on Terra Novus. I introduced him to Cally as my head of operations.

"We'll find them," Brix says darkly. "I won't rest until we do. I promise you that."

I nod mutely at his reassurances, not trusting my voice to be steady enough for a reply.

"Let's go," Aurora says, turning to leave. "We'll be dropping back out of FTL soon, and we need you to lay in the coordinates for the Shroud."

Brix and I follow her out and up the nearest grav chute to the gunship's command deck. Another jolt kicks through the deck while we're striding down the corridor to the bridge.

Heavy blast doors part with a rumble, revealing a breathtaking vista of stars. We cross the deck to the primary control stations in the center of the bridge, and Aurora gestures to the co-pilot's station. Brix drops into it, pulling up a star map on the main holo display.

I watch as he zooms out and pans the map over to a particular star system. It's just 10.3 light-years from Pyria, out in uninhabited space. "The Veragas System?" I ask, reading the name as it's highlighted on-screen.

"That's our old location," Brix confirms as he zooms in and picks exit coordinates in orbit above the system's only habitable world: Cevax II.

I've heard of it in passing, though I can't say I've been there or taken the time to read up about it.

"Locked and loaded," Brix says, spinning away from the controls. "ETA, twenty-two hours and thirteen minutes. This tub is as slow as a garbage hauler! But I guess we are dragging two derelicts along for the ride."

Aurora scowls. "The *Augur* isn't derelict. She just needs re-fueling."

Brix holds up his hands in surrender. "My apologies, Aurry. Didn't mean any offense. Hey, speaking of re-fueling, we've got some time to kill. Mind pointing me in the direction of the mess hall?"

I point to the ceiling with my index finger. "Should be one level up. I'll take you."

"Thanks, Reaper," he says, using my nickname from our days in the Paladins. I earned it by being a cold and efficient killer, supposedly able to carry out my orders with no hesitation or remorse. I did things for the Coalition that would turn other people into jiggling puddles of shame. Unfortunately, or *fortunately*, depending on how you choose to look at it—I grew a conscience somewhere along the way and began to question the agendas behind what I was being ordered to do.

Aurora follows us off the bridge, but heads for a different grav chute, saying, "You two go ahead. I'm going to fix the *Augur's* airlock and refuel her."

"Don't blow us up!" Brix calls jokingly after her.

Aurora disappears wordlessly down the grav chute. We step into ours, going up, and the field buoys us steadily to the next deck, spitting us out right in front of the mess hall.

"That's convenient," Brix says.

I follow him in with a sick weight in my stomach. It wasn't that long ago that I was eating pizza in bed with Aurora, and I'm not the least bit hungry now. I'm just here to pick Brix's brain and to find out what he knows about Cally's abductor. I'm assuming that whoever jacked Aurora's double is the one who abducted Cally, but that's a fair bet.

Brix sits down to a plate-sized piece of lasagna and starts digging in. He cocks an eyebrow at me while working through his first mouthful.

"You not gonna eat?"

"Not hungry," I reply.

He frowns and sets his knife and fork down. "Shit. I'm sorry. Look at me stuffing my face, with Cally out there…" He shakes his head and pushes the plate away.

"Eat," I insist, pushing the plate back.

Brix makes a face, staring at his food like he's just lost his appetite.

"You want to help?" I ask.

Brix eyes me curiously.

"Tell me what you found after Aurora's double got jacked. I'm assuming you looked into it. Do you have a suspect?"

Brix grimaces. "You'd think so, but it's just like I told Aurry, we've got nothing. Whoever they were, Aurora knew the person, because she let them into her quarters; there was no sign of forced entry, and you know those doors are all self-locking.

"Could have been hacked. Like your comms."

"Maybe," Brix agrees. "But there was no sign of a struggle, either, which means that Aurora was taken completely by surprise. Someone breaking in unexpectedly would have made her shoot first and ask questions later, don't you think?"

"What about the surveillance logs?"

"Holo feeds all over the base were scrambled for twelve minutes, right around the time that Aurora got jacked. Her ship took off six minutes after that, and we have a recording of her in the hangar, walking out to her ship, unaccompanied.

"Eventually someone correlated the security

malfunction to Aurora leaving, and we tried reaching her on the comms to see if she knew anything about it. She never answered. Then we discovered that the computer systems in her room were all badly scrambled, like from an EMP blast, and we put two and two together. We contacted Aurora on Pyria to let her know what had happened to her double, and then I guess she told you."

I nod along with that. "Okay, so someone tampered with the security system on the Shroud, then they broke into Aurora's quarters or were *let in* by her. They took her by surprise with an EMP attack, jacked into her body, and then copied their neuro data over hers, walking out in her skin—all in less than twelve minutes."

Brix nods. "It had to be another bot to pull it off that fast. And they had to have their shields up to protect from the EMP they used on Aurora."

"Agreed," I say. "But what happened to the jacker's old body?"

"They could have doubled," Brix suggests. "Then walked out one after another, going in two separate directions."

"That tracks," I say. "But it would have to be one of our hunters. Security would have flagged the intruder otherwise. I assume you checked the logs, just in case?"

Brix nods. "Nothing unusual detected."

"Hmmm. I'll have to get a look at those logs."

"I didn't bring a copy with me," Brix says,

"but we can dive into them when we reach the Shroud."

"First thing," I agree. "Regardless, we have a traitor in our midst."

"It could have been someone impersonating one of ours," Brix says. "If you jack one bot you can jack another."

I shake my head. "No, as you pointed out, a bio couldn't copy their neurodata to a bot in just twelve minutes, and we do checksums for all our bot hunters before they enter the Shroud to avoid exactly that type of infiltration. What we don't do, is checksums when they leave. If we did, we would have realized that the Aurora leaving the Shroud wasn't the same as the one who entered it."

"Shit..." Brix mutters. "I guess we'd better start running those checks."

"Better late than never," I mutter. "But that's even more confirmation that this was one of ours. It's less likely that an infiltrator would know about the loophole in our security."

"I guess not," Brix says.

I'm stroking my jaw, deep in thought. "That means we have a list of suspects: all of the bot Templars who were on the station at the time that the cameras got scrambled. One of them was hired to pull this job and abduct Cally."

Brix reels back in his chair as if I just slapped him. "But who would even go for something like that? We're choosy as hell with our recruitment process. Templars are crusaders for justice. We're all there because we want to make the galaxy a better place, not because we need the credits."

"Someone must have joined up under false pretenses," I reply. "We might be able to narrow the list of suspects by looking at all the bots who joined our roster recently."

Brix nods grimly. "I can do that from here."

"Let's flag anyone who joined in the last six months and work our way back from there," I suggest.

"Got it."

It's an arbitrary cut-off point, but we've got to start somewhere.

I push up from the table with my hands.

"Where are you going?" Brix asks me.

"Gonna shut my eyes for a minute. Something tells me I'm not going to get another chance to rest for a while."

"Sweet dreams, Reaper," Brix says as I turn to leave.

Reaper. My old moniker rattles around inside my head as I ride the grav chute down to the ventral airlock where the *Auger* is docked. Deus help whoever took Cally. When I catch up with them, they're going to wish I was the Grim Reaper.

Death will be the last thing I treat them to.

CHAPTER 17

"**T**his is it," Brix announces from the gunship's nav station. "Reversion to real space in five minutes."

I nod wordlessly with the announcement, glancing at Aurora. Her glowing orange eyes blaze into mine. Her cheek twitches into a fraction of a smile. I return the sentiment with a squeeze of her hand, then find myself staring at our hands, which are clasped tightly between our control stations. We are each other's lifeline right now: trapped in our worst nightmare, we've got to hang on to something, or we'll slip into despair. The whole reason we retired was to prevent something like this from happening. And now it's happened. Cally is gone, her life in the hands of monsters who want nothing better than to see her and us suffer.

I tear my eyes away from Aurora and let out a stale breath. It's been twenty-nine standard hours since Cally's abductors jumped through a rift to parts unknown. Too long. I can almost *feel* the trail growing cold. It's like there's this rubber band between us that's being stretched longer and longer as time goes by, and if enough time passes, it's going to snap, and then I'll never be able to find her.

My skin prickles with that thought. My veins sing with fire, my mind buzzing with impotent rage. Every inch of me feels electrified.

I have to resist the urge to scream.

Patience, Cade. Patience.

As if reminding myself of what I lack will make it any easier to acquire. The wait has been slowly driving me insane.

We reached the comm buoy at the Shroud's old location five hours ago, waited two more hours for our escort to show up, and now with our comparatively slower FTL drive, it's been almost another three.

I was hoping we might be able to ride in aboard the escorting ship and maybe shave an hour or so off the final leg of our trip, but the Templars sent a whole squadron of interceptors to bring us in, all of them one-man vessels.

Probably for the best. We know that the Shroud's previous location was compromised, and leaving the gunship behind, or setting the autopilot to follow along at a slower pace, would have been an extra risk.

Our escort is also our backup, just in case the mercs that followed Brix are somehow following us, too.

The weird thing about that, though, is that we spent the past day scanning every inch of our ships and their systems, checking for trackers and comm taps. The search came up clean—even on Brix's ship—which means those mercenaries somehow followed Brix the old-fashioned way. Maybe they got lucky by dropping out of FTL right on top of him.

It seems like too much of a coincidence to me. Following ships through FTL is never that precise, but I guess in the absence of any proof, I'll have to chalk it up to blind luck for now.

"Reverting in three, two... one."

A flash of light rips through the bridge, dazzling my eyes. My vision clears, and I see a strange, rainbow-colored world dead ahead with bright yellow rings of dust. I can see thin white clouds down there, and the surface is pocked with dark blue lakes that look like old impact craters.

"Welcome to Charon Prime," Brix says. "The Templars' new home."

I don't see any sign of the Shroud in orbit, either a visual or a ping on sensors. Must be on the dark side.

But then I notice the trajectory that our escort has set: they're flying straight in, rather than preparing to slingshot around to the far side of the planet.

"They landed it?"

"I guess so," Brix says with a heave of his massive shoulders. "Must be semi-habitable."

"Hmmm," I reply.

"It will make it harder for someone to find us," Aurora points out.

"And harder to escape if they do," I reply.

"Hey, it's not all bad," Brix insists. "At least we'll get to stretch our legs in real gravity for a change... Ho, and check this out: the air's breathable with a filter mask! You know what that means? We get to air out the station. About damn time, too. The place has been smelling like a tobra for months."

"Hmmm," I say again. I don't like the idea of being pinned down by a gravity well. Especially not since we suspect Cally's abductor might have doubled when they stole Aurora's body. If so, the traitor could still be on board, just waiting to call in a fleet of mercenaries once we get there.

Then again, the Shroud's supposed to be on lockdown, so that wouldn't be so easy. And if the original traitor is still on board, then they might know where their double took Cally.

I take a deep breath and steel my nerves for what's to come, whatever that may be. We have to stay focused and prepared for the unexpected. We've come too far to run into another dead end. Somewhere down there we're going to discover the clue that will lead us to Cally.

With a grim determination, I shoot up from the captain's chair. "See you down there, Brix."

"What? Where are you going?"

"We'll get there faster in the *Augur*."

Aurora jumps out of the co-pilot's chair, already headed for the exit.

"What about Nevos and his crew?" Brix asks as I follow Aurora out.

"Keep them in stasis for now," I reply.

"Copy. See you on the ground, Korbin."

* * *

The Shroud sits on a colorful alien field, overlooking a cliff to the water-filled basin of an ancient impact crater far below. The station looms over Charos Prime like a giant metal specter, with its vast matte black hull blocking out the greenish-blue light of the now-setting sun.

The station's shape is unmistakable, an immense sphere at its center, glittering with lights from hundreds of compartments spread across sixteen different levels.

Spokes radiate from there to an outer ring with hangars full of the Templars' ships.

Massive landing struts with clawed feet have folded out beneath the sphere and all along the outer ring to support the structure on the planet's surface.

Not many space stations are designed to land on planets, but we wanted to maximize mobility and keep our enemies guessing, so we purchased an old colony ship and fixed it up to suit our needs.

Back when it was used to colonize planets, the station's ring used to rotate around the central sphere to provide artificial gravity on long voyages. But now we have grav generators to tell us which way is up or down, so we gutted most of the ship and re-worked it to suit our needs.

The Shroud is equally at home on a planet's surface as it is in space. It can even float on a lake or an ocean, or anchor itself to the bottom.

Aurora takes us in, aiming for bay 3C, which flight control designated for us while we were still up in orbit. Harsh lights illuminate the empty hangar bay. Our landing pad is glowing green, with a sequence of flashing glow strips guiding us in.

I take in the scenery with half an eye as we glide toward the empty berth.

The rainbow colors that we saw from orbit are owed to the vast ridges left behind from all the overlapping impact craters that carved up the surface of Charos. Striated layers of dirt and rock each have their own colors, and wherever vegetation grows, it seems to take on those same pigments, perhaps drawing them up from the soil and rock below. Wherever rivers flow down from rocky heights, the same forces are at work, carving through striated layers, revealing more of the same bands of color.

It's a strange planet, that's for sure. One thing about it caught my attention: whatever expedition charted this planet, they didn't stay long. They marked it with a class five hazard rating, citing extremely dangerous fauna, and moved on.

Figures that the Templars would pick the most dangerous planet within a hundred light years to pitch their proverbial tents.

The *Augur* glides into the hangar and settles to the landing pad with a ringing *thunk.*

Aurora powers down the ship and jumps out of the pilot's chair. I'm right behind her, our footsteps ringing in tandem in the corridor. We hurry down the ramp to the lower deck and veer left to the airlock. Both sets of doors open with our approach, revealing the hangar beyond.

I'm not surprised to find a welcome party already waiting for us at the bottom of the landing ramp, but I *am* surprised to find that I don't recognize either of the two hunters who've come to greet us. Have I been away that long that no one who knows me has bothered to come and greet me on my return? By now the news must have spread through the station that I was coming.

Maybe none of the hunters I knew are still with us. When was the last time I came to the Shroud? Ten years ago, at least. And we do tend to cycle through our personnel faster than most guilds.

"Aurora!" one of the two Templars calls out, waving and grinning as we hurry down the ramp. It's a petite female bot with glowing fuchsia eyes, pale skin, and short, spiky indigo hair. My holoband identifies her as *Pixie Dust (Bot).*

Aurora smiles tightly and waves back. Under the circumstances, the carefree exchange between them sticks out like a wart on a puffer's backside, but then I realize that Brix hasn't made public the details of Aurora's body-jacking and Cally's abduction.

The man standing beside Pixie is anything but petite. My holoband marks him as *Kraug Hammer (Augment).* Like most hunters, Kraug and Pixie are broadcasting their call signs, and not their real names.

Kraug is an augmented bio who looks like he could be competing to be the next Mr. Galaxy. With long black dreadlocks, he stands at least seven feet tall with arms as thick around as my thighs. He's tanned to a deep bronze, with plenty of laugh lines and crow's feet to suggest a good sense of humor.

Aurora and I stop at the bottom of the ramp, and Pixie rushes forward to pull my wife into a hug, saying, "Damn, girl! You're back soon!" She withdraws quickly, saying, "That must've been one quick contract. Either that or your guild rating needs an adjustment."

Aurora nods and smiles tightly at her friend.

I'm studying Pixie carefully, wondering if she could be the original instance of the bot we're looking for—the one who jacked Aurora's double and took Cally.

Kraug makes no move to introduce himself, while I stand around awkwardly, resisting the urge to tap my foot while I wait for someone to make the formal introductions.

Pixie takes in Aurora's grim, silent demeanor, and her face suddenly falls. "What's wrong?"

"Nothing," Aurora says brightly, but the lingering look that passes between them leaves me wondering what might have been said over their integrated comms.

Pixie nods and her attention drifts to me, looking me up and down like I'm a piece of meat. A fresh grin springs to her dark pink lips. "Who's your handsome friend?" she asks while licking her lips. Maybe I *am* just a piece of meat to her.

I'm broadcasting my civilian ID, Corvus Hale, and we've never met, so there's no way Pixie could know who I am, but the fact that she didn't guess that I might be Aurora's husband makes me realize Aurora hasn't advertised that she's married or has a family. At least she took sensible precautions to keep us insulated from her double life.

For all the good that ended up doing. Somebody here, somewhere, knows what happened to Cally.

"This is Corvus Hale, a good friend of mine," Aurora says.

"Oh, I'll bet he's *good*," Pixie says, still staring at me. Bots aren't supposed to be this flirty, but I'm guessing it's a part of Pixie's old personality from when she was a bio. Either that, or she's realized that sexuality is just another weapon, one to which bios like me are uniquely vulnerable. She's obviously never met a bio like me. I don't like to be led around by the nose, or any other part of my anatomy.

"We're in a bit of a hurry," I put in, realizing that this welcome party wasn't arranged by Brix to get us situated.

Pixie makes a face.

Kraug speaks up in a deep growling baritone. "We're on lockdown, and Corvus is new, so I'll have to escort you in. Will Corvus be staying with you?"

Aurora nods, and Pixie wags her eyebrows at us.

"Lead the way," I say, nodding to Kraug.

He nods back and turns to lead us across the empty hangar. The hangar boasts three empty pads besides the one where we landed the *Augur*, each of them big enough to take a corvette-class ship.

To my dismay, Pixie falls in beside us. "I'm surprised they let you land at all with the Shroud on lockdown," she says.

Aurora shrugs. "Urgent business. And we won't be leaving until the lockdown is over."

"Oh, I guess that makes sense," Pixie says.

She follows us out into a long curving corridor that runs between the hangar bays. To our right, the inner wall of the station's ring is wall-to-wall viewports, with an uninterrupted vista of the spherical black hub in the center of the Shroud. Lights glitter brightly. A darkening blue and purple sky flashes with a bolt of lightning that reflects off the top of the dome. Then comes a rumble of thunder, and fat raindrops streak across the viewports.

With the station on lockdown, the corridor is deserted. No one coming and going right now. Our escort hung back with Brix and the gunship. They're probably just landing now.

Kraug veers to the right and a broad set of blast doors rumble open, revealing a long, straight corridor down one of the spokes to the central hub. The corridor is flanked by walls of viewports on both sides, and two moving pedways that run in opposite directions.

Kraug steps onto the one that's rolling in the direction we're headed and doesn't skip a beat, having now doubled his regular walking pace, which was already considerable thanks to his unusually long strides.

Pixie is chattering incessantly in Aurora's ear the whole way, mostly one-sided small talk. Aurora responds with short, one and two-syllable answers, or nods mutely in response.

Pixie doesn't seem to take the hint. Then again, maybe this is their usual dynamic—with Pixie yipping around Aurora's ankles, and Aurora mysteriously tolerating her presence. Maybe.

What the hell do I know?

I clench my teeth, realizing just how little I know about my wife's double life.

Finally, we reach the grav lifts in the middle of the echoing concourse at the core of the hub, and Aurora bids her sycophantic friend goodbye, saying that *I'm* tired and need to go to bed.

Pixie hesitates, then winks at us. "Oh, *I* get it," she drawls. "It's all right. We'll catch up later, Sistah!"

I sigh as the lift doors slide shut. "You're friends with *her?*" I ask, eyeing Aurora skeptically.

"That's right," Aurora says, but then sends me a more detailed explanation over my holoband.

Pixie has other qualities that I appreciate. Loyalty, for one. And being a chatterbox makes people underestimate her, but Pixie is my eyes and ears on this station. She's tapped into everyone's business. If there's anything suspicious going on, she'll know about it.

I send a reply back silently via my neuralink, *But you dismissed her? Shouldn't we be asking her about what happened to your double?*

Aurora answers: *When she asked me what was wrong, I asked her about the lockdown, but she doesn't know anything other than that there was a security malfunction, and the Shroud's previous location was compromised.*

She could be lying, I point out.

And now you know why I dismissed her, Aurora

replies.

The lift opens up on the top level, on deck sixteen, where Aurora and I have our quarters. Kraug steps out, and we follow him into an abbreviated, stone-lined foyer. Sculpted marble fountains bubbled in lighted alcoves to our left and right, and a heavy set of terantium-alloy doors waits at the end.

I remember living here for a couple of years when Cally was a baby and the Templars were just getting started. A memory flashes through my mind's eye: Callista running giggling through this foyer with me chasing after her, pretending to be a hungry xeno monster. She slams into the doors, smacking on them with her little hands, screaming, "Mommy! Help! The monster is going to get me!"

But Aurora doesn't hear her or she isn't there, and I sweep Cally into my arms, gobbling her tummy up with tickles.

My eyes are stinging as that memory fades. Aurora is gesturing impatiently to the doors, but they're not opening for her.

Kraug explains. "Brix changed the security codes after what happened. Give me a second, I'll send them to you."

So Brix *did* send someone to get us situated. I wonder if we can trust Kraug, but our suspect is a bot, not a bio, and Kraug has Brix's confidence, which I guess should be good enough for me.

"Thanks," Aurora says.

"Wait." Kraug's green eyes flick to me as if to ask if I can be trusted. "What about Nightmare?" he asks.

Aurora hesitates. "I thought Brix would have taken her in. At least to keep the crime scene clean."

"His quarters aren't set up for that. She's a beast, Aurry, you know that."

"Nightmare?" I ask.

"She's a sweetheart," Aurora objects and waves the doors open. The entrance parts with a swish, and Kraug falls back steadily with his hand on his sidearm.

That's enough warning for me. Suddenly I'm on high alert, my eyes scanning the big, open living area of our sprawling quarters. The lights are off, but dim green illumination is pouring in through wraparound viewports, reflecting off polished white sparkstone floors.

Aurora walks in, clicking her tongue and whistling. "Nightmare! Hey, girl!"

Then comes the sound of claws scrabbling furiously for purchase on the stone floors as something big comes boiling from the hidden recesses of our living quarters. The distinctive shriek of a wraith sets my teeth on edge, and my blaster leaps clear of its holster.

CHAPTER 18

"You have a pet *wraith?"* I ask, backing up slowly just as an ink-black shadow appears on the far end of the living room. It's yipping and chittering excitedly, four thick legs ablur, its claws gouging fresh furrows into the stone. Crisscrossing streaks run across the soft sparkstone floors in all directions, a testament to the fact that it has been living here for some time. Two wiry forelimbs are curled up to the monster's chest beneath a massive flattened head with broad, slavering jaws and long, protruding fangs.

Four golden eyes fix upon me and narrow slightly before sliding back to their real target: Aurora. The creature must weigh at least as much as Kraug.

Nightmare closes to within twelve feet of Aurora and then leaps into the air. My wife opens her arms and plants a foot behind her to brace herself before the wraith slams into her.

Even with that preparation, the two of them go sprawling to the floor, and Aurora is pinned beneath its substantial bulk. A long pink tongue snakes out, licking Aurora's face and growling ominously. Aurora is protesting loudly and battling with the beast, telling her to get off, but the wraith isn't listening.

Nightmare. She is certainly the stuff of nightmares. Wraiths are incredibly deadly creatures, with four eyes, two in the front of their skulls and two on either side, giving them almost three-hundred-and-sixty-degree vision with the visual acuity of an eagle. It can probably see better than Aurora in the dark, but it doesn't need to, having the ability to echo-locate with soft clicks. Venomous spikes run from the tops of their heads to the tips of their tails, which they can shoot at their prey, disabling them with a potent neurotoxin from up to fifty feet away. On top of that, they're semi-intelligent and possess a rudimentary language that can be translated to versal with specially calibrated translators. I can see that Aurora has attached one to Nightmare's collar, which makes me hopeful that we can reason with the beast. But just in case we can't, I take another two quick steps back, falling in beside Kraug at the entrance of the grav lift.

I deftly flick my blaster to the stun setting, hearing a soft click and hiss as an air-fired tranq dart slots into the lower barrel of the plasma blaster.

Aurora finally succeeds in pushing the wraith off her chest, to which Nightmare chitters and squeals in protest.

"Missed you," the translator says in a husky female voice. *"Where go?"*

"I missed you, too, Night," Aurora says. "You don't remember what happened?"

"Bad person shoot Nightmare with tail spike."

Aurora nods and scratches the wraith behind one of its big triangular ears. "I'm sorry, Night."

"She means a tranq dart," Kraug whispers to me.

"Aurora smell like food," the wraith adds with a series of clicks, pacing around Aurora and snorting loudly as it sniffs the air around her. The wraith's nose is a series of flaps in its chin and throat that look vaguely like the gills of a fish.

Standing on all fours, the top of its head comes up to Aurora's shoulder or the bottom of my chest.

Aurora nods to me. "You are smelling my husband's scent."

The wraith stops sniffing and its giant head swivels sharply to me. She stares quietly with all four of her yellow eyes narrowed. Nightmare pads through the open doors, approaching steadily with her long whip-like tail lashing the stone floor. Her spikes rattle as they stand up like the hackles on a dog's back.

"Not understand word, husband. Is friend?"

Nightmare asks.

"He's my mate," Aurora explains.

"Mate?" Nightmare says slowly, still approaching quietly.

"No sudden moves," Kraug whispers to me as he pushes my gun down.

I frown and nod at that, reluctantly holstering the weapon. If Aurora isn't stopping the wraith from greeting me, then it must be at least reasonably friendly.

The wraith stops about a foot away from me and lifts its massive head, drawing in a rattling breath. A long flat pink tongue the size of a shirt darts out and slops over my right cheek, leaving a sticky trail of drool that tingles uncomfortably against my skin. A mildly acidic analgesic that makes being eaten more palatable to the prey. I quickly wipe the alien saliva off on my sleeve.

Nightmare growls contentedly and licks its lips. My hand tightens on the grip of my weapon.

"Mate taste good," Nightmare says.

"He is not for eating," Aurora says quickly. "Understand?"

Nightmare stares fixedly at me. Kraug's hand flashes down to his sidearm, and mine comes inching back out of its holster.

Aurora sprints over to us and tugs the wraith back by its collar. Aurora drops her mouth beside its ear, speaking louder and more insistently, "Understand?"

Nightmare releases a loud snort that sprays

me with alien snot. *"Understand,"* she agrees, and her spikes rattle once more as they settle along her back. She turns on the spot and slaps me with her tail. I feel one of her spikes prick my leg through my jumpsuit, and it immediately goes numb. I stagger sideways almost falling over, but manage to catch myself on the door jamb of the grav lift.

"Nightmare!" Aurora bellows after the wraith.

A low chitter reaches my ears. *"Was accident."*

"Sorry," Aurora mouths to me. "She's not used to being around bios."

"Just as well," Kraug mutters. "They wouldn't last long. Are you sure you want Corvus staying here with you?"

"She'll come around," Aurora insists. "Come on. Let's see if the jacker left any clues behind." Aurora leads the way into our quarters, and I limp after her. Some of the feeling returns to my leg, and pins and needles cascade from my hip to my toes.

Kraug moves to help me, but I wave him off.

Nightmare skulks away, heading for the corridor to the bedrooms at the far end of the open living space. Her tail swishes angrily, rasping and clattering against the walls and furniture as she goes.

Our quarters are capped with a gridded dome of palladium glass that flows down to the deck, giving us an uninterrupted view of the sky, now dark purple and fading fast with the night. In between the dark, shadowy streaks of the clouds, I can see the planet's rings, a bright green arc slashing across the sky like a cosmic scythe. A handful of stars are out and twinkling, some of them big and bright enough to be neighboring planets.

My gaze drops back down to see that Aurora has already homed in on the scene of the crime. A shattered glass table and a broken crystal sculpture in the middle of the living room, right beside the curving glass dome.

"Brix told me there were no signs of a struggle," I point out as I join her there.

"There weren't," Kraug insists, coming to stand beside me with massive arms crossed over his chest. "That must have been Nightmare's doing."

"She acts up every time I leave," Aurora agrees, and turns away with a sigh.

Glow strips in the gridded frame between the panes of glass in the dome gradually swell to life. I blink a few times, forcing my eyes to adjust to the change in brightness. Turning in a slow circle, I scan the space for clues, but besides the broken table and sculpture, the only thing I see that's amiss is that Aurora has redecorated since we shared this place with Cally. Most of the furniture has changed to meet a bot's needs. The kitchen has been gutted and walled off, replaced by a sealed room whose purpose I can't guess without going inside. There's no dining table. Comfortable couches and chairs have been swapped out for more practical, utilitarian designs. A giant plush black pillow sits on the floor in one corner of the room, right beside the door to the emergency airlock that leads to our private hangar and the small, armored shuttle we used to keep there. On the other side of the airlock is a charging pad for Aurora.

I limp over there, a thought occurring to me. "Are we sure that the intruder didn't come in through here?"

Kraug and Aurora follow me there.

"We checked the airlock. There were no signs it had been used, and the station's sensors would have detected any unusual activity outside the station."

I look pointedly at Kraug. "How do we know that? If they managed to hack the security system, they could have hacked our sensors, too."

"Except that they didn't," Kraug says. "Sensors were functioning normally the entire time."

"They could have been cloaked," I suggest.

"Even then, we would have detected the airlock opening."

"Someone could have overridden the sensors in the doors."

"Maybe," Kraug replies, his tone doubtful. "They were working normally when we checked them."

I test the controls now, opening the inner set of doors and stepping into the airlock.

Checking the outer panel, I find that the hangar is pressurized, and I trigger that set of doors open, too, revealing the boxy gray bulk of our shuttle.

Turning back to Aurora, I ask, "Does Nightmare remember where the intruder came from, or where she was when she got shot?"

"She was in the primary bedroom," an even deeper baritone than Kraug's answers from the open door to our quarters.

Turning in the direction of the voice, I see Brix come in through the front door that we left open.

Once more, I hear the scrabbling of claws on stone, and the wraith streaks out of the corridor, yipping and chittering as she did when Aurora called for her.

Nightmare barrels into Brix, knocking him over and showering him with kisses, just like it did with Aurora.

He grumbles and protests, eventually prying himself off the deck. He spends a moment furiously wiping off acidic alien slobber on his sleeves. "Every damn time!" he mutters. "Scrag it, Nightmare!" he exclaims as he flings sticky greenish gobs of drool from his hands. "You *know* you're not supposed to slobber all over bios! We're gonna run out of synthskin treating the chemical burns from your bad manners."

Nightmare crouches low to the ground, her ears flattening to her head. She whimpers softly and whistles through her nostrils, turning and slinking over to her bed beside the airlock. She flops down, eliciting a noisy *whoosh* from the cushions. Her forelimbs unfurl and she covers all four of her eyes with her giant paws as if she's so ashamed that she can't even stand to look at Brix. For a terrifying alien predator, she is surprisingly subdued around him.

"He feeds her when I'm gone," Aurora explains, reading the confusion on my face.

"Wraiths bond tightly to their masters," Brix adds, walking over to us. "She was dying in a gutter on Kazir when Aurry and I found her."

"Nightmare sorry..." the wraith's translator mutters through a series of soft clicks.

"It's okay," Aurora soothes. "You just got too excited."

I jab a thumb over my shoulder to the open airlock. "Aurora's jacker might have broken in or escaped through here. All they'd have to do is hack the sensors so that there'd be no record of the airlock opening. If that's the case, we might not be dealing with one of our own."

Brix peers skeptically into the open airlock and the hangar beyond. "Escaped how? With what ship? Your shuttle is still there, and there isn't room for another ship to land in there with it."

"They might not have needed a ship," I point out. "Could have been cloaked and crawling around out there. A bot wouldn't even need a vac suit."

"We have sensors in the hull to detect even the slightest vibrations," Brix says. "Even if we couldn't see an intruder out there, the Shroud would *feel* it."

"Could have been another malfunction. How would you know if the system wasn't reporting anything?"

Brix's brow furrows so deeply that it wrinkles his bald scalp. "We'll run a system diagnostic and see if we spot any anomalies."

I nod and mentally shut both sets of doors to the airlock. "See what you can find in the station's systems and send me a report as soon as you can. Also, check in with our accountants and find out if they've traced the money from Hadros yet."

"I'll get right on it," Brix says. "We should have some answers soon. In the meantime, you and Aurora should try to relax. Head down to the rec center, or grab a bite or a drink on the mess deck and take your minds off things."

I shake my head vigorously at his suggestions. "No time for that. We're going to scan every inch of this place and search for clues."

Kraug nods to me. "I can stay and help if you want."

I'm about to accept the offer when Aurora shakes her head, saying, "We could use some privacy. It's been a difficult time, and my husband is still adjusting to the fact that I've been leading a double life. We appreciate the offer, though."

Kraug's green eyes blink once, his body too still, expression unreadable. "Of course."

I sense a subtle undercurrent of distrust between him and Aurora, even though she has clearly told him about me. But maybe that's the problem. Kraug is one of the few people here besides Brix who even knows that Cally exists.

But again, we're looking for a bot, not a bio.

Or are we? It could be a bio packing the necessary hardware to enable the rapid transfer of neurodata...

"We'll catch up with you later," I add, nodding in turn to Kraug and Brix. "Let us know as soon as you find anything."

"Of course," Brix replies.

The two of them march out together, and Aurora shuts and locks the doors behind them with a wave of her hand.

"You don't trust them," I say.

"Not Kraug, no," she replies. "About a year ago we caught him working contracts on the side for the cartels."

"You're scorching my jets."

Aurora shakes her head.

"Then what the hell is he still doing here?"

"There were extenuating circumstances. He claimed the jobs were part of an undercover operation to expose a group of slave smugglers operating out of the neutral zone."

"Was it true?"

"He provided the information that allowed us to take down two different bases and rescue almost fifty people, half of them underage kids."

I wince at that, thinking of our underage daughter. But Aurora is right. The connection could be significant. What if Kraug was just covering his ass after we caught him? His ties to those slavers might have been real. And if he was working with slavers once, he could be again.

"We need to look into him," I say.

"Yes," Aurora agrees. Her gaze slides away from mine. "Night, are you sure you didn't see anything?"

One paw leaves her eyes, and two golden orbs flick between us.

Clicks and growls issue from her. *"Nightmare hear heavy sound. Wake from sleep. Bad person walk quiet to room. Nightmare run out. No face. No smell. Shoot Nightmare with tail spike. Nightmare scratch and bite. Then sleep."*

"You bit it?" Aurora asks quickly. "What did it taste like?"

"Not taste good."

"Sounds like a bot," I conclude.

"Or a bio wearing armor," Aurora replies. "Let's look around. If Nightmare scratched and bit the intruder, we might find something we can use."

I nod along with that, wondering to myself what we could possibly find. A few flakes of paint or alloy? Some bit of generic synthskin flayed off a bot's chassis? But I suppose that would at least give us the bot's apparent ethnicity.

Nightmare removes her other paw from her face and slowly rises from the bed. She paces along behind Aurora, sniffing at the floor. Aurora raises the lights to full brightness, dazzling my eyes and making the stone floors sparkle brightly with colorful flecks of silica.

I make my way around the opposite side of the living area, checking dusty corners, behind potted plants and sculptures, under the carpet beneath the broken coffee table in the living room…

Besides the dust and a collection of wiry black bristles ejected from Nightmare's coat, I don't see anything.

"Did your sweeper drone break down or something?" I call to Aurora. Looking up, I see the doors to the room that Aurora closed off where the kitchen used to be are now open.

"Brix must have shut the cleaner down to stop it from clearing away any evidence!" Aurora calls back to me.

I find myself wondering again about what's in that room, but my curiosity can wait. Moving on, I reach the corridor to the bedrooms and hurry down it, remembering that Brix and Nightmare both described the altercation with the intruder as taking place around the primary bedroom.

The decoratively paneled walls are scuffed

with scratches from Nightmare's spikes. The floors are also gouged with scratches from her claws. Looking back, I see a crisscrossing track of those scratches running to the door, making me think that Nightmare has a habit of running out at top speed to greet people when they arrive. But there's something else that catches my eye. No dust. No shed hairs. The sparkling stone floors are completely clear of debris in the corridor.

I drop to my haunches with a frown and run my hand across the floor. It comes away clean. No dust or shed hair. It could be that Nightmare's frequent sprints to and from the door have carried all of the dirt and hair from the corridor to the living area. Maybe. But how long has it been since Aurora's domestic drudge cleaned the floors? There's too much accumulated dust and hair in the living area for it to have only been shut down a couple of days ago. Maybe Nightmare broke it. Given the shattered table and sculpture in the living room, that seems likely.

I straighten and continue down the corridor, checking periodically for dust and hair. The whole length of the passage is clean, even in the corner where it hooks a 90-degree turn to the left. But that's impossible. Even if the wind of Nightmare's eager welcomes has carried all the dirt from the corridor, there should at least be a pile of dust and hair in the corner.

Unless...

The cleaner was busy vacuuming the corridor when the intruder came in, and then it got knocked out by the same EMP that took Aurora's double offline. Maybe.

Or the intruder deliberately ordered the drudge to clean the corridor after jacking Aurora's double, and then it shut the cleaner down afterward, making it look like the EMP disabled it. Brix might have booted it back up to check its logs, or to see if it vacuumed up any evidence. The bot's dust bin could have been emptied. But even so, why clean the corridor?

Nightmare said she scratched and bit the intruder. Could she have bitten into a bio and sprayed the corridor with blood?

But Nightmare said that the intruder didn't taste good. Would she have described it that way if she'd bitten into human flesh?

Something isn't adding up here.

"Find anything?" Aurora asks suddenly.

I startle at the sound of her voice close beside my ear and turn around to see her and Nightmare standing right behind me.

"Night, you said the bad person didn't taste good. Why?"

"Bad blood."

A quiet thrill shoots through me. "So there was blood?"

"Blood bad," Nightmare says again.

"Synthetic blood?" I wonder, looking to Aurora.

She slowly shakes her head. "A bot pretending to be a bio? That's going a bit far, don't you think? What would be the point?"

I shrug. "To prove that you can bleed and fool people into thinking you're *not* a bot. Or maybe to get through security systems with DNA samplers."

"Maybe..." I agree, my mind still spinning through possibilities. The light bulb goes off in my brain a few seconds later. "Or it was a bio with an altered body chemistry."

"An augment," Aurora whispers.

"Like Kraug," I add.

CHAPTER 19

Kraug bristles at our accusation. We summoned him and Brix back to our quarters to confront him with the evidence. Brix looks confused, but wary, studying his right-hand man with new eyes.

"I swear on my mother's life, I had nothing to do with it," Kraug says. He nods to Nightmare. "Do I smell like the intruder?"

Nightmare rocks her head from side to side, her version of a human shaking their head. *"No smell."*

"Well, I took a sanisteam a few hours ago," Kraug grumbles.

Nightmare pads toward Kraug, lifting her chin and sniffing loudly.

"Human smell," she declares.

Kraug looks confused. "So which is it? Human smell or no smell?"

Aurora explains, "She's saying you smell like a human, but the intruder didn't smell like anything. We think the jacker was wearing armor or a vac suit. Nightmare claims she sank her teeth into the intruder. She says they tasted bad. Specifically, their blood did."

"So? What does that mean?" Kraug asks, shaking his head and sending dreadlocks rustling across his massive shoulders.

I explain, "Could be some type of modified bio chemistry. Like yours."

Kraug frowns. "*That's* what has you accusing me? We have a hundred and sixteen hunters on station right now, and at least thirty of them are augmented bios like me. You'll need to cast a wider net if you want to find someone with bad-tasting blood."

"There's more," I insist. "You were recently involved with a group of slavers in the neutral zone."

"Because I was trying to bring them down from the inside! Which I did, by the way."

"Only after we discovered your involvement," Aurora says. "You could have been covering your tracks."

Kraug's jaw drops. "*Aurry,* you *know* me. You recruited me for scrip's sake!"

Aurora scowls. "The problem is, I know all of you, but someone had to have betrayed us."

"What about your airlock theory?" Brix asks quietly, nodding to the emergency airlock in question. "As Corvus said earlier, it didn't have to be one of ours if they somehow snuck in directly."

"You tell me," I reply. "Did you find anything from the system diagnostics?"

Brix slowly shakes his head. "We're still working that angle."

Kraug grates out an irritated sigh. "There's an easy way to resolve this." He pulls up his right sleeve and extends his arm to Nightmare. "Bite it."

Nightmare's eyes widen hungrily and she bares her teeth in a nasty grin. She sniffs experimentally at his arm and gives it a lick.

"Are you crazy?" Brix snaps. "She'll rip it off!"

"So tell her to bite softly," Kraug replies. "Aurry?"

She appears to hesitate.

"There has to be a better way..." Brix mutters.

"Just get it over with," Kraug insists.

Nightmare looks to Aurora for permission, and she nods. "Small bite."

"Bite small. Yesss..." She rumbles eagerly. Her spikes rattle as they rise. She takes a quick step toward Kraug... and then pounces on him, grabbing his outstretched arm with both of her forepaws. She chomps down between them, and blood spurts around her lips.

Kraug unleashes a muffled cry but clamps down on it with gritted teeth. Blood seeps around Nightmare's jaws, pitter-pattering to the deck in a steady rain. Her back set of eyes sink halfway shut as if she's relishing the taste.

"All right, that's enough!" Brix roars, stalking angrily toward Nightmare.

She abruptly releases Kraug's arm and ducks low as she darts away behind Aurora.

I frown at the unusual behavior from the deadly xeno, thinking that this wraith might have been abused by her previous owners on Kazir.

Kraug rips off his other sleeve and wraps it deftly around his bloody arm to staunch the flow from deep, interlocking puncture marks that wrap around his forearm in two curving arcs from Nightmare's upper and lower jaws.

"So?" Kraug grunts. "What's the verdict?"

We all look to Nightmare. She's busy licking Kraug's blood from her paws like a cat. *"Taste good,"* she mewls.

Kraug sneers at Aurora. "Anything else, Boss?"

Aurora sighs and waves him away. "Get yourself down to the med bay and patch up that arm."

Kraug wordlessly turns to leave, and a heavy silence fills the room. The doors rumble open, then shut behind Kraug.

Brix is studying us thoughtfully. "What makes you think it was a bio all of a sudden? It's more likely that a bot would taste bad— if Nightmare got a taste of hydraulic fluid or coolant, for example."

He's got a good point, and that would also explain why the intruder might have cleaned up the corridor before they left. "Just covering our bases," I explain. "Kraug's connection with those slavers was the real smoking gun."

"Look, I get it," Brix sighs. "Your daughter's missing and every minute counts. It's making you desperate, but don't waste time jumping at shadows. We've got a pretty good chance of following the money on this one. One of our forensic accountants has an in with a top-level exec at the Bank of Kazir."

My spirits are suddenly soaring with that revelation. "Are you serious?"

"Dead serious," Brix replies. "We're looking through the Hadros Group's transfer records now. Won't be long before we find something."

"Good work, Brix," Aurora says. "That's really good news."

At some point, sensing the mood in the room, Nightmare slunk off to one of the bedrooms, but now I see her scurrying back. She has some scrap of brown fabric sticking out between her teeth. Maybe from a shoe or a piece of furniture that she chewed up in Aurora's absence.

She spits it out at Aurora's feet.

"What is that?" Brix asks, pointing to it.

"Skin," Nightmare explains.

Aurora picks it up to examine the scrap of fabric more closely.

"Looks like some type of leather," I say, stepping in for a closer look at the wrinkled brown material.

"Morlskin," Aurora confirms.

"Is that a piece of a mag-seal?" I ask, pointing to where a dark black strip is still attached on one end.

"It must have been ripped off a jacket," Brix says quietly as he crowds in between us.

"Where did you get this?" Aurora asks, dropping to her haunches in front of Nightmare and holding the scrap of leather under the nostrils in her chin. Nightmare snorts and turns her head away, baring sharp, interlocking rows of teeth.

"Bad person," she says, confirming the connection for us.

"Do you recognize it?" I ask, taking the scrap from Aurora and handing it to him.

"Lots of hunters own brown morlskin jackets..." he says. "Including you, Korbin. But, if I had to take a shot in the dark... there is one hunter who wears one like a uniform."

"Vance Baleros," Aurora says.

Brix nods. "And he's a bot."

"Is he here?" I ask quickly.

"Let me check..." Aurora says. Imagery flickers brightly over her eyes. "Internal sensors show him in his quarters."

"Check where he was when your double was jacked."

"The logs are scrambled, remember?" Aurora asks. "But... according to the system, he wasn't in his room before the malfunction. He was on the mess deck. After the malfunction he was back in his quarters… and he hasn't left since."

That puts a knot in my brow. "You mean he hasn't left his room for two straight days? Why the hell not?"

"Let's go ask him," Brix suggests.

Aurora's glowing copper eyes clear. "And while we're at it, we can see if there's a piece missing from his jacket."

I'm already running for the door.

* * *

We arrive at Vance's room on level ten. Brix overrides the door controls, and Aurora and I both draw our sidearms. The three of us storm into a small compartment. We're standing in a modestly appointed living room with a small kitchen area that probably only ever gets used for Vance's bio guests. A single, sleek white couch sits between two small blue armchairs arrayed around a glass coffee table. A single rectangular viewport takes up most of the far wall behind one of the chairs, giving a view overlooking the cliff where the Shroud is landed. The lake at the bottom of the crater basin gleams darkly with a pale green light cast by the planet's rings.

My eyes are drawn to an empty charging pad by the window. There's no sign of Vance anywhere, and by now he should have heard or detected his front door opening.

"Vance!" Brix bellows.

No reply.

"Let's check the bedroom," I whisper.

Aurora beats us there, aiming her gun into the room. I crowd into the open doorway behind her, peering over her shoulder.

Vance is standing on another charging pad, right beside the bed with its crisp, unwrinkled blanket and sheets.

His eyes are glowing blue, but they're not tracking us as we step into the room.

"Vance!" Brix tries again, but there's still no reply.

We're looking at an empty shell. Vance must have transferred his neurodata to Aurora, then sent his old body down here with only a few scraps of rudimentary code to guide it. That means we're not going to find any clues in its neural net.

"Lights," I snap at the station's AI, and light strips swell brightly in the ceiling. Vance is wearing a brown morlskin jacket. The bottom corner of it has been ripped off.

Aurora fits the piece that Nightmare tore off to the empty space.

"Looks like we've found our guy," I mutter.

"Or his old chassis, anyway," Brix mutters.

"I'm going to jack in and see if I can find anything," Aurora says.

"Be careful," I reply, watching as my wife reaches behind her neck, flips open a compartment, and reels out a thin transparent cable. She opens a matching port behind Vance's neck and goes suddenly still with her glowing orange eyes pulsing brightly.

"So?" I ask after waiting impatiently for a few moments.

"Nothing!" Aurora hisses through her teeth. "He wiped all his data. The only thing in here is some basic navigation software that he used to send his body down here after jacking mine."

That puts a deep frown on my face. We've made some progress, but having a name to put to Cally's abductor is less useful than I had hoped. Vance is long gone, and he's probably ditched Aurora's body for another chassis by now.

"Well, at least now we can stop the witch hunt," Brix sighs.

"He could have had an accomplice," I point out.

"What?" Brix looks almost offended by the suggestion. "How do you figure?"

"How else did he cause that system malfunction?"

"He had to have access to the system, but that doesn't mean he had help," Brix replies. "I'm sure if we track his movements over the past week or two we'll find a point where he entered the control room and jacked in with a virus."

"Look into it and let us know what you find," I suggest.

Brix nods. "Count on it."

Aurora unplugs from Vance and turns away with flashing orange eyes. It takes me a second to realize that her eyes are flashing because she's busy scanning through reams of data. Probably doing a deep dive in the Shroud's databanks to dig up everything she can on Vance.

While we're waiting, I cross over to Vance's body, checking for bite marks that could explain the bad taste that Nightmare reported.

Opposite the right side of Vance's jacket with the missing corner, I notice four parallel tears where Nightmare's claws slashed it open. Those tears continue down to his thigh on the same side, but there's no sign of teeth marks.

Lifting the jacket around the missing corner, I see that the white shirt underneath is stained dark blue with some type of coolant fluid, and there are dozens of puncture marks from Nightmare's teeth. Synthskin is self-healing, so there's no sign of damage beneath the shirt.

"Night got a mouthful of coolant," Brix mutters.

"Bad blood," I reply, remembering the wraith's description. Straightening, I turn to see if Aurora has finished looking into Vance yet. "Find anything?" I ask.

Aurora nods absently. Her eyes stop flickering a moment later. "Vance was a bio before he joined the Templars, affiliated with the Legion. He died on a job, then came back as a bot. Apparently, dying made him question all of his life choices, and he wanted to turn over a new leaf. That was what brought him to us. Two years ago. Brix passed his application on to me, and I approved him on a probationary basis. For the first year, we spoon-fed him a string of low-paying contracts, testing him to see if he'd go off the rails to get a bigger payday. We didn't even let him into the Shroud. After that year, we conducted a review and found that he'd kept his nose clean, sticking only to the contracts that we gave him. So we signed him on permanently and brought him here. For the past year, it's been the same story. He never took any contracts that didn't come from our job board. He's ranked 139 out of 209 on our roster, and has an SGR rating of 4390."

The SGR is Zero and Krom's Standard Guild Rating Index, established by two legendary hunters almost fifty years ago. There are more than ten thousand active hunters listed on that index today, across nine different guilds, including our own. The SGR is what establishes a bounty hunter's base rate of pay, and it also helps prospective clients negotiate the bounty when a contract is exclusive rather than open. But Vance's rating is hardly impressive.

"He's just an average hunter," I conclude. "So how the hell has he managed to run circles around us?"

"He took you by surprise," Brix suggests quietly. "You weren't expecting it."

"No." I shake my head. "I don't buy that. If he was operating alone, he's not skilled enough to have pulled all of this off. Where would he have even gotten the credits to bribe those patrollers?"

Brix shrugs. "People fall ass-backward into money all the time."

"Or someone hired him and they're the ones who bribed Nevos," Aurora suggests.

"If that's the case, then why not hire someone who's a better match for us? Aurora and I are both in the top one hundred of the SGR. Or we were before we retired, anyway. Whoever is behind this had the credits to afford a better hunter. They paid two million to Nevos and his crew, and they weren't even the main act.

"Put yourself in a hypothetical employer's shoes," I say. "You need a man on the inside, so you pick someone off our roster. Why pick someone with an impeccable record? As far as we can tell, Vance is a straight edge, so how could they possibly know that he wouldn't simply turn around and report the plot to us?"

"They must have had something on him," Brix replies. "Some kind of threat against someone that he cares about."

"Maybe..." I agree. "Or there is no employer, and this is personal. Remember the comms we got from Cally's abductor just before they jumped out? The jacker was taunting us. It seemed personal. Does Vance have any family that we could have done something to?"

Aurora answers, "A mother and father, both deceased with DNRs."

That's interesting, I think to myself. DNR

stands for *Do Not Resurrect*. It means the person in question does not want to come back as a bot under any circumstances, and legally, they cannot be resurrected by anyone else if there's a DNR in place.

"How did they die?"

Aurora hesitates for a fraction of a second. "Natural causes. Old age."

I stroke my jaw, considering the matter. "So there's no way Vance could be holding a grudge over that. He doesn't have a spouse, or lover, or any kids?"

Aurora shakes her head. "Not that we know of."

"There has to be someone out there," Brix insists. "Like you said, why else would he do this? Either it's personal and it's revenge, or someone got to him by threatening people he cares about."

"But why taunt us? The abductor made it seem like they were behind this."

"Could have been part of the job," Brix says. "He might have been reading someone else's script."

"Yeah. Maybe..." I agree. "But there's another possibility that would explain why they used a sub-standard hunter with a clean record to get to us. Say someone is threatening Vance. They get him to come back to the Shroud, carrying some other bot's neurodata. Once he's passed the security check, he overwrites his own data, essentially jacking himself. And then whoever it is jacks Aurora and leaves the station in her ship. That would also explain the gloating message from Cally's abductor."

Aurora sighs. "So it could still be anybody, and this doesn't give us any new leads."

"It might give us a lead if we can find Vance's family," I reply. "If *he's* behind this, then we must have done something to someone that he cared about. And if he was hired to let someone else into the Shroud, or to abduct Cally himself, then the real mastermind had to have gotten to him somehow. And you don't scare an immortal bot by threatening them directly, so it had to be someone Vance cares about, and probably a meatbag with a DNR, which would mean that they don't get to come back if Vance didn't give in to the threats."

Aurora and Brix are both nodding along with my reasoning.

"Makes sense," Brix adds.

I start ticking off our leads on my fingers. "Number one, find out what we can learn from the Hadros Group's transaction logs. Number two, we see if we can find anyone that Vance might have cared about, deceased or living, who can help us understand his part in things."

Aurora frowns at that. "I already checked our records and government registries. Besides his parents, he didn't tell us about anyone, and no one is officially registered under his name."

"Ask around," I suggest. "See if your friend,

Pixie, knows something, or at least knows who he was close to at the Shroud. Someone here might know something."

"And if not?" Aurora presses.

"Then we dig deeper and ask around at his old guild. Maybe he didn't tell us about his family, but told someone there."

"Good idea," Brix says. "While you're working that angle, I'm going to check in with our system engineers to see if they've found anything to explain the surveillance malfunction. We're going to turn up something soon. I can feel it." Brix tries on a reassuring smile, but it looks cold and dead to me. Probably me projecting my feelings onto him.

A muscle jerks in my cheek as I watch my old buddy leave. I'm feeling anxious about being so disconnected from this investigation. We're waiting on Brix and his people to feed us our next clue.

I tear my gaze away from the open door to Vance's room, looking back to my wife. "Let's go find Pixie," I suggest.

Aurora's eyes are flickering once more with reams of data. After a few seconds of silence, her gaze clears, to stare pointedly at me.

"What is it?" I ask.

"Do you trust him?" Aurora whispers.

"Who? Brix?"

She nods. "He runs this place twenty-four-seven, and his standard guild rating before that was right up there with ours. We've had attempted reprisals before. By skilled operators. Mercenaries, bounty hunters... you name it. So how does someone like Vance run circles around him and jack into his security system to cause a comprehensive malfunction for twelve whole minutes, and somehow, two days later, Brix is *still* looking into it?"

"He's like family," I insist. "He would never hurt Cally. And we go back a long way. I'd trust Brix with my life. We ran dozens of ops together while we were in the Paladins. He must have saved my life at least five times, just as I saved his. And besides, what motive could he possibly have? I might not know if Vance has any family out there, but you and I both know that Brix doesn't. He rarely leaves the Shroud, and besides the occasional hookup with one of our own, he's a lone operator."

"No, you're right. Damn it..." Aurora grimaces and shakes her head. Her expression quickly crumbles into a miserable look, and a single tear slides down one cheek.

I step quickly over to her and pull her into a hug. "Hey. We're going to figure this out soon. We'll find out who took her, and then we're going to get Cally back."

"You promise?" Aurora breathes in a shaky whisper that piles hotly against my ear. Once again, I'm amazed at just how realistically she can simulate human functions and reactions. If not for her glowing eyes, and the fact that I know she's a bot, I might never be able to tell the difference.

"I promise," I whisper back. Withdrawing from that embrace, I reach up under her chin and turn her lips to mine, kissing her emphatically and inhaling her scent. She even smells and tastes like a real human.

That brings to mind Nightmare's testimony: she said that the *bad person* didn't smell like anything, and had no face. Vance must have been wearing a synthetic holo mask to hide his features, which is consistent with Aurora's corrupted memories of the encounter. He probably also disabled his scent emitters, if his chassis even has them. But why does Aurora remember that Vance was wearing a holo mask and not that he was wearing a brown morlskin jacket?

I withdraw sharply from her, looking back to Vance. "Do you remember what he was wearing?"

Aurora frowns, her gaze drifting out of focus as she searches her memories. "No..." She slowly shakes her head. "It was dark. All I can see is a blank, featureless black face."

"Was he wearing a jacket?" I ask.

"Maybe, I don't know. It's too dark," Aurora says. "Let me enhance the imagery... No, too blurry. He's in the background, and my eyes were focused on something else."

"On what?"

"Can't see it. It's just a blank, black blur, moving too fast to track. Probably Nightmare. Then I get hit with an EMP."

"Why would your eyes be focused on Nightmare if there's an intruder in your quarters?"

Aurora frowns. "I didn't think of that."

"Try reconstructing the imagery with predictive algorithms," I suggest.

A moment later, Aurora mutters a sharp curse. "There was a second intruder. He's wearing a vac suit! Black, with a helmet. Vance is in the background, also wearing a helmet. He's headed for the bedrooms, probably to deal with Nightmare."

"So Vance did have an accomplice," I conclude. "And the fact that they were wearing a vac suit means they might have come in through or left by our private airlock."

"That's the direction they're coming from," Aurora says.

"And they're probably also a bio," I point out. "Bots don't need to wear vac suits. That means they had to have used a neuro-jacker to take over your double, so there could even be a third player in all of this. But I'm willing to bet Vance is just there to distract us. They wiped his data to make us think that he's the one who took over your double, and I bet they left that piece of his jacket behind on purpose. It's too sloppy otherwise."

Aurora lets out a strangled noise. "But that means we still have no idea who did this!"

She's right, but at least now we know we're looking for two people instead of one. In theory, that means we have twice as many trails to follow, and they had twice as many tracks to cover up. Somewhere along the line, one of them will have screwed up and left a real clue that will lead us to Cally.

"Let's go talk to Pixie about Vance. See if he had any family."

"You just said he's a dead end," Aurora objects.

"Someone still had to threaten him to get him involved. If we can find out who did the threatening, we might turn up a real clue."

CHAPTER 20

I'm sitting in a dark, quiet corner booth next to Aurora in the Cosmic Cask, one of the Shroud's two bars, on level 9, the mess deck. It's a decorative spot, with actual whiskey casks hanging from the ceiling repurposed as chandeliers. Neon blue and purple lights illuminate the bar. A gleaming silver drudge bartender stands behind the counter, polishing glasses and watching his patrons with glowing green eyes. Only a handful of people are down here with us, discussing their business in booths like ours with noise-canceling fields activated to protect their privacy. A towering gridded wall of curving viewports beside us looks out over the station's outer ring to Charos's night sky. A jagged purple flash of lightning catches the corner of my eye, reflecting briefly off the crater lake below. Rain starts up again, streaking the viewports with snaking lines of moisture.

Pixie sits opposite us, sipping a fruity red

cocktail from a fluted glass. She's a bot, but she must be used to keeping up with the social mores of meatbags like me. Aurora is, too, but she's all business right now, so she didn't order anything. She's laser-beam focused on just one thing: getting our daughter back. I am, too, but I need something to bring me down before I explode, so I'm nursing three fingers of my favorite 12-year-old Bowmore Scotch from Earth.

"Vance, huh?" Pixie muses, while stirring her drink with a metal straw. "I never would have pegged him for a traitor."

We told her that Aurora got jacked in her room, which is safe enough to share, but not about Cally. Pixie's loyalty to Aurora aside, she's plugged into the rumor mill, which means she's got loose lips.

Maybe it doesn't matter anymore who learns what. After all, the worst has already happened, but once we get Cally back, if everyone here knows about her, it won't take long for that news to spread, and pretty soon we'll find ourselves in a hundred new sets of cross hairs.

We *did* live here with Cally for a couple of years before we retired, but we only brought her here when she was six months old, and back then the story was that she was an orphan we picked up on a job. We said we were waiting to find her a home. And then eighteen months later we retired and disappeared. Since then our roster has been recycled a few times, and by this point,

I can count on one hand the number of people connected to the Templars who know that we have a daughter. But with Aurora's frequent comings and goings, it only would have taken her getting tailed to Pyria once to find out about Cally and me.

Aurora fixes her friend with a hard look. "Pixie, we think someone got to Vance. Do you know if he has anyone he cares about, on or off station, who could have been used to threaten him?"

Pixie makes a face. "What, you mean like a family?"

Aurora nods.

Pixie shakes her head. "Not that I know of. But it's not the kind of thing that people around here would share. Hunters don't like to blab about their personal lives."

"Yeah..." I nod, swirling the ice cubes in my glass before taking a big gulp.

"Do you know anything about the system malfunction?" Aurora asks next.

"The missing twelve minutes of holo data?" Pixie asks.

"Yes."

We didn't tell her how long the Shroud's surveillance system was offline, so the fact that she knows it was twelve minutes is proof of Pixie's value as an informant.

"There's got to be at least a dozen people and drudges who have access," Pixie says. "I could name them for you, but I suppose you probably already have that list."

Aurora nods.

"Sorry I can't be of more help," Pixie says.

"Maybe you still can be," Aurora says.

Pixie's eyebrows dart up as she takes a long sip from her drink.

"What about Brix?" Aurora asks.

I find myself frowning at that. She's questioning his loyalty again. As far as I'm concerned, he's beyond reproach, but I've been out of the game for a long time. Aurora has been here, living a double life for the past four years. I'm starting to wonder if she knows something about Brix that she hasn't told me.

"What about him?" Pixie asks.

"Would he have access to the surveillance system?" Aurora presses.

"You know that he does... but why would he jack you?"

Aurora shakes her head. "I don't know, but he would have had the means and the opportunity. All that's missing is the motive."

"Motive is everything," Pixie replies.

"Does he have any family off station?"

"Brix?" Pixie laughs prettily. "He's a lone wraith," Pixie says. "Speaking of wraiths, how's Nightmare?"

"She's good," Aurora replies shortly.

A call begins trilling through the bone conduction speakers in my holoband. It's Brix.

I answer with a thought, and his head and shoulders appear before my eyes.

"Corvus, I have some developments to share. Meet me in the control center with Aurora as soon as you can."

I nod. "We'll be right down."

The comm ends, and I drain my glass and stand up from the booth. "We have to go," I say.

"Already?" Pixie asks. "We just got here!"

I nod and pay the tab via my holoband. "Brix just called. He has something."

Aurora stands up beside me. Pixie frowns. "You suspect he could be involved, and yet he's feeding you intel?"

"We don't suspect him," I reply, feeling the need to defend my friend.

"We suspect *everyone*," Aurora adds ominously.

Pixie gapes at her. "Even me?"

I disable the noise-canceling field, and we step out of the booth.

"I'll be in touch," Aurora says as we turn to leave.

"That was a little harsh, don't you think?" I whisper to her as we breeze out of the Cosmic Cask.

"No," Aurora replies. "Until we get to the bottom of this, we're better off not trusting anyone."

"Do you trust me?" I ask.

"Of course I do. Don't be a scrigg," Aurora

replies as we stride down the corridor from the bar.

"Good," I reply.

We pass the entrance to the mess hall, weaving around the few other hunters coming and going. Some of them wave or nod to Aurora.

Silently over a text, I ask, *"Is there something you need to tell me about Brix?"* The station has eyes and ears everywhere, so we can't discuss the topic openly. In the booth we had the privacy field engaged, but casting suspicion on Brix out here in the open is a bad idea if he really is involved.

"No, but he's your *friend,"* Aurora writes back. *"I didn't serve in the Paladins with him, and he's never saved my life. The fact that he is in a position to pull off something like this, and that he's the only one here who knows about Cally and our double lives on Pyria is suspicious enough all by itself."*

"Okay, so why now?" I reply. *"He's been in charge ever since we left fifteen years ago. If he's secretly been out to get us all this time, why betray us now?"*

"Something had to have happened recently," Aurora writes. We reach the grav lifts and wait quietly for the nearest one to open.

"Except that it couldn't have happened recently," I point out. *"The ship that took Cally was called the* Korbin's Folley, *and her abductor said that I took something of theirs, so now they're taking something of mine. I've been retired for fifteen years, so whatever I did to provoke this, I did it a*

long time ago, and that rules out Brix. He's been with us since before Cally was even born."

"Old history makes for dusty skeletons," Aurora replies. *"He could have been playing a long con."*

The lift opens and we step in, finding it empty.

"No one waits that long for revenge," I argue as the doors slide shut behind us. *"Not unless they're still maneuvering themselves into position. Look, I get it: we have a new suspect and we have no clue who it could be, so it makes it seem like it could be anyone, but they were wearing a vac suit, right?"*

Aurora nods.

"Brix wouldn't need to use a vac suit or our emergency airlock to get to you. He could just knock on the front door, and you'd let him in without a second thought."

"Let's see what kind of leads he's turned up," Aurora says audibly as the grav lift opens on level five, the command deck.

I follow her out, wondering grimly what we're about to learn from Brix.

CHAPTER 21

Brix is the only one in the command center with us. I wonder if that's because he doesn't know who to trust. I'm surprised Kraug isn't there, but there's probably some bad blood between us after we accused him of jacking Aurora. No pun intended.

Aurora and I are watching holo feeds on a wall of displays. The feeds are from the station's security cameras and sensors, tracking Vance all across the Shroud just before the surveillance outage. He is seen leaving his quarters an hour and six minutes before the outage. He's wearing the same brown morlskin jacket we found a piece of. Cameras track him going to the concourse on level eight, then out to his ship in Hangar Bay 9D. He stays there until just seven minutes before the outage and then comes back up. He's riding alone in one of the main lifts, coming from the concourse on level eight with a helmet tucked under his arm. There's no sign of his accomplice in the black vac suit—more confirmation that they came in through the emergency airlock.

"That's all we've got," Brix says as the feeds go blank. "Once the system returns, Vance is back in his quarters, and as you know he didn't leave his room after that. We tracked him through the logs for the past six months. He never had direct access to the security system."

"So who did?" I ask.

"It's a short list," Aurora says. "The system is automated, and access is read-only except from the server room. We don't have anyone actively watching the feeds or regularly updating the code. Who last accessed the server room?"

"Janus Savage, our systems engineer, and that was four months ago. We're already checking him out—quietly because we don't want to spook him into covering his tracks, but so far, there's no sign of any suspicious activity."

"Hmmmm," I mumble. "What about a power outage? Someone could have cut a conduit or overloaded the circuit, or simply powered the system down from here."

"It wasn't powered down, because we noticed the outage immediately, and we tried everything to get it back," Brix explains. "As for physical sabotage, there wasn't any, and the system is highly redundant. You can't cut power to all the cameras and sensors from any one location."

"Then it had to be Janus," Aurora says.

Brix appears to consider it. "It's possible that

he was used unwittingly to deliver malicious code or a system jacker drone."

"Is Janus a bio?" I ask.

Brix shakes his head. "Bot."

"Then wouldn't his integrated sensors have detected a jacker drone hitching a ride in with him?"

"Hard to say," Brix replies. "It could have been dormant, running on minimal power, then dropped off his clothes before he left."

Aurora plants her hands on her hips. "So you brought us up here just to tell us that you haven't found anything?"

"I didn't say that," Brix replies with a grim smile. "The surveillance angle is a dead end for now, but our accountants found a lot of dirt when they started digging." Brix gestures to the screens and a host of digital files take the place of the scrambled holo feeds.

"Our contact at the Bank of Kazir came through. First up, is the Hadros Group. Their account was opened two years ago, at the same time the corp was founded. Almost immediately after that, Hadros received a payment in the amount of one hundred million credits from Icarus LLC on Kazir. That's where the money came from to bribe Nevos and his crew."

My eyes are skipping over the financial records, scanning them for clues. "What's that?" I ask, pointing to a series of highlighted transactions for one million credits, paid like clockwork in the middle of each month. I recognize the name of the payee. "Horizon Holdings. That's the Syndicate. My old guild."

Aurora looks surprised. "Hadros has a bounty hunter on their payroll?"

Brix nods. "And judging by the size of those payments, he's got to be in the top one hundred of the SGR, just like the two of you. Payments go back almost two years, the same as Hadros itself. Ten to one, that's your guy. Or girl," Brix says with a nod to Aurora. "Whoever jacked you and took Cally, it wasn't Vance. He was part of it, that's for sure, but he doesn't have the skills to pull off a job like this on his own. He had to have an accomplice."

Interestingly, Brix has reached that conclusion without even knowing what we found lurking in Aurora's corrupted memories of the incident. I'm tempted to tell Brix, but Aurora gives me a little shake of her head as if she knows what I'm thinking. She still doesn't fully trust him. But so far she has extended that mistrust to everyone here, even to her friend, Pixie, who she claims is unfailingly loyal.

"What is Icarus?" Aurora asks, suddenly changing the topic. She's staring at that giant lump-sum payment to Hadros at the top of one of the screens. "That was the seed money for this whole operation."

Brix answers, "Officially, it's an exploration and pharmaceutical research company, but they're all about finding new stims beyond habited space. They're not directly affiliated with any of the cartels or pharmaceutical companies, but they sell their formulas to the highest bidder, and you can pretty much guess who that will be when it comes to hot new drugs and stims. Keri Pharma or Solaris, depending on the legality of the substance in question."

I frown at that. "So Icarus paid a massive sum to buy someone else's discovery, probably something that needed further in-house development before they could sell it to one of the big pharma corps or stim cartels."

"My thinking exactly," Brix says.

I go on. "Then we're looking for an explorer or a prospector. Someone who would have had the opportunity to find a rare organic compound or symbiotic microbe with useful properties."

Aurora pulls her ruby-red hair out of its ponytail, letting it cascade freely over her shoulders. "Either that..." she muses. "Or else, Hadros is an extension of Icarus itself. In which case, *they're* the ones behind this, and Hadros is just the front that they're using to pay for it."

"Also possible," Brix agrees. "It's a privately-owned company."

"No kidding," I growl. "Who owns it?"

"Now that's where things get interesting," Brix replies. "Icarus was founded by two former Coalition researchers, Ivy Rox and Aster Stavros, both of whom were evicted from Cath space during something called the Hadros Incident, forty-five years ago."

"The *Hadros* Incident?" Aurora asks sharply. "That *can't* be a coincidence."

"No, it's a clue," I agree.

"A deliberate one," Brix adds. "Someone wanted us to make that connection, which means you two need to be real careful going forward."

"The *Hadros* Incident..." I mutter. "When I first heard the name Hadros, I thought I recognized it from somewhere. I think that might be it, but I can't remember any specific details about it."

Aurora gives me a sharp look. "You didn't mention that to me."

"I wasn't sure it was worth mentioning. It felt like déjà vu. Us meatbags get things mixed up sometimes."

Brix arches an eyebrow at me. "Well, it's old Coalition history. I wouldn't be surprised if the name seems familiar."

"Not to me," Aurora says.

Brix regards her steadily "Forty-five years ago, you would have been, what?"

"Fourteen. Still a bio," Aurora says.

"Exactly," Brix replies. "So you had other things on your mind than politics. Cade is seven years older than you, so he would have been twenty-one."

"I was already a Paladin by then," I add. "But

this doesn't feel like some bit of trivia that I forgot. It feels like… an itch deep inside my brain that I can't scratch. Something important."

Brix favors me with a deepening frown. "That sounds like a scrub trace to me."

I nod my agreement. The Paladins have a bad habit of sending their people on missions so deeply classified the operators can't even be allowed to remember them. So they'd regularly scrub our brains to erase any evidence that could later tie back to them or our government.

"Well, that's just scragging fantastic," Aurora mutters. "Do *you* recognize the name?" she asks, nodding to Brix.

I know why she's asking him. She wants to know if he could have been there with me. And if he was, then that makes him an even bigger suspect than before.

"Not in the way Cade is describing," Brix says. "But that doesn't mean much. Not everyone experiences scrub traces, and not every time they get scrubbed. It's a random side effect. Sometimes you're left with vague recollections, like phantom pains from a missing limb. And sometimes, the memories just disappear."

Aurora narrows her eyes at him, but he doesn't appear to notice.

Brix nods to her. "Let's say the Hadros Incident is the key to all of this. Assume Cade was there, working on a mission with the Paladins. Afterward, they scrubbed his memory, which is why the name sounds familiar, but he can't directly remember why. Now, forty-five years later, someone comes after him because of *something* that happened on that mission."

"But forty-five years is a hell of a long time to be nursing a grudge," I point out. "Why only go after me now? And why *me* specifically? Why not my commanding officer, or even higher up the chain than that, to the politician who gave the orders?"

Brix shakes his head. "Short of breaking into the Paladins' archives, I don't know if we'll even be able to figure out who those people were, but it's possible that whoever this is has already found them and exacted vengeance. Maybe they spent forty-five years working down the chain of command until they finally found you."

"What does public record have to say about the Hadros Incident?" I ask.

Brix waves to the screens and the financial records vanish, replaced by a series of articles and news recordings—muted, but subtitled. They're discussing an incident in the Hadros Sector.

Brix points to the screens. "The line to the public was that the Coalition had a research facility out on the edge of Cath Space. They were studying old Priors tech, but no one knows what exactly. Then the Cath found out about it, and I guess they got pissed that we were edging too close to their sacred territory.

"They annexed the entire Hadros Sector, boarded the research facility, and sent all of the researchers packing. But something went wrong along the way; their ship malfunctioned or ran out of fuel, and they never made it back. It caused a huge political incident between the Coalition and the Cath, with the Coalition accusing them of executing everyone.

"Finally, a passing cartography vessel detected the researchers' distress signal in the heart of the Hadros Sector. After some tense negotiations, a rescue vessel was allowed to go pick them up. Guess who was among the scientists that they rescued? The founders of Icarus, along with a few other notables—including Christophe Zabelle of Zabelle Enterprises, and Gina Keri of Keri Pharmaceuticals, which we all know is a front for the Solaris Cartel."

"Zabelle Enterprises?" I ask, wondering if there's any way that Nadine could be after me again. But no, in this timeline, I never did anything to her or her family. As a result, research into FTL rifts is a lot farther along, but as far as I know, it's still highly experimental. Still, I wonder if there's a connection. After all, Cally's abductors jumped through a rift to throw us off their trail.

"Solaris and Icarus are pretty similar names," Aurora points out.

"Agreed," Brix says. "But there's no connection

besides their founders' common experience of being stranded out there in uncharted space."

"But Solaris would have all kinds of motives to come after us," Aurora points out.

"Yes, but more indirectly," Brix says. "If they have an issue with you, or specifically with Cade, it'll be because you founded the Templars who have been getting in the way of their operations from day one. It wouldn't look quite as personal as this does."

"Any chance that Gina Keri is behind Hadros?" Aurora asks, still not giving up on that angle.

Brix shrugs. "Maybe? Who knows?"

But I'm skeptical. "Why would Icarus pay Hadros, AKA Solaris, a hundred million credits? The money is flowing in the wrong direction. Solaris pays Icarus for promising new stims, not the other way around. Icarus could be involved, but I doubt that extends to Gina Keri or Solaris."

"They have their own in-house R&D department," Aurora insists. "If the Solaris Cartel developed something, gave it to Hadros, and then Hadros sold it to Icarus, that would explain the flow of credits."

Brix snorts at that. "What happens when Icarus tries to sell the formula, only to find out that Keri Pharmaceuticals is mysteriously absent from the auction and somehow already has the street market cornered? That sounds like a declaration of war to me."

"Maybe it was," Aurora says.

"All to get revenge on Cade?" Brix asks dubiously.

"And to steal a hundred million credits from Icarus," Aurora suggests.

Most stims can be reverse-engineered once they hit the streets. Some of them are hard to synthesize and have to be grown like *Glo,* but either way, Icarus probably makes more money by selling legal patents to pharmaceutical companies like Keri than they do by selling illegal stims to the cartels. It's hard to believe Icarus would buy a formula to something for a hundred million credits without also buying the patent, and that means Keri Pharmaceuticals would be shooting itself in the foot if they're secretly the ones who sold it to Icarus. Unless, of course, the compound turned out to be useless for legal drugs, in which case the patent would be worthless anyway. Keri would have passed the formula directly to their evil twin, the Solaris Cartel. But after that, would they try to trick Icarus into buying the patents?

"It's a lot more convoluted that way around," I decide.

"But possible," Aurora insists.

"What makes you like Solaris so much for this?" I ask.

"Because this has their fingerprints all over it," Aurora says. "Human trafficking is their gig."

"And Icarus has ties with them," I reply. "It's the same thing. We'll start with Icarus, see if we can find out who they were paying via Hadros, and for what." I look to Brix. "Any ideas where we can find Ivy Rox and Aster Stavros?"

Brix nods grimly. "Icarus is headquartered in the Apex Tower, the tallest building on Kazir. Ivy and Aster's private residence spans the top twenty floors. Everything else below that is Icarus."

"Well, that makes them easy to find," I reply.

"They'll have a lot of security," Brix points out.

"Not a problem," I reply.

"We could try going through official channels," Aurora says.

"If we do, then we won't be able to interrogate them," I reply. "And for all we know, they're the ones who took Cally."

"Maybe," Aurora agrees.

Brix crosses his arms over his chest. "They must know something. If not about the Hadros Group, then maybe about the Hadros Incident. They might even remember why Cade was there, and what he did to trigger all of this."

"Assuming the Coalition didn't get to them and scrub their memories, too," I point out. Changing tracks, I say, "There is one other angle we should look into. Vance. Have you checked his accounts with the Templars?"

"No sign of a pay-off, if that's what you're thinking," Brix says. "But he's been making semi-regular payments to someone out in the Neutral

Zone ever since he joined our roster. Nothing too big or flashy. A thousand credits here. Five hundred credits there. And then all of a sudden, the day before yesterday, he sends twenty-three thousand two hundred and six credits. He emptied all of his accounts in one go."

Aurora scowls. "He probably knew we'd seize his funds as soon as we discovered his involvement. So he sent his nest egg somewhere else to make a fresh start with a new name and a new face."

"Maybe," I agree. "But then what about all the previous transfers? It sounds more like he was supporting someone. Maybe a wife and kids."

"A son," Brix confirms.

"How do you know?" I ask.

"He left a message on his ship for his son. Remember, surveillance showed him going down there just before Aurora got jacked? That's what he was up to. The time stamp on the recording confirms it. And the comm number for the recipient is registered to Margrave in the Neutral Zone."

"Was there anything useful in the message?" Aurora asks.

"Just the usual sentimental stuff."

I run a hand along my jaw, considering it. "He sent all of his credits to his son just before he betrayed us. Sounds like he was getting his affairs in order before they perma-killed him."

"He might not be gone," Aurora says. "He

could have copied his neuro data and resurrected in a new body."

I'm shaking my head before she even finishes that thought. "Whoever planned this wouldn't leave a loose end like Vance lying around. He was meant to die and stay dead so he couldn't tell us what he knows."

"His son might know who was threatening him," Aurora says.

"Assuming the son is still alive," Brix adds.

I grate out a sigh. "Exactly. Still, it's worth looking into. Do we have a name?"

"No. Vance was sending the money via a popular transfer service: the Credit Bureau. They require names and IDs for transfers, and you have to pick up the transfers in person, but we're not privy to that information from here. You'd have to get a look at their records."

"Or ask around at their branches," Aurora says. "Margrave is lightly populated. It probably only has one Credit Bureau."

"It does," I confirm. "Or it did, the last time I was there."

"You've been there?" Brix asks.

"Once upon a time, on an op with the Paladins. Back then it was a hellhole, infested with raiders and mercenaries."

"They've cleaned up a bit since then," Aurora says. "Not much, but enough that some decent people call it home."

"All right. We have two solid leads to check." I

clap Brix on the shoulder. "Thanks. This is really going to help us find Cally. Send us the raw data when you get the chance. We'll look it over between jumps."

"Already done." Brix holds out a small black wafer the size of my thumbnail. I accept the data chip and slip it into a mag-sealed pocket in my jumpsuit. "I guess you'll be headed out soon?" he asks.

"Immediately," Aurora confirms.

"Where are you going first?" Brix asks. "Margrave or Kazir?"

Aurora shakes her head. She's already headed for the door. "We'll figure it out along the way."

"Good luck out there," Brix adds.

"Thanks," I reply as I follow Aurora from the control room. I have a bad feeling that we're going to need it. The Hadros *Group* was paid by Icarus, and Icarus was founded by two scientists at the heart of the Hadros *Incident,* which I was probably involved with, even though my memories of it were likely scrubbed. The motive behind Cally's abduction almost certainly lies in those missing memories. I might be able to find a copy of them in classified Holo Files in the Paladins' archives. If I could get a look at those records, I'm sure I'd know exactly who is gunning for me, and why.

The problem is, breaking into those archives would be next to impossible. The Paladins' compound on the Moon has to be one of the most secure places in all of the Coalition, and even if I could get in there, I don't have the time to plan an op that elaborate and dangerous.

This leaves me following the trail of breadcrumbs that Cally's abductors left. And at least one of them—the one that leads to Icarus —was left there deliberately. Why else would her abductors name their shell corp the Hadros Group? They wanted me to tie them to the Hadros Incident and from there to Icarus's founders, and maybe even to Solaris and Gina Keri of Keri Pharmaceuticals.

Somehow, all of it is tied together.

I just can't see how yet.

CHAPTER 22

We're back in our quarters, gathering some of Aurora's personal effects, but mostly we're here to pick up Nightmare.

She's yipping and chittering around Aurora's heels, bouncing around like she wants to play.

"Down, girl!" Aurora says as she ducks into the room that used to be the kitchen. This time I follow her in—

And find that it's been converted into a fully-equipped armory with every kind of tech, weapons, and armor imaginable.

I whistle appreciatively. "Nice collection…"

"Take anything you think we'll need and stack it in those hovercrates," Aurora says, pointing to three of them lined up on the left side of the room.

"I'm on it," I reply. As I set to work, pulling weapons and equipment off the walls, I notice that Aurora grabs two silver rings from a hook near the door. She clips one around her wrist, and the other around Nightmare's neck.

A restraint collar.

The wraith whimpers and all four of its yellow eyes appear to wince. *"Nightmare be good."*

"Sorry, Night. It's the only way they'll let me walk you to the hangar," Aurora replies while holding the wraith's massive head between both of her hands. "I won't use it unless I have to, okay?"

"Don't use," Nightmare mewls, her ears flattening to her head. A split second later, her eyes are back to sparkling and her ears are pointed once more. Her tail swishes across the floor a few times. *"Food?"* she asks brightly.

"Oh, right! You must be hungry," Aurora says.

Nightmare bounds out of the room, sending an entire aisle full of ammo and charge packs wobbling. I manage to steady it.

Aurora follows the wraith out.

As I'm going over Aurora's collection of armor, jet suits, and exosuits, I notice one that's familiar. It's my old exosuit. Matte black and form-hugging. The helmet has a distinctive orange visor, polarized and highly reflective. This exosuit has one of the most sophisticated cloaking shields that I've ever seen, as well as a powerful integrated weapon that's unequaled anywhere on this side of the galaxy: a directable, self-replicating swarm of nanites. It's alien tech, dating back to the Priors. A parting gift from my old friend, Alpha, the benevolent ruler of the enigmatic Cath.

A few minutes later, Aurora comes in just as I'm finishing up.

"I see you found your old exosuit," she says, pointing to it.

"Help me pack it into one of the crates," I reply, nodding to her.

"You're not going to wear it?" she asks.

"Not yet. Better to save the power cells."

Aurora and I hoist the suit off the mounting brackets and carry it to the third crate, where I have already laid another pair of more generic exosuits with integrated cloaking shields.

"What have you got so far?" Aurora asks as we finish packing in the alien suit.

I point to the stack of weapons in the first crate. "Repeating blasters, mag-silenced bolter rifles, plasma blasters, tracking stun darts and explosive rounds, weaponized drones, EMP rifles, SAM launchers, RPGs, discrete explosives and a few high-yield devices, two auto-turrets..." I move on to the next crate. "Breach kits, camo kits, tracking kits, comms jammers, jacker drones, bio masks, holo masks, air filter masks, synth-prints, and blood for any biometric barriers... And then in the third crate, two armored vac suits with cloaking shields."

"So, a little bit of everything," Aurora concludes.

"Exactly."

The lights dim to a bloody red, and battle

sirens split the air. My blood runs cold and my eyes bulge as if someone just dumped a hypo full of *blitz* into my system.

Brix's voice booms out over the station's intercom. "General Quarters, general quarters! This is not a drill. All Templars to your ships and action stations. We have hostiles inbound!"

Aurora's eyes widen sharply.

"How the hell did they follow us?" I roar.

"Let's go!" Aurora gestures sharply to the crates, and all three of them seal up and hover six inches off the floor.

We race out of the armory with our gear trailing behind us, and almost crash into Nightmare. She's pacing in circles and whining pitifully with her ears flattened to her head.

"Loud! Hurts!" she shrieks as she wraps her forelimbs around Aurora's legs, pinning her in place.

"Nightmare, let me go!" Aurora cries. "We have to get out of here!" She pries the wraith's arms free and sprints for the door. Two more crates are waiting there, both of them refrigerated. Must be food for Nightmare.

The front door slides open, and we run out and down the foyer to the grav lifts. It's a short wait since our quarters have priority in the system. The doors slam open, and we crowd in with Nightmare and all of our gear, barely leaving an inch of floor space between us. That's good because the lift's sensors will detect it's full and it won't try to let anyone else in. As I access the control panel on my holoband, I notice that Aurora toggled the privacy switch just in case.

I select the concourse on deck eight, and the lift promptly drops away beneath our feet. I'm suddenly weightless as the lift accelerates faster than Charos's gravity. My feet briefly leave the floor before my grav boots automatically kick in, yanking me back down. Nightmare whimpers sharply, and curls herself around Aurora's waist before she can slam into the ceiling.

The lift slows rapidly with a whirring screech from its brakes. With the station on high alert, the lifts are all moving faster than usual. The doors part with a *swish,* revealing the concourse already bustling with activity. At least fifty other hunters beat us down from the mess deck and crew quarters on levels nine through fourteen. They're sprinting to the six corridors that radiate like spokes from the spherical hub in the center of the station to the twelve hangar bays. I dash for the corridor at the two o'clock position, just off-center to our right. *Bays 3&4* are marked in peeling white paint above the opening. My holoband highlights that text, making it glow brightly.

I'm running at a flat sprint, but Aurora quickly pulls ahead of me with Nightmare and the five hover crates loaded with our supplies. Can't beat bots and apex predators for speed.

Another bot races by me as I'm chugging

along with my legs burning and my lungs screaming for air. A blur of spiky indigo hair is enough to identify her. It's Pixie. She flashes a grin over her shoulder, revealing bright purplish-red eyes. "Try to keep up, Corvus!"

Aurora reaches the airlock to Bay 3 and flashes through the open doors. We're on the surface of a planet, so no need to guard against depressurization right now.

Pixie runs through after her, followed by me and two other hunters, both meatbags.

As I aim for the ramp of the *Black Augur,* I notice Pixie is heading for a modified Beluga light transport. That might explain why she was waiting here with Kraug when we arrived. Maybe she was already here because her ship was, and she recognized the *Augur* as it came in.

Racing up the ramp, I fly through the airlock, up the next ramp, and down the corridor to the *Augur's* cockpit.

Nightmare is pacing behind the seats, adding the muted drumbeat of her paws to the muffled sirens that I can still hear roaring through the open airlock from the hangar. The airlock rumbles shut, cutting off most of the noise.

I duck an accidental swipe of Nightmare's tail spikes and drop into the co-pilot's station beside Aurora. Wraith spikes shriek as they drag across one of the bulkheads, carving fresh scratches into the alloy.

"Night, go to bed before you break

something!" Aurora snaps at her.

"Nightmare scared!" she shrieks back.

I glance over my shoulder to see her lying flat on the deck with her forepaws over her eyes and her whole body shivering so violently that it makes the spikes on her head and spine rattle. Her tail is still swishing restlessly, but at least now she's more subdued. For a deadly wraith, Nightmare sure is skittish.

"Hide under the bed!" Aurora suggests, but Nightmare doesn't budge.

Aurora grates out a sigh. "Sometimes, I wonder why I rescued you."

Nightmare whimpers softly, but doesn't answer that.

Aurora's hands fly over the controls, cold-starting the reactor with a rising *whir*. I buckle my harness just as the *Augur* leaps off the deck and turns on the spot to face the buzz-shielded opening of the hangar. A luminous blue haze separates the inside of the hangar from Charos's atmosphere.

I deploy the controls for the Augur's weapon systems and drum my fingers restlessly on the armrests as I check the power distribution levels on my holoband. I sneak some extra power away from our shields to make my job easier. Going into battle without my own ship to pilot makes me feel like a spare wheel, but there's not much I can do about that right now. My old corvette, the *Cloven Hammer,* is busy gathering dust with an orbital storage company around one of the outer planets of the Pyros System.

The comms chime with an incoming message from a ship called the *Trickster.* I notice it's a beluga-class transport, and patch it through. Pixie's voice crackles over the speakers, saying, "I've got your six, girl."

"Just try to keep up," Aurora replies. She slams the throttle for the grav lifts to the max, and the *Augur* speeds out of the hangar. The buzz shields sizzle softly against ours as we leave the protection of the Shroud.

Aurora noses up sharply, and cruises on for a few seconds before igniting the main thrusters with a meaty roar that plasters me to the back of my seat. Nightmare yips sharply in alarm, her claws digging in with a sound like nails on chalk as the sudden acceleration sends her sliding to the back of the cockpit.

"I told you to hide under the bed," Aurora mutters, even as she turns up the dial for the inertial dampeners, pushing them to the max. The chest-squeezing sensation of acceleration fades abruptly, and I drag in a deep breath.

Dozens of red enemy target boxes pepper the sky above us as sensors pinpoint them for us. I check the grid to see fifty-six enemy signatures, ranging in size from one and two-man fighters to corvettes like the *Augur.* They even have a harbinger-class assault frigate designated, *Voidreaper,* which is the real eye-popper on the screens. It looks like an entire mercenary enclave has been hired to take us out, and they've got the firepower to do it. Nothing to identify their affiliation, but I'd bet good money these are the same mercenaries that jumped Brix.

The Templars' ships are racing out from the Shroud all around and behind us, their running lights and thrusters blazing brightly against the night.

"Contact, twelve o'clock high," Pixie announces. "Fifty-two thousand klicks and closing."

"I see them," Aurora replies, reaching across the dash to augment the power to our forward shields.

"That frigate is already within laser range," I point out. "We need to focus fire on it to drive it off before it starts trading salvos with the Shroud. We're pinned down by the planet's atmosphere *and* its gravity. Landing down here was a bad idea."

"Maybe, but the atmosphere's also shielding us," Aurora points out. "It'll scatter lasers, and burn up shells from rail cannons."

Just then, as if both sides were secretly listening to our conversation, fat red laser beams from heavy batteries go flashing by us from the Shroud. A split second after that, dozens of equally heavy lasers answer back, slicing down through the clouds. Like that the darkness of the night turns to crimson fury.

I toggle a friend-foe overlay in *Augur's* combat computer to make sense of it, turning the Shroud's lasers green and the enemy's red.

A quick look at the grid and the orders coming in over the Templars' command channel reveals Brix's battle strategy. All ships have been ordered to defend the Shroud from incoming ordnance and enemy fighters. Meanwhile, the Shroud is busy lifting off with boiling clouds of dust, drifting over the cliff and bleeding altitude to reach the surface of the lake at the bottom of the crater below. I have a feeling Brix is planning to take the station underwater to shield it further from enemy fire. But that will also take the station's defensive batteries out of the fight. He's digging in rather than running away. That strategy could work if the enemy doesn't have reinforcements coming, but of course, we don't know that.

I consider the layout of the battlefield while crunching the numbers on both sides. Ninety-seven Templars are in the air, which is about double the number of enemy ships. The mix of ship classes is roughly equal, and the *Augur's* combat computer has given a strength rating of 176 to the enemy force. Ours is rated at 232, but the Shroud has a rating of 72 by itself, so if we take them out of the fight, our forces are about even. Their frigate has a strength rating of 80. It's also big, slow, and vulnerable if we can get in close enough to hit it with our rail cannons and missiles.

But if we hunker down here below atmo, wasting time on defense while the Shroud goes into hiding, that frigate is going to pin us down. Those heavy lasers on the frigate are well-suited to cutting through atmosphere, and we're too slow down here to dodge them.

"Defense is the wrong play here," I say, nodding to the comms display with a transcript of Brix's orders. Aurora had the command channel muted, but I'm sure she's been paying attention peripherally.

"How do you figure?" Aurora asks. "If they take out the Shroud, the Templars are finished."

"And if we don't get up to orbit and take out that frigate while we have the chance, it'll pin us down and take us all out. We have greater numbers, we need to press the advantage, not play it safe. He's going to get us all killed."

Aurora hammers the right rudder pedal, firing lateral jets and scooting us out of the way just as a heavy laser beam blazes down from orbit, narrowly missing us.

"So tell Brix that!" Aurora snaps at me.

Triggering the comms, I switch to a private channel and hail Brix.

His face appears, looking tense. "What's up, Korbin?"

I repeat my concerns to him, but he just shakes his head. "We need to protect the Shroud at all costs. If we try for orbit now, they'll drain our shields from a distance and once we're close enough, they'll overwhelm our point defenses. It won't take more than a couple of missiles getting through to crack us like an egg. In the lake, their lasers won't get to us, and their ordnance will be buffered as well. Our ships will intercept their fighters and missiles in atmosphere, and once we've whittled their numbers down, we'll send our squadrons up to chase off that frigate."

"By then we'll be lucky if we have a third of our ships left," I object.

"Better than two-thirds left and no base of operations for them to come back to. The Shroud lives and the Templars go on. It dies, and they scatter to the wind. You know that."

"We can always buy or build back a new headquarters," I insist. "Our people are more important than the hollow shell that houses them."

Brix arches an eyebrow at me. "Half of our hunters are already bots, and the rest will come back as bots when they die. Put it that way, and our losses don't seem to matter that much. Besides, put strictly in terms of operating capital, we're not equipped to replace the Shroud. It's worth more than all of our hunters' ships combined. Now, unless you're giving me a direct order...I suggest you trust my judgment on this."

I look to Aurora, wondering whose side of the discussion she's on. "I'm with Korbin," she says, settling the argument. "Break for orbit and hit that frigate with everything you've got."

Brix hesitates. "Are you sure about this, Aurry?"

"Do it," she insists. "We're taking command of the air group from here. We'll leave the interceptors to cover the Shroud on its way up. She'll make it. Bruised and battered, maybe, but she'll make it. Get the FTL spun up and ready, and send everyone the coordinates. We're bugging out as soon as we can."

"Yes, ma'am…" Brix replies. "I'll designate an alternate in the Neutral Zone, just in case we *don't* make it."

"Always the optimist," I reply dryly. "Let's get it done."

Brix nods grimly and ends the comms from his end.

"Time to blow your cover, Cade," Aurora says.

"What?" I blink at her.

"This was your plan, so you get to conduct the orchestra." She triggers the comms once more. "Attention all Templars, this is Aurora Velez aboard the *Black Augur.* I'd like to introduce you to Cade Korbin, my husband, and co-founder of the Templars, now officially coming out of retirement. From here on, he is in command."

Suddenly the channel is alive with exclamations from the Templars.

"Cade who?"

"Say again, *Black Augur?*"

And Pixie, aboard the *Trickster*, "*Good friend,*

my ass! I guess this means he's off limits..."

"Welcome back," someone else says. It's Kraug Hammer, aboard the *Titan.* I don't remember him from before my retirement, but somehow he remembers me? Maybe he's just being polite.

I clear my throat before answering their replies. "Cade Korbin here. Javelin Squadron, hang back and keep the Shroud covered. All other vessels, form up on our wing. We're going after that frigate."

"Copy that."

"Forming up..." Kraug says.

"Got your six."

"On your wing, *Augur.*"

"Oh, I just love it when a man knows how to take charge," Pixie adds, drawing an eye-roll from my wife.

"Is she always like that?" I ask after shutting down the mic.

"Don't let it go to your head," Aurora says, scowling as she jerks the *Augur* into a spiraling climb to evade a sputtering stream of fire from an incoming corvette. "She's like that with everyone."

"She wasn't like that with Kraug."

"Because she's already *had* him. You're fresh meat."

I snort at that. "What kind of friend hits on your husband?"

Aurora doesn't reply to that. This is probably a side of Pixie that she hasn't had to deal with until now.

I push those thoughts from my head to focus on the distribution of enemy forces above us. I'm looking for vulnerabilities in their formation, a way to punch through and get to the frigate. They're coming at us in a dribbling stream, with each vessel moving at its own peculiar top speed. No real formation other than to hit as fast they can. If we line abreast and match speed with our slowest ships, we can focus fire on the leaders as soon as they come into range. We'll overwhelm their shields and take them out instantly, one after another.

I get back on the comms to communicate that strategy, but instead of line abreast, I order our ships into a concave wall that will put each of us approximately equidistant to the nearest enemy vessel. Our formation bursts through the clouds into clear skies with the stars glittering all around us. Ships are trailing out ahead of us on all sides, jumping and juking around with automated evasive maneuvers that are designed to make them hard to hit at this range. Heavy lasers are still trading back and forth between the *Shroud* and the *Voidreaper.* Red and green forks of cosmic lightning.

Now and then a glancing hit causes one of our ships' shields to flare brightly. Fortunately, a combination of the planet's atmosphere and extreme range is scattering those beams, making them less deadly. At this range, it only takes about a sixth of a second for lasers to reach us from that frigate, but a combination of AI-powered evasive patterns and extremely agile thrusters allow most ships with small cross-sections like ours to make themselves hard targets. That'll change once we get closer to the frigate, but it will force them to stop firing on the Shroud and focus on us instead, and our combined firepower at that point should be enough to overload their shields and start burning holes in their hull. But before that happens, we have to pass through a deadly head-to-head engagement with a wave of their smaller ships. All fifty-five of them.

No, fifty-four, I correct myself as one of their fighters winks off the grid. The Shroud accidentally vaporized it with a pair of lasers that were intended for their frigate.

The enemy appears to notice the problem with their dribbling formation just a few seconds before we reach effective laser range. *Too late.* A cold smile creases my lips as I seize the gunnery controls in both hands and activate the comms to give the order. "All ships, weapons free!"

CHAPTER 23

The first six enemy ships disintegrate under our combined assault. The subsequent ones fall back as fast as they can until their formation resembles ours. Now we're trading blows more equally across a narrowing gap of forty thousand kilometers.

I feed targets to the Templars two and three at a time, focusing our fire in several directions at once to take them out faster.

Aurora jumps and skips the *Augur* around to evade enemy fire, but plenty of lasers still hit us, splashing across our shields with fading crimson fury. Somewhere behind us, Nightmare is curled into a shivering ball, whining piteously with each impact.

Before long those impacts fade into muffled silence, only to be replaced by the distant booms of Templars' ships exploding one after another. The enemy is focusing their fire, the same as we are, and rapidly expanding fireballs bloom on all sides of us, with little to no warning. Some of the pilots manage to eject before their ships explode, drifting down with jet suits, or the grav lifts in their ejection seats. They aim for the Shroud, which is rising steadily beneath us. Tractor beams will yank those pilots into the hangars and airlocks. But other ships vanish so completely that their pilots are vaporized right along with them.

Realizing that outcome is becoming more and more likely for our ship, my skin prickles with dread. I'm still wearing the pressure suit I was in before we landed on the Shroud, but I left the helmet under my seat. I yank it out and slip it over my head, securing the seals with a twist. At least now, assuming I survive our ship's demise, I can eject safely into vacuum.

But that's if we reach outer space before we're destroyed. We're steadily racing to the edge of Charos's atmosphere at a rate of twenty-two klicks per second.

Enemy forces are down to a strength rating of 149 on the targeting grid. Our number is a heftier 205. A muffled boom to starboard and a burst of fiery light takes our rating down to 197. Moments later one of our targets cracks in two, and then its antimatter containment fails and the debris turns into projectiles. A chunk smashes through an enemy corvette. Its thrusters go dark, and the lights in its cockpit flicker out. Derelict. The enemy rating is 142 now.

Attrition is wearing each side down at an almost equal rate. Leaving the AI to handle our weapons, I scan the list of the nearest enemy ships, looking for our next targets. One of those ships catches my eye, and my gaze fixes sharply upon the name and SID code of the vessel: *Korbin's Folley.*

I almost don't believe my eyes.

A hissing crunch from the combat computer indicates enemy lasers just bled through a weak spot in our shields, causing a damage report to flash up on one of our screens.

I ignore it, still gaping at the ship in question.

"Cade, we're losing pressure in the galley," Aurora warns. "Lock it down, and deploy a repair drone."

Instead of doing that, I target the *Folley*, highlighting it on Aurora's screens.

"That's the ship that took Cally!" Aurora thunders.

"We can't let them be destroyed," I add. "Break formation and go after them. I'm giving command back to Brix."

Aurora nods silently and peels out of formation, aiming directly for the *Folley*. I give our automated-weapons a new priority: to disable, rather than destroy, and our dual megawatt lasers begin lashing out at the enemy ship's reactor and thrusters.

That done, I get back on the comms to the

Shroud and leave the channel open to the rest of the Templars so they can overhear what I'm about to say.

"Everything all right up there, *Augur?*" Brix answers.

"We're handing command back to you. We just found a new lead, and we have to follow it. Hope you understand."

"Copy that, *Augur*. Same strategy?"

"Affirmative."

"Understood. Good hunting, *Augur*."

I nod to the screen as Brix's face fades to black, leaving a running transcript of ongoing comms between our forces in his place.

"They're making a run for it!" Aurora warns.

She's right. The *Folley* is racing away from Charos Prime, heading for open space. There's no FTL inhibition field out here, so they could jump out any second if their drive is already spun up and ready.

I try hailing them, but this time there's no reply. Not that I suppose it would help. We already tried bargaining with Cally's abductors.

"We'll track them," I say, pulling up the jump scanner.

"Not if they hop through another rift!" Aurora replies.

That possibility worries me, but not every planet has a collection of rifts in orbit. Running a quick scan of the area, our sensors detect just two, and none of them are close enough for the

Folley to use.

I relate those details to Aurora and she looks mildly relieved.

"Their jump drive is charging!" Aurora warns.

The *Folley* begins glowing brightly on our screens. Just seconds from jumping out.

I run the jump scanner to predict a possible destination from their current heading. A list of possibilities flashes up on the nav. Just three of them intersect systems with habited planets. The nearest one is a system and planet that I recognize: Margrave. That's the same planet where Vance's son lives. Or at least where his comms number is registered. Can't be a coincidence.

A heavy laser slams into us from the *Voidreaper,* and damage alerts shriek through the cockpit, drawing my gaze to the engineering panel. Shields are at twenty-one percent, and there's a fresh, gaping hole in our ship—the sleeping quarters on the lower deck. Dumping all the power from weapons into shields, I deploy two more repair drones to deal with it and spin up our FTL, destination: Margrave.

The *Folley* blazes brightly and vanishes from our screens.

"Track that jump!" Aurora says.

"On it," I say, setting the jump scanner to work. According to the fading wake of tachyons in their jump stream, the *Folley's* heading and possible destinations are the same as before. I target the jump stream and set our nav system to follow it. Our sensors can't detect anything in real space while we're traveling through FTL, so we won't be able to see them if they drop out early. But we will be able to see the end of their tachyon trail and deduce accordingly that they've dropped out of FTL.

Our jump drive spins up with a rising whir.

"Sixty seconds," I announce, just as a timer pops up on a secondary display.

Aurora is putting us through a series of dizzying evasive spirals to avoid a killing blow from that enemy frigate. Good thing, too, because they seem to have dedicated at least one of their heavy laser batteries to taking us out. Fat crimson beams stab through the void around us, narrowly missing.

Even a glancing hit could disable us at this point. Our shields are still recovering at fifty-three percent.

"Ten seconds!" I announce.

The ship's computer chimes in soon after that: "Three, two—"

The cockpit blazes crimson. The canopy explodes with a *boom* and an inverted shockwave of air and shattered glass racing out into the void.

CHAPTER 24

I'm tugged hard against my seat restraints by the rushing air. My suit's air intakes seal off, leaving me breathless for the split second that it takes for emergency hoses to snake out to the back of my helmet and flood my lungs with cool air. My skin tingles and then burns from the radiation of the laser, but it's only for a fraction of a second before our jump drive engages, catapulting us into FTL. Nightmare is a giant black blur, tumbling end over end toward the swirling tunnel of light beyond the shattered cockpit.

An emergency buzz shield engages, sealing off the ship with a translucent blue haze, but that won't be enough to stop Nightmare's momentum.

Aurora catches her by the tail and yanks her back the other way. Then air comes whooshing back into the cockpit as the doors behind us open up, and vents begin dumping in the fresh atmosphere from our emergency reserves. The cockpit re-pressurizes in seconds, and I manually disengage the air hoses from the back of my helmet.

"That was close," I mutter, rolling my shoulders to work out some of the knots put there by my near brush with death. I wince as the movement causes my suit to chafe against burned skin.

A molten patch of terantium alloy on the deck between Aurora and me indicates where that laser slashed through our cockpit. About a foot to the right and it would have blown off my leg.

"Are you okay?" Aurora asks.

"No okay! Scared!" Nightmare says, leaping into Aurora's lap.

I smile tightly as she battles to push the wraith back down.

While she's busy dealing with the terrified creature, I turn my attention to the jump scanner. So far the tachyon stream ahead of us is uninterrupted. No sign of the *Folley* dropping out of FTL early. I wonder if they really are headed for Margrave. If so, then they're taking us straight to one of our other leads: Vance's son. That can't be a coincidence.

Now that I have a chance to breathe, those coincidences are piling up and turning into a knot of worry between my eyes.

A *thump* puts an end to Aurora's battle with her terrified wraith. Nightmare yelps indignantly and slinks off to the back corner of the cockpit, curling into a ball once more. Aurora looks at me with a frown. "You should head down to the med bay and get yourself patched up." She nods to a shiny patch on my left arm where my vac suit melted slightly, probably fusing with the skin underneath.

"Not yet," I reply, waving away her concern. "How did those mercs find us?"

Aurora slowly shakes her head. "One of our ships must have had a dormant tracker on it."

"Maybe," I reply. "But then the Shroud would have detected the outbound comms and the breach of lockdown protocol, and we would have had more warning about the attack."

Aurora shrugs. "They had to have tracked us somehow. It could have been Brix, you know. He could have called in those mercs at any point along the way, or even from the Shroud. Like I said, he has the means and opportunity. We're only missing the motive."

A heavy sigh grates out of me at the thought that one of my oldest and most trusted friends could be behind all of this, but without any actual evidence to point to him, I'm reluctant to agree with Aurora's suspicions. "There's an even bigger problem. What was the *Folley* doing with those mercs?"

"They were hired along with whoever took Cally," Aurora says.

"Yes, but why send that particular ship after

us, and then have it turn tail and jump away from the fight? They're baiting us."

"So you think we're flying into a trap," Aurora concludes.

I nod. "Yes."

A flicker of movement catches my eye. Two of our repair drones are crawling around on the nose of the *Augur*, maneuvering big sheets of palladium glass into position and securing them with nanite-infused repair gels.

Without looking away from me, Aurora flicks off the ship's artificial gravity to make their job easier. I'm suddenly weightless and my stomach begins churning uneasily. Nightmare yips in alarm, scrabbling for purchase with her claws. She drifts up to the ceiling. Her lanky forelimbs uncurl from her chest wrapping around Aurora's neck like a bristly scarf. Aurora ignores her. "So, what should we do?"

I consider the question. Someone is leading us around by the nose. The question is why? The answer seems obvious to me: like a cat toying with a mouse, they're torturing us. Dangling leads in front of our noses like proverbial carrots. What was it that Cally's abductor said to us just before they jumped away through that rift? *"Tag. You're it."*

So that's what this is to them: a game. If we want to win, we have to be less predictable and start following clues that weren't specifically laid out for us.

"What do you want to do here, Cade?" Aurora asks. Her glowing eyes are wide and full of uncertainty.

CHAPTER 25

It takes me a minute to make the decision. Do we stay on the *Folley's* tail, or break off now before we fly into a trap?

Following the ship that took Cally is a tantalizing lead. But knowing that it is being dangled deliberately in front of us makes me decidedly less eager.

"Pull us out of FTL," I say.

Aurora hesitates. "Are you sure?"

It takes a physical effort to nod my head. "Yes."

Aurora hauls back on the jump lever, disengaging the FTL drive, and the whirling tunnel of colored light vanishes, the stars returning to static points.

I unbuckle from my restraints and stand up, my feet pinned to the deck by my grav boots despite the zero-G environment. "Plot a jump to Kazir," I say as I'm turning to leave.

Aurora nods, her expression wincing. She looks about as miserable as I feel. "Where are you going?"

"To the med bay."

Walking down to the med bay is excruciating. As I move, my vac suit tugs and pulls where it fused to my skin, coming unstuck and peeling off the top layers of my skin in the process.

In times like these I really miss the old *stim-dripper* implant in my arm. Right about now it would be dumping painkillers into my system to dull the pain. After I retired, I didn't see any point in maintaining old implants like that one. And that's not the only thing I'm missing. I've lost my edge. I need to think.

Mercenaries followed Brix to Pyria. Then the same ones followed us back to the Shroud, and the *Folley* was right there with them. They're all involved, on the same payroll as Nevos and that unknown bounty hunter who jacked Aurora.

The *Folley* jumped through a rift, which means they could have taken Cally almost anywhere in an instant, but then how did they get to Charos in almost the same amount of time that it took us to fly directly there?

By crunching those numbers, I can get a ballpark radius of how far the *Folley* must have been from the Shroud when they dropped out of that rift. My heartrate picks up, anticipation building. There are some extra variables to consider—like the individual FTL speeds of the *Folley* versus the *Augur*, how long we spent aboard the Shroud, and our detour with Nevos and the *Iron Helix.* On the *Folley's* end, I have to put an estimate to how long it might have taken to drop Cally off somewhere before joining the battle at the Shroud. Unless they had her aboard that frigate... That would make my strategy of targeting the frigate tragically ironic.

But no, getting Cally killed would spoil the fun for whoever is using her to toy with us.

Crossing into the med bay, I stop beside the treatment bed and quickly strip out of my vac suit. Excruciating waves of pain make my head swim dizzily. I do my best to ignore just how much of my flesh is peeled away with the suit. The *Augur's* medibot rolls over to treat my wounds, spraying them with synthskin and injecting me with painkillers.

"Please lie down, Mr. Hale," the bot intones. "You could pass out and hit your head."

"We're in zero-G," I mutter, glaring at the bot.

Artificial blue eyes brighten and then dim. The bot's blank, rubbery white face pinches into a scowl. "Gravity could be restored at any moment. Please lie down."

Rather than argue more, I do as I'm told just to shut the machine up. Lying down is an awkward feat in zero-G, but the bot helps me out by activating a weak grav field in the treatment bed.

Pinned in place by partial gravity, I stare up into the glaring lights of the med bay and get to work with my holoband, crunching numbers.

Thirty-three hours and sixteen minutes have

passed since Cally's abductors jumped away from Pyria. The rift jump means they would have reached their destination almost instantly. I can only assume if they intended to track us to the Shroud, that they had another ship waiting on the other end to take Cally off their hands, either that or the other end of the rift was close to the planet or station where they planned to leave her.

Since the *Folley* is Aurora's modified heavy fighter, I happen to know that its FTL speed is 0.72 light years per hour. They couldn't have taken less than thirty minutes to drop Cally off, even if they had another ship waiting. So the maximum distance between Charos and the Shroud is the distance that the *Folley* could travel in about thirty-three hours. That gives me a maximum radius of 23.76 light years from Charos Prime.

Pulling up a star map on my holoband, I draw that radius around Charos Prime and scan the inside of that circle for any inhabited star systems that are lawless enough for slavers to operate freely.

I find a couple, including, and especially, Margrave in the Neutral Zone.

Breaking off our pursuit of the *Folley* feels like even more of a mistake now. But I have no way of knowing that the *Folley* didn't simply rendezvous with another ship in deep space and hand Cally over to them. That ship could have plotted a jump almost anywhere else in the galaxy while we were en-route to the Shroud.

That's much more likely, due to the unpredictable nature of rifts. They couldn't possibly find one that conveniently connected Pyria to a slavers' base, but they could have sent ships through that rift just ahead of the *Folley* and had them waiting to receive Cally.

I scowl and angrily swipe away the star map on my holoband. I'm not going to figure out where they took her with a lucky guess.

A tell-tale jolt kicks through the deck with the *Augur's* transition back to FTL.

A few seconds later, I feel the weighty return of full gravity plus the light field projected by the treatment bed. The repair drones must be done sealing the cockpit. The medibot disengages the bed's grav field, and announces, "Treatment complete."

I sit up and check myself over. Glossy translucent patches of synthskin cover ragged red patches of flesh on my left arm, lower abdomen, and left leg.

Swinging my legs over the side of the bed, I turn to face the door to the med bay just as Aurora comes in. "A little over twenty hours before we reach Kazir," she announces.

That draws a heavy sigh from my chest. Hurry up and wait. "We'll use the time to come up with a plan to get to the founders of Icarus."

Aurora regards me dubiously. "We'll have to

study their movements before we can do that."

"Not necessarily," I reply, smiling darkly back. Cally's abductors aren't the only ones who can dangle bait, and I think I have just the thing to attract the likes of Ivy Rox and Aster Stavros.

PART THREE: DEATH HAS A NAME

CHAPTER 26

Forty-Six Hours Later...

Kazir, Alliance Space

Now wearing my secret weapon, the alien exosuit that Alpha left me, I stand before a fluttering scrap of construction wrap, staring into one of Kazir's glittering artificial canyons. The whole planet is snarled with chugging lines of air traffic and swirled with the tangled ribbons of elevated streets. Kazir is a tidally-locked moon of Kaz; the gas giant dominates the skyline above the thin wisps of cloud and pollution that thread between the tops of the tallest spires. The giant planet is mottled with greens and blues that flow in mesmerizing patterns. It bathes Kazir in an eerie blue-green twilight that rises and falls with the moon's orbit around its bloated parent.

My gaze tracks back down, and I step out the empty window, past the tattered construction wrap, to the ledge. My head spins as I peer down into the hazy glow of the abyss. Kazir is affectionately known as Vertigo City by the locals. I've got a head for heights, but even I can appreciate that nickname.

Neighboring buildings shine neon lights into the endless well of darkness below me, illuminating at least a kilometer before vanishing into obsidian realms of shadow. With surface gravity that's only one-quarter of galactic standard, it's easy to build impressively tall buildings on Kazir.

No matter how far down you go, it always seems like there's more city below you. It's practically impossible to find the natural surface anymore. And even once you've reached the spot where it used to be, there's still more than a hundred sub-levels left to go. Those levels are swarmed with vagrants, stim-baked lunatics, and a motley collection of the galaxy's worst lowlifes. KPD refuses to assign patrols in the under city anymore, and city workers have to hire private security just to perform routine maintenance.

Besides the human predators, Kazir plays host to plenty of alien ones. I'm not surprised Brix and Aurora rescued Nightmare here. People like to keep wraiths as pets because they're notoriously deadly, but they're also fickle. Forget to feed one, and they'll bite your arm off the next time you toss them a treat. I can only imagine how many of them got turned loose by their mangled owners. Now there's a thriving population of wraiths in the under city.

The shiny upper levels are draped in a thin veneer of security, glitz, and luxury that attracts tourists far and wide, but the farther down you go, the more dangerous it gets, and the more that veneer gets stripped away until only the filth remains.

Unfortunately, that's where I have to go now. Into the filth.

Call Aurora Velez, I sub-vocalize to my holoband.

The thin black circlet that's clipped around my forehead places the call. I wait, counting how many times it rings through the bone-conduction speakers before she answers.

On the third ring, Aurora's gorgeous face appears in the top right of the holo display projected by my holoband. I can see her hands moving over the controls of the *Black Augur*. Her fiery orange gaze tightens with a hint of a smile as she sees me. My visual is relayed to her by a combination of AI-generated imagery and live feeds captured by my holoband.

"Ivy's and Aster's bot doubles are Oscar Mike," she says.

"Good. Are they alone?" I reply.

"So far."

"What do you know," I mutter dryly. "I guess one out of two isn't bad. Send me the tracking data and I'll be on my way."

"On it..." Aurora replies, her glowing tangerine eyes darting from mine to study her screens. "Damn it. I've lost them. They must have found the tracker."

Aurora planted a tracker on Ivy's left boot yesterday, during a separate outing from Apex Tower. The device is tiny and unobtrusive, and we only activated it recently, but I guess Ivy noticed it once it started broadcasting her location.

"Well, it doesn't matter," I decide. "At least I know where they're headed."

"Be careful, Cade. It could be a trap."

"It is, but I'm the one springing it."

Aurora nods. "Don't get too cocky."

She ends the comms from her end, and I step closer to the edge, contemplating the kilometers-long drop into the abyss.

I told Ivy and Aster to come alone and in person to meet with me but of course, high profile, high net-worth meatbags like Ivy and Aster all have remote-operated bot doubles that they can safely use for situations that are too dangerous for them to risk their actual necks.

So I contacted them via a pre-recorded message, delivered anonymously to their residence in Apex Tower. In the message, I was wearing a bio mask set to display my real face, back before I retired and visited a sculptor to permanently alter my features. I also disabled my vocal modulator so that I was using my actual voice for the message. The hope was that something about me might trigger a scrub trace in Ivy's or Aster's memories and thereby help to sell my story.

Then I proceeded to lay out the bait: I told them that I know what happened out in the Hadros Sector, why the Coalition wanted to cover it up, and how they can profit from the information. Then I dropped my own name, hoping that they would at least recognize that, if not my face and voice. And finally, I asked them to meet with me alone, in person, in a particularly dangerous zone of Kazir's sub-levels.

Aurora criticized my plan at first. *"How can you be sure that they don't already know what happened in the Hadros Incident? If they're behind Cally's abduction, then it's probably because they recovered their memories, and whatever happened out there is their motive."*

But I told her, *"If they are behind it, then they'll come, if only to taunt us and get us chasing our tails again. And if they aren't behind it, then they'll be too curious to pass up the chance to find out what I know."*

Aurora replied, *"Either way, they'll know that this could be a trap, and the sub-levels are too dangerous for them to visit personally. They'll use remote-operated bots, and we can't interrogate empty shells to find out what they know."*

But then I explained the other part of my plan, and why we *want* them to send their bot doubles to the meeting.

Afterward, Aurora had to admit, *"It's not a bad plan. If it works."*

We're about to find out, I think grimly to myself.

My comms buzz with a message from Aurora.

"Found them," Aurora says. "I guess they didn't notice the tracker. Must have been passing through an EM-shielded area. They're on sub-level twenty-two and going down. Looks like a private lift coming from Apex. I'm pushing live coordinates to your holoband now. Let me know when you get them."

Two small blue boxes appear below me. Beside them, I read the targets' distance: a whopping two thousand two hundred and eighteen meters away, below the glittering spire of Apex Tower which soars high above the surrounding buildings, its upper levels wrapped in neon blue clouds which are lit up from within by the tower's external illumination.

"Targets locked," I confirm.

"Good. You ready for the plunge?" Aurora asks.

I nod and draw in a deep breath of Kazir's faintly honeyed air. My suit isn't pressure-sealed at the moment, since the air is perfectly breathable, but stim use is so pervasive here that the lingering fragrance of them never seems to fade. Every whisper of wind brings a slightly different flavor and a subtly different shade to my mood.

"Ready as I'll ever be," I say through a deep exhalation. "You have a lock on *my* tracker? Just in case I need backup?"

"I've got you. Last chance to send *me* down instead," Aurora says.

"Would if I could. Ivy and Aster are expecting to meet with me."

Aurora sighs. "Just be careful, Cade."

"I know how to look after myself, Aurry."

"I know," she replies.

A whistling roar precedes the appearance of a darkly gleaming shadow. The y-shaped fuselage of the *Black Augur* drifts down to eye level with me. It's facing me with its two blocky main thrusters rotated straight down, but dark and dormant rather than roaring with blue fire. The ship is idling on its grav lifts to abide by sub-orbital traffic laws. The front end where the cockpit sits is a sloping twenty-foot wall of palladium glass, freshly repaired from our brush with that mercenary frigate.

I toss a sloppy salute at Aurora.

A bright blue rectangle appears at the top of the sloping wall of glass as the cockpit canopy turns transparent, and I see her sitting at the controls, bathed in azure light. She waves and blows me a kiss. I peripherally notice a smaller picture-in-picture version of her miming the same actions over our comms.

I perform a quick check of my two DX-22 laser

pistols, tugging on them to make sure they're firmly mag-locked into their holsters. They're not budging. Reaching around behind my head, I check the Arkan X12 Shotgun on my back. It's firmly clipped to the mounting brackets.

I disengage my grav boots with a mental command, and suddenly I feel dangerously untethered in Kazir's light gravity.

I place my armored hands together and raise them above my head—

And then I spring off the ledge, diving headfirst into the abyss.

CHAPTER 27

The wind whips around me with deafening fury. I dial down the audio-pickups in the helmet, and the sound fades to a hair above silence.

Even at a quarter of standard gravity, my holoband tells me I have less than a minute to reach terminal velocity, which is about double what it would be on Earth thanks to Kazir's thinner air.

Neighboring buildings cast fuzzy, feeble light into the growing well of darkness. A thick layer of polluted fog swells below, choking out the light and cutting visibility to zero. Just before I part that miasma like water, I activate a sensor overlay to see any potential obstacles. Yellow-shaded buildings and elevated streets appear all around me, but nothing directly ahead. And then that polluted fog comes curling through the filters in my suit. I catch a whiff of the moldering urban decay. The rancid reek of garbage and sewage almost chokes me. Nearly vomiting from the stench, I bump up the suit's air filters to 100%, relaxing as clean air mercifully fills my lungs.

The altimeter on my holoband scrolls down rapidly. That number, along with my velocity —over three hundred klicks per hour—begins blinking red and urgently beeping at me.

I'm still nowhere near terminal, but it's time to prepare for landing. Somersaulting to get my feet beneath me, I snap my legs straight and fire my modified grav boots in full reverse to slow my fall. Blood immediately rushes away from my head, making me see stars, and the unbalanced thrust has me slowly spinning in circles, threatening to send me veering into the lowest levels of Apex tower. Thrusting out my hands with the palms facing down, I activate supplemental grav lifts. The flight computer does the work of balancing thrust between my boots and hands, keeping me erect and steady as I descend.

I'm slowing rapidly now. The artificial surface comes racing up beneath my feet. Thanks to my sensor overlay, I can make out a scattering of yellow-shaded civilians walking along that moldering avenue in both directions. Here and there, a landed air car whistles into or out of a parking space.

Even down here, in the rank, dangerous ghetto built along the fraying boundary between the glitzy upper city and lawless under city, Kazir never sleeps.

My velocity scrolls rapidly to zero. The miasma parts and the patched and crumbling street appears. Flickering blue-tinged street lights provide intermittent illumination.

Pedestrians barely glance upward, too busy seeking safety as they scatter at the sound of my arrival, making room for me to land. I glance at the circular mini-map in the top left of my display, checking for red enemy blips, but they're all civilian blues. A quick look at the threat detectors around the cross hairs in the center of my field of view gives me a more detailed sitrep. Five potential hostiles, all armed and dangerous and watching my descent. White target boxes highlight them through the murky air. They're not civilians, nor enemies, but something yet-to-be-determined.

I activate a power-hungry personal deflector shield and drift the last twelve feet to the ground.

My right hand smoothly drops to the grip of one of my DX-22s. I give it a tug to disengage the mag-lock and mentally flick off the weapon's safety.

I take in those five lingering scumbags with a sweeping glance. They have hungry eyes, dirty faces, and crudely-assembled laser pistols. Two are bots with glowing irises. One is a cyborg by the look of his gleaming silver arms and legs. And two are regular meatbags like me.

I draw my weapon and wave it casually at them. The two meatbags fade into the fog, obviously deciding that I'm not worth it, but the bots and the cyborg linger. Then they appear to notice just how heavily I'm armed and armored, with all the latest and greatest tech, and then they, too, slink away, joining the flow of pedestrians who already made way for my landing.

I re-holster my weapon but don't mag-lock it this time.

My unconventional entrance into the underworld had the desired effect. Anyone with a brain will know that I'm more trouble than I'm likely worth.

I could have gone with a low-key approach and ridden an elevator down here like any old scrigg, but then there would be a holo recording floating around of me entering that elevator. I'd probably also have picked up a tail of at least a dozen lowlifes on the way down.

Like this, I'm going to save myself a lot of wasted time cracking heads.

Pulling up my targets' tracking data, I see that Ivy and Aster are on the move. Looking down, I zoom in on their location and pull up a wire-frame schematic to see that they are busy heading down another elevator. Our rendezvous is on sub-level ninety-seven, in an old abandoned red-light district known as Lucky's Grotto.

I turn to my right and sprint down the

street to the nearest public elevator. Once again, the crowd parts with my approach, but it's still slower going than I would like, and I'm left ducking elbows and even knees from over-sized augments, bots, and cyborgs.

Lurid neon ads for seedy establishments flash up and flicker to life on my holoband as my gaze strays too close to their windows and doors.

I quickly set my holoband to filter and block those spammy advertisements, but I can do nothing to blank out the scantily-clad bots and meatbags who are physically standing outside, making cat-calls and explicit comments to lure me into their establishments.

The thought of Cally winding up in a place like this makes my skin crawl and my blood boil. I can't allow that to happen.

The door to a bar slides open ahead of me, and a pair of drunken brawlers tumble out, both meatbags, bleeding and battered from smashing each other's faces with their fists. The object of their scuffle emerges behind them, screaming for them to stop. It's a pretty young woman with glowing pink eyes.

After a few seconds of shouting at the two men to no effect, she appears to lose her patience, and yanks both of them into the air by the collars of their shirts, holding them apart and dangling out of each other's reach.

I wonder what kind of twisted love triangle has got those two so riled up. Pushing those thoughts from my head, I switch my focus to my own business.

I reach the public elevator just as it's opening to let in a couple of grim-looking scumbags with e-inked tats that come to life as I look at them. One is a glowing blue snake that slithers around the wearer's arm, tightening like a boa. The other guy has a few drops of blood dribbling from the corner of his right eye like tears. That catches my attention instantly. It's a tat from the *Locusts*, one of the more notorious street gangs on Kazir, and they in turn work for the Solaris Cartel. I could let them have this elevator, but I don't have time to wait for another one, so I fix each of the men with a meaningful glare as I step in after them. They can't see my eyes behind the visor, but they can see my head turn fractionally to look at each of them.

"Take the next one," Teardrops says with his hand on the hilt of a plasma blade. Each teardrop represents a kill, and his are still dribbling away.

I use my holoband's police-scanner to pull up his rap sheet, but it's completely blank. He must have paid to have it scrubbed, or else he's using a biomask and a fake ID.

"Seems to me like there's plenty of room," I say, casually taking another step to stand opposite Teardrops and his buddy.

"Oh yeah? Well, it seems to *me* like you think you're a real big boy in that jet suit."

Jet suit, exosuit—he probably doesn't know

the difference. A jet suit will make you fly, and it's legal for civilians to use, in certain places, with the right operator's license. An exosuit is the same, but with heavy armor and shielding, and an integrated exoskeleton to augment the strength and speed of the wearer. Being that it's alien tech, this suit is technically neither, but its nearest human equivalent is an exosuit.

Without looking away from Teardrops and Snakearm, I pull up the elevator controls on my holoband and select sub-level ninety-seven.

Someone else comes barging through the open doors just as they're sliding shut. It's a burly-looking cyborg with two gleaming metal fists and a ragged scar slashing through a glowing red eye that replaced the original one. Tucked under one arm is a tiny-waisted meatbag with blonde hair and augmented skin that looks like plastic. She's giggling and stumbling while she dangles from his arm. Obviously wasted.

Teardrops stops them with an upraised hand and slowly wags his index finger from side to side. "It's out of service," he growls.

The cyborg comes up short, muttering something in his girl's ear. She sobers up instantly, and together they dart out of the lift.

"Last chance, big boy," Teardrops says, gesturing to the doors as they begin sliding shut once more.

"I'm in a hurry," I reply.

The doors thump ominously as they shut, and

the lift slides sideways into a vertical shaft that we'll share with dozens or hundreds of other lifts that are both coming and going like vertical lanes of traffic that run between the city's tallest buildings. For a split second, I feel myself become weightless as the lift accelerates faster than the planet's gravity, but then its own grav field engages, and the sensation disappears.

"Big mistake," Teardrops says. I see personal deflectors shimmer to life in a blue haze around him and Snakearm. Both of them draw blazing orange plasma blades that hum and crackle in the relative silence of the elevator.

Teardrops steps sideways away from his buddy, maneuvering to outflank me.

But I'm already making preparations of my own. I've been making them ever since I noticed those bloody teardrops.

"Don't worry," Teardrops says. "I hear that coming back as a bot is a blessing in disguise."

And then they come in swinging, taking full advantage of the confined space and our close proximity.

CHAPTER 28

I duck Teardrops' blade, spinning away from him, and catch a glancing blow from Snakearm that is mostly absorbed by my shield.

Then both of my palms flash up, and I fire the suit's grav lifts at full blast, sending the two goons slamming into the opposite side of the lift and making it shudder violently. Snakearm accidentally slices off the front of his right foot with his plasma sword, but he doesn't appear to notice.

Teardrops deactivates his weapon and smoothly draws his sidearm—an illegal plasma blaster. That's an instant disintegration if it gets through my shields. There'd be nothing but a pile of ashes left for the police to examine. Not that they would bother. We're already deep into the under city.

"Here's what you're going to do—" Teardrops says. Snakearm appears to notice that a part of his right foot isn't following his leg anymore, and he starts screaming. "Shut up!" Teardrops snaps at him.

"I'm listening," I say, with my hands relaxed at my sides. I could draw either one of my DX-22s and pop off a shot on the overload setting to end this scrigg's life despite his personal shield. He'd also get off a shot, though. My shields are strong enough to take it, but trading fire from overpowered energy weapons in an elevator car, while racing straight down a hundred stories, with dozens of other cars moving at high speed above and below us is a great way to turn myself into a pancake.

"Disable your shield, take off your armor, and lay your weapons on the ground," Teardrops says. "We'll take your gear and you get to stay a meatbag."

Snakearm nods eagerly, doing his level best to sneer at me rather than bawl like a baby from the searing pain of his severed foot.

"And if I refuse?" I ask mildly.

The elevator is getting close to level ninety-seven. I find that interesting because it means that Teardrops and Snakearm didn't bother to pick a destination of their own. Maybe they were just waiting for someone to come in that they could rob. Maybe someone in particular. I guess I scragged with their plans.

"Hurry up, or I'm gonna shoot you, and end this slagging conversation."

I shrug. "Well, at least that will shut you up."

Teardrops' eyes flare angrily at me. "Slag this!" he roars, and pulls the trigger, but nothing happens. His expression turns to comic disbelief. He flips the weapon on its side, checking its safety.

"The fuck?" he asks of no one in particular. The weapon begins glowing white-hot at the grip, and he drops it with another expletive.

Snakearm draws his own sidearm. It also starts smoldering in his hand, and he drops it with a shriek of disbelief.

They haven't noticed the dark haze of foreign particles swirling around them, or the slightly metallic tang to the air. Their inattention was understandable at first. The alien nanomachines left my suit in snaking streams that slithered out surreptitiously along the floor.

Both men recover quickly, drawing their plasma swords again. The lift screeches to a stop and then jerks sideways as it reaches level ninety-seven.

Teardrops and Snakearm lunge at me, and I send the hazy black cloud of nanites streaming up their noses and into their ears. Their eyes roll up in their heads as blood comes trickling out. They collapse on the floor, their blades deactivating as their hands slacken on the hilts of the weapons. I don't believe in killing unless the target deserves to die, but these two would just go back to preying on innocents if I left them alive. Chances are, one or both of them will come back as bots, anyway, but maybe they couldn't afford the exorbitant fees that the resurrection companies wanted to charge for a couple of high-risk scriggs like them. Hopefully, they stay dead.

The elevator chimes and the doors rumble open. With a silent command from my neuralink, the diffuse black swarm of nanites retreats to me, flowing like a liquid over my armor until it settles into a solid outer layer once more.

I leave the elevator with a smug sense of satisfaction at having made this little corner of the galaxy a slightly cleaner cesspool than it was before.

Re-focusing on the task at hand, I see that I've emerged in a filthy alley barely illuminated with blue and orange glow strips and the pulsing red lights that once heralded the nature of this district.

As the elevator doors thud shut behind me, I quietly draw both of my DX-22s. Dead ahead, I can see the two small blue target boxes that represent Ivy and Aster. They're no longer moving, which means they've reached the coordinates for our meeting place—six hundred and two meters away.

I take a moment to examine my surroundings and check for signs of imminent threats. Just because Ivy and Aster sent their bot doubles doesn't mean that they came alone.

The air in the alley is choked with grimy

steam and loud with the clanking and chugging of Kazir's ancient atmosphere generators. The ground is cluttered with soggy bits of debris and garbage that lie in congealing black puddles that appear to have been regurgitated from blocked sewer pipes. Good thing I'm filtering the air. It's probably foul enough to knock out a tobra.

Looking up, I see a tangled nest of pipes and conduits vanishing endlessly into red and blue-tinted clouds of condensing water vapor. It's as if the walls of this corridor are ancient skyscrapers that were used as a foundation for the towers above.

Satisfied that the alley is abandoned, I begin creeping steadily down it, careful to keep my footsteps quiet.

The discolored doors to old establishments look like they've been welded shut. Windows have either been hastily sprayed with castcrete, or left broken and gaping into unfathomable voids.

I hurry past those openings, peering briefly into them to make sure that nothing is about to leap out at me. But neither my eyes nor sensors are detecting anything. I'm also watching the darkened arrows of the threat detectors to either side of the cross-hairs in the center of my holo display, as well as the small flat circle of the minimap in the top left. A green diamond in the center represents me. As I walk, the gray outlines of buildings scroll steadily around me.

I've set the scale to keep everything within a five-hundred-meter radius in view. Colored dots on that display will indicate different types of lifeforms detected by my suit's sensors: red for enemy, green for friendly, yellow for neutral, and blue for my objective. Two small blue dots come inching in at the top of the map as I come within five hundred meters of Ivy and Aster.

So far there's no sign of anyone down here except for me and them. I'm surprised it's so lifeless given the sub-levels' reputation as a haven for the dregs of society. I expected to see *something*: stim-pushers, hookers, beggars, and homeless, maybe even a drunk or two lying passed out beside a garbage chute. But there's nothing alive down here—

Unless you count the rockrats. A few of them skitter about, squiggling in and out of old sewer grates. They're lumpy, four-legged creatures, about a foot long, with an oval body, wrinkled skin, and patchy white or black fur. They have a nasty set of claws and sharp teeth arrayed around a circular orifice at both ends of their bodies.

The blue target boxes ahead of me indicate that Ivy and Aster are still four hundred and sixty-two meters away. Figuring that's close enough, I engage my suit's cloaking shield. My arms and legs shimmer, becoming perfectly invisible, then shaded green by the sensor overlay so that I can see what I'm doing.

Worried that I might not be the only one who's cloaked down here, I send streams of nanites ahead of me like the silver beads from an occlusion scanner to check for invisible obstructions. The Priors' nanites are much smaller and less obtrusive. They won't be immediately seen or recognized, so I'm not worried about triggering an alarm from any hidden security teams that Ivy and Aster sent down ahead of them.

About a minute later, the minimap flashes in warning, along with my threat detectors. A pair of yellow dots pepper the map ahead of me, along with the shaded silhouettes to accompany them —all humanoid shapes. I re-designate them as enemies, and the shaded silhouettes turn red.

So, I've found the security cordon. The nearest two are pinpointed with target boxes that appear on either side of an intersecting alley about two hundred meters away. I can see from the shading that they're armored (their silhouettes are too bulky for clothes), armed with rifles, and cloaked (since the shading is translucent), but there's no telling if they're bots or bios, or even if they've also detected me— although, I doubt it. My suit's sensors are much more sensitive than the average human tech, and my cloaking shield is also more advanced.

I only detected these two through their cloaks because my nanites physically ran into them, just like the drones from an occlusion scanner.

And speaking of, I can see something glittering faintly in the air up ahead, directly between those two guards. They've activated an occlusion scanner, and they're just waiting for some invisible hostile to go waltzing blindly through it.

Seeing that I don't have any other angles immediately available to approach the meeting with Ivy and Aster, I look up—into the tangled nest of pipes and conduits above. Firing my grav lifts on low power, I drift up into that shadowy maze. Rather than walk along those rickety pipes and risk making a sound that would give me away, I continue with grav lifts, flying slowly over the alley where the guards laid their trap. No sign of alarm from the guards.

I instruct some of the nanites I sent from my suit to linger around those two but send the bulk of them on with orders to find any other cloaked hostiles down here.

I drop back down to the street level a hundred meters from the perimeter that the guards established. Moving quickly now, I hurry down the alley to the meeting with Ivy and Aster.

By now they'll have realized that I also sent a remote-operated bot double. Aurora is probably using it to keep them occupied, maybe even having started the interrogation without me.

More red blips pepper the minimap around me as my nanites encounter the rest of Icarus's security forces. All of them are cloaked and blocking the various alleys and streets that lead to and from the abandoned club that I designated for the meeting with Ivy and Aster.

Ultimately I reach a black, slime-crusted door, behind which my targets appear to be lounging on a couch that I can't see. Sitting across from them is a yellow-shaded humanoid signature; the bot that's meant to be me.

Two perfectly visible gleaming black guard bots are flanking the door: no faces, no skin, just cold hard metal, and glowing red eyes. They look like combat models. One of my boots crunches over something. Both sets of eyes blaze suddenly brighter, and their arms snap up with integrated weapons already deployed.

Occlusion scanners send bursts of glittering silver drones boiling into the air a split second before I leap off the ground to evade them, firing the grav lifts in my boots, and sending nanites to deal with the bots. The tiny alien nano-machines from my armor drill directly into the bots' neural nets, and both of them abruptly sag, their heads drooping, the light fading from their eyes.

The nanites go after the whirring silver beads from their occlusion scanners next, and within seconds the whole cloud comes crashing down, tinkling softly like metallic rain.

I land amidst the debris and step carefully to the slime-crusted door. Ivy and Aster are still seated on that couch and my bot is on the chair. There's no sign that they've been alerted.

Yet.

I could simply tap into the remote feeds for my bot double and take over from Aurora at this point, but I want Ivy and Aster to see that I've busted through their security cordon, and to know that means they've been outmaneuvered.

Not that they should care—this is why they sent their remote-operated doubles. But there's something crucial they don't know about the bots that they sent down here—or rather, the VR pods that they're using to control them.

The final piece of my trap is about to be sprung.

CHAPTER 29

*L*ocked.

The prompt appears, asking me for a twelve-character passcode to open the door.

I don't have time to hack it, but there's a faster option. Streams of black nanites swarm from my suit, worming their way into the door jamb. A clearly-defined circle appears, glowing white hot along the right edge of the door, about halfway up. The molten patch oozes down, leaving a hole that I can use for a handle. Nanites stream back to me, and I reach into the hole they made to yank the door open. It resists stubbornly, shrieking as I drag it open. I wince at the noise and freeze. Old machinery chugs away in the background, pumping freshly-generated atmosphere into the air.

Ivy and Aster jump up from the couch, their shaded silhouettes turning in my direction.

They heard the door.

My cover is blown.

Not that it matters much. I give my nanites orders to neutralize Icarus's guards, putting them into a deep sleep, and for the bots, temporarily interrupting the power supply to their neural nets. The red blips on my minimap wink off one after another, and I slip quietly through the door.

Sprinting up a short flight of stairs to the room where Ivy and Aster are, I burst through a broken door to see that my targets are busy running for one of the other exits.

I draw both of my DX-22s, aiming one at each of them. The weapons are not a part of the suit, but they're equally invisible, thanks to a coating of the very same nanites that are responsible for the suit's cloaking shield.

"Freeze," I shout at them, deactivating the cloak and trading it for a personal deflector.

The abandoned club is empty but for debris and garbage. A few pieces of old furniture sit in a sunken lounge, a shattered chandelier lies in pieces in the middle of the foyer where I'm standing, and a bunch of broken bottles decorate the wall behind the bar. Two glow panels are still flickering, providing weak illumination for the space. And my bot double is staring blankly after the targets, only now rising from the armchair where it was seated.

Both Ivy and Aster stop and slowly turn. Neither one of them has the glowing eyes of a bot, even though that's exactly what these doubles are. They were hoping to disguise that fact while pretending to have complied with my demands that they come alone and in person.

"Not another step," I warn.

Ivy is tall and slender with straight dark hair cut short and bangs across her forehead. She has clear blue eyes. Aster is olive-skinned and shorter with a thick black beard that I can tell he's using to hide a weak chin. He has unnerving silver eyes that he couldn't have been born with and has thick, shaggy hair.

I wonder if I'm looking at my daughter's kidnappers. And if so, what could have possibly motivated them?

"Well, well, who d'we have here?" Aster asks in a thick, twangy accent that makes me think he grew up on a backwater somewhere far beyond the major trade lanes.

"Cade Korbin," I reply, setting my visor to clear.

Both Ivy's and Aster's heads slowly turn to look at my double. An ironic smile springs to Ivy's lips. "I thought this was Cade Korbin?"

"No, you didn't," I reply.

"No," she agrees, her grin vanishing, and eyes glittering like two chips of ice. "You realize you can't threaten us with blasters. We're not actually here. Give us one good reason why we shouldn't simply unplug right now."

Aurora comes striding up the rotten wooden steps from the sunken lounge, and I hear one of the boards groan ominously under the remote unit's weight.

She sets the holo mask to relay her features instead of mine, and glowing copper eyes blaze to life in the middle of suddenly petite feminine features, but that does nothing to change the bot's short golden brown hair.

"Recognize me?" Aurora demands.

"Should I?" Ivy asks with a furrowed brow.

"You jacked my double from the Templars' headquarters."

"Templars? Vigilantes?" Ivy looks at her partner. "My, my, Aster what could we have done to deserve their sanctimonious wrath?"

"You know what you did," Aurora intones.

"This conversation is boring me, Aster. Let's go, shall we? Let them exercise their delusional demons on our empty metal husks. This was a waste of time."

"I couldn't agree more, sweetheart," Aster says.

I smile grimly behind my helmet, waiting for them to unplug.

"Aster... are you having the same... difficulty that I just experienced?"

"'Fraid so darling. We got ourselves an issue of a technical nature. It would appear we are locked inside our pods. Your doing, I assume, Mr. Korbin?"

My smile widens. "When one of your maintenance bots went haywire yesterday and damaged two of your VR pods, you probably should have gotten suspicious, but of course, you didn't, because the staff wouldn't bother you with such a mundane detail. It was easy to figure out the brand of the pods, locate the nearest service center, and jack their comms so that we were the ones who answered your call. Those VR pods aren't just programmed to keep you from disconnecting. They're also fitted with neural probes so that we can find out exactly what we want to know, and whether or not you are lying."

"Aster... I can't seem to contact anyone for help," Ivy says.

"Your comms are being actively blocked by the pods. The only signals that are allowed out are the ones between you and the bots that you brought down with you." Aurora explains. "And as for your bot doubles... it's just a pity that the commands to activate their integrated comm systems have to be routed through the VR pods first. We're blocking those, too."

"What do you want?" Aster demands. "Hurt either one of us in any way, and we'll come after you with the full might of our empire. The Templars' reputation will be ruined. You'll never work again. And I will personally ruin you and your bot partner."

"Let's not get to trading threats," I say. "By now you know that we neutralized the guards you brought down here, so you know what we're capable of. All I want are a few answers to a few simple questions."

"Ask," Ivy hisses.

"You paid the Hadros Group one hundred million credits, about two years ago. Who were you paying, and what was it for?"

Ivy's expression flickers uncertainly. She looks to Aster who looks equally perplexed. "We were buying a promising new stim that someone had discovered out in uncharted space. I can't say who we bought it from, because we don't know. But we were able to verify the value of the sample. I can't say much about it, since it's still under development. Why do you care?"

"That money was used to finance an operation to kidnap our daughter," I reply.

Ivy's hand flies up to her mouth to cover a gasp.

"What does that have to do with us?" Aster growls.

"You're saying it wasn't one of you, using Hadros as an anonymous front to come after us?" I ask.

"Of course it wasn't us!" Ivy snaps. "Why would we go after a little girl? That's barbaric."

Little girl. Interesting. Ivy doesn't know Cally's age.

Aurora looks at me and gives her head a slight shake. "The probes confirm it. They're not lying."

I double-check the data myself, pulling it up on my holo display. Aurora's right. So far, no lies from either of them. These two are innocent. At least, innocent of this particular crime. They still sell the formulas for potent new street drugs to the stim cartels.

Time to drill down to something that they might know about. "What about the Hadros Incident? What do you know about that?"

Aster heaves a sigh. "Not much, I'm afraid. The Coalition scrubbed us. I assume you know more, or at least... you claimed to when you set this meeting up."

"I know the official story. That's about it," I reply. "It was bait to see if you were involved with our daughter's disappearance."

Ivy huffs angrily. "Well, now that you know we're innocent, you can let us go. Before you dig yourself a grave, yes? Good luck finding your daughter. I do hope for her sake that you succeed."

"Not so fast. Hadros Group. Hadros Incident. You must have made the connection. Weren't you curious about it?"

"Not really," Aster says. "We returned from there with plenty of samples ourselves, so we knew that Hadros is teeming with potential for new stims. We haven't been able to get out there again, thanks to the Cath, but... well." Aster spreads his hands. "It seemed reasonable that someone had infiltrated the sector and returned with something that might be of use to us."

"Fine, but here's the thing," I say. "I was there. And something I did made someone else who was there come after me and abduct my daughter for revenge. I know the two of you were also a part of the incident, and that you indirectly or directly financed her abductors. But if that wasn't deliberate, then we're looking for one of the others who were in Hadros with you, so I need names."

"And you think, after all these years and our brains being scrubbed, that we even remember who else was there?" Aster demands.

My screens flash, indicating a lie.

"Aster… just tell them," Ivy says.

He glares at her but gives in with another sigh. "Well, it's not exactly a state secret! You can look it up on the galnet and figure it out for yourself. Let's see… Christophe Zabelle, of Zabelle Enterprises… FTL Research, yes, that makes sense, since we were officially there studying rifts. Who else… ah, yes, well this one I already knew, Gina Keri. You may have heard of her…"

"The head of the Solaris Cartel," Aurora growls.

"Rumors, I assure you," Aster says, waving a hand at her.

"Facts," I insist.

"What about her?" Aurora presses.

"Well…" Aster frowns and his silver eyes slowly widen, as if something just occurred to him. "Now that I think about it, she might be the one you're looking for."

Aurora glances pointedly at me as if to say, *I told you so.* But that's always easy to say in retrospect. She had a hunch, not proof.

"What makes you say that?" I ask.

Ivy is scowling at Aster. "You mean we bought a stim from Keri? Don't we *sell* to her?"

Aster waves his partner's objections away. "Which is why I don't mind pointing the finger at Keri—not that I'm talking out of my ass, mind you…" He adds, looking quickly at me.

"Get to the point," Aurora snaps at him.

"Well, it's just that about three years ago, she came to us, in confidence, to ask what we remembered from the incident. Of course, we told her the same as we're telling you, that it's all a blur, yada yada.

"Then she explained that she'd been having these nightmares about a daughter that she'd never had. In the dreams, they were in a lab together, working on something. I guess the girl was older, maybe eighteen or twenty-something, probably working with her mother as part of some grad research."

I can feel my blood growing colder with each passing second that Aster talks. But I don't dare to interrupt him.

"Well, supposedly we were there, too," Aster says. "So she thought maybe it had something to do with the Hadros Incident, which we were all a part of, and that made her think that she really *did* have a daughter and that for some, unspecified reason the Coalition scrubbed away every single memory of the girl.

"Now, I hate to be a snitch, Korbin, but if Gina somehow found out what happened out there, and in the process, she learned not only that she did have a daughter, but that you, Mr. Korbin, ex-Paladin and government assassin, maybe had something to do with her daughter's demise, or even just her memories of the girl being erased… Well, then I suppose I could see why she might have abducted your daughter in revenge."

I'm busy scanning the metrics from the neural probes that we inserted into their VR pods, but everything Aster just said is reading as true. He's not just spinning a story to get me to back off.

"Thank you," Aurora mutters. "We have what we need."

Rather than try to extract the generic bot that we used for my double, Aurora simply unplugs, leaving it standing frozen there like a statue.

"Are you going to release us now?" Ivy demands of me. "We've told you everything we know."

I nod mutely, unable to summon the energy for a reply. Hearing that one of my dark ops might have caused the death or disappearance of an innocent girl, and in turn, led to our daughter's abduction, has sucked all the wind out of my lungs and turned my feet to lead. All my pent-up righteous fury is fast giving way to a sick, sinking sense of guilt. The motive behind Cally's abduction is about as simple as they get: an eye for an eye.

"You can open your pods now," I mutter, after disabling the overrides that we installed.

"I hope you find her," Ivy says.

Aster isn't as generous. "If you tell Gina that we pointed you in her direction, we won't just deny it, we'll come after you ourselves."

Rather than reply, I re-activate my cloaking shield, and drift away into the shadows, moving as quickly and quietly as I can.

By the time I'm halfway back to the nearest elevator, I have my emotions in check, and I'm once again focused on the task at hand. I still don't know exactly what I did, and until I do, I can't assume that I deliberately hurt an innocent girl. It could have been an accident. Or collateral damage. But Gina Keri isn't the sort of reasonable person who's likely to care much about that distinction.

At least now, we know who we're dealing with.

My comms buzz with an incoming call just as I enter the lift. I accept it without even checking who it is, and Aurora's voice comes crackling to my ears.

"At least now we have a name," she says.

"Yes," I agree.

"Get back up here as soon as you can. We have a lot of work to do."

"Copy that," I reply, ending the connection before Aurora can chime in with my conscience and start blaming me and my bloody past for whatever has happened to Cally.

Pushing self-recriminations aside, I switch my focus to the target, struggling to piece together a plan.

Gina won't be easy to get to. And what's worse, she's been leading us around, dropping clues and leads the whole way. She wants us to find her. Maybe not this fast, but she wasn't planning to stay anonymous forever. And that means if we're not very careful, we're going to wind up walking straight into a trap.

CHAPTER 30

I'm back on board the *Augur,* stripped down to my jumpsuit, sitting in a lounge with Aurora and Nightmare, at the aft end of the upper deck. We're in a high orbit over Kazir with the autopilot engaged, safely ensconced in the planet's FTL inhibition zone so that no mercenaries or bounty hunters can drop out of FTL and ambush us.

Aurora is sitting on the couch kitty-corner to mine with Nightmare lying across her legs as she gently scratches the bristly fur on the side of the wraith's head. I'm cupping a hot mug of black coffee, squinting through the steam at the two of them. Aurora is waiting for me to spell out our next move, to come up with some genius plan that will get Cally back.

But I'm not sure what our move is from here. Gina Keri is a dangerous woman to go after, and not easy to get to. More so, now that I know just how badly we're being baited. She wants us to find her, and that means she's ready for it.

I'm missing something. I know I am. It's right under my nose. I can feel it. I take a long slow sip of my coffee, burning my mouth in the process.

"So? What's our move, Cade?" Aurora prompts me.

I shake my head. "I don't know. I need time."

"Cally doesn't have time."

I fix Aurora with a hard look. "You don't think I know that? If we make the wrong move here, it's over. She'll have us right where she wants us, and we lose everything."

Aurora lets out a grating sigh and looks away. Nightmare hisses and her tail lashes the couch, scratching straight through the tough material.

"I need to sleep on it," I say.

"That cup of coffee is a good start."

"Figure of speech," I add, waving her concerns away.

"Fine." Aurora gives me a tight, shallow nod and nudges Nightmare off her lap. The wraith lands soundlessly and then mutters something I can't hear through her translator.

"I'll be in the cockpit if you need me," Aurora says.

I nod and take another sip of my coffee, watching as she leaves with Nightmare padding after her. After a few minutes of trying to distract myself with hot coffee, and failing, I stand up with a growl and cross the lounge to the corridor, heading for the cockpit. I can't think of a better place to be.

I can hear Aurora arguing with Nightmare up there, and that noise chases me away. I need some time alone to think. I duck left into the primary sleeping quarters and shut the door behind me.

The room holds a bed with a small desk beside it. A couch lines the wall beneath a rectangular viewport. The door to the head is open, and I can see a slice of the sink and toilet.

I go straight to bed, turn down the lights, and set my coffee on the desk. Then I flop down on the mattress with my grav boots on. I'm staring up at the glow panels in the ceiling, my hands crossed over my chest. My heart is racing erratically, making my palms sweat.

I'm missing something. We were supposed to go after the *Korbin's Folley* to Margrave, not come straight here. Maybe that means Gina isn't ready for us yet. Maybe we were supposed to be chasing our tails for a few more days and Gina needed that time to finish her own preparations.

Maybe.

But what would we have found at Margrave? Vance's son, and maybe the mercenaries who were hired to help abduct Cally. Vance's son might have led us to the bounty hunter from the Syndicate who was paid a handsome sum to jack Aurora and kidnap Cally. And that would have led us where?

Probably to the same place, eventually. Here,

to Kazir, and then to Gina Keri.

I'm still following the breadcrumbs she laid out, just putting the pieces together faster than she intended.

And there's some key piece of this puzzle that I haven't figured out yet.

I need to start from the beginning.

Aurora's double got jacked at the Shroud. The jacker was a top 100 bounty hunter from the Syndicate, working with one of our own, Vance Baleros, who was likely being threatened via his son to get his cooperation. The Syndicate hunter would have needed Vance's help to get aboard the Shroud and maybe also to cause the twelve-minute malfunction that covered their tracks. But Vance didn't have access to the Shroud's surveillance system. It's unlikely he could have caused the malfunction without help.

But why go to all of that trouble in the first place? Why not jack Aurora somewhere else, while she was on a mission, for example? It would have been much easier and required fewer moving pieces.

But then I wouldn't have as many clues to follow. Maybe I wouldn't have any at all. No way to lead me around by the nose.

A deep frown furrows my brow.

Think, Cade. Think...

After Aurora's freshly jacked double left the Shroud, she went straight to Pyria and abducted Cally. The abductor jumped through a rift to get away, making sure we couldn't follow. Brix was already en-route at that point to Pyria. We met up with him in deep space, only to discover that he'd been followed and jumped by mercenaries.

Then we flew back to the Shroud with him, and somehow those same mercenaries followed us again.

Either our ship or Brix's had to have a tracker on it, but we never found the tracker, so either it dropped off somewhere along the way, or...

There was no tracker.

Maybe Aurora is right. If Brix is in on this, then he could have deliberately contacted the mercs and made it look like they'd jumped him at our rendezvous. Then he contacted them again to tell them where the Shroud went.

That would also explain the system malfunction at the Shroud. Brix had access. He could have easily caused the 12-minute system failure that allowed Aurora to be jacked in her quarters.

But there is one other person who could have done both of those things with equal ease.

Aurora herself.

That thought hits me like a grav sled full of neutronium ore.

It would also explain why Aurora pointed the finger at Brix: to keep me from realizing that she was the only other person who could have set all of this up.

But why would Aurora abduct our daughter?

What motive could she possibly have for doing something so twisted? Unless she didn't know she was doing it. Gina might have found a way to jack her at our home on Pyria, maybe when Aurora met up with her double in that secret hangar below our house. Then Gina could have scrubbed away any trace of what she'd done. But if she managed to do all of that, why would she relinquish her control over Aurora? Both my wife and her double could have been equally compromised this entire time, and that means Aurora didn't really reveal her secret life or the fact that her double had been jacked. That was Gina, laying out the first breadcrumbs for me to follow.

Shit. I sit up quickly, my head light and spinning, my nerves sparking with adrenaline. This has all been a game from the start. It makes sense. Gina Keri has been leading me around with clues, baiting me the whole time. She's been in control of the situation from the start, and the best way to stay in control would be to have someone right beside me, feeding me misinformation, or at least interpreting the available information to send me in a specific direction.

Gina wouldn't want me to find a way to outmaneuver her. She would want to stay ahead of me, and to know what I'm planning just as soon as I do, then use Aurora to deliver me on a platter for the culmination of her revenge.

But...

I could also be wrong.

It *could* still be Brix working his own angle to help Gina and hurt me.

But if that were the case, then he should have insisted on joining us and tagging along as a third wheel. Instead, he stayed back at the Shroud to keep things running just as he always has. Aurora set him up, making it look like he could be involved by having those mercs jump him before they followed us to the Shroud. And then she pointed the finger at him before anyone could point a finger at her.

Very clever.

Of course, whoever jacked her had to have studied Aurora's neuro data carefully, or else retained access to it, to play the role without me or anyone else getting suspicious. But that's easy enough I suppose, assuming they had the time and space they needed to crack Aurora's encryption.

Whatever the case, I need more than suspicion to go on. I need to disable her and get in with a neural probe to find out if I'm right. And I need to do it without Aurora realizing what I'm up to.

The problem is, she's up in the cockpit, no doubt monitoring every inch of the ship. Whoever jacked her will be suspicious of me, wary that I'll figure this out and try to turn the tables.

The only way for me to do that now is to trigger an EMP grenade beside her or to shoot her with an EMP rifle while her shields are down. Then I'll have a short window of opportunity to power her down and go to work with a bot jacker. But all of that gear is below deck, in the armory. I'd need an excuse to go there.

Alternatively, I could use the nanites in my exosuit to disable Aurora through brute-force methods, but I left my suit in the airlock, and I won't be able to get back to it now without raising suspicions.

I need a good excuse. A reason to arm myself. But that shouldn't be too hard under the circumstances.

Swinging my legs over the side of the bed, I plant the soles of my boots on the deck with a ringing *thunk.* Activating my holoband with a thought, the glowing displays swirl to life, and I toggle the comms to contact her.

"Aurora, I'm going back down. We need to do some recon around Keri Pharmaceuticals, to see if we can at least locate Gina."

"Already ahead of you, Cade."

A tickle of apprehension swirls through my gut, twisting it up in knots. "What do you mean?"

The door swishes open, and Aurora appears silhouetted in the opening.

I do my best not to react, but Aurora's sensors have almost certainly detected the sudden spike in my pulse and blood pressure at the sight of her. If I'm lucky, she'll think it means I'm just happy to see her. My hand twitches toward my sidearm.

Glowing orange eyes harden.

"Well? Where is Gina?" I ask, keeping my voice steady and even.

Aurora smoothly draws her sidearm and levels it at my chest. "I'm right here, Cade."

Gina pulls the trigger, and a bright flash of light dazzles my eyes just before I plunge into a deep well of darkness.

CHAPTER 31

I come to after an indeterminate amount of time. My head is pounding with a splitting headache focused around the left side of my skull. My eyes crack open, only to wince shut from the bright lights glaring down at me.

A rhythmic beeping sound makes me think I've been hooked up to some type of life signs monitor or maybe to some other type of life support equipment.

Where am I? What happened? I take a moment to gather my thoughts. Gina. She was the one who jacked Aurora. And she shot me. *She must have been watching me have my 'aha' moment over the* Augur's *surveillance feeds.* She wouldn't have needed any captions to understand what she was looking at: me, finally putting two and two together.

I try to move—

And a sharp pain erupts from my left shoulder. The left side of my head, left shoulder… I probably hit them when I fell off the bed after Aurora stunned me.

"Good. You're awake," a deep female voice growls loudly in my ears, seeming to come from everywhere at once. *"Now we can begin."*

I force my eyes open again, blinking back tears to get an idea of where I am, only to find a curving glow panel directly in front of my face.

Smooth alloy walls surround me. I'm lying in a stasis pod. Or a resurrection chamber. Or… a coffin.

That beeping noise is speeding up now. It's my heartbeat. Definitely a life signs monitor.

The glow panel swirls, and I feel myself plunging into a waking dream. This is a VR pod.

Suddenly I'm not lying down, but sitting upright in the cockpit of a ship. My hands are on the controls as we fly directly toward a glassy sphere of distorted space-time that looks like a giant FTL rift. My hands are moving of their own accord, making subtle adjustments to power levels and engines. I try to move my hands for myself, or simply to arrest their movement, but nothing happens.

My head turns to the co-pilot. He's saying something, but whatever it is, I can't hear it. My heart rate spikes again at the sight of him. It's Brix Rylo. He's wearing a sleek black suit of Coalition combat armor with the helmet off and tucked under his seat.

"Do you know where you are?" the voice in my

ears asks.

"Who are you?" I demand.

"I already told you that, Cade. I'm Gina Keri. Please try to keep up. Focus. Where are you?"

I pry my tongue off the roof of my mouth. It's as dry as a venusian desert.

"I don't know," I admit.

"Wrong answer. Try again."

"A Coalition shuttle," I say.

"Better," Gina says. *"What else?"*

Recognizing a few of the displays, I add, "It has a cloaking shield engaged, so it might be a Javelin-class." Seeing the range on the FTL computer, I add, "It's one of the long-range variants."

"Good. Now, where *are you?"*

My head turns back, away from the co-pilot. I can feel my mouth moving, but I can't hear what I'm saying. The audio has been muted.

Suddenly I realize what this is. This is a memory. My memory. It's the missing one that will explain everything. My holo files from the Paladins. How in the galaxy did Gina get this? But right now, the *how* is less important than the *why*.

This time around, I'm just a spectator, being forced to relive the events passively.

My eyes flick to a jump timer, counting down from four and a half minutes. The ship's current location is ominously listed as *Unknown*.

"I don't know where I am," I insist.

"Let me fill in the blanks for you," Gina says. *"You're fleeing from alien hostiles in a neighboring galaxy after botching the rescue of six Coalition researchers, one of whom is my daughter, Lucia."*

"Aliens? A neighboring... *galaxy?*" I ask. "That's impossible."

"Is it?" Gina asks. *"What is that giant rift doing in front of you? Where do you think it leads?"*

She waits a second for me to come up with a likely answer.

My gaze shifts again, giving me a good look at the sensor grid. It's teeming with red blips. Hostiles are everywhere, chasing us, but I can't tell from that if they really are *alien* ships. The only sentient aliens that we know of are the Cath. I venture that as a guess.

"Wrong," Gina says. *"The Cath are waiting for you on the other side. Which is where?"*

"Hadros," I reply.

"Good. At least that particular clue wasn't wasted on you."

"Where is Aurora?"

"Which one?" Gina challenges.

"The *real* one."

"Ah. Well, that all depends on you."

"And Cally?"

"Same answer, but don't worry. This doesn't have to end badly. I'm not the monster you must think I am."

"What do you want?" I demand.

"What do I want?" Gina asks shrilly. *"I want*

my daughter back! I want you to finish the job you were sent to do forty-five years ago! You were supposed to rescue us, and you failed. Not only that, you gave the order to leave my daughter behind."

"I..." I'm struggling to remember what the hell she's talking about, but I can't. None of this looks or sounds familiar.

"You don't remember. I know. Neither did I. But that's okay. That's why you're here. Brace yourself. This will hurt... a lot."

A searing pain erupts behind my eyes and my head feels like it's about to explode. The pain increases abruptly, drawing a gritted scream from my lips.

Images and memories flash before my eyes. Mission prep with my team on the Moon... then leaving the Coalition with Brix, Pixie, and Kraug aboard an ERAS-3 Javelin-class shuttle to rescue eight Coalition researchers from a distant research facility in the Hadros Sector. It's an alien facility left behind by the Priors, code-named *Terminus Station.*

The Cath were threatening to annex the station and that entire region of space, so we were dispatched to destroy Terminus and evacuate the researchers. It took us almost a year in FTL just to get there, more than six thousand light years from Earth.

When we finally reached the unnervingly familiar toroidal station, we found six of the researchers missing: only Cristophe Zabelle and

Ivy Rox were still aboard. They told us that the other six had taken their two shuttles through an FTL rift that was being generated at the center of the facility. That rift led straight to a neighboring galaxy—the Small Magellanic Cloud.

The researchers sent a shuttle and three of their people through the rift to explore, but it never returned. Then they dispatched a second shuttle to find and rescue the first. Cristophe and Ivy suspected that the Priors themselves might be found in the galaxy on the other side of that rift, and they wanted us to go there to find and bring back their missing colleagues. I left Pixie and Kraug behind with orders to blow the station if we didn't return in twenty-four hours.

It took most of that time just to locate the missing shuttles. We found the crew of the second ship busy staging an elaborate rescue for the crew of the first. When we arrived, they were skulking in the feathery green underbrush of an alien-inhabited world, surveilling a colony that resembled a giant termite mound. Alien ships were everywhere—misshapen ovoid fighters and lumbering behemoths with spikes, curving superstructures, and tentacled projections that made them look like living creatures.

The missing researchers from the second shuttle, Aster Stavros, Gina Keri, and another woman, Masra Kander, believed that these were the Priors, even though we'd never found any artifacts from them that remotely resembled these organic, almost insectoid vessels.

They shared with us holo recordings of the beings inside the colony: bulky two-legged creatures with bright red eyes and thickly-plated bluish-gray exoskeletons. Where a human's mouth would be were a ragged series of gill-like flaps that made them look like they were always grinning maniacally. Beneath that was a beard of fine, translucent hairs and thicker tentacles that dangled from their chin. Aster explained that these were sensory organs that in conjunction with their ears, allowed them to echo-locate like a wraith. I said that they looked like demons. None of the others disagreed.

Aster and Masra went on to explain that these beings were the original organic species of the Priors which later ascended to digital consciousness and artificial bodies, ultimately building the orbital rings, solar-collecting Dyson spheres, and toroidal stations like Terminus that we found scattered around the Milky Way. The biological beings that they'd started as hadn't been wiped out in the process of that transition. They'd simply left—or maybe *fled*—through Terminus, to the Small Magellanic Cloud.

But none of that mattered to me at the time. I was there to get these researchers home and to destroy Terminus Station. And now I had an even better reason to destroy it—not just to prevent the station from falling into the Cath's warmongering paws, but to stop a second alien power from joining galactic politics.

Gina had other ideas. She wanted me and Brix to sneak into that oversized termite mound with our cloaking armor, to rescue her missing daughter and the other two researchers who'd been captured with her. Brix and I argued that they were probably dead, but Gina countered that argument with the tracking info and life signs data from their neuralinks. All three of the researchers were still alive and well.

The problem was, I'd set a clock when I left Terminus: twenty-four hours, and we were out of time. So we dragged Gina out of there. She fought us the whole way, but eventually settled for a compromise: we would return to Terminus, tell Pixie and Kraug not to blow the station, and then we'd make a second trip to rescue her daughter, Lucia, and the other two researchers. I agreed to that, but it was a lie. I was just trying to shut her up and make sure that she didn't do anything stupid to compromise our mission.

Brix and I took Gina to our shuttle to keep an eye on her, while Aster and Masra flew their vessel back. Despite keeping both ships cloaked the whole way, the Priors spotted us and gave chase.

Now we definitely couldn't come back for a second attempt at a rescue. Gina blamed me. She wanted me to swear that I would keep my word, that I wouldn't blow up the station until we rescued her daughter, which of course I couldn't promise to do.

She insisted that she would go back and rescue Lucia, with or without our help.

Brix stabbed a finger at the grid to indicate our pursuers. "If they can see us through our cloaking shields, then they'll see you return. You'll be killed or captured as soon as you cross the rift."

I agreed with that sentiment even as I tweaked the power balance in the reactor to goose the engines and get us the hell out of there just a little faster.

"Aren't you Paladins?" Gina demanded. "You're trained for covert insertions into hot zones!"

"Not this hot," Brix muttered.

"Rescuing you was a secondary objective," I added. "We've got five out of eight. If we try this again, we risk losing more of you or losing Terminus to the Cath, or to whatever the hell these bogies are. This is as good as it's going to get. At least you're alive. You have a backup of your daughter's neuro data, right? Bring her back as a bot."

But that wasn't good enough for Gina. She lunged for the controls, and Brix put her down with a tranq dart to the chest. He locked her in one of the stasis pods, getting her to sleep early.

"Now do you understand what you did?" Gina growls in my ear.

"I do," I reply. "But I was only following orders.

This wasn't personal."

"It was my daughter! Of course, it was fucking personal!"

I wince at the force of her outburst.

"Revenge won't change anything," I add quietly.

"That's where you're wrong. This isn't revenge. And it will change everything."

"What?" My brain is going into overdrive now. "What are you talking about?"

"Shut up and keep watching, and maybe you'll figure it out."

I clamp my mouth shut and do as I'm told.

We made it through the rift, back to Terminus, and I had Cristophe Zabelle shut down the rift before our alien pursuit could follow us. Then we got the researchers packed into our shuttle along with their gear and any of the Priors' artifacts that weren't nailed down. One of which, I see myself taking an interest in and asking about—it's a black disk, about the size of my palm, with alien symbols that glow to life around the edges when you touch it.

"We think it's the Priors' version of a comm unit. Rift-based, so it's instant across any distance," Cristophe Zabelle explained. "We haven't exactly figured it out, but…" He shrugged. "If we can, it'll be a game changer. No more FTL relays. No comms delays or risks of interception. Can you imagine?"

I nod along with that and hand the device

back to him, already losing interest. Comms are already almost instant, traveling over FTL relays hundreds of times faster than physical ships can manage with their FTL drives, but I suppose there's always room for improvement.

We finished setting the charges to blow the station and hurried back to the hangar and the shuttles—

Just in time to see Cath soldiers come boiling out of half a dozen shuttles of their own, flooding the hangar. We're surrounded and forced to lay down our weapons. They're all wearing form-hugging suits and helmets that shimmer brightly like they're mirror-plated. It's some type of refractive armor, designed to deflect energy weapons.

One of the Cath strides to the fore. It's wearing a more familiar-looking black exosuit with a glossy orange visor. It towers over me since the Cath are much taller than humans. The suit it's wearing reminds me of *my* exosuit, the one Alpha left with me as a parting gift.

The visor clears, and I see that it's just another Cath inside, with big lidless yellow eyes, and a black-furred triangular head with a broad mouth full of sharp, jutting teeth. It says something to me in a series of chirps and growls.

A familiar voice translated: "He says, you are trespassing in their territory, and he demands to know if you are the one in charge."

"I am," I admitted. My eyes darted nervously

to the circle of alien soldiers who are busy aiming their mirror-plated sidearms at us. "My apologies for trespassing. We were just leaving…"

I realize that I didn't recognize the exosuit or the voice, because back then, Alpha and I hadn't met yet.

The suit shimmers and then flows away from its Cath wearer in an amorphous black cloud of nanites, leaving the Cath with a sleeker version of its armor. Now a vaguely humanoid shadow stands beside it, still buzzing in a fuzzy black cloud of nanites. It has a head, two arms, two legs, and two bright silver pinpricks for eyes. In this vaguely humanoid configuration, a voice rolled smoothly from the cloud, echoing slightly: "I am Alpha, friend Cade. I am the leader of the Cath."

"Alpha…?" I repeated slowly, looking back and forth between the Cath and the shadow standing beside it.

I realize that I'm trying to figure out if I'm dealing with one entity or two, and which one is which. My gaze settled on the shadow rather than the alien wearer of the nanite-infused suit. "How do you know my name? And why did you call me a *friend?* Do I know you?"

"Not yet," Alpha said. "But you will."

I realize now that Alpha was alluding to the fact that we'd already met in the future. He knew me, even if I didn't know him yet. He'd traveled back in time through the Gateway just before

I destroyed it, somehow altering the course of major events, including the Cath's extinction.

"What do you want?" I hear myself ask him.

"What do *I* want? I want you to leave," Alpha replied. "The Cath want to execute you, very publicly, which will start a war, but I have convinced them to let you go—on one condition: you will not detonate your explosives, which I know you are thinking about doing as we speak."

"And why would I do that?" I asked.

"Because if you do, then *you* will start a war. Now, what will it be, friend Cade? Will you trust me, or kill yourself and set the galaxy ablaze, leaving others to pick up the pieces?"

I hesitated. "How do I know you won't use Terminus to open a rift and launch a first strike against us?"

"How long has the Coalition been here, studying this facility?"

I shrugged, probably not wanting to reveal any more intel than I had to.

"Your people haven't learned to control this station in all of that time, and neither will the Cath. But to answer your question, you'll just have to trust me. Neither of us wants a war."

"I don't even know you. How can I trust you?"

"But you *do* know me, Cade. Many years from now, we will meet, and I will help you save your daughter and the woman you love."

"I don't have a daughter."

"Yet," Alpha said. "So, friend Cade, what will it

be?"

It took me a while to answer that.

"We'll leave," I finally decided.

"I am glad," Alpha replied. "Before you go, you will help us to disarm and remove your explosives."

"Do I have a choice?"

"No." The shadowy specter forms a hollow curve where a mouth would be. A smile. Even with what I know now, that Alpha is a benevolent entity, it still looks creepy as hell.

The scene fades to black, leaving me alone in darkness with my thoughts.

"I don't get it…" I mutter. But then I do. "Wait. You think we can go back in time to save your daughter?"

"Aha. You're not a scrigg after all," Gina replies.

"But… we destroyed the Gateway at Nexus. It doesn't exist, and as far as you're concerned, it never did." I'm not sure how much of this Gina knows or could possibly know. After Alpha and I destroyed the Gateway, it never even existed in this timeline. But then again, I guess it doesn't take a genius to infer its existence from my mysterious conversation with Alpha.

"What in the galaxy are you talking about?" Gina demands of me. *"We're going to Terminus Station, and you're going to convince your friend, Alpha, to help us use it to go back and fix your mistake."*

Suddenly I realize why Terminus Station

looked so familiar when I saw it in my missing memories. Terminus Station and the "Gateway" that I destroyed are identical, both of them are massive rift generators that can open portals between distant points in space—

Or time.

CHAPTER 32

When the pod opens, I'm confronted by a carbon copy of the woman from my missing memories. Gina Keri. She's flanked by a pair of combat bots. I recognize Gina by her gaunt cheeks, shoulder-length brown hair, green eyes, and her tall, slender figure. Gina is the type of woman who prides herself on cultivating a foreboding appearance rather than an attractive one. She looks as if she hasn't aged a day from the woman I saw in my memories, but chronologically she must be older than me. She's scowling, and her gaunt cheeks are deeply shadowed in the dim light. I quickly take in the space and see we're in the remote ops center aboard a much larger ship than the *Augur*. I'm lying in one of at least fifty VR pods. The *Augur* only has four.

"Get him on his feet," Gina orders.

One of the combat bots reaches in and yanks me roughly from the pod. My injured shoulder aches sharply with the mistreatment.

"Where am I?" I ask, nearly tripping as I step over the side of the pod.

"Aboard my dreadnought, the *Venator*."

I blink at that, not particularly surprised to learn that Gina has an old decommissioned warship. Probably a whole fleet to go along with it.

"Follow me," Gina says, and turns sharply on her heel.

The two bots don't give me much of an option, each of them seizing one of my arms in cold iron grips and yanking me roughly after her.

We're moving quickly for the exit. I struggle to keep up to avoid being dragged by the bots, but they don't release me.

"Where are we going?" I demand.

"Aft. To the stasis tubes."

"Wha... wait." I'm panting from pain rather than exertion. Those bots are squeezing the life out of my arms.

Gina stops and turns just before the exit. The bots jerk me to a halt. She regards me imperiously. "What?"

"Where are Aurora and Cally?"

Gina smiles thinly at me but says nothing.

"I'm not going to help you without seeing some proof that they're okay. Both of them."

"I thought you might say that," Gina says. She reaches into a mag-sealed pocket in her jumpsuit and holds out a holoband. "Put it on."

One of the bots releases me, and I reach for the device. Slipping it around my temples, I turn it on with a thought and try to toggle the comms.

But Gina is remote-controlling the holoband with hers. She places the call for me, patching through to another part of her ship—

The Brig.

I'm looking down into a cell with two bunk beds and a sink and a toilet between them. A pair of familiar-looking women are sitting on one of the beds. Shoulders hunched. Bright red hair and blonde identify them as Aurora and Callista.

"Cally!" I shout.

She looks up into the camera that I'm watching them through. "Dad?" she asks, reaching up to flick locks of blood-matted hair out of her eyes. There's a bruise around one eye and blood crusted over that eyebrow, but otherwise, she seems fine.

Aurora looks up now, too, her face stricken, but not injured like Cally. She's not wearing the same clothes as she was aboard the *Augur*, which makes me think this is Aurora's double. Not that it matters which of them Gina restored, so long as all of her memories are there and she's no longer a prisoner in her own body. "Cade, it's Gina Keri. She—"

"I know. I'm going to get you out of there," I reply.

"Are you..." Aurora glances about furtively, obviously worried that someone could be listening.

"She captured me, too," I explain.

Aurora's face falls dramatically, and Gina laughs, and the sound echoes over both ends of the call, revealing that she's been listening in. That draws a scowl from Cally.

"Cade... she's going to kill us," Aurora says. "I mean perma-kill us."

"Not if he does what I have asked him to," Gina puts in. "Don't worry. I'm sure he won't fail... *again*."

Aurora's brow furrows in confusion, and Cally slowly shakes her head.

"What is she talking about?" Aurora asks.

"It's a long story," I reply. "Look, I'm going to figure this out, okay?"

"I know," Aurora says. "I trust you."

"I love you both. We'll be together soon."

The feed cuts out just as Cally and Aurora are reiterating my sentiments.

I fix Gina with a scowl. One of the bots removes the holoband from my forehead and hands it back to her.

"Let them go," I say. "I'll still help you. You have my word."

Gina slowly shakes her head, regarding me with a sad smile. "You need to stay motivated, Cade. I can't have you deciding to sacrifice yourself on this mission, thinking that at least your family will be safe. No, if you fail, they die."

"Now, let's go. Time's wasting." Gina laughs

lightly at that, and the combat bots jerk me into motion once more. As we exit the remote ops center and join a broad corridor, I notice that the lights are turned down low everywhere, and the ship appears to be deserted. I put that together with what Gina said earlier—that we're going to the stasis tubes—and I realize the crew must already be asleep. It's a long way to reach Terminus Station.

Shit. I won't even have time to think this through before we get there. I'm going to be frozen the whole way.

My mind goes into overdrive as I try to think of a way out of this. I don't know if Alpha will agree to help us. Just because he and I have some kind of connection, doesn't mean that he'll agree to help me alter the past. And for all I know, that's not even possible.

I seem to recall some tricky issues with backward time travel—like the paradox that if I go back in time to save Gina's daughter, then I wouldn't have any reason to go back in time and save her, and Gina wouldn't have had any reason to abduct Cally or to jack Aurora and force me to go back and save Lucia. But surely Gina knows all of that, so how can she possibly think that this will work?

Alpha only managed to change the past because we destroyed the Gateway at Nexus *after* he traveled back in time. The facility existed in a superposition of the past, present, and future, so by destroying it, we stranded him in the past, but we also undid everything that ever happened because of its existence. In this timeline, it's like the Gateway never even existed. Unfortunately, it turns out there was more than one of them.

It's actually a good thing that Alpha stopped me from destroying Terminus. The Priors who used it to leave our galaxy all those eons ago never would have left if I had succeeded in blowing that station to bits.

My blood runs cold. Is *that* what Gina is after? If she destroys the station, then the Priors never would have left the Milky Way, and chances are we would all be slaves in their empire right now—or worse. They could have wiped us out entirely.

But if Gina simply wanted to destroy Terminus, she wouldn't need me to help her. She's hoping to leverage my friendship with Alpha to get what she wants. That's the only reason she targeted me for this mission. But then why lead me on a merry chase across the galaxy looking for my daughter? Why not simply cut to this part? I decide to ask her that, while I still can.

"I may have misspoken earlier when I said this isn't about revenge," Gina replies. "What I meant was, it isn't *only* about revenge. I wanted you to suffer the way I have suffered, even if it would only be for a few days instead of years. And that also helped you to understand the stakes. If you don't save my family, then you won't save yours, and by now you know how serious I am about following through with that threat."

Gina waves two heavy blast doors open at the end of the corridor, revealing a massive chamber with aisle upon aisle of stasis tubes, their curving glass frosted and illuminated from within to reveal the human and cyborg members of the ship's crew. Bots can simply power down or go into standby mode to make the trip seem shorter.

I'm led straight to a dark, empty tube at the end of the fourth aisle. Gina activates it, and the bots shove me roughly inside.

"Sweet dreams, Korbin."

My upper lip twitches along with a muscle in my jaw.

"What about Cally?" I ask. She's a bio like me, so she'll also have to sleep for this trip—unless Gina intends to keep her and Aurora locked up and awake that entire time.

To my relief, Gina gestures to another empty pod beside mine. "She's on her way here."

"I want to see her."

Gina clucks her tongue. "I'm afraid I've surpassed my daily limit for maudlin displays of affection. You can see her when you wake up."

I'm tempted to burst out of the pod and make a play for Gina's sidearm, but the two bots standing between us will be much faster than me.

For now, I can't see any way out of this. I'm going to have to see it through, and hopefully, figure out a way to convince Alpha to help us when we get to Terminus. There *has to be* a way to change the past without creating a paradox that will undo it all and put me back at square one.

The bots step back as the cover of my stasis pod swings shut. Gina is waving and smiling sarcastically. Frigid steam hisses around me in billowing clouds. The cover *thumps* shut, and a safety harness folds out, clamping lightly across my chest and thighs. A needle slides into my neck, pushing a cocktail of stasis-prep solutions and sedatives into my veins. My body grows numb and my mind begins to fade, spiraling down into oblivion.

CHAPTER 33

This time, when I wake up, I'm surrounded by Gina's people. They're everywhere: helping me and others out of the pods, wrapping a heating blanket around me, checking my vitals, then doing the same for Cally. I wait a few seconds for her to recover from the confusion and the violent chills of hibernation sickness before I wade through the crowd with my escort of combat bots to greet her.

She has a thermal blanket wrapped around her shoulders like me, but she's still shivering.

"Cally!" I shout.

Her head jerks to me. "Dad!" She comes running—only to be yanked back by one of the combat bots standing next to her.

They hold us about six feet apart, never letting us get close enough for a hug, or to even properly speak to one another. I grit my teeth and glare at the bot on my left. "What do you think we're going to do here? We're surrounded." But the bot's glowing red eyes and gleaming face are as stolid as ever. I'm asking for empathy from a lifeless drudge.

Gina joins us, her hands clasped in front of her. She smiles thinly at me, then nods to Callista. "You can see that your daughter is alive and well."

Cally glares at her.

Gina snaps her fingers to one of the bots holding her, and they begin dragging her roughly away.

"Wait! Just give me a second, would you?"

"Let me go!" Cally protests.

Gina shakes her head sadly. "Like you gave me a second before dragging *me* back to your ship, away from *my* daughter?"

"Where are you taking her?" I demand, craning my neck in a feeble attempt to keep eyes on Cally through the milling sea of crew.

"Back to the brig, of course," Gina replies. "Don't worry, Aurora is there, waiting for her." Gina holds out her palm, producing a hand-held holo projector. Imagery materializes above her hand, looking down into the same cell where I saw Aurora and Callista before. Aurora is pacing the deck.

"Was she awake the whole time?"

"Why would I go to sleep for more than three hundred days, yet leave a very dangerous, very angry woman *awake* for all that time aboard my ship?"

I grunt angrily for an answer.

"Come," Gina says. "We have work to do." She turns and leads the way out. The bots escorting me yank me along after her. We join the stream of thermal-blanketed masses busy flooding from the stasis deck amidst the handful of resurrected bots who came down here to wake them.

Three hundred days. We must be in the Nidus System already. Maybe already hiding behind the gas giant that Terminus Station orbits: Icarus.

Now, in hindsight, with my memories restored, all of this makes sense, but I'm still not sure how to actually *do* what Gina wants me to. Even assuming that Alpha agrees to help me, there are some practical impossibilities when it comes to time travel. I can't break the laws of causality. If I go back and change how this all played out, then there'd be no reason for me to go back and change it.

But surely Gina isn't that stupid. She has to know that what she's asking is impossible. Which brings me back to the way that I changed events: destroy the time machine, and you undo everything it ever did, because it's there in all times, simultaneously, and if you destroy it in one moment, it disappears from all of them. It's a crazy loophole that doesn't even make total sense to me, but I have to accept it because it happened. The only way I was able to retain my memories of the past timeline was by making sure that I wasn't too far from the time machine when it was destroyed. I got caught in some kind of temporal shockwave that superimposed my memories, and now I'm one of the only living people who know that time travel is even possible. Unfortunately, Alpha is the other one, and technically so is Gina. Alpha alluded to his time-traveling adventures in my memories, which Gina recovered.

Gina leaves the main corridor, leading me up a ramp to the deck above. From there she proceeds to a grav lift, which stops five levels up and opens directly into a command center of sorts. It's empty, but for a handful of people and about twenty combat bots guarding them. The crowd of bots parts, and I'm shocked to see that I recognize the people here: Brix. Pixie. Kraug. *Shit.*

This is my strike team from the original mission to Terminus. But if they're here...

"Korbin's here," Kraug growls.

The rest of them turn. Pixie forgoes her usual flirtations and fixes me with a scowl. Brix looks apologetic.

"I did my best, Chief," he says. "The mercs were too much for us. They captured the Shroud."

And all of you with it, I think. But that was Gina's plan from the start. She wanted all four of us together for this. If I hadn't taken her bait and followed the *Korbin's Folley* away from the battle, I'd have been captured right along with them. Or killed in the attempt to lead the Templars to victory. That's probably why Gina had that ship fly away from the battle in the first place. She couldn't risk losing her pawn.

I'm jerked to a stop a few feet away from Brix. He called me *Chief,* as in *Chief Operations Officer.* So he remembers now, too. I'm guessing they all do. Each of us was involved, to greater or lesser degrees, in the Hadros Incident. And I suppose it seems like some twisted kind of justice to Gina that the same four operatives who dragged her away from Lucia should be the ones to undo that mistake now.

If it even was a mistake. Assuming it's possible, saving Lucia and getting her back from the Priors won't be easy. Or safe. Back then they tried to follow us through the rift, back to our galaxy. They were just waiting for someone to open a portal back to the galaxy they left all those eons ago. We really don't want to go back in time now just to kick off an alien invasion.

"Where's Aurora?" Brix asks.

"In the Brig," Gina supplies.

"And Cally?" he presses, wincing as he asks. Maybe afraid to know the answer. I can't believe I let Gina make me doubt him. Brix is like an uncle to her.

"Also in the Brig," Gina says. "Can we get on with this?"

Kraug grunts and rolls his massive shoulders. His dreadlocks have been cut short—I'm guessing to better fit his head inside a vac suit. Or maybe they froze and shattered in stasis.

Pixie's glowing fuchsia eyes are narrowed on me. "So, Chief, what's the plan?"

I look to Gina, deferring the question to her, and she gives me a small, sarcastic frown, placing a hand on her chest. "What are you looking at *me* for? It was *your* mistake that brought us here. Now you want me to tell you how to fix it, too? Aren't you Cade Korbin, former Paladin and legendary bounty hunter, founder of the Templars? Surely you can figure this out for yourself."

The way her mouth quirks up in the corners tells me she already has a plan, but she wants me to come up with one of my own, maybe to see whose is better, or to validate her strategy... or just to make me look like a scrigg.

I look around quickly, taking in the room where we find ourselves. Control stations line the bulkheads. A broad wall of viewports looks out into a sparkling sea of stars that could be anywhere. Two more control stations are arrayed in front of those viewports, one each for the captain and the XO. A big, glowing holo table stands behind those two seats for mission planning. But all of the control stations are empty. Gina is the only one here besides us and her combat bots.

I realize what that means. She hasn't told her people what this is all about. At least, not everything. Probably for the best. We don't need the whole galaxy learning the ins and outs of time travel.

I pull my thermal blanket tighter around my shoulders. "First of all, we need access to Terminus. Where are we right now?"

"Close, but not too close," Gina says. "The Cath have an entire war fleet guarding the station."

"Well, that's what I'm here for, right?" I say. She targeted me, not just because I'm responsible for Lucia's fate, but because she saw from my memories that I have a special connection with Alpha. That he considers me a friend. So surely, Alpha will want to help me out of the bind that I'm in now. To save my wife and daughter.

Gina's eyebrows elevate, but otherwise, she doesn't react to the question, still not willing to reveal any of the elements of her plan. More games. If she weren't such a twisted slagger, this would be much simpler.

"We have to contact the Cath and ask to speak with Alpha," I say.

"That would give our location away," Gina points out.

"Then we use a comm buoy," I reply.

"I can do one better than that," she replies. She reaches into her jumpsuit and produces a familiar palm-sized black disc. The same one I saw in my memory. The one Cristophe Zabelle described as a Priors' comm unit. Instant communications, impossible to intercept. Maybe also impossible to track.

She touches the top of the device and those glowing alien symbols appear around the edges. She taps a specific sequence with her other hand and the device chirps.

More chirping ensues.

Gina waits. A small smile is frozen on her lips.

"Who is this?" a familiar voice answers, deep and clipped with a strange, alien accent.

"I am a friend of Cade Korbin's. He's in trouble and he needs your help."

"I'm listening," Alpha says.

Gina holds the device out to me. I take a step closer. "Alpha, it's Cade."

"Friend Cade. It has been many years. What do you need my help with?"

I suck in a deep breath and look at Gina, wondering how much I'm allowed to say.

She shrugs. I guess she doesn't care if Alpha knows everything.

So I start at the beginning. "You remember when we met aboard Terminus Station in the Hadros Sector?"

"Of course," Alpha replies.

I explain about Gina's daughter being stranded in the galaxy on the other side of the rift, and then I tell him about Aurora getting jacked and my daughter being abducted, ending with Gina's involvement and what she expects from me... and from him.

"You're asking for a very big favor, friend Cade."

"I know."

"And you know that the past cannot be changed. At least, not intentionally."

Gina arches an eyebrow at that.

I hesitate. "There has to be a way."

"Perhaps there is," Alpha admits. "Are you close to Terminus?"

Gina nods.

"Yes," I say.

"Then come. I will meet you on board, and we will find a way to resolve this that makes everyone happy and doesn't lead to any... apocalyptic outcomes."

CHAPTER 34

As it turns out, Gina parked her Dreadnought half a light-year from Terminus. Now I'm sitting in the pilot's seat of a fresh-off-the-shipyard ERAS-4 Javelin-class shuttle. It's a whole generation more advanced than the one I used to reach Terminus all those years ago. It's also a *Coalition* vessel, with all of the latest tech, including an enhanced cloaking shield that will hopefully hide us from the Priors this time around. I can't imagine how Gina got her hands on a ship like this, but then again, she shouldn't have been able to gain access to the Paladins' holo files, either. She must have some very interesting connections to have put all of this together.

"Coming up on Terminus now…" Brix announces from beside me.

The dark side of Icarus inches steadily away, and the fiery mottled surface of its day side scrolls into view, drawing a bright crescent across the starfield ahead of us. Moments later,

Terminus itself appears: a darkly gleaming black torus with no visible viewports or lights shining out. Countless smaller specks are glittering around it. Cath vessels with their mirror-plated armor. Zooming in for a better look, I see the alien fleet in greater detail—sleek, aerodynamic ships with no visible gun emplacements or viewports. Somewhat like the station itself, but the Cath's ships are shiny and silver and the ancient space station is black and almost invisible against the void. The open center of the ring-shaped station is clear of any distortions, so it's not currently generating a rift.

"ETA?" Sia Dust asks, leaning into view from where she sits in one of the auxiliary control stations behind us.

"Ten minutes and counting," Brix replies.

Kraug makes an irritated noise from the seat behind his. He's annoyed at getting dragged back into this after so many years. Maybe he blames me for it.

Why not? Pile it on, guys.

I blow out a shaky breath and pat down the mag-sealed pocket in my jumpsuit. I'm reassured to feel the disc-shaped outline of the palm-sized alien comm unit. It's the only link I have back to Cally and Aurora. Gina promptly relocated her fleet after we left the *Venator,* and there's no telling where they are now. Scanning deep space for ship-sized blips half a light-year away is essentially impossible, and that means the only way I'm getting back to my family is if I'm bringing Gina's daughter with me, ready to make a trade. And that's how it's going to have to be. Gina never told me *her* plan, and Alpha has yet to reveal his, but I know that there's only one way that we can do this without violating causality in some way that would prevent us from traveling back in time in the first place.

We have to go and rescue Lucia from the past, then bring her back with us to a time slightly after the one we left. Like that, we'll still have had a reason to go back and save her, since we're only returning with her *after* we left. Gina won't get back all of those missing years with her daughter, but she will get her daughter back, and Lucia won't have aged more than a few hours or days.

It's the best I can do, and I suspect a shrewd woman like Gina knows it. She's waiting for me and Alpha to confirm that this is the only way. I'm supposed to check in with her via the comm unit before I leave, so she'll still have a chance to veto any plans she doesn't like.

One of the massive hangars on the side of Terminus begins rumbling open, but there are no buzz shields active behind the doors, meaning the hangar isn't pressurized.

I see another ship already landed inside. Just the one. A small, teardrop-shaped one-man fighter. And a humanoid figure is standing beside it in a familiar suit of black armor. Too short for there to be a Cath inside. Alpha came alone to greet us. That probably means he's keeping the Cath in the dark, too. Just like Gina. I guess he kept his promise, that the Cath wouldn't learn how to use Terminus.

Good thing.

But how did he get here so fast? Or was he already here? Is that because he never left, or because he's everywhere, having replicated the swarm of nanites that contain his awareness, filling the entirety of the Cath Imperium? An involuntary shiver rocks my shoulders at the thought. Good thing he's on our side.

"You good?" Brix asks, eyeing me skeptically.

"Yeah," I reply, nodding and swallowing thickly.

I land the shuttle beside Alpha's ship and retrieve my helmet from under the pilot's seat, slipping it on and twisting it to engage the seals. "Let's go," I say, jerking my chin to the exit as the others rise from their seats and put on their helmets. None of us are armed yet or wearing the suits of cloaking armor that Gina provided. After all, if we can't trust Alpha, this mission will be over before it can even begin.

CHAPTER 35

"**Y**ou are correct, friend Cade," Alpha says, inclining his helmet to me. "The past cannot be changed." The glossy orange visor of his helmet is a mirror, revealing the four of us standing in front of him on the ink-black deck of the hangar. "You can only save Lucia Keri by bringing her back to this time. Or rather, to a time slightly after this one. I can help you do this, by using Terminus to open the necessary rifts, but that means I have to stay behind. I cannot help you rescue Lucia. At least, not directly. And it would be inadvisable for me to join you. The risks of revealing my existence to the Priors are simply too great. They would stop at nothing to destroy me."

"We'll manage without you," I say.

"I hope so, friend Cade. For your sake."

"How soon can we leave?" Brix asks.

"Almost immediately, if you are ready?" Alpha's helmet turns imperceptibly, directing the question to each of us in turn.

"Born ready," Kraug says, smacking a fist into his palm.

"*In omnia paratus,*" Pixie mutters.

Ready for anything. I glance back at her. *Are we, though?* I wonder. I'm not so sure.

"What can we expect to face?" I ask. "Any intel you can provide?"

"When they left, my biological forbearers were not as technologically advanced as the ascended branch of our species, but they are still more advanced than your human empires, or the Cath. You will need an edge if you are going to sneak into one of their colonies and rescue Lucia."

Brix cocks his head to one side. "Like what?"

"The suit you gave me," I suggest.

"Exactly," Alpha replies.

The cloaking tech built into that armor is far better than anything we've ever developed.

Alpha turns and gestures to his ship. A rectangular outline appears on the side of the teardrop-shaped vessel, then sinks into the gleaming side of the ship and slides out of the way. A ramp telescopes down to the deck. Moments later, four bullet-shaped pods sail down the ramp. They're not mirror-plated like the ship, but smooth and gray like polished rocks taken from a river. All four capsules settle to the deck, somehow managing not to roll out the hangar door despite their rounded shape.

The nearest one opens with a hiss, revealing an exosuit that looks identical to the one I have, and to the one that Alpha embodies now.

"These will get you in without being seen, but you'll have no way to hide the captives once you reach them, so you'll have to fight your way out. The armor will help with that, too. Cade can explain how to direct the swarm embedded in the suits. It will be your only advantage. Unfortunately, they will recognize this technology, and they will know that their enemy lives."

"Their *enemy?*" Brix asks before I can.

"They left this galaxy, but only after ensuring that they had wiped out all of the ascended Priors. They remained biological lifeforms for a reason. Their fierce devotion to an ancient religion made ascension and digital consciousness an anathema to them, and they waged a holy war against us. Unfortunately, we were not prepared for it, and they won."

"But *you* survived," I point out.

"Being the sole survivor of my people does not diminish their victory."

"What a fascinating history lesson," Pixie mutters. "Can we get this over with? I have a life to get back to. Assuming I survive, that is."

I glance at her. She's a resurrected bot. Also an ascended digital being. I wonder if this conversation is striking too close to home. Maybe she's nervous about facing a fanatical alien species whose beliefs drove them to wipe out all the ascended members of their own kind.

"Take the suits aboard your shuttle," Alpha says. "Show your team how to use them. I will open a rift to a time just after the one you left forty-five years ago. The Priors will be on high alert after chasing you to the rift, and I will have to shut it down immediately to make sure none of them slip through here, to this time."

"Wait, how will you know when to open the rift to let us come back?" Pixie asks.

Alpha looks pointedly at the disc-shaped bulge of the Priors' comm unit in my pocket. I pull it out and hand it to Alpha, shrugging as I do so. "It's linked to Gina Keri's." After she linked my comms to hers, Gina showed me how to activate the device, by pressing the top of it. That will open a channel to her, but not to Alpha.

He touches the device and the glowing alien symbols appear. Tapping a sequence of them results in all of them glowing blue. He removes a matching device from his belt and I see that it's glowing blue as well.

"What about Gina? We're supposed to check in with her before we leave."

Alpha nods and hands my comm unit back. A data-sharing prompt appears on my HUD. I accept it and see two distinct sequences of alien symbols appear at the bottom of my screen. The top one is labeled *Alpha*. The bottom one is labeled with an expletive that would make a sexbot cringe.

"Got it," I say, minimizing the image from my display. Turning to Brix and the others, I nod, and say, "Let's get this done."

"Hooyah," Kraug mutters.

"Good luck, friend Cade," Alpha says. "I am afraid you will need it."

CHAPTER 36

After a brief demonstration of the nanite suits to the others, we're back in the cockpit of the shuttle, now fully dressed in the suits and ready for action. The armor Alpha gave us came with matching black sidearms, but as I demonstrated to the others, the nanites can flow over other surfaces, coating almost anything with the same degree of cloaking and active shielding as the suits themselves possess. That came as a relief to Kraug, who's determined to bring the shuttle's entire armory with us. He can't even sit down for all the weapons he's carrying.

I have the Priors' comm unit in my open hand, and my visor raised so it can pick up my voice. No clue how to tap in remotely over more conventional comms. I've tapped Gina's comm code into the device, and now I'm listening to it chirp as it makes a connection.

"Korbin," Gina answers. "That was fast. I

assume you've worked things out with your alien friend."

"Yes," I reply. Then I explain the plan to her, hoping as I do so that she's not going to veto it and insist that we rescue her daughter and bring her back to the same time that she left.

"That is the only way to save her?" Gina asks.

"It is," I confirm.

"Very well. Bring Lucia back to me here, and I will return your family to you. An even trade. Although, some would say that I'm giving two for the price of one."

Scowling angrily at the device in my hand, I have to bite my tongue to avoid rising to the bait.

"I'll be in touch soon," I say. To her, the wait would be a matter of minutes. Not a lot of suspense involved. For me, this op could easily take several days. It took nearly a full day the first time around, and I didn't have to infiltrate an alien colony back then.

"I'll be waiting," Gina replies. "Don't let me down Korbin. I *will* kill them if you fail. Or perhaps I'll find a more creative fate for Callista. She's a valuable commodity, after all. It would be a shame to let all that potential go to waste."

I end the connection with an angry stab of my thumb.

A hand lands on my shoulder, squeezing gently. The advanced haptics in the suit makes it feel almost like I'm not wearing armor at all. "She's just stoking you up," Pixie whispers.

"Maybe," I agree. But something tells me it's not a bluff. Not with someone like Gina Keri. She said it herself, back when she was pretending to be Aurora: human trafficking is one of the Solaris Cartel's main enterprises. Gina wouldn't bat an eye before selling Cally as a slave.

The alien comm unit chirps and vibrates subtly in my hand, turning blue. I touch the top of it to answer the call, and Alpha's voice comes rumbling through it.

"I'm about to open the rift. Are you ready?"

"We're taking off now," I reply, setting the comm unit on a flat part of the dash.

"Standing by," Alpha replies.

Grabbing the controls of the shuttle, I notch the grav lifts up with a whirring roar, and the shuttle jumps off the glossy black deck. I turn us on the spot to face the opening of the hangar and the hellish red swirls of Icarus below. I nudge the main throttle up gently, sending us roaring out into space.

It only takes a minute to maneuver us into position above the hollow center of the toroidal station.

"Ready," I say.

"Opening the rift now..." Alpha replies.

The inner circumference of the station shimmers brightly, and then a glossy bubble of distorted space-time appears, growing swiftly larger from the center of the station. Little eddies and swirls appear within the bubble, along with flickers and flashes of light.

"That doesn't look safe," Pixie mutters.

"What do you care?" Kraug asks from where he stands behind his empty chair in the back of the cockpit. "You die here, and you'll just come back in a new body. If you haven't already."

He's referring to the fact that some bots have a system in place whereby they'll automatically resurrect if they don't check in from time to time with their resurrection centers. A lot of bios and cyborgs have the same system in place. Even I used to, back in the day when there was an even chance on any given day that I might get iced on a job. After traveling for almost a year to get here, it's a pretty good bet that Pixie has already come back in a new body.

"I'll live on in a new instance of my data," Pixie objects. "That's just as unnerving as the thought of transcending from bio to bot probably is to you."

"Then let's make sure you live long enough to re-integrate with your resurrected double," Brix suggests.

Kraug grunts at that.

The rift appears to stabilize, with the eddies and swirls smoothing out, and the flashes of light subside, leaving behind a clear, glassy sphere of distorted space suspended in the open center of the station.

"Cade," Alpha says. "You need to go now. Before any of the Priors make it through."

I slam the throttle past the stops, the thrusters roar, and our shuttle careens toward the rift.

CHAPTER 37

We cross the rift in a flash. The transition is instant and seamless. When the view clears, the stars ahead of us are painted lightly in the dark blues and purples of a nearby nebula.

"Well, that doesn't look like the Milky Way," Brix mutters.

"No," I agree, checking the sensor grid. It's teeming with unidentified gray blips. I designate them in the system as hostiles, and they all turn red.

Our cloaking shield is engaged and the thrusters are now offline, so we're invisible. Unless we do something to reveal ourselves.

A quick look at the rear screens shows the rift shrinking into oblivion behind us, leaving an unruffled patch of bluish-purple space behind us. In theory, we're still in contact with Alpha over the comms... but how? That has to be one hell of a comm unit to stretch across galaxies and forty-five years.

"Alpha?" I whisper. "You still there?"

Silence.

"Oh shit," Brix says.

"I am here, Cade."

There is a repeating echo to his voice and more than a little static, but he heard us. My chest deflates with a shaky sigh. "We're through," I reply. "I'll contact you as soon as we're on our way back."

"I'll be waiting," Alpha replies, and the echoes cut off suddenly as he ends the connection.

The glowing blue disk fades to black, and I slip it into a compartment on my belt. That done, I scan the grid for the rocky gray-green planet where I now remember finding and rescuing Gina and Aster all those years ago. It's a relief to have my missing memories back, even if the process of restoring them felt like a mauler was clawing around inside my head.

I'm relieved to find the planet right where we left it at 1.72 astronomical units from the rift that we just exited. We've arrived here barely fifteen minutes after the time that I left with Gina and Brix forty-five years ago. It's a calculated risk, coming here *after* we left. It means more time will have passed with Lucia in captivity before we arrive. The Priors could have executed her already. But Alpha assures me that they'll want to keep her and the other captives alive to study them.

I just hope he's right. If I return empty-handed, or worse, with Lucia in a proverbial body bag... I know that Gina will take it out on my family.

But there was no other way. We couldn't risk coming here earlier and accidentally bumping into ourselves. According to Alpha, an entity from the future meeting with itself in the past could have catastrophic results. Not the least of which is that the Coalition would learn, through my altered memories of the original op, about Terminus Station's potential as a time machine. They never would have accepted that we failed to destroy the facility and allowed it to fall into the Cath's hands. They'd have sent every ship they had in a desperate bid to take control of Terminus.

And then the war that I, Alpha, and the Cath have so far managed to avoid would suddenly spring into existence.

Something about all of that makes me think Alpha lied to me about time travel. Or maybe he didn't explain himself properly. The past *can* be changed. Maybe not intentionally, but we can still wreak a lot of accidental havoc, and that's deeply troubling.

What could we do here, without intending to, that might later change the course of events? I don't want to get back to the future only to find that the Priors somehow returned and conquered everyone. But maybe if we're lucky, they can't. I don't see any toroidal rift generators around here.

Pushing those concerns from my mind, I focus on the task at hand, plotting a micro-jump to the planet where Lucia is being held. The Priors could detect that jump, even with our cloaking shield engaged, but I'm hoping the shuttle's wake diffusers will keep us hidden— at least long enough for us to land somewhere close to the colony and get this scrigg's errand underway.

Time to find out.

I start spinning up the jump drive, and my hand finds the jump lever.

"Moment of truth..." Brix says as the jump timer ticks down to zero.

I slam the jump lever forward, manually engaging the drive. A flash of light tears through the viewport, and suddenly we're careening down a tunnel of swirling, multicolored starlight.

CHAPTER 38

The shuttle drops out of FTL in high orbit with a jolt and a muffled sigh from the reactor. I'm already nosing toward the planet, scanning passively for signs of the giant termite mound that is the alien colony.

The surface of this planet is deeply rippled with impossibly high gray mountains capped with snow and fissured with dark blue rivers of glacial run-off. Deep lakes pool between ranges, running further down into the planet's only ocean. Somewhere on the feathery green plains of a plateau overlooking that ocean is the Priors colony.

"There," Brix says, pointing to a big bright blip of EM radiation on our sensors. I mark the spot and pull up slightly, aiming for a shallow descent toward the distant green diamond of the waypoint I set.

No signs of pursuit yet, so I guess the jump wake diffusers did their job, muffling our signature from enemy sensors.

The Priors' fleet is still almost a full astronomical unit away, having chased my original mission from the planet, so I'm sure that also helped keep us undetected.

We hit the upper atmosphere and it begins roaring angrily around us. I'm worried about lighting up the sky like a meteor, so I compensate with grav lifts to reduce our speed and make a slower approach. The noise quickly fades to a soft whistling.

"So far so good," Brix whispers.

"Don't jinx us," Pixie growls.

I'm not superstitious, but even I'm nervous about this. If we get spotted on our way down, this mission is over and we'll be joining Gina's daughter as the Priors' captives. Assuming we aren't incinerated in the sky.

I wonder how adding our presence here would change the past. The Priors would have thought we escaped, only to discover us, or our remains, hiding in their backyard.

Pushing those thoughts away, I focus on our descent, using every possible technique I can think of to hide our approach.

At just two hundred klicks from our objective, we reach the upper layer of clouds: a thick, angry carpet of dark gray thunderheads that rolls on as far as the eye can see. It completely conceals any sign of the surface below. The shuttle's nose plunges through a thunderhead the size of a mountain just as lightning forks all around us, purpling the black sky in a dozen or more places and dazzling our eyes before hammering our eardrums with primordial explosions. Fat drops of rain streak across the cockpit canopy.

The sky is quickly growing darker as we fly toward our objective, but that has more to do with the colony being on the dark side of the planet than with the weather. The sun is busy sinking below the horizon behind us.

High winds buffet our shuttle, and soon they're tossing us around like a cork bobbing on a choppy sea.

"At least the storm should cover our approach," Kraug says.

"Will it?" I ask.

A muscle jerks in Brix's jaw and Kraug mutters a curse. They just figured out what I'm talking about.

The storm might help to cover any sight or sound of the shuttle's descent, but rain and cloaking shields don't play well together. You can transmit light and EM radiation from one side of a cloak to another, but *rain* will run right off our armor like the solid surface that it is. We'll be visible to the naked eye, if not to sensors.

"We'll have to wait for the rain to stop," Pixie decides.

"Yes," I agree. Hopefully, that won't take long.

The clouds part below us, revealing a shadowy sprawl of jagged mountain ridges and water-filled valleys. Lightning flickers down, bruising the sky before reflecting off gleaming glaciers and shadowy lakes.

The dark spire of the Priors' colony is dead ahead, a mountain in its own right, perched on a plateau above the distant black canvas of the planet's ocean.

"Do we have a name for this place?" Kraug wonders aloud.

"It's bad luck to name an uncharted world," Pixie says.

I glance over my shoulder. Kraug's frowning dubiously at her. "How's that?"

"My dad worked with a cartography guild," Pixie explains. "They always waited until *after* they left to give planets a name... lest they get stranded there."

Seems like a case of mistaken association to me. Of course, any explorers who wind up stranded on an uncharted world will eventually give the place a name, but that doesn't mean that the very act of naming it was what caused them to become stranded. Cartographers' superstitions aside, I venture a suggestion.

"How about Thanatos?"

"The Greek god of Death," Kraug mutters. "Death has a name, and it's a planet. Thanatos." He nods once, smiling. "I like it."

"Now you're just fucking with me," Pixie says.

I toss a wry smile over my shoulder. "In my defense, you make it easier than it should be." *A superstitious bot,* I think to myself. *Takes all kinds, I suppose.*

Pixie scowls, and Brix snorts and shakes his head. "Let's hope you don't prove her right."

A grim silence falls with that warning.

I'm dropping altitude quickly now as we make our final approach. The target is fifty klicks away. I'm planning to set down just beyond their perimeter, wherever that is. Hopefully, I'll be able to make that call right. I'd hate to flatten a copse of trees right beside a couple of Priors out for an evening stroll. The storm probably reduces the odds of that, but you never know with aliens. Maybe they're nocturnal with a penchant for singing in the rain.

The shadowy specter of the Priors' colony appears. No sign of lights shining out into the darkness, which probably means that they're quasi-blind burrowers used to living underground. They're used to the darkness. Either that or they're scared of the local fauna.

At one klick out, I'm hovering above a feathery field of shoulder-high grass, checking sensors for signs of threats. Besides a handful of fighter-sized ships lazily circling the top of the colony's central spire, I don't see anything. Those ships have running lights on, and they're flashing floodlights around.

Well, that settles it. The Priors aren't blind. But they don't like windows. I guess I'll figure out why once I'm inside.

"Good a spot as any," I say. "The grass is high enough to cover our approach."

"You've got that backward," Brix says. "They'll see us making lines through the foliage."

He has a damned good point. With those fighters watching from above with a bird's eye view, it won't take long to spot four snaking lines racing toward their colony.

I take a moment to scan the terrain for bald patches or trampled areas that would make for a better approach, but there aren't any. "Suggestions?" I ask, glancing back at the others.

"One of us drops the other three right on top of the target," Kraug says. "We cut a hole or sneak in behind the locals."

That's not a bad idea. If the Priors haven't seen us through our cloaking shield this far, they're not likely to spot us just because we flew the last kilometer to their colony. And it presents us with a good opportunity to get closer to the captives. That glorified termite mound looks to be readily scalable—or at least, the dome-shaped base of it is. We could crawl around on the shell until we're right on top of the captives, cut a hole, as Kraug said, and drop down right on top of them. If we use the grav boosters in our suits, we could fly right back out of that hole and into the open airlock of our shuttle. A quick, clean extraction, and no need to shoot our way out like the action heroes in a holovid.

"Let's do it," I decide.

"Who's hanging back to fly the ship?" Brix asks.

None of us volunteers. We're all former Paladins, and staying out of the action to pilot the getaway car, so to speak, is more spineless than any of us can stomach. But one of us has been more vocal about the dangers than the rest, and in lieu of a volunteer, it falls to me to assign one. "Pixie."

"What? Why me?" She sounds offended, but the way her mouth is trembling with a hint of a sheepish smile, I can tell that she's relieved.

To spare her ego, I reply, "Because Brix and I have more experience with covert insertions, and Kraug is a beast if it comes to a fight."

Pixie scowls. "And that makes me what, exactly?"

"A damn good pilot," I reply, standing up to relinquish the shuttle's controls to her.

"He's right. You're better than any of us. Quicker reactions and better at multitasking. You can juggle power levels, firing solutions, shields, and evasive flight patterns without even breaking a sweat."

Pixie accepts the compliment with a frown, taking my place behind the controls.

"Let's get down to the armory," I say, heading for the exit.

"Way ahead of you, Chief," Kraug says, reaching behind his back and un-clipping a repeating plasma blaster the size of one of my legs. He's betting heavily on us having to blast our way out through a horde of aliens.

I really hope that he's wrong.

CHAPTER 39

Armed to the proverbial gills, we're standing in the airlock, waiting for Pixie to finish bringing the shuttle into position.

I'm on edge, half-expecting to hear the thrusters roar because we've been detected and Pixie is going evasive.

But that doesn't happen. Instead, all I hear is the steady whisper of the grav lifts as we inch toward the alien spire.

My right hand grazes the butt of the sidearm that came with the suit. A semi-automatic laser pistol with a stun setting, packing fifty-six shots per charge. It's not completely alien tech, and not completely human either. Some kind of hybrid model that Alpha invented over the eons of his immortal life.

Brix went with a more typical automatic laser rifle that we used to use in the Paladins. It's spectrum shifted and mag-silenced, like our sidearms, so he can fire without revealing himself. Clipped to my back is a much heavier weapon. Not as ridiculous as Kraug's, or as concealed as Brix's, but close. With no idea what kind of personal shields or intrinsic armor the Priors' chunky blue-gray exoskeletons might provide, I went with a guided flechette cannon. The flechettes fire in a tight cone, homing in on all the designated enemy targets in sight. It's like an antique slugthrower loaded with buckshot, if the pellets were all pointy like bullets, had explosive tips, and were able to guide themselves to their targets.

It's not exactly a *legal* weapon, but neither is Kraug's plasma blaster. And Gina Keri doesn't exactly run a *legal* operation anyway.

I'm trying to wrap my head around how anything we are doing falls under the definition of *legal*. Nope, nothing except drawing breath, and under the circumstances, even that might come into question.

We aren't supposed to be here.

I remind myself, once more, why we *are* here, and refocus on the task ahead.

Besides the flechette cannon, I'm wearing a belt full of various types of grenades, and of course, the suit itself is a weapon, with its directable swarm of alien nanites.

Between all of that, we might actually be ready for anything.

"In position," Pixie whispers over the ship's intercom. We wouldn't dare to use regular comms this close to the enemy base. We're down to hand signals and tight-beam, line-of-sight contact. But preferably just hand signals.

"Have you located the hostages?" I ask while Brix and Kraug double-check the charges on their weapons.

"Affirmative. Human life signs are distinct enough from the xenos that you shouldn't have trouble tracking them, but I don't know if the sensors in your suits will be strong enough to detect them through the walls. Their locations might not update after this."

"Got it," I reply, just as a trio of blue diamonds appears on my HUD. They're almost directly below us—five *hundred* and sixty-two meters down. That puts a frown on my lips as I realize the true scale of the alien structure. It's massive. If the dome at the base of the spire is more than five hundred meters high/deep, then I can only imagine how tall the spire itself must be. No wonder it looked like a mountain. It must extend several kilometers above the rest of the structure.

"I doubt the captives will be moved before we can get to them," Brix says, adding some optimism to the equation.

"What about hostile signatures?" I ask.

"I'm not getting more than a handful... nine or ten, all near the outer edges of the colony," Pixie says. "But that doesn't mean much, since I can't do an active scan without giving the shuttle away, and they're probably not emitting any active signals, either."

Not like our people, I think to myself. Good thing they've got those neuralinks. Their brain implants are sending out steady pings, with all three of the captives having activated their emergency locators the instant they were taken hostage.

"Send us whatever hostile tracking data you have, too," I reply. "Better than nothing."

"You sure? They're gonna move around, and paying too much attention to where they *were* could give you a false sense of security."

"More information is always better than less," I reply.

"Copy that..." Pixie says.

My HUD populates with nine red-shaded silhouettes of varying sizes and locations around the outer shell of the colony. Seeing that none of them are particularly close to us, I re-focus my attention on the blue diamonds that indicate our objective and contemplate the long way down. I hope we can find a grav lift or drop tube inside. If not, five hundred meters down means one hell of a lot of stairs or winding tunnels...

"Let's execute this shit," Kraug says, grunting as he picks up our breach kit. It's a hefty two-hundred-plus pound hover crate with handles on the sides that's meant to be maneuvered in zero-G, and usually by more than one person. We can't use the crate's grav generator, since it's not emission-shielded like our shuttle. We'd be lighting ourselves up on the Priors' sensors.

Down here on Thanatos, that crate must be even heavier than usual, since gravity is a little higher than standard, at 1.21 Earth G's —according to the readings from my suit. Of course, Kraug being a massive cyborg, probably thinks it's light. And our suits are strength-enhanced, woven with synthetic fibers that move dynamically with our muscles to make us both stronger and faster. The net effect is that I actually feel lighter than I would in standard gravity without the suit, but I can still feel my heart working harder than usual. Unfortunately, there's no way to aid the blood flow unless you're a bot like Pixie or a Cyborg like Kraug.

"Stand by for my signal," I say, stepping to the outer doors of the airlock. Brix and Kraug appear on either side of me. I nod to Brix, and he inclines his helmet to me.

"Activate cloaking shields," I say to them.

Our armor shimmers and turns a translucent green, indicating that we are now invisible to the naked eye and most types of sensors—occlusion scanners and their alien equivalents aside.

I can still see the human-tech weapons clamped to our backs, and the breach kit in Kraug's hands, but in a matter of just a few seconds, the translucent green overlay flows over them like water. That's the alien nanites from our suits, spreading out and forming a thin layer on top of the ordinary alloys and composites below.

Incredible. If the Coalition or the Alliance were ever to discover and harness this tech, I'd hate to see what would become of the business of war—or crime for that matter.

"We're ready," I say.

The doors spring open, revealing the outer *crust* of the alien colony below. The surface is porous and rocky-looking, nearly black, and almost exactly the consistency of the giant termite mound that I likened it to. Pixie has us hovering just a few feet above the colony, so we step right out of the airlock, and perch precariously on the gently sloping dome. The central spire is about fifty feet away. We're invisible, but I'm still reassured by the absence of any windows, doors, balconies, or viewports.

Kraug gets the breach kit settled on top of the dome, and Pixie moves the shuttle until it's directly overhead. We gather around the breach kit, using our bodies and cloaking armor to shield what's going to happen next. The breach kit begins sputtering with muted blue fire around the edges as it cuts a hole in the rocky material beneath our feet. My breath catches in my throat at the sight of that. This is a calculated risk. No way to hide the emissions other than to stand in front of them and hope for the best. Breach kits are designed to be as quiet and inconspicuous as possible, but it's still possible to detect the heat signature.

My gaze snaps up, staring straight through the transparent green overlay that covers our shuttle, to the alien fighters flying in lazy circles around the spire above us. They're still sweeping their floodlights around the perimeter below. If one of them sees something and comes to investigate, they could fire off drones for a closer look. Or even deploy their version of occlusion scanners to check it out. A vision flashes through my mind's eye of tiny alien drones splashing over us like a wave and lighting us up on enemy grids...

CHAPTER 40

The breach kit stops sputtering, and Kraug signals that it's done, then looks to me, waiting for my command. I nod once, and he triggers the hatch. The top of the breach kit parts and a hazy blue buzz shield appears to keep in whatever alien mix of air they've got inside this place. Can't assume it's the same atmosphere and pressure as we have out here. But that shield is releasing even more emissions that we can't hide. Kraug peeks over the opening, then gives us the all-clear. I signal for him to take point, and he lowers himself deftly through the hatch. My eyes are still on the sky, tracking those alien fighters as I usher Brix through ahead of me.

Still no reaction from up above.

Maybe our shuttle is enough to hide the signature.

Hurrying to the hatch, I peek over it—into a dark, cavernous space below, that's only vaguely illuminated with a dim, purplish light. Grabbing the edges of the opening, I swing my legs over and then let go, activating my grav boots to buffer the landing, and mentally triggering the hatch shut in my wake. With the hatch shut, the breach kit is once again cloaked by the layer of nanites from our suits, and the buzz shield vanishes as soon as it's no longer needed to hold in the air. Before my feet have even touched the ground, my sidearm has cleared the holster, and I'm sweeping it around. Brix and Kraug stand to either side of me with their heavier primary weapons drawn and aimed.

A quick visual and passive scan of the area reveals no sign of hostiles, but we're in a long, winding corridor or tunnel of some kind, which means we could be standing in a high-traffic area without even knowing it. The tunnel almost looks natural, like this could be a lava flue, with the walls made of the same porous rock as we cut through on the outside. But the floor is different, padded like a shag carpet with a spongy black material.

The surfaces in here are all glistening as if wet, and that dim mauve lighting is coming from luminescent crystalline veins marbled throughout the walls and ceiling, yet curiously, not the floor.

I lift one foot and notice that the flattened imprint of my boot, which sank in about half an inch, is rebounding very slowly.

"I'm getting life signs from it," Kraug says

over tight-beam comms. He nods to the fading footprint that I'm still staring at.

He's right. I'm getting them, too. Not a pulse, or anything that obvious, but the carpet is made of organic compounds, and it's giving off chemical signatures that are consistent with respiration. This carpet, living or not, is responsible for maintaining the atmosphere inside. It's like the spongy pads of moss growing on rocks back in a forest on Earth, but more uniformly distributed.

"This shit's gonna give us away," Brix mutters. My footprint is *still* fading but almost gone now. I realize it takes about a minute to completely disappear, so if someone happens to be a minute behind us, they'll not only know that we're here, they'll be able to follow us with ease.

"Let's pick up the pace," I say. "Keep comms to essential only." By way of example, I resort to hand signals, indicating my visor with two fingers and flipping them around to point at the ground ahead of us. Both Kraug and Brix nod, having got the message. *We need to keep an eye out for* alien *prints.* The spongy floor is both a liability and an advantage. We can use it in conjunction with our sensors to gain advance warning of any hostiles up ahead. And that's a big relief because the passive scanners in our suits are doing a shit-poor job of seeing through these walls. I'm not picking up a single alien signature so far, but I happen to know the shuttle detected at least nine of them in here.

I don't want to think about what that means for our chances of reaching the captives without being detected.

The corridor winds down, and around, and then down some more. Every so often there are these puckered black orifices that look like... well, not pretty, anyway. Passive scans indicate more corridors and chambers behind them.

But no sign of actual Priors occupying those spaces.

"What's with all the biotech?" Kraug mutters over tight-band as we pass another puckered doorway.

"Can the chatter," I snap.

"The place is deserted, Chief," Brix adds, gesturing off-handedly to the gentle curve of the tunnel and the unblemished carpet of alien moss ahead of us.

He's right, but I don't trust it.

"All the same. Maintain comm silence."

We continue down, with me and Brix on point and Kraug bringing up the rear. We're getting farther away from the captives, even though we're gradually going down. Realizing how long it could take us to reach them at this rate, I decide to take a calculated risk.

Calling a halt, I drop to my haunches and place a hand against the wall. Activating one of the sensors in my suit, I detect pulses of low-frequency infrasonic sound waves through the structure. Moments later, a shaded-blue outline of the facility appears with waves of ever-brighter, crisper, and farther-reaching details. The longer I hold my hand against the wall, the better the schematic gets, with my suit constructing the imagery from the echoes of those vibrations. But I'm also risking that something detects the epicenter of the sound waves, so I remove my hand after just a few seconds.

I beam the scan over to Brix and Kraug, and all three of us spend a moment studying it while keeping half an eye on both ends of the tunnel.

"Looks like there's some kind of vertical shaft through there," I say, pointing to a puckered black doorway up ahead and to our right.

Signaling for them to follow, I creep steadily toward the portal. The door doesn't open with my approach, and I don't see any control surfaces or likely-looking trigger points. No sign of hostiles beyond or anywhere nearby, so I'm not too worried about blasting through with mag-silenced lasers, but maybe there's a better way.

I try forcing it open at the center by pushing the barrel of my pistol through—

The membrane swiftly dilates, folding away into a baggy, wrinkled ring.

"Oh, that's gross," Kraug gasps.

"Now you know what it's like to be a piece of shit," Brix mutters.

I really wish he hadn't put such a fine point

on it, but he's right. It's like we're navigating the bowels of some disgustingly obese alien monster.

Beyond the door is a roughly circular chamber with small black pools of water spaced evenly around the floor, and one larger one in the center. The pools are glowing with the same purplish light from the veins in the rocky tunnels, but it's brighter below the water. Signaling caution to the others, I lead the way toward the nearest pool and aim my weapon in. It seems to go down endlessly, and the schematic I constructed earlier confirms it: each of these circular pools is a long drop, straight down through crystal clear water. The schematic shows other tunnels branching off them, some hooking upward, or down, and terminating in large open spaces. This is what I've been looking for: the Priors' equivalent of an elevator. Just one problem. It's flooded. And we didn't bring any oxygen tanks for our esteemed captives.

"This isn't going to work on the way back up," Brix says.

"No," I agree, busy tracking one of these nine water-logged tunnels down to a point that's almost directly beside our objective. "But it's going to get us there." Our exosuits have a good nine hours of air left, so it's no problem for us to go underwater.

"You think we're dealing with an aquatic species?" Kraug muses.

I know why he's asking. We haven't seen the Priors yet. And there might be a good reason for that: maybe we haven't entered their real habitat yet.

I remember those gill-like mouths and beards of tentacles that I saw in my holo files, and I realize that's exactly what the Priors are. But I doubt they're strictly aquatic. "Amphibian," I decide. Which means we have to watch our backs everywhere. "Ready for the dive?" I ask, turning to regard each of them.

They both nod.

"We'll have to go headfirst. Doesn't look like a lot of room to maneuver once we're inside." Which of course means we won't be able to turn around and swim back out if we run into trouble.

I nod back and lead them over to the particular tunnel that I tracked all the way down to the captives.

"You know, Korbin…" Brix begins, "When I joined the Templars, you really should've warned me about spelunking in alien intestines. A heads-up woulda been nice. Might want to think about it for new recruits."

I can't see Brix's expression through his helmet or his cloaking shield, but I can tell he's grinning like a wraith. He's secretly enjoying this. It's probably been a while since he's been out on a real mission—always hanging back to run things at the Shroud.

"At least, they won't see our footprints in the

water," Kraug says.

He makes a good point.

But if they evolved any even halfway decent senses in whatever primordial soup they crawled out of, the Priors are going to *feel* us coming in the water currents. And they might even smell us, too.

Somewhere I read once that a shark can smell a drop of blood in the water from over a mile away. Imagine that. I wonder what the Priors can do?

Not wanting to give it too much thought, I unconsciously draw in a deep breath. "Let's do this," I say, letting it out shakily. And then I put my hands together, holding my pistol out like a spear gun ahead of me, and dive headfirst into the tunnel.

CHAPTER 41

I'm swimming down and down into the endless amethyst depths of the tunnel. No sign of hostiles swimming up toward us or in from the adjoining corridors as we pass them. It's not getting any darker along the way, and the suit is protecting me from the changes in pressure. But the weight of the water above me is still pressing heavily on my mind.

We've gone down about a hundred meters already, with four hundred and change left to go, and that's a very long way to come back up, with no clear path for the ascent. If we're extraordinarily lucky, the captives will still be safely ensconced in whatever pressure suits they used to leave their shuttle. But doubts are busy crowding my mind: I recall that the first shuttle and its crew of three from Terminus Station were already missing for a week when I arrived. There's no way the air in their suits lasted that long unless they took filtration equipment that they could use to recharge their tanks from the available mix of gases down here. Possible, but... would the Priors have let them keep the very equipment that they would need to escape? It seems more likely that they would have picked a hermetic chamber that they could adjust to the needs of their prisoners.

We came prepared for this, of course, bringing spare air masks with compact liquid air tanks stuffed into the storage compartments on our belts. The air on this planet isn't breathable to us, nor is it breathable in the corridors above this water-logged labyrinth, which I suspected even if I couldn't verify until we got inside, so we knew to come prepared with air supplies for the prisoners.

But here's what we didn't foresee: the need to bring complete pressure suits for the captives. It's one thing to bring a portable air mask in a pouch on your gun belt, quite another to completely insulate someone from the intense pressures inside a very deep volume of water. Ascending from a depth of five hundred meters will force us to go up very slowly, taking incessant breaks along the way to decompress. Even then, I'm not sure that the three people we came to rescue would survive. It's even worse on a planet like Thanatos with higher than standard gravity.

So, we need a dry route to come back up, and so far I haven't found one. Granted, I haven't studied the entire schematic, but our chances of getting out are not looking good right now.

These concerns are interrupted by a big, darting shadow swimming across the tunnel ahead of me. I immediately freeze up, twitching my wrists slightly to track the target.

The alien is naked. No sign of a weapon. But if its sheer size and rippling muscles are anything to go by, it can probably rip me apart with its bare hands. This creature makes Kraug look like a light-weight.

Somehow the images I saw in my missing memories failed to convey how physically impressive the Priors are.

It's there and gone in a second; no sign that it detected us floating invisibly above it. I think I spotted fins along its back and its arms and legs. It probably has webbed feet and hands, too.

I wait a full minute to make sure it doesn't come swimming back the other way—and to be sure that it was alone—before continuing down the tunnel.

The next two hundred meters are completely uneventful, leaving me to wonder what that means. Maybe the shuttle failed to detect more than a handful of Priors down here because the colony is abandoned. Or maybe the colony isn't finished yet. Or the colonists have yet to arrive.

Whatever the case, I'm glad we're not running into Priors at every turn. It gives me hope that we'll have time to find another way back.

The final stretch of the dive goes by in just a few minutes. We cross half a dozen adjoining corridors, but don't run into any more Priors.

That's a damn good sign as far as I'm concerned. But where does this tunnel end?

I get my first clue when I hit the bottom only to find that the passage curves sharply back up the way we came, forcing us to ascend. About forty meters later, we emerge in a dry chamber like the one we entered above.

No Priors here either, but plenty of other tunnel entrances, so we can't afford to stick around. This is some kind of transit hub, which means it's going to be busier than the other parts of the colony.

After crawling out onto the spongy black ground, I kneel beside the opening and help Brix and Kraug clamber out. Soon the three of us are all standing with our primary weapons drawn. This time I'm going with the flechette cannon. We're out of time for subtlety.

I turn and point directly toward the three blue overlays of our objectives, which are now, finally, at the same level as us, and just on the other side of the curving rock walls of this chamber. My sensors are giving me a live read on them, too, and the blue diamonds have been replaced with accurate shading that accurately corresponds to each of them and their sizes and postures. Two ordinary-looking men and a young woman. All three of them are lying down, not moving. That sends a chill down my spine, but my sensors aren't reading them as dead. Maybe they're just sleeping...

We hurry to the puckered doorway in the transit hub and push through into a corridor with another door directly in front of us. This one looks even nastier than the others: thicker and puffier like it's diseased or inflamed. But I have a feeling that just means this door is reinforced. Pushing into the center of it gives a different response. The barrier clenches up like a fist.

"We might have to blow this one open," I mutter to the others.

"With pleasure," Kraug replies. Brix and I step back as he levels his plasma blaster at the living barricade.

"Watch for collateral damage," Brix says, quickly tracing a circle between the three captives on the other side.

Kraug nods tightly, plants his feet wide and grabs the massive rifle in both hands. I notice he's aiming off to one side to avoid splashing the prisoners with fire or scalding debris.

He pulls the trigger, and a blinding stream of discrete plasma packets stutters out, slamming into the barrier and drawing actual screams of agony from the living doorway.

It bursts into flames and shrivels away from the assault, dribbling fat blobs of flaming meat on the spongy floor.

An opening appears, big enough for us to squeeze through. "Go, go, go!" I shout to Kraug.

And then he's through. I barge in after him with Brix on my heels—

To see another door just like the one we blasted through a moment ago. "Looks like an airlock, Chief," Brix says.

"What do you wanna do here?" Kraug asks.

"Blast it. They'll have to hold their breath until we can hand out the masks."

"The air in here could be toxic," Brix says.

"Sensors didn't flag anything," I reply.

"Our sensors aren't calibrated to detect every possible threat. The effect of exposure to alien pathogens is unknown."

I'm shaking my head. "Even if it *is* an issue, they're probably already contaminated. We can scan and treat in the shuttle's med bay."

"Copy," Kraug says. He pulls the trigger again, incinerating the second doorway and drawing another wail of agony from whatever creature is responsible for these doorways in the alien colony. That leaves me to wonder how it's making the sound, but there's no time to figure it out.

I'm the first one through the door. I deactivate my cloaking shield and activate my external speakers at the same time to assure these three that we're friendlies.

I needn't have bothered. The three of them are

lying in a raised pool of water, floating on their backs, with some type of glossy black octopus wrapped around their heads and faces. Fat, venous trunks of flesh trail from each of those octopuses to a lumpy mound of flesh floating between them in the middle of the pool.

"What in Deus's name is that?" Brix whispers, aiming his rifle at it.

It looks a bit like a giant brain to me. But something about the setup makes me think it could be a biological version of a computer. Those trunks leading to each of the captives are like bundles of wires. The fleshy tentacled things covering their faces are keeping them fed and breathing, otherwise, my sensors would be reading three *dead* humans in front of me right now.

"How do we get them out of there?" Kraug asks.

"Only one way to find out," I say, striding purposefully toward the pool. Clamping the flechette cannon to my back, I reach for the small black handle of a plasma blade and flick it on. A bright nine-inch orange beam of fire crackles to life above the hilt, washing my armor with heat.

CHAPTER 42

I vault over the raised edges of the pool, which turns out to be relatively shallow, at least around the edges where I am. Wading out, I pick one of the two male researchers—just in case. Grabbing the thick trunk of flesh in my free hand, I lift it from underneath, bringing as much of it out of the water as I can. Damn, it's heavy. At least as thick as one of my thighs, but at about ten meters long, this tentacle is a beast all on its own, let alone the horrific bulk that it's tied to.

I hesitate, waiting for a reaction from the mountain of flesh in the center of the pool.

Nothing.

Okay. Here goes.

I plunge the blade in, slicing straight through in one clean stroke.

The pool floods with a gout of ink-black blood, and the brain-monster begins to thrash. The severed tentacle washes me with blood, and I hear a shrill cry from the beast.

Massive waves heave toward me, shoving me violently back against the edge of the pool. Water sloshes over the side and a giant alien stands up on four even thicker tentacles than the ones it had attached to the human captives.

The thinner appendages release the other two captives, and they immediately begin thrashing and gasping for air, but I don't have the luxury of wading over to give them the air masks we brought.

One of the small tentacles lashes out and smacks me in the chest. The hand in the center spreads out and wraps around my torso with surprising force before yanking up and tossing me straight into the air. The ceiling of the cavern is a good thirty feet up, and I cross the gap in an instant, slamming into the rocky ceiling with enough force to make my ears ring inside my helmet. And then I feel myself beginning to fall, my arms and legs thrashing for something solid to arrest my momentum. An involuntary scream tears from my lips before I remember to engage the grav boosters in my suit. I make a controlled landing and draw my flechette cannon.

Kraug is already pounding the monster with plasma fire, and Brix is firing a steady crimson stream of high-powered lasers at it. The beast is somehow absorbing it all, losing giant, flaming chunks of flesh in the process, but it's not dying as fast as I need it to.

Worse yet, the beast's mindless thrashing is

putting Lucia and her two colleagues at risk.

One of the two male captives makes it to the edge of the pool and begins scrambling out—

Only to get seized from behind by a tentacle, and hoisted high into the air.

Taking barely a second to aim, I fire a booming burst of tracking flechettes at that tentacle. They pepper the meaty appendage with explosions, severing it with another gout of black blood. The man falls twenty feet, screaming and flopping around like an idiot before his screams are cut off with a smack and he lies still, face-down and floating.

Lucia is thankfully smarter than that. She's wading away from the monster as slowly and gently as she can, hoping to avoid drawing its attention.

Kraug cries out in alarm as a giant leg tentacle bursts out of the water and smacks the plasma blaster from his hands.

Brix ducks another swipe that's aimed at him.

I spring off the ground to do the same, using grav boosters to fly—

And firing flechettes steadily at center mass.

They're homing in and exploding, pocking the lumpy hide of the creature with bloody black holes. And then it rears up to greet me, revealing what's hiding underneath: a vast, sucking maw with concentric rings of teeth, and a dark ring of what might be eyes around that.

It's going to swallow me whole.

I instruct my nanites to go to work, sending streams of them straight for the eyes. The monster lets out a resonant shriek but doesn't back down. Tentacles lash out, wrapping around me with enough force to squeeze the air from my lungs, even through the suit. It's pulling me in steadily.

Firing flechettes straight into the throat, I'm gratified to see a series of bloody explosions preceding me down the gullet of the monster.

And then I'm surrounded by gnashing teeth, and I lose my grip on the rifle. I hear the power cell overloading with a *pop.* My suit will be next, cracking open like an egg...

Sharp spears of fire come grinding through, piercing me all over. Damage alerts spring up on my HUD, the warnings scrolling steadily...

And I realize that I'm not going to live through this. And that means Cally and Aurora are as good as dead, too.

CHAPTER 43

I can feel my mind fading, growing hazy for lack of oxygen...

And then, suddenly, the grinding pressure disappears and I'm falling free...

Only to land with a mighty splash. And a much bigger one slamming down behind me. I feel a massive weight sinking above me, and barely manage to kick my way free before it drags me down and pins me to the bottom of the pool.

More splashing as I swim for the edge of the pool. I suck in a few ragged gasps from my suit's air supply and set the suit to work sealing off holes and making repairs with the nanites that supply the adaptive and regenerative features of the armor.

I can even feel the suit tightening up around my injuries to slow the blood loss and keep me alive. As soon as I feel solid ground beneath my feet, I burst out of the water and cast about quickly to get my bearings.

Kraug is wading out of the water right behind me with two blazing orange plasma swords, one in each hand. The three-foot blades retract into the hilts and he clips them back to his belt. "You're welcome," he says.

I nod my thanks and check on our captives. To my relief, Brix is busy tending to Lucia where she sits on the edge of the pool, and she's already wearing one of the air masks that we brought. But the two male researchers are both lying motionless in the water. My sensors read both of them as dead. The one I cut free never came back to consciousness, and the severed octopus hand is still clamped over his face. Did he suffocate with that thing attached to his face?

I push down a wave of guilt with a grimace. There was no way I could know that he wouldn't wake up when I cut the proverbial cord.

Running over to Brix and Lucia, I catch her eye and say, "We need to get you out of here. Do you happen to know of a way up that doesn't involve ascending through half a klick of flooded tunnels?"

She nods quickly. "The way we came in. I can show you."

I almost sigh with relief. "Great. Brix, you take point. I've got Lucia."

"Copy that," Brix says.

"How do you know my name?" Lucia asks as I grab her by the arm and yank her to her feet.

"Long story," I reply. "Your mother sent us to

rescue you."

"My *mother?*" Lucia sounds confused. "Then you're not the Paladins who were coming to evacuate us from Terminus?"

"Yes and no," I reply. "Come on!" I tug at Lucia's arm to catch up with Brix and Kraug.

"Wait! What about..." She trails off, staring at her dead colleagues. Based on the crimson stain that surrounded the one who's lying face down in the water, it appears that he bled out, which means it wasn't the fall that killed him. Those tentacled octopus hands must have spikes or teeth in them somewhere.

"They're gone," I snap at her. "You need to worry about yourself right now."

Lucia nods once, her blue eyes wide and frightened.

"Korbin! We need to bug out, *now!*" Kraug booms from the doors we came in by. "We've got incoming!"

Not bothering to keep a low profile, I run an active scan as I head for the doors. I'm getting shaded signatures all over the place now. Hundreds of oversized amphibians are running or swimming down toward us from surrounding tunnels.

I race out behind Brix and Kraug just as half a dozen Priors come boiling through the door of the transit hub directly opposite this chamber.

Kraug sprays them with plasma and Brix adds a stream of lasers, sending them scattering back into cover.

"This way!" Lucia cries, racing out ahead of Brix.

"Slow down!" I shout at her, but she's not listening. Cursing between gritted teeth, I burst after her in a loping sprint, doing my best to ignore the sharp pangs and buckling muscles in my wounded legs. A wave of nausea and dizziness comes over me, but I push through and shake my head to clear it.

Having lost my rifle in the belly of the beast, I draw my sidearm instead. Pulling slightly ahead of Lucia, I scan for signs of hostiles ahead of us. "Get behind me!" I snap at her, gasping from the pain more than exertion.

Lucia favors me with a frown. "Do *you* know the way out?"

"So give me directions! You're not wearing armor. I am."

"Lot of good it did you," Lucia quips, obviously having noticed how I'm limping and struggling to keep up with her.

Teenagers are the worst. I bet Lucia and Cally could share notes on the finer points of sarcasm.

I can hear Brix and Kraug hanging back, laying down booming volleys of covering fire. Tossing a look over my shoulder, I'm just in time to see multiple flashes of plasma grenades going off. That puts a raging wall of flames between us and our pursuit. Taking the chance, both Brix and Kraug turn and come running. Together we dash around the corner. Lucia points up ahead to another puffy black door like the one that guarded her chamber.

"Through there!"

"Are you sure?" I demand, wondering how she could have come in through that door without burning it to slag like we did.

"Yes, I'm sure! That's the way they brought us in," she replies.

So they didn't blunder in here like the naive scriggs that I took them for. They were captured and then brought inside. Better, but not by much. They never should have landed here in the first place. As soon as they realized they'd made contact with an advanced alien race they should have turned tail and burned like hell back the way they came. Sure would have saved me a lot of trouble if they had.

"How much further?" I ask Lucia as we reach the barrier.

"Not far," she replies.

"But we're still underground!" Brix objects while aiming his rifle back the way we came, checking for signs of pursuit.

"He's right," I put in. "The dome is only about a hundred meters high. We went down five hundred and sixty before we found you."

"So where are we going to get out?" Brix asks. "In hell?"

"After this, that would be a vacation," Lucia says. "It comes out at the base of the cliff. Those flooded tunnels you were navigating? They're fed by natural spring water and they lead to the planet's ocean. That's where the Priors spend most of their time, hunting in schools like packs of sharks."

Kraug ignores us, hefting his rifle at the door and swapping out the depleted power cell for a fresh one. "Brace for contact," he warns. "Hostiles on the other side."

"Copy," Brix says.

Running a fresh scan, I see what he means. A wall of six Priors, standing in a row about fifty meters from the door and blocking the exit.

"Get yourself into cover," I snap at Lucia, giving her a shove toward a rocky corner on the left side of the door. Kraug aims for the right at an angle that should avoid putting him in the line of fire as soon as the door starts peeling open.

"We good to go?" he asks.

"Light it up!" I reply.

A stream of plasma turns the door into a shrieking, shriveling husk. It peels away from the right edge, and the first of the Priors blocking our way come into view. I pop off a couple of lasers at full power, aiming for his head, but these guys are armored with bulky crystalline suits. My shots bounce off, seeming to splinter as they refract harmlessly into hundreds of smaller beams.

And then the Priors are shooting back, and a

flickering violet stream of lasers catches Kraug in the side. He spins out of the line of fire and plasters himself against the wall. Brix fires back, shooting as he runs, but his shots are splintering like mine did, and drawing bright flashes of light whenever they don't. It's some combination of refractive armor and energy shields. I duck out of the line of fire after Brix and catch a glancing beam across my hip. The suit's shield deflects it, but drops from a hundred percent to seventy-two, leaving me to wonder what a direct hit might have done.

A quick look at Kraug's smoking armor gives me an idea.

"Now what, Chief?" he gasps through the pain. For a cyborg to have overloaded his pain regulation implants, it's got to be bad.

"Use the nanites," I suggest. "No sense risking our necks on this."

"Nanites?" Lucia asks.

Glittering black streams flow out from us. I hear alien chitters and screeches as they call out in alarm at the sight of it. I wonder if they know what it is. After all, it was the ascended branch of their own species that invented the swarm.

Guiding the nanites onward, I pull up a visual from mine so that I can properly watch the confrontation. Several of the Priors are firing directly into the swarm to little or no effect. One of the others comes running out to greet our attack, shrieking like a witch.

Once he's halfway to the swarm, the others stop firing and drop to the floor, curling their armored bodies around each other, facing away from the runner.

A queasy flood of apprehension explodes in the pit of my stomach. "Pull them back!" I shout at the others.

"What?" Brix asks.

"Now!"

The swarm reverses course, but it's too late. The shrieking Prior dives straight into the thick of it. A split second later, his armor glows as bright as the sun, and a scalding wave of fire billows through the damaged door, incinerating what's left of it. Lucia cries out in alarm and pain and flees from the heat. But she's not on fire, so it's probably just a nasty sunburn.

As for the swarm—

Our nanites were vaporized by the blast.

Realizing we've got nothing to lose, I activate the comms. "Pixie! We're at the bottom of the cliff. We're pinned down and could really use some air support."

No reply.

I look to Brix. Kraug is sagging against the wall, curling over his wounded side and looking like he's just a few seconds from passing out.

Brix gives his head a slight shake. "Looks like we're on our own, Chief."

"Wait," I reply.

It's one thing to intercept a comm signal;

you can do that on a cloaked ship without giving yourself away, but actively transmitting is another matter, and Pixie has strict orders to stay hidden.

"Here they come..." Kraug warns in a gritty whisper. He aims his plasma blaster one-handed at the opening, waiting for them to come into his line of fire. The barrel is wavering back and forth drunkenly. Good luck hitting anything like that.

"Contact rear!" Brix roars just as my audio pickups detect a flurry of armored footfalls coming up behind us. We don't have any cover from that direction. Plucking grenades at random from my belt, I wind up and toss them one after another. They roll and bounce around the corner, then explode with flickering booms of plasma, shrapnel, and EMP pulses and waves of stun darts. Brix tosses a few of his own, while Kraug lays down a haphazard stream of fire to hold off the advancing soldiers from the front.

My sensor overlays show the Priors dropping and curling their bodies over each other to weather the assaults, just like they did when their suicide bomber went *boom.*

About ten seconds later Kraug's rifle clicks dry. "I'm out!" he roars.

And I toss my last grenade with a lackluster *pop,* unleashing a wave of stun darts that don't have a prayer of making it through the Priors' armor.

"They'll take us alive!" Lucia calls out into the

ringing silence that follows.

I frown inside my helmet, wondering how that's any better.

"Then what?" I ask.

"Then you'll wish they hadn't," she says with her eyes tearing up and her face contorting miserably. "Shoot me. *Please.*" She comes walking unsteadily toward me, heedless of passing into the enemy's line of fire.

"The hell I will!" I snap, and burst out of cover, slamming her back into the deck. "What the fuck is wrong with you?"

Lucia shakes her head, blinking tears and flinging them away with her hands. "You wouldn't ask me that if you were the one who was captured a week ago."

The heavy cadence of rushing footsteps returns, and I know it's game over.

We're done. We failed. And I know what that means for my family.

If that isn't bad enough, Lucia's grim warnings are starting to make me fear for myself for the first time since Cally was abducted.

"If you're not going to do it, I will," Lucia growls. And with that, she lunges for my weapon.

CHAPTER 44

I manage to jerk the gun away a split second before she pushes my finger against the trigger. A bright red laser screeches out into the wall beside her head, leaving a smoking black scorch mark that narrowly missed burning a hole through her eye.

I recoil from her and turn the gun on the approaching soldiers behind us. They've stopped in a row behind us, blocking the way back. Their heads are almost brushing the ceiling where it curves down to meet the walls, which makes me think they must be almost nine feet tall.

Brix comes backing over to me, his rifle aimed at them, but not daring to pull the trigger. Not like our lasers ever did anything to them anyway. We should have grabbed plasma blasters like Kraug.

Brix lets out a shaky breath. "Chief, if you've got some top-secret plan to turn the tables here, now would be a damn fine time to put me out of my suspense."

Kraug tosses a plasma grenade to give the soldiers on the other side something to think about, but I can see their red-shaded silhouettes wading right through the blast, evidently no longer scared of what we can do to them. Whatever that armor is that they're wearing, it's stupidly strong.

Running out of ideas, I thrust my hands up above my head. "Okay. We surrender. Let's just talk. You want something from us? Information?"

"What makes you think they speak Human?" Kraug asks. He means *Versal,* but I get the point.

"They do," Lucia whispers. "They were studying us."

I look sharply at her. "Why?"

"Why do you think?" she snaps back at me.

One of the Priors behind us steps forward, signaling to the others. It utters a sequence of shrill chirps and wails that remind me vaguely of a whale song from Earth.

I wait patiently for the translation, grateful that this is working. I've bought some time. Now I just have to figure out what to do with it.

The translation never comes. Instead, I hear booming reports echoing behind me and turn to see all five remaining Priors vanish in quick succession. Another superheated shockwave makes Lucia yelp, and a fat red laser sneaks through the ruined doorway, slamming straight into the Prior who addressed me on the other side. He disintegrates into flaming chunks, and the others scatter, shrieking, falling against the walls and the spongy floor in their haste to take cover.

Realizing that blast must have come from a starship, I burst into action, yanking Lucia into my arms, and sprinting for the exit. Brix is right behind me, and Kraug struggles to keep up, limping and favoring his wounded side.

I hesitate, giving him a chance to catch up. My overlays reveal that the remaining Priors behind us have recovered from their fright and they're giving chase.

We're not going to make it if we have to wait for Kraug.

"Go!" he booms at me. "I'll slow them down." Turning back the other way, he draws his plasma swords again and ignites them with a flick of each thumb. Dashing into the cover of the ruined door, he waits to ambush them.

"Korbin!" Brix thunders. "We have to go!"

There's a lump in my throat the size of a wraith egg, making it impossible to muster a verbal reply. This is the second time Kraug is saving my life, and it will be the last.

Sprinting after Brix, I meet him at the final door. It's been blown open, revealing a dark, violent ocean that's busy scraping the rocky beach raw with frothing twenty-foot waves.

And nothing else.

"Where is she?!" I ask as I barrel out of the doorway and down a dusty path. I *do* spot a Javelin-class shuttle in the distance, landed, and not cloaked, about two hundred feet away, down the left side of the beach.

"There! We can take mine!" Lucia suggests.

I don't like our odds running all that way across open ground, with no cover between us and our pursuers, but if we have no choice—

A doorway shimmers and opens directly in front of me, cutting off that thought.

"Get in, you scriggs!" Pixie cries over our shared comms.

I don't need to be told twice. Using the grav boosters in my armor, I leap across the intervening space. Brix lands in the airlock right behind me, and then the doors thump shut, and I hear grav lifts whistling sharply as Pixie pushes them to the max to get us out of here.

Setting Lucia on her feet, I wave the inner doors open and sprint up the ramp to the command deck of the shuttle. My injuries are feeling better now. Not sure if I should thank what's left of the nanites in my suit for that, but whatever the case, I'll take the win.

I land in the co-pilot's chair beside Pixie, breathing hard. Feeling suffocated by the can on my head, I twist it off and suck in a breath of mercifully clean air that isn't tainted with the sour tang of my own sweat and blood. She fixes me with an angry look. "Where's Kraug?"

Before I can answer, Brix and Lucia come stumbling in. "He gave us the chance we needed to escape."

She spares a glance at the sensors and her eyes flash brightly. "He's still alive!" Pixie shrieks.

My gaze snaps to the grid, and I notice that she's right. There's a *live* human signature behind us, and it's surrounded by alien ones. No sign of weapons' fire, so he must be subdued or out cold. Lucia was right. They wanted to take us *alive*.

"They'll torture him in ways you can't even imagine," Lucia whispers. "And soon they'll know everything that he does."

Pixie's jaw grows slack. "What? Why would they *torture* him?"

"I don't know!" Lucia cries.

"Well, fuck that," I growl. "Get out of the pilot's seat."

Pixie jumps up and I take her place.

"What are you doing?" Brix asks.

I yank the flight yoke to the side, banking back around until the dark, frothing canvas of the ocean takes the place of stars and sky. The storm must have passed while we were inside the colony.

I drop back down to the same level as the shattered opening at the base of the cliffs, then prime an AP rocket, and give it Kraug's tracking data to lock onto.

"They could detect us if you—"

I pull the trigger before he can convince me

otherwise, and a small tracking warhead goes scudding out on a bright ribbon of propellant. I wait there, hovering above the beach for several precious seconds until the rocket reaches its target...

And then all of the life signs ahead of us wink off the grid—human and alien both.

"*Vita brevis*," I whisper, citing the second half of the Paladins' motto.

A flurry of squawks issue from the combat computer, drawing my attention to the blinking threat detectors at the top of the HUD. Hostiles are targeting us from above. The starfighters circling the spire. They saw us. That small act of mercy for Kraug might have cost us the mission.

"Hang on to something!" I warn the others, just before I activate an emergency power preset to pour every available megawatt into the engines.

Pixie drops into the co-pilot's station, and Brix and Lucia hurriedly strap in behind us. I fumble one-handed with my own restraints. Our inertial dampeners and artificial gravity have been cut back to bare-minimal levels, but we'll live.

Yanking the stick straight up, I slam the throttle past the stops, and the breath leaves my lungs in a whoosh as we put Thanatos in our rear-view screens.

Enemy lasers crunch and sizzle against our hull, effects that are mostly simulated to make sure they won't be ignored.

"Taking damage!" Pixie warns.

I flick off the cloaking shield and engage deflectors. Our cover's blown to hell, anyway.

CHAPTER 45

We scream into orbit with all three enemy fighters on our tail and no signs of shaking them. Our shields are holding, but that's mostly because the Priors have shitty aim. Thank Deus for small mercies.

"Get Alpha on the comm!" I shout, snatching the alien comm unit off my belt and handing it to Pixie. A thin layer of nanites flows away from it, falling away like gunpowder and settling against my suit.

"How?" Pixie cries. "I don't know how to use this thing!" The device comes to life in her hands, alien symbols glowing brightly around the edges. It's glowing blue, which means it's already linked to Alpha's.

"Just touch the top with your thumb, and wait for it to connect!"

Pixie does as she's told, and the comm unit pulses faintly, chirping as it connects. A moment later, I hear Alpha's voice come echoing through.

"Are you ready?" he asks.

"Yes!" I shout at him. "Open the rift! We're inbound hot. I'm spinning up the FTL for a micro-jump to get us back to the coordinates where we came in." A quick look at the jump timer tells me we have almost six minutes to go for that jump. I relay that info to Alpha.

"Good," Alpha replies. "I will begin opening the rift. Are you being followed?"

Another look at the grid reveals the three fighters chasing us, but no sign of any other ships. I remember the war fleet that we saw on the way in and wonder absently where they went. "Just three interceptors." Enemy lasers hiss violently against our shields as if determined to make their presence known. Our shields are holding at fifty-six percent. Not great, but... I think we're going to make it.

"We'll handle them on this end," Alpha says. "Good luck, friend Cade. I will see you aboard Terminus for the hostage exchange."

"Copy that," I reply.

"Hostage exchange?" Lucia asks.

Pixie fixes me with a sideways look. "We should tell her."

"No," I reply.

"Tell me *what?*"

"She deserves to know what kind of person we're handing her over to."

"Handing me over?" Lucia demands. "What the fuck? I thought you said that my *mother* sent you?"

"She did," I reply.

"Then what are we talking about?"

"We're handing you over to her, that's all. The hostage exchange is none of your business."

"My mother abducted someone?" Lucia asks in a shrinking voice.

"My daughter," I snap. "Now drop it."

And for a miracle, Lucia does drop it.

"Look, I'm sure she's a great parent," Brix says. "I mean after she went to these lengths to save you, it's a fair bet that there's nothing she wouldn't do for you, kiddo."

Lucia doesn't say anything else, and we reach our jump point with twenty-nine percent still left on our shields. I engage the jump drive. A bright flash and a swirling tunnel of light, and then we're reverting to real space right in front of a big, glassy black marble of distorted space-time.

As we pass through it, it looks like someone is turning the starfield inside out around us. We trade the bluish-purple nebula for the clear star-speckled black of space.

A distant red speck appears, then quickly swells to millions of times its size as we race across time and space to greet it. Now the forward canopy is completely dominated by the angry red and orange swirls of Icarus.

A quick look at the grid reveals we weren't followed. I let out a breath I didn't realize that I was holding, and sag wearily against my restraints.

"We made it."

"You sound surprised," Brix quips. "We're Paladins. You know we always get the job done."

"Kraug didn't," Pixie adds.

"We'll bring him back," I say.

"Welcome back," Alpha says. "Please meet me in the hangar. I have already arranged for the exchange to take place there. They're sending Callista and Aurora over now—" A data transfer request pops up from Alpha, and I accept it. A blue target box appears around an ordinary-looking Type-7 Corvette, inbound hot to Terminus Station. "Once we have verified that your family is well, we will send Lucia over," Alpha explains.

"How in the galaxy did you get her to agree to *that?*" I ask, surprised to hear how lopsided the exchange is going to be—all in our favor, with no guarantees for Gina.

"Simple," Alpha says. "I did not give her a choice."

It's then that I notice the sensor grid isn't exactly empty of threats. Gina's entire fleet is here, within spitting distance of Terminus, and it's *surrounded* by the Cath's glittering silver ships.

A smile quirks to my lips. Alpha has been busy while we were gone.

CHAPTER 46

I'm standing on the deck of the hangar bay with Alpha, an honor guard of armored Cath, and Brix, Pixie, and Lucia Keri. The hangar is pressurized this time around, so I have my helmet off and tucked under my arm. We need to see *who* comes off that transport. Not that Gina can't fake it and have secretly jacked Aurora again. But this time, I know what to look for, and it won't be hard to confirm that it's really her.

I start tapping my foot. Then clenching and unclenching my fists. I think I'm more anxious than I've ever been in my entire life. If I weren't wearing my armor, I think I might explode. The thought of seeing Cally and Aurora again, both of them alive and well... it's overwhelming.

And that makes me realize just how pessimistic I've secretly been about a happy ending to this mess.

But I can thank Alpha for that. Again. He really is a *friend*. Having said that, we should probably try to see each other more than once every forty-five years. That puts a smile on my face.

"Here they come," Alpha says.

The corvette breezes through the hazy white wall of the Cath's version of buzz shields. The y-shaped vessel spins around on the spot, turning to face us with its engines. Getting ready for a speedy escape with Lucia.

In case we are planning a double-cross, or because Gina is?

That turns my smile into a scowl. This had better not be a trick.

But I can't imagine how that would turn out well for Gina. She has to play by our rules this time.

Standing beside me, Lucia is bouncing on her toes and biting her nails, looking about as nervous as me.

"Take it easy, kid," I say.

She glances at me with wide eyes. We already broke the bad news about this little rescue: that she's returning to a time forty-five years *after* the one that she left.

"My mother never would have done something like this," she says, shaking her head.

"Well, she's done a lot worse," Brix says. "I mean... this is the tip of the iceberg, you know. She practically invented human trafficking. We're just lucky we've got you so we don't have to chase down every slave trader in the galaxy to find Callista."

Lucia's eyes grow even wider. "You've got to be scorching my jets!"

Pixie fixes Brix with a disapproving scowl. "What he means to say, is that grief screws with people's heads, so... I guess, cut your mother some slack?"

Brix looks at her like she's just sprouted a second head. "Slack? You're joking, right?"

Pixie clamps her mouth shut, obviously not wanting to continue the argument.

But something about what they've just said is bothering me. Gina didn't *know* that she'd lost her daughter until two years ago, so how could *that* be the catalyst that turned her into the criminal mastermind she is today? The Solaris Cartel precedes her finding out about Lucia by about three decades. Maybe four.

"What's wrong?" Alpha asks, his helmet turning to stare implacably at me.

I look to Lucia for the answer. "What do you mean your mother would never do something like this?"

"She's a human rights activist! Bot rights, too, for that matter. Abduction? It's just... it doesn't make any sense."

"Well, she wouldn't be the first person to put on a holier-than-thou facade," Brix mutters. "Those robes have been worn by a lotta hypocrites."

"It wasn't a facade with her," Lucia insists.

"She volunteered with a fringe enforcement unit for an entire year in the neutral zone, risking her life to help put a stop to slavery! Now you're telling me that she's behind one of the biggest slave trades in the galaxy? I mean... are you sure you have the right Gina Keri?"

And there it is. That's exactly what's wrong here. Alpha stiffens suddenly.

"We have to leave. *Now.*"

"What?" Brix roars. "We're not done yet!"

The corvette drops its landing ramp and two familiar-looking figures stroll out with a squad of cartel enforcers aiming rifles at their backs. Fearing that this is a trick, I can't take it any longer. I break into a sprint, running toward them. I need to *know* if these two are Aurora and Cally.

"Cade!" Brix calls after me. "Slow down!"

Lucia comes running alongside me, keeping up easily thanks to the lingering pangs of my injuries. She's frowning deeply. "Is that them?" she asks, jerking her chin to my family.

"It is."

"Cade," Alpha says quietly, his voice echoing tinnily through external speakers in the helmet that I still have tucked under my arm. "We have a problem."

"If that's not them, she's *not* getting her daughter back." But even as I say that, I wonder if the Gina we've described cares about her daughter at all. But why would she do all of this if she didn't care?

Lucia's convinced that Gina is not the same woman she used to be. But forty-five years is a long time, so she can't possibly say that. And who knows if getting stranded in the Hadros Sector fucked with her head. Or maybe it was the Coalition, who wiped her memory...

Shit. That would explain how she got access to the Paladins' classified holo files. For all I know, that's it: she could be a Coalition agent, brainwashed into a totally different person. And that would mean it's no coincidence that she's running the biggest cartel in the Free Systems Alliance. That's actually a great way for them to destabilize their adversary. Let the Alliance waste resources fighting organized crime instead of building up their fleets. And it makes the Alliance's ideology look like a poor alternative to the so-called utopian society in the Coalition.

"You figured it out, didn't you?" Alpha whispers to me through the helmet. "Get your family, and get out of here."

"What if it's not them?" I ask.

Lucia is frowning deeply at me as we cover the last twenty feet to reach Cally and Aurora.

"That's what we're here to find out."

"You have them surrounded," I whisper back, slowing to a limping walk and waving smilingly to my family. "What are you afraid of?"

"I detected an anomaly in the station's logs. A ripple in the rift when you were flying back through it."

"What does that mean?"

"It means you *were* followed, Cade. You just didn't see them. And neither did I."

I stop dead in my tracks. "The Priors. That's what this has all been about? Getting them back to our galaxy?"

"I am afraid so, friend Cade."

"But..." I put the helmet on to keep the conversation private. "The Coalition wouldn't want that. Why would they want to kick off an alien invasion?"

"Because, Cade, they're afraid of me. And of the Cath. And I am the sworn enemy of the Priors who have returned. They will stop at nothing to defeat me."

"So leave! Let the Cath govern themselves."

"If I do that, the Cath *will* go to war with the Coalition. I'm the only thing holding them back from their war-like natures."

Well, isn't this a fine shitstorm, I think to myself.

"Cade!" Aurora cries. She twists off my helmet and kisses me roughly on the lips. "Why did you put that on?" she asks, her glowing copper eyes searching mine. Cally crashes into us next, and the reunion becomes a group hug.

Lucia looks on with a small, sad smile as if she's afraid she won't have anything remotely similar when she sees her mother.

"It's Aurora this time," Alpha says tinnily

from the helmet.

"How can you tell?" I demand.

"I did the checksum already. Put the helmet back on, Cade. We're not done talking."

Aurora frowns at that. "Kind of needy, isn't he?"

I roll my eyes at that and mouth an apology. "Give me a second." I put the helmet back on. "What?" I snap at Alpha, angry at him for ruining this moment for me.

"You need to finish the exchange. Send Lucia up the ramp. Gina can't know that we may have figured this out. If she learns the truth, she's going to tell the Priors that the jig is up, and they'll come straight here to take control of Terminus. If it falls into the Priors' hands…"

So I have to send an innocent girl to her monster of a mother who probably isn't even her mother anymore. "Got it," I reply shortly. Yanking the helmet off, I wave to the enforcers at the top of the ramp inside the corvette and then look at Lucia with a heavy heart and a very fake smile. "It's your turn."

She nods quietly, looking torn and preoccupied. "Okay. I'm glad it all turned out for you."

I catch her by the arm as she's leaving and whisper in her ear. "Play it cool. Pretend you're overjoyed to see her again. And when you get a chance, look up the Orion Shipping Co. at Terra Novus. Go straight to Orion Station. Tell them your name. They'll be expecting you."

"Why?" Lucia whispers back.

"Because I'm going to need your help to prevent a galactic war."

"Hey!" one of the enforcers shouts down to us. "What's going on?" I release Lucia and she nods mutely, looking confused, but grimly determined to do what I've asked.

I retreat quickly with Aurora and Cally, running back over to Brix, Pixie, and Alpha.

Pixie and Aurora have a mini-reunion of their own, and Pixie even sheds a few tears. Brix joins in with a bear hug for her and Cally. The two of them stayed out of the exchange on my orders. Only me and Lucia were allowed to go out and meet Aurora and Cally, and we were unarmed. Adding anyone else to the mix would have meant risking a laser bolt to Cally's back.

Alpha sidles over to me just as the corvette's landing ramp goes telescoping up and the ship blasts out of the hangar at top speed, carrying Lucia back to Gina. Alpha nods and whispers again, this time not bothering to speak over my helmet speakers. "Good job, Cade. Now let's hope that girl doesn't blow it before we have a chance to use her to stop the war."

"Yeah," I agree, blowing out a long, ragged breath. But I'm not sure how optimistic I'm feeling. Having a mole close to Gina to figure out what game the Coalition is playing is only half the battle. What we need is to find a way to stop them from stoking two alien powers against each other—and then to stop those alien powers from turning their sights on the human ones instead.

I drift back to my wife's side, slipping a hand into hers, and pull Cally into a one-armed bear hug of my own.

Whatever the galaxy's fate, at least my little piece of it is safe.

For now.

GET JASPER'S NEXT BOOK FREE

Nightstalkers

A post-apocalyptic invasion story.

(Coming June 2023)

Get a FREE e-copy if you post an honest review of this book on Amazon (https://geni.us/CK5review)

And then send it to me here (https://files.jaspertscott.com/nightstalkersfree.htm)

Thank you in advance for your feedback!

KEEP IN TOUCH

SUBSCRIBE to my Mailing List and get two FREE Books! (http://files.jaspertscott.com/mailinglist.html)

Follow me on Amazon:
https://www.amazon.com/Jasper-T-Scott/e/B00B7A2CT4

Follow me on Bookbub:
https://www.bookbub.com/authors/jasper-t-scott

Look me up on Facebook:
https://www.facebook.com/jaspertscott/

Check out my Website:
www.JasperTscott.com

Follow me on Twitter:
@JasperTscott

Or send me an e-mail:
JasperTscott@gmail.com

MORE FROM JASPER T. SCOTT

Keep up with new releases and get two free books by signing up for his newsletter at www.jaspertscott.com

Note: as an Amazon Associate I earn a small commission from qualifying purchases.

Architects of the Apocalypse

Planet B | Worlds Collide | Apokalypsis

The Kyron Invasion

Arrival | New World Order | End Game

From Beyond

From Beyond | Signal | Survival

The Cade Korbin Chronicles

The Bounty Hunter | Alien Artifacts | Paragon | The Omega Protocol | Bounty Hunters

Final Days

Final Days | Colony | Escape

Ascension Wars

First Encounter | Occupied Earth | Fractured Earth | Second Encounter

Scott Standalones (No Sequels, No Cliffhangers)

Under Darkness | Into the Unknown | In Time for Revenge

Rogue Star

Rogue Star: Frozen Earth | Rogue Star: New Worlds

Broken Worlds
The Awakening | The Revenants | Civil War

New Frontiers Series
Excelsior | Mindscape | Exodus

Dark Space Series
Dark Space | The Invisible War | Origin | Revenge | Avilon | Armageddon

Dark Space Universe
Dark Space Universe | The Enemy Within | The Last Stand

ABOUT THE AUTHOR

Jasper Scott is a USA Today bestselling author of over forty sci-fi novels. With over a million copies sold, Jasper's work has been translated into various languages and published around the world.

Jasper writes fast-paced books with unexpected twists and flawed characters. He was born and raised in Canada by South African parents, with a British heritage on his mother's side and German on his father's. He now lives in an exotic locale with his wife, their two kids, and two Chihuahuas.

Made in United States
Cleveland, OH
16 November 2025